CHRISTO

Cas Erchamion

Prologue

Picture an arctic landscape at night. Not one with bleak, flat ice sheets and icebreakers carving a path to some unknown destination but a mountainous vista untouched by modern civilization. Above it, *aurora borealis* lights up a clear, evening sky amidst more stars than most people know exist above their cities and towns. Under the stars, a snow capped mountain towers above a deep stretch of rocky shoreline. A small portion of the mountain side, cleverly disguised as natural rock, slowly opens to reveal a huge doorway.

A sleigh, just a tiny dot in the snow, waits patiently for the stone gates to open. It's not a simple sort of sleigh pulled by maddened huskies across endless, flat Arctic tundra but the kind one would expect to see being pulled by well groomed horses in pre-industrial Europe. This sleigh, however, is being pulled by several large reindeer of a size and aggressiveness normally associated with the word *vengeance* and much less with the word *venison.* In addition, everything about the sleigh is black. The skis are black, the half-covered carriage is black and the thick leather harnesses around the reindeer are black. However, owing to the universal convention of having a touch variety on any vehicle, the heavily leathered seat on which the large driver sits, is red. It's the kind of sleigh that could make an arctic vampire weep in appreciation. Behind the reins, a heavy-set figure wrapped in a dark, crimson cloak guides the sleigh through the massive, stone doorway. As it vanishes into the darkness beyond, the stone gates slowly close behind it.

The interior of the dark cavern is not a rough hewn affair with icy stalactites and still pools of glacial water. On the contrary, its filled with an endless array of grand halls, rooms, galleries and kitchens. Every nook and cranny carved from the roots of that snow-capped mountain is warmly lit by an innumerable variety of braziers, strange glowing crystals or simple oil lamps.

The reindeer driven sleigh slows to a stop at the center of an enormous, dome-like vestibule. Bristling and neighing with steam pouring off them, the reindeer look around to the driver. The tall driver steps off the sleigh, pats the lead reindeer on the neck and walks briskly towards stone steps.

In front of the sleigh is a horseshoe-shaped ring of stone steps lit by tall, brass braziers casting warm hues about the area. The sleigh driver ascends the stone steps towards a set of huge oak doors. As he approaches them, the doors burst open and the driver's crimson cloak billows out behind him in answer to the sudden gust of warmth. Emerging from them are two children at a run followed by a concerned but amiable looking woman in deep blue robes. She is dark haired, leans on a staff of white birch wood and smiles at the sleigh driver.

The children are no more than six or seven years old and run full speed at the sleigh-driver. One is a boy with long, ginger locks and the other is a girl with dark hair like the woman behind her. They are wearing bright green pajamas and floppy red slippers that would better suit someone nine feet tall with feet to match.

"Daddy!" The children shout.

The large man scoops the children up at once with two large arms and laughs.

"Ho-ho-ho!" He bellows. "I'm home."

This is a story about a jolly old boy's life as a young man. I know what you are thinking - you are thinking this is a story about *him* but it's not. This is a story about *them*. After all, *he* is one of *them*. Furthermore, this is a story about a strange place and some peculiar events that happen at a specific time for an important reason. Judging by the happy scene just described, one could speculate that everyone lives *happily ever after* but let's not get ahead of ourselves. After all, *happily ever after* is a point of view. More importantly, *happily ever after* a phrase largely associated with endings. This story, on the other hand, is all about beginnings. And those beginnings start 2000 years ago in the city of Jerusalem.

Chapter 1: Lamb with a side of Blessing

Not to put too fine a point on it, crucifixion is widely considered to be one of the most terrible forms of execution. The term literally means fixed to a cross and pretty much describes what the unfortunate individual must undergo. It's also the source of the word *excruciating* and not a difficult stretch to see it often associated with the word *anguish*. If there was a contest for *The Most Terrible Executions in History*, it would surely be at the top of a long, grisly list. Oh sure, the Chinese did terrible things with burning oil and the Aztecs did their infamous, heart-rending work but crucifixion lasts a long time. For that reason, it is considered to be exceedingly horrible.

On a pleasant summer evening, on a hill outside of Jerusalem about 2000 years ago, three men were suffering death by crucifixion. They were being guarded by two Roman officers. Against the cool, blue evening sky, their ghastly silhouettes loomed over the hill. The hill, called Golgotha, was a crucifixion site reserved for those who were unacceptably naughty or upset the wrong politicians. It has been said that watching someone die on the cross is almost as bad as being nailed to one. On the other hand, no one in recorded history has ever come down from a cross and said "OK, now let me try watching a crucifixion then I'll compare the two." Regardless, people believed it was a horrible experience for everyone all 'round so soldiers often found themselves on *death watch* as a kind of disciplinary punishment. Curiously, watch duty for crucifixions was mandatory in Roman-occupied Jerusalem at this time. This was remarkable because no one in the long and bloody history of execution ever escaped after being nailed to a piece of wood.

Standing on the hill beneath the three unfortunate men were two Roman officers on night watch. They were not at all happy for being there despite the pleasant evening and stood silent vigil for a lengthy period of time.

After a while, the larger of the two unhappy officers sighed and squinted in the moonlight as he looked up at one of the three dying men.

"He wakes, Erik."

Leaner and younger than his counterpart, Erik looked up at the central convict with the crown of thorns and nodded. "He will linger longer than most, I imagine." He sighed and shuffled his feet.

In addition to their plumed officer helms, polished bronze breastplates and red cloaks, they bore spears. The fact they were officers was also notable because night watch on Golgotha was only assigned to low ranking soldiers. This meant the two officers were unacceptably naughty recently but not enough to be nailed to a cross themselves.

Erik stared up at the dying men and tried not to imagine what it would be like to die in such a manner. His ice-blue eyes were piercing but not at all wise. Rather, they were filled with that peculiar reflection of innocence trying to grasp complexity. His short, light-brown hair and cleanly shaven face made him appear rather boyish beside his dark complexioned partner.

Erik's companion, on the other hand, had the three universal qualities that all women seem to have a programmed desire for – tall, dark and handsome. Actually, in Roman times these three qualities were somewhat different - tall, pleasantly tanned and handsome enough to forgo wreathed vegetation as a hat-accessory.

Erik sighed and lazily repositioned his pole arm.

"What's on that feeble mind of yours?" Said Erik's companion.

"How many of these have you seen Longinus?"

"Too many." Said Longinus, elder and larger of the two. "I was irritating Pilate long before you joined our merry band, remember?"

Erik nodded silently. Despite his talent for annoying Pilate, Longinus would always be protected because his father was a powerful man in Rome. A magistrate, in fact.

They remained silent for some time. A sparrow flitted past, chirping as it went about its business. The night was unusually humid and quiet. There seemed a dampening of noise on the hill despite the occasional weeping and moaning of the dying men.

"This is no way to die." Said Erik flatly, spitting into the dirt.

Longinus didn't respond but stared up at the three men with a grim expression.

"C'mon. Really, it is. At least in the coliseum a man can die in combat. Die like a man."

Longinus sighed as a sparrow flew past again. "But that one isn't a man. He's the *son* of man."

Erik snorted. "Whatever that means. It got him nailed to that cross, damn fool."

Longinus stretched and yawned. "Alright, time for patrol. Lies or tails?" He said, taking out a coin from some place within his cuirass.

"Caesar."

Longinus flipped the coin and it landed in the dirt at their feet with a *clink* sound. "Tails it is. My rounds."

He sighed and straightened his weathered armor. "I'll be a little while negotiating these outcrops. Don't go doing anything exciting without me." He kicked a nearby pebble and trudged off into the darkness.

"I'll make sure they don't escape." Erik whispered loudly to him as he vanished into the night. It was a dry expression, he knew, but he couldn't help it. It was the only way he could deal with such dispiriting duty.

A cool breeze swept across the hilltop, breaking the close air. Erik shivered and looked around. In the foreboding silence, he brooded over his duty and looked up at the dying men once more. He hated crucifixion. It was a cruel death but not one for thieves or political dissidents.

Longinus hated it, Erik knew. However, as current commander of Jerusalem's law enforcement infrastructure, he begrudgingly admitted that crucifixion played an effective deterrent for law breakers. Despite Pontius Pilate's apparent thirst for frequent capital punishments, Longinus urged all the men under his command to exercise restraint. He reminded the young soldiers that their jobs were not to dispense divine justice from the heavens or any other such nonsense. Their jobs were to maintain peace. *"Order, education and diplomacy,"* Longinus would often say, *"are mightier than spears, arrows and shields."* The expression sounded curiously like a quote but whom he was quoting, Erik never enquired. For those reasons, Longinus was respected among most of the soldiers stationed in the city.

A sound startled Erik and he turned suddenly, peering into the darkness down the hillside.

"Long? You there?"

Although it was somewhat faint, he could have sworn he heard a muffled a thump of some kind.

"This isn't the time or place. Not funny at all." He whispered loudly.

There was no reply.

He looked up, wondering if perhaps the convicts were struggling but they were silent and motionless now. A full moon, moving slowly across the night sky, was now positioned directly behind the head of the central convict. It would have been a brow-raiser any other time but at this moment something else toyed with Erik' attention. He frowned and tightened his grip on his spear. Peering around the dark summit, his instincts were telling him the thick silence was menacing.

The air was chillier now and a feeling of impending engagement fell upon Erik. A nameless fear grew in his stomach and he felt his attention being drawn to his immediate surroundings. His heartbeat echoed heavily in his ears and he felt a peculiar sensation of being encumbered and suffocated. A cold sweat drenched his brow and he shivered. Oddly, he thought he could smell roast lamb, his favorite food.

He heard a footfall behind him and spun around with his spear ready. Three hooded figures emerged from the gloom. One of them appeared to be carrying Longinus' spear.

"What in Hades! Who are - ?"

But Erik didn't have time to finish his sentence. One of the figures waved an arm and whispered something. Erik dropped like a sack of garlic, completely unconscious. His spear and shield clattered against some rocks.

The three figures stepped over Erik' unconscious body and walked slowly to the central convict. Their robes were dark blue and each carried a walking stick made of white birch wood.

One of the three stepped closer. "Nazarene." He said softly.

The man on the central cross opened one eye and then another.

"*You.*" He said with a hoarse voice, as he looked at each of the figures. *"Three of the four riders, he sends. Betrayers. Halaam. Why have you come here?"*

"Does your crown displease you my lord?" Said the man flatly.

"*Our conversations are over. There is no more to discuss. Leave us. We will not meet again.*" Said the dying man, his voice strained and wheezy.

A second figure stepped forward. "You will not succeed where he failed." He said softly. "Your father has abandoned you."

The air around the hill was still and humid once more. No sound of swallows, insects or anything alive penetrated the silence. The Nazarene considered this for a moment and stared at each of the men.

"Curious. You know I will live on in martyrdom. My followers will see to that. They will bring my message to humanity."

A third carrying Longinus' spear stepped forward. "It matters not. The fourth rider is coming. When he arrives he will be displeased if you destabilize the gates. You will not reach the makers. You will not succeed where he has failed. You will only die here. That is all." He raised the dangerous end of Longinus' spear and pointed it at the crucified man.

Hear me, son of Erik.

Erik blinked and raised his head from the dirt. He stared around in confusion for a moment then focused on the three figures in front of the central cross. He could have sworn he just heard his father's voice. The moon lit up the hillside and he could clearly see the figures although they appeared to be motionless. They didn't react to his recovery but stared fixedly up at the crucified man.

"W-what?" Erik stammered.

"*Erikssen look at me. I am about to die.*"

He looked up at the dying man. The fact that he knew Erik's name wasn't nearly as shocking as having the strength to say anything at all. Regardless, Erik stood up and staggered forward, keeping his eye on the robed figures. They stood motionless and seemed to completely ignore his presence.

"They must have blackjacked me or someth - " He started to say as he looked about the area for his spear and shield.

"Here I will die. It is a price I must pay on behalf of my kinsmen for desecrating this paradise you so richly take for granted. Before I pass from this place, a boon I would ask of you."

"What in Hades is going - ?" Erik asked glancing sideways at the motionless figures but his question was interrupted.

"Silence!"

The deafening command exploded in Erik's mind and he cowered instinctively.

"Come closer Erik. They cannot hear us."

Wary of the motionless figures and driven by curiosity, Erik stepped forward and looked up.

"The spike – take it from my feet so that I may pass from this realm quickly."

Erik military training suddenly came back to him and he shook his head. "I cannot. My…d-duty..." His sentence trailed off.

"*Yes, I know.*" Said the dying man soothingly. His eyes were closed now as if in meditation. *"I can feel your commitment to duty. It is a sign of your humanity. Beastliness is weak in you."*

"Please do not ask me." Erik pleaded, glancing fearfully at the three, motionless figures beside him. "And who in Hades are they?"

"They cannot hear us. They are temporarily...elsewhere."

Erik was beginning to feel frustrated. He was quite sure the men *were* standing right behind him and not *elsewhere.*

"Look." Erik turned slightly, keeping an eye on the figures. "I didn't like what this whole business was about. If it were up to me, you would be doing community service but

I am a officer. I follow orders. You have been condemned, whether I agree with it or not. Please do not ask this of me."

"*The pain is unbearable.*" Whispered the man urgently. "*Quickly brother before they awaken. I beseech your mercy. Take the nail from my feet and I will pass away. You will bear no shame nor will your kin. Your duty will be fulfilled.*" He looked down and Erik could see desperation in his eyes.

Erik hesitated. He hated crucifixions but on the other hand, what harm would it do? As young and naïve as Erik was, he understood the meaning of the request. Crucifixion was devised to make felons suffer greatly and for a long period before their inevitable death. By removing the spike from this man's feet, the physics of the whole situation would change. In his weakened state, the man's lungs would surely collapse under the weight of his torso and his passing would be quick indeed.

"I will do this for you." Said Erik quietly. "Longinus wouldn't care anyways. He hates crucifixion as much as I and helping you die faster is a humanitarian act."

Erik looked at the spike buried in the wood of the crux through the man's overlapped feet. He winced at the wound, guessing it was extraordinarily painful.

"*Now, brother, take it out.*" The man whispered urgently. "*You will find it quite easy to remove, as a sliver plucked from thy palm.*"

Erik stepped forward and touched the spike with trembling fingers. Dried blood coated its surface and it felt cold to touch. Slowly, Erik pulled the spike from the crux wood. It slid out easily and the man's feet sunk.

The dying man released a great sigh and smiled down at him.

"*Bless you.*" The sound of his voice was clear and loud in Erik's mind. "*Bless you and all of your kin. For this service your bloodline shall be long and prosperous. Take you, your wife and unborn child from this den of hopelessness and let them mature beyond the fens of*

Caesar." The man drew a strangled breath and began to wheeze.

Erik stood frozen, staring at the man in amazement. The fact that he knew about his wife and unborn son was trivial compared to the fact he was speaking to Erik without opening his mouth. He was not imagining it. The man was speaking to him in his mind.

Keep you that spike for it is a key to your future. Never lose it. The stains of my blood shall make it thy shield against age, thy skein for weaving hope, and thy sword for smiting beasts. Remember you well this axiom for your bloodline must champion its course: blessed are the meek, for they shall inherit the earth.

Erik looked down at his shaking hands which held the bloody spike. It was too much for him and his mind did somersaults trying to make sense of it all. He mouthed the words, still echoing in his mind: *Blessed are the meek.*

"No!" One of the hooded figures suddenly leapt forward and screamed at him. "What have you done? What have you there?" He attempted to reach out and take the spike from Erik' hand but a sliver of lightning erupted from the spike. The figure recoiled and massaged its hand, snarling unintelligibly.

Erik nearly dropped the spike and looked around wildly. The three men advanced on him, albeit somewhat cautiously now.

"Longinus! Where the hell are you?" Erik shouted as he backed away and looked around for a weapon larger than a nail.

"You!" Shouted the one who carried Longinus' spear. He pointed it at Erik. "You... are one of them! This cannot be! How could we have missed a Hurum?" He spat the words and looked at the others as if one of them were to blame. Then he turned his attention to the man on the cross.

"You will never find the makers." He snarled at the dying man. "The gates are closed! The nefilem are lost. When *he* arrives we will go home!"

"Betrayers of the first promise," the crucified man said softly, *"watch as I demonstrate what your leader could not do himself."*

The hooded figure holding Longinus' spear stepped forward quickly, knocking his companions out of the way. Before Erik could react, the man stabbed the spear upward and with great force, impaling the Nazarene deeply in the torso. Blood, crimson and warm, gushed down the spear.

"No!" Erik heard himself scream. He felt his legs carry him forward but one of the others landed a blow from a staff to the side of his face. Erik was knocked off his feet. He dropped the spike and collapsed unceremoniously several yards away with his head spinning from the blow.

"No." Said Erik weakly from the ground.

The crucified man convulsed and he exhaled violently as his thorny crown fell from his head. His body sagged and went limp. The hooded figure withdrew the spear and hesitated. Blood flowed freely from the horrid wound and coursed down the spear shaft in a subtle network of crimson streams.

Erik sat speechless in the dirt, stunned by viciousness of the execution. He watched the three figures continue to stare up at the central cross as if waiting for something to happen.

Then a bright, yellow light seemed to grow from within the gaping wound in the man's side. Brighter and brighter it grew in intensity, engulfing the body and then the immediate surroundings. The hooded figures staggered back, blocking their faces from the light.

The third dropped the spear in the dirt and screamed. "He has found a way! Master we cannot stop him!"

A tempest of wind and static energy swirled about the summit of Golgotha. Lightning peeled across the sky followed by an ear splitting thunderclap. Erik sensed a kind of vacuum in the air. A swirling updraft of sand and gravel stung his face and cheeks as he staggered around the area. The tempest grew to such intensity that Erik' mind reeled and he called out to Longinus once again. The light blinded him and he was forced to his knees, sheltering his face with his hands.

A voice suddenly boomed in Erik's mind.

This façade is over. It was deep, cold and seemed to come from a vast distance. *Go back to your wife, primate, and pray to Jupiter that we do not cross paths again.*

Erik shivered as the unwelcome presence left his mind. He didn't understand the meaning of the words nor who spoke them. Blinded by the intense light and groggy from the blow to the side of his head, he chanced a look up at the cross and half-imagined a hooded figure leaning over him, silhouetted against the blinding tempest. It was larger than the others and carried a lantern which swayed and gleamed in the raging storm of light and cloud. As consciousness slipped away, Erik thought he heard the sounds of rapidly approaching footfalls.

Chapter 2: Night Cap

"Erik."

The voice stirred Erik's consciousness. It was soft and familiar. A hand clasped his. His hand…something was in his hand…the spike!

Erik gasped and lurched forward. His head spun but he was home. He sank back into the softness of his bed and looked bleary eyed at his lovely wife sitting next to him. Her grey eyes glistened and her long, dark hair was lightly matted to her cheek in lieu of newborn tears.

"Aurelia." He said, smiling weakly.

"Shh, rest now." She whispered, kissing him on the forehead. "I'll go make something to eat for my hero." She winked and slipped from the room.

Erik watched her leave then sank deeper into his bed. He tried to recall the previous evening then it all came back in a rush. He thought of Longinus, hooded figures on Golgotha and then the spike.

Erik sat up and looked around. In the soft candlelight of his makeshift home, he surveyed the simple room from windowsill to bedside table. He reached over to a stool near the bed where Aura placed his robes and cuirass. The heavy breastplate fell to the floor with a loud *clang* as he searched his robes for the spike.

"What are you doing in there?" Aura called out from the pantry.

"Nothing, sorry." He replied in the way that all husbands do when they are, in fact, *doing something.*

Aurelia came back in the room. "Take it easy. You need your rest. Longinus will be here later. He'll be pleased to see you are alright and probably wants to talk."

Erik felt a little panic driven as he rummaged about the small room. "Dear? Did you find me clutching anything when I was brought here or did you see anything fall out of my robes or armor?"

"No. I saw no such thing. Was there something valuable in your possession?"

Erik nodded. "Valuable? Yes." Then he turned his attention to the window. A sparrow landed on the sill and attempted to join their conversation with occasional 'chirp'.

"Are you alright?" Aurelia asked, coming to stand at the foot of his bed.

"Come here." said Erik, gesturing for here to sit down.

Aurelia sat, staring at him quizzically. "What is it?"

"Aurelia. Tell me about how I arrived back home. Is this the next day?

"This is the second day after you were brought home." She sighed and looked at him with concern.

Erik was struck with the sudden and hopeful notion the night on Golgotha was all a dream. All that happened - the spike, the hooded strangers - could have just been an elaborate nightmare.

"Tell me how I came back here."

Aurelia didn't respond right away but continued to stare at Erik with concern. After a moment she shrugged and related to Erik all that had occurred.

"Longinus brought you here two mornings ago. You seemed to have contracted brain fever. I sent for the apothecary and he confirmed our suspicions. Since then, you have been here in bed."

"What about Longinus? Did he seem…strange?"

"He was concerned of course. As your Commander, he has excused you from duty until you are fit to return. As your best friend, he has been here both nights with Cassie, hoping for your speedy recovery."

"I see." Erik frowned and scratched his chin. "Did he say what happened?"

"Yes. He said you were ambushed by insurgents while he went on patrol. You apparently stood your ground and were overcome. He said you took a blow to the head and became feverish when you arrived back home on a stretcher."

"I'm sorry." Erik said quietly. "I don't recall." He put a hand to his temple, remembering the white staff that had knocked him off his feet. Then he smiled weakly in a vain attempt to banish his wife's concern and placed a gentle hand on her pregnant belly.

"Umm…I've been having the strangest craving for roast lamb."

Aurelia looked at him sideways. Her lips curling into that devastatingly cute smile that always leveled Erik's resolve. He knew that *she* knew he was changing the subject and decided to play along.

"I'll see what I can get." She pulled a brown shawl over her tanned shoulders and bustled out of the room.

Erik sighed as he watched her depart. He imagined her silky brown hair laughing at him as she swept from the room. He was indeed a lucky man to be her husband. Falling back into his bed, he closed his eyes and recalled the voice in his mind. *Blessed are the meek...*

"Erikssen Fisherman! Attention!"

Erik was yanked out of the dreamy comfort of rest to an altogether disoriented version of wake. '*Attention*' was a word used by authority. His soldiers' training took over his motor-skills at the authoritative command and he stood up straight out of bed. Bleary eyed, he swayed in the discomfort of consciousness and blinked at the source of the command.

Laughter filled the tiny bedroom. Erik realized where he was.

"Good afternoon, soldier!"

Erik turned to see his grinning Commander. "Long! You scared the hell out of me. I thought I fell asleep at post again."

"Relax Erik. Just wanted to see if this cushy time-off was softening you. I have to keep you on your toes, you know. That's my job."

Erik sat down on his bed before dizziness made the choice for him. "What happened?"

Longinus grinned down at him and shrugged. "Don't know exactly. They came at me from behind and I was out like a lamp. Insurgents of some kind, I'm guessing. Corporal Corn is asking questions around town on behalf of Pilate, for whatever good that will do. Good to see your alive. How are you feeling?"

"Alright, I guess. Aurelia's been pampering me."

"Oh, poor you." Longinus mocked as he looked around the room.

"Some mead, sir?" Asked Erik as he prepared to get up.

"Sure." Longinus nodded. "Bring the whole skin. We're going to need it."

Erik stood up, yawned extensively and left the room to search the pantry. He returned with two brass goblets and a bulging skin of mead. Longinus took the skin and poured each of them a healthy portion.

After draining his cup, Longinus sighed. "You gave me a bit of a scare up there."

Sunlight bathed the small room in warmth as Erik stared into his goblet. "Yeah, I heard what happened. Loyalists or something?"

"Looks that way but I need to hear your side of it. Pilate is fairly vexed. The Nazarene was not to be touched."

Erik hesitated. He didn't exactly know where to begin so he just poured it all out, even the conversation with the Nazarene. Longinus listened patiently to Erik as he recounted the events on Golgotha a few nights before. When Erik finished, he stood up and walked to the window sill where he stood for a few minutes in silence, brooding over what he had just heard. Sunlight glistened off his polished cuirass as he turned to Erik.

"Well?" said Erik.. "What do you think?"

"Well one thing is for sure." Longinus sighed and poured himself another goblet of mead. "Pilate thinks I was the one who stabbed the Jew-king. He thinks I wanted to put the man out of his misery. There's blood all over my spear so it doesn't look good." Longinus looked serious and shook his head. "Sounds like you saw the whole thing."

Erik nodded. "I was there. Three men were talking to him. Then they killed him. So what about you though? What happened?"

"As I said, they came at me from behind. During patrol, I heard a noise from the embankment at the far end of Golgotha. I thought it may have been ravens or whatever but decided to investigate just in case. A few minutes later I tripped on a rock in the darkness and fell. I jammed my knee into the ground and hit my head. Not sure how long I was out. Sometime later I got up and staggered around in the darkness looking for my spear. I couldn't find it anywhere and decided to let it go 'till daybreak. Then I headed back to you and found you all banged-up and the Jew-King bleeding all over the place."

"Nothing sounds too unusual about that. I mean, before reaching me." said Erik, frowning into his half-empty goblet.

"No not really - except for one thing."

Erik looked up.

"I found my spear."

"Where?"

"Embedded in the Jew-Kings' torso." Longinus sighed "Pilate wants to have a word with me over it. That's not going to be fun at all."

Erik and Longinus stared at each other in silence. After short time, there came a noise from the kitchen and Aurelia entered the room.

"Longinus!" She embraced Longinus in a hug. "When did you get here?"

"Just a little while ago."

In walked another woman, Cassiopeia, Longinus' wife and Aurelia's best friend. She was a tall, shapely woman and notoriously jealous of her man.

"What trouble are you up to then?" she said, stepping closer to her husband.

"Nothing dear. Just catching up and making sure this northerner can be on duty tomorrow." Longinus grinned innocently.

Cassiopeia sneered in mock disapproval at Longinus and playfully slapped him on the behind. She winked and nodded at Erik.

Aurelia and Cassiopeia (as everyone called the two women about town) were best friends and had met their husbands at the festival of Compitalia a few years before. Aura was a dark-haired Etruscan with gorgeous grey eyes that could see everything Erik was thinking. Erik suspected she was tougher and much more intelligent that himself but she always made him feel pampered. For this reason, he loved and respected her more than any woman he had ever met.

Cassiopeia, Longinus wife, was a fiery tempered Greek lady. She had little love for the empire but fell hard for

Longinus at the beginning of their courtship. She was an opinionated woman who spoke her mind freely and Longinus loved her for it despite her uncommon graces. Her Hellenistic charm seemed to captivate him and their passion for each other was immeasurable. She was just the woman a man like Longinus needed. Were Cassie a man, she undoubtedly would be Commander of the Eastern Legions of the Roman Empire by voice alone. They made a formidable couple.

As for Longinus, he was Commander of Pontius Pilate's peacekeeping force in the city and Erik' best friend. As the third son of a Roman magistrate, he was sent to the far reaches of the empire for cultural experience. No doubt he would become a higher ranking officer someday, possibly a Legatus.

As a boy, Erik remembered meeting his friend by a large river outside the city known for its abundance of fish. Longinus would have been about fourteen at the time and struggled with outdoor activities. Erik, realizing the young man was new to the Judean frontier, offered to help. Being the adopted son of a fisherman and thus educated in survival skills, Erik learned to fish at an early age. Longinus welcomed the assistance and paid close attention to Erik. He wasn't arrogant or even remotely embarrassed that a child of younger years was showing him how to do something. They quickly became close friends and in exchange for teaching him frontier skills, Longinus returned the favor by showing Erik how to read and write.

When Erik was fifteen, Longinus showed him how to *woo* women. This confused Erik at first because he didn't know what a *woo* was nor how to *woo* in the presence of a lady. He soon learned, however, and it was a truly an invaluable skill that Erik suspected came naturally to his wealthy and handsome older friend. Erik smiled in spite of himself at the memory and looked at his beautiful wife.

After a few years, Longinus was a man and an officer under Pontius Pilate, the Prefect of Judea. A few years later, Erik was chosen for a posting within Pilate's compound. This was considerably surprising to Erik because he didn't apply for the position in the first place. Longinus had something to do with that, he was sure.

Although Longinus was Erik' senior in age and rank, there was good camaraderie between them. They seemed to think the same way. They both loved Rome and their jobs as peacekeepers for the Republic. 'Long and 'Rik' (as they were called about the city) were always welcome in the wine houses around the city and quite popular with the clientele. They would drink, eat and joke with common folk, then be the first ones on duty the next morning conducting exercise drills with the rest of Pilate's men.

Erik, being able to read and write thanks to Longinus, was quickly promoted through the ranks. Regardless, Erik rather disliked Pilate and thought the man often abused his power for luxuries.

"Alright you." Cassie poked Longinus in the ribs. "We've got to go and let Erik rest. He's been staring into space for five minutes now."

Longinus and took on the voice of an indentured servant. "Would your graces be in need of anything before the Lady and I go home and spend the evening making bab-*ouch*!"

Cassie stepped on his foot.

"-err, baked goods?" He smiled weakly.

Aurelia blushed and laughed. "No, we're fine you two. See you tomorrow."

"I'll be there early tomorrow." Said Erik.

Aura escorted them to the door of the tiny home and whispered in Longinus' ear. "She's ready." Aura nodded towards the exiting Cassie while patting her own pregnant belly.

Longinus looked down as Aura patted her belly and dawning comprehension flashed in his eyes. He smiled wickedly and chased his wife out the door. "Quick dear, quick!"

Aura smiled as she listened to Longinus speeding his wife home through the streets. She turned to look at her husband and smiled wickedly.

"You need some exercise, young man."

The soft candlelight of Erik and Aurelia's home went out...

****Jingle*Jingle*Jingle****

Later that evening, Erik found it difficult to sleep. Something weighed on his mind and it was in the shape of an iron crucifixion spike.

Careful not to wake Aura, he slipped from their house and quietly navigated the streets of slumbering Jerusalem to the outer walls. Once there, he bribed a gatekeeper with some smoked fish and mead from his pantry and disappeared into the darkness beyond. He could have just ordered the man to open the gate, he was an officer after all, but he wanted to keep his investigation quiet.

Outside the city walls, the moon and stars did little to light the hill of Golgotha. It was an eerie place and reeked of death despite the refreshing crispness of the evening breeze. Erik shivered and pulled his hooded cloak closer around him as he relived the events some days before. Jagged, twisting shadows and the occasional bustle of rodents and other nightlife made the place all the more unsettling. Erik was not the sort to believe in Gods or the rituals surrounding them but he did fear them. For that reason, he was a little on edge in a place where hundreds had died.

He *had* to find the spike but wouldn't be able to explain why. He simply felt an instinctual desire to keep it safe. He looked around in the dark and bent low. He dared not use a torch or lantern up here for fear of attracting unexpected company. Getting down on all fours, he stretched out his hands and swept them over the dirt and stone in an area that looked familiar. A sparrow landed near his hands and chirped. He shooed it away as he examined the area.

As he continued to rummage in the dirt, Erik recalled the crucified man told him the spike was important, like an heirloom. He snorted at the prospect of passing down a pointy hunk of iron to his son someday and imagined himself saying 'here you go son, take care of it!' Then he recalled the silhouetted figure call him something. *Primate* was it? What in Hades was a *primate* anyways?

He continued searching for some time, running his hands over certain areas of the rocks and dirt. Then suddenly he put his hand on something rather odd. It was a foot.

"Stand up, friend. I am only a man."

Erik jumped up startled. "What! Who?" He exclaimed, peering into the darkness at a hooded figure a few yards from him.

"Easy friend." Said the hooded figure in soothing tones. He removed the hood and stepped forward. Erik stood his ground but said nothing.

"Looks like you were searching for something." Said the man. He was about thirty years old and bearded in the Jewish fashion. His dark eyes glittered despite the dim lit surroundings and his manner appeared to be friendly. His tattered, brown cloak and shoddy sandals identified him as a tradesman or a laborer. As he stepped into the dim moonlight, however, Erik could see the man's eyes were puffed and swollen.

"I am an officer. I lost something here yesterday." Said Erik flatly. "But I'm sure it is of no value to you." He quickly added.

The man nodded and surveyed the ground critically. "Many valuable things are lost up here, officer."

Erik smiled grimly. He chose to ignore the man's biting reference. "What is your purpose here citizen?" Asked Erik, using the neutral tone of an officer.

"I was merely out for a stroll. I couldn't sleep." He said.

"You came up *here* for a stroll? It's not exactly a sea shore."

The man paused as if to consider this. "An interesting point, if I understand what you are implying, officer but I'm sure the sea has claimed many more lives than Golgotha." Then he looked around with curiosity. "I wonder if I shall find myself up here someday? Lose myself, rather."

Erik frowned. The man was soft spoken and intelligent, even kind. It was puzzling. A typical trader would be easier to deal with and send back to the city but Erik' curiosity and comfort in the man's presence pressured him to let the man stay.

"Ah, yes." The stranger said suddenly, bending down. He lifted a stone and pulled something out from underneath. "Looking for this?" He held out an iron spike.

Erik mouth fell open as he grabbed the spike from the man's outstretched hand. He knew immediately it was the one he was looking for. It had dark stains on its surface and although he couldn't explain it, it seemed to *feel* right.

"How?" He exclaimed, unable to mouth the obvious question.

"Just a lucky guess, I suppose. Odd trinket though."

Erik clasped the spike to his breast. "Blessed are the meek." He whispered to himself. Then he caught himself and wondered why he said that.

The man smiled and looked up into Erik face. "Indeed?"

"Thank you, citizen." Erik faced the man. "If you ever need a favor, just let me know and I'll see if I can help. My name is Erikssen Fisherman. I am stationed in Antonia under Pontius Pilate."

The man nodded. "My pleasure. Perhaps we shall meet again someday." He bowed and turned, strolling away into the darkness while Erik continued to stare at him. Then the man stopped and turned around.

"Curious isn't it?" He said tilting his head.

Erik stared at him. "What is curious?"

"'Blessed are the meek.'" He said, repeating what Erik had whispered to himself.

"What do you think it means?"

"Children, I think but I'm not exactly sure." He paused as if to consider some more. "Could be children." He shrugged and turned away, disappearing into the darkness.

Erik stood alone with his thoughts for a while. *Children*, he thought. Then his mind drifted to visions of his beautiful wife and unborn child.

After one more look around the hill, Erik smiled and clasped the spike in his hands. The man found it. It was under a stone. Without that man's help it would be there forever.

A sparrow flew past and chirped as it went about its business. The stars were fading and the horizon was a deep crimson signaling the approach of dawn. Erik turned and hurried back down the slopes of the hill towards the city gates. He hoped his wife had not wakened to find an empty bed. He hoped she was not worried about him. He hoped she would not ask why.

The man watched Erik from the shadows and, satisfied he would not be disturbed, returned to the top of Golgotha. He waited patiently for some time until the sound of footfalls made him turn.

"Hello, brother." Said a young man with long black hair, walking up to join the other. He was handsome and wore a simple linen robe. He carried a walking stick which tapped the hilltop stones as he approached.

The man turned and stared in shock for a moment. Then he bowed respectfully. "Hello indeed, my lord. Its been nearly forty years!" He whispered loudly. "We have missed you."

"Hello young emissary. And why would you come to such a grim place, at such a dark hour?"

The man hesitated. "I grieve for him. He was my friend and my teacher. He was one of the best of us."

"Do not grieve, young emissary. He is...elsewhere."

"Do you think he achieved an opening?" The man paused and rephrased the question. "Do you know of this *opening* he spoke of?"

"I do but that is a matter yet to be seen." The young man sighed and looked around the hill. "There are more immediate concerns for us. How fair other areas? Do you have anything to report?"

"I do." The man sighed and scratched his beard. "War, disease, famine, pestilence are on the rise in various locations around the Empire and it's vicinity. Saja reports Asia is also not well. Maurice tells the same story of other continents. I have never seen or heard of it's like."

The young man considered this for a moment and nodded. "I have seen it before."

"What does it mean, my lord?"

The young man looked at the older one and considered the question for a few more moments. "It means an old enemy may have returned. One that you are far too young to know about."

The man looked shocked. "An enemy? One of the Hurum?"

"No. He is much older and much more dangerous."

The man considered this. "What must we do, Enlil?"

"For now, do what you think is best. I suggest keeping an eye on that officer for now. The Nazarene gave him a key. Either he or his unborn son will use it, I cannot foresee which."

"Who are they? Are they Hurum?"

"No. But for some reason *he* wanted one of them to reach Abanis."

The man sighed. "Will they be important in some way? Will they stand with us against this old enemy you speak of?"

The younger smiled slightly and looked back to the city of Jerusalem. Dawn was approaching and dark shadows grew on the western side of Golgotha. "Yes. I believe so but our enemy is both cunning and powerful. I sense one or both of them will need assistance."

The older man nodded. "I was told three imposters came here in the night. I'm still trying to find out who they were. They certainly wouldn't be emissaries."

"Namtar and his two brothers are missing. I suspect they have been...used."

"Used?" The man looked alarmed. "What does that mean?"

"Sorry brother. I'm not sure. For now, watch the officer and his older friend. They may need your assistance before long. As for myself, I will be taking a pilgrimage of a sort and will not return for some time. Please tell no one of this meeting. Farewell, young emissary." He said kindly.

The man looked depressed but nodded quietly.

The younger stepped forward suddenly and placed a hand on his shoulder. "Be at peace, Peter. He loved you and would not wish you to be saddened by his departure. Have faith."

The young man turned and walked away, twirling the walking stick in a nonchalant way that made the other man feel oddly encouraged just by watching him.

"My lord?" Peter said suddenly.

The young man turned. "Yes?"

"Is, uh, *was* the Nazarene really your son?"

The young man considered this and tilted his head to the side. He smiled conspicuously for a moment and tapped the side of his nose. With a wink and a nod he vanished into the shadows.

Chapter 3: Speared Quail

At this general point in the history of Judea, the city of Jerusalem was a strategic hill fortress under the control of the Roman Empire but ruled by a pack of *Herods*. In Imperialist fashion, the Roman Empire approved Herod the First's kingship and even gave him a gaggle of soldiers to take control of the region. The Prefect (or Governor or Procurator, if you prefer) of Judea at that time was Pontius Pilate. Surely some, if not all of you out there have heard that name before so let's get some facts straight. Pilate housed himself in the port city of Caesarea but often stayed at the Fortress of Antonia in Jerusalem. A special company of soldiers were stationed at the fortress under his command and many of them referred to Antonia as 'Pilate's Compound'.

The rule of Pilate was one of difficult circumstances. Frequent revolts and insufficient forces at the edge of the Roman Empire caused Pilate no end of worry. In reality, however, Pilate was a minor governor under the Syrian governor Vitellius. Most governors had control over legions of men but Pilate had a relatively small auxiliary force at his disposal led by a few Cohorts, Equestrians and Centurions. One of those cohorts was the notoriously insubordinate Longinus. This made him irritable. Not only because he had a small number of men but because a substantially wealthier family in Rome had planted the young whelp in his midst to make his life miserable. Pilate resented having Longinus around and was constantly losing face in the man's presence.

Another irritation to Pilate was his superior, the Syrian Governor, who couldn't be counted on in an emergency. The Roman governor of Syria was rumored to be distracted from his duties with Horace the Poet. According to one of Pilate's cohorts, the governor spent far too much time with Horace and not nearly enough time governing. If there was an incident in Judea, Pilate would be less likely to receive reinforcements and more likely to receive a sympathetic sonnet.

Erik and Longinus had served in Jerusalem for some time under Pilate. While other Commanders were on missions between Judea and Syria, Longinus was left in command of a substantial number of men in Jerusalem. Longinus had promoted Erik to consort to assist him with the day to day management of Pilate's forces within the city. Unlike some other officers, Longinus and Erik were lucky to have residences in an opulent quarter of the city, thanks to Longinus' family.

In his small house, after returning from Golgotha, Erik prepared to meet Longinus. They planned to meet just before sunrise and he had little time.

Aura yawned and blinked blearily in the dim lamplight of the bedroom. "You're up early."

Erik was hastily buckling up his cuirass and packing a backpack with some dry rations and a wine skin. He smiled at her. "I'm going to meet Longinus early this morning. Things are not so peaceful around the city with the death of that…" He paused. "…man a few days ago."

Aura stared at him. "His was a political death and an unnecessary one. You know Pilate forced it…" She trailed off and yawned again. It was too early for such topics. She raised her eyebrows. "What's that?"

Erik was stuffing a long, thin object wrapped in oiled skin in his cuirass. "This? Oh just a little…thing I picked up. Any mutton left?"

Aura frowned but decided to let it slip. Whatever it was, she was too tired to wonder. "Wrapped and ready near the door. Take it all. You'll need your strength."

"OK. I'm off." Erik leaned over to his wife and kissed her. "See you later this eve."

Aura smiled sleepily. "Mmm-K." She rolled back over and closed her eyes.

Erik slipped out into the pleasantly cool morning air and proceeded briskly into town. The city was always quiet at this time and he breathed deeply. He rather enjoyed the early morning hours when the inky blackness of the night sky gave way to a rich, blue hue heralding a new day. As birds chirped, announcing a slowly brightening morning, he stopped and marveled at eternity up in the sky.

He suddenly wondered if the gods looked down on earth in wonder and admiration as he did of the heavens. Shaking his head to clear the morning cobwebs from it, he continued a brisk pace into the slumbering city.

As he walked he noticed a man sleeping in a gutter some yards from the street. A suddenly flash of anger entered his mind and he saw another man's face arguing with him over some fish down at the market. Erik stopped and blinked in confusion as he looked at the man. Images flashed in his mind as if they were his own memories. He suddenly felt ill, as if he'd drank too much wine the night before. Confused and nauseous, Erik hastened away from the area and continued towards the markets.

He rounded the last corner and saw with relief his friend leaning against a fountain in front of the gate to Pilate's compound. Longinus was eating a pomegranate with great enthusiasm and saluted casually as Erik approached.

"Pomegranates! Fresh from Athens!" He patted a bulging side pack. "Good for the wife, if you know what I mean." He smiled devilishly at Erik who didn't respond but looked worryingly around the vacant city square. "Hey, you OK? You look a little pale."

"It's nothing." Erik shuddered slightly and shrugged. Longinus tossed him a ripe pomegranate. Erik realized something and looked at his friend. *He's worried about me.* He thought as he bit into the juicy red fruit.

"Eat up. Let's go for a walk." Longinus gestured down the main market street winding further into the city. He strode off, tossing the remains of pomegranate over his shoulder. Erik fell in beside him and gripped his pilum firmly as he looked about the deserted streets.

"Oh come on," said Longinus, glancing sideways as they walked. "No one is going to bother with me here and now." He raised his hands to the city at large. "They don't hate us here. Much."

"Yes sir." Erik nodded. *Yes, but how much did they like us?* He thought as he bit into the pomegranate and wiped the crimson juice from his chin. An officer of Longinus' rank was rarely seen walking, much less strolling through the streets at the crack of dawn without any men. It was reckless but Erik decided to let the matter slide.

As they walked Erik glanced down at Longinus' spear. It gleamed in the early morning light and Erik guessed his friend had polished it well, especially after the night on Golgotha. It was a formidable weapon and even more so in his friends' capable hands. Normally, officers of Longinus' rank carried an eagle-crested war sword - a symbol of their station. Longinus wore one at all times, sheathed at his side but the spear he carried belonged to his family.

A notable navy officer who fought in Egypt, Longinus's uncle passed away a number of years ago in Germania. The spear was delivered shortly after with instructions that it become an heirloom of Longinus' family. Thereafter, he treated it well, going to great lengths to maintain and keep it free of blemishes.

The two friends passed from residential areas into slowly awakening market streets. Erik passed Longinus a hearty chunk of smoked meat and they ate in silence as they walked. After a time, Erik decided to break the silence.

"So?"

"Yeah." Answered Longinus. "Well, I don't know." He tossed a mutton bone into an alley and looked around the city street. "We just don't have the manpower to go searching for mysterious hooded figures who speak strangely. If we see them, we'll deal with the situation." He sighed and looked hard at Erik. "The Jew king is already dead. Your alive. I'm alive. Let's be about our business. OK with you?"

"Sure." Said Erik, tossing some remaining shreds of mutton meat to an inquisitive dog. The mongrel inhaled the mutton and continued to stare longingly at the two men.

"Besides," Longinus continued walking down the street. "You're going to be a father. Deal with that first and then we'll talk about strange things that occur on crucifixion hills. Got it?"

"Agreed." Erik nodded and felt a sudden wave of relief flood over him. He didn't want to talk about the Golgotha matter either. Something about the whole evening made his skin crawl, like a bad nightmare. "So, what's the surprise?"

Longinus stopped and smiled wickedly.

Erik knew that look. It meant they were going skip duty. He liked the idea already, whatever it was.

"You and I are going hunting and fishing today. I've notified the ranks. As far as anyone is concerned, we are off doing some diplomatic duties. Is that ok with you, citizen?"

"Sure." Erik grinned. "Can't argue with a good hunt."

Longinus turned to scan the marketplace and pointed to a chariot-coach across the vacant square. "And we're taking *that* to get out of the city." He beamed at Erik.

A driver stood leaning against the side of the coach yawning in the dim light of the morning. The magnificent stallions snorted and rustled impatiently in their reigns.

"I've arranged a bit of transport for us. We should get going. The market will open in a little while and I don't want too many people to see us leave."

Erik was impressed. A coach of such quality was well beyond the monthly pay of an officer.

"Well, well, well." chided Erik in mock cynicism. "Must be nice to be the son of a Roman politician. Did *Pater* pay for this?"

Longinus winced at the remark and punched his friend playfully in the arm. "Alright, alright. Just come on."

They hurried across the square and boarded the carriage. Once inside Longinus knocked on the painted wood roof to signal the driver. The driver, still yawning and blinking in the dawn, guided the horse-drawn carriage through the outlying city streets.

As they rounded the last corner near Pilate's compound, however, they heard commotion coming from the gate. A crowd had gathered in front of the massive, iron-braced doors leading to the compound's courtyard. Longinus pounded on the carriage ceiling signaling the driver to stop and exchanged a quick glance with Erik.

"Looks like we're not going anywhere. C'mon."

Longinus bolted out of the carriage as it slowed, followed by Erik. The two men grabbed their spears and shields from the top of the carriage and surveyed the situation.

There seemed to be a small riot taking place. Torches bourn by the protestors danced angrily in the dawn mists. Three guards at the gate were trying to defuse the situation but mobs, whether large or small, need an authoritative voice to interact with. Longinus and Erik gripped their spears tightly and ran across the roadway to intercept the crowd.

"Free him! Free him! He is innocent!" Shouted a young woman with long black hair and large, almond shaped eyes. She threw a stone at one of three Roman guards standing in front of the gate. They were fresh soldiers from Rome and looked worried as they tried to calm the mob. The stone struck a guard in the face and he staggered back. The crowd, which at first was greatly agitated, seemed to lose some of its conviction at the sight of blood flowing from a wicked gash above the guard's eyebrow. The stricken guard fell back holding his hands to his face as the other two stepped into the gap to protect their fallen companion.

They made a grab for the woman as others in the crowd tried to hide her. One guard, much larger and stronger than the others thrust aside several dirty, malnourished members of the mob and yanked the woman forward. He threw her to the ground where she spat on his sandals and faced him defiantly. He raised his spear and roared.

"Miscreant!" He bellowed and thrust down but as he did so another spear deflected the strike. The guard's spear skewered the dirt beside the woman and the crowd fell suddenly silent.

"Enough!" Shouted Longinus. His eyes flared in anger as he surveyed the crowd. Even Erik, coming to stand beside him, started at the forceful command.

The guard who meant to strike the woman turned in anger and suddenly caught himself.

"Who dares this insol – err – Commander, sir, I - I didn't see you, sir. This crowd has assaulted Pilate's gate." He gestured to the silent crowd who looked at Longinus with a kind of awe.

Erik noted this as he peered into the faces of the people. *They are in awe of Longinus. One person beloved among them has been cruelly accused and sentenced to death.* He shook his head as strange thoughts formed in his mind and returned to the present.

"You!" Longinus commanded, pointing at the soldier who raised his spear menacingly at the woman still kneeling in the dirt at his feet. "Take this injured guard to a doctor. I will deal with this." The guard saluted immediately and took the injured man away from the commotion, leaving one soldier behind. Then he turned to the people at the gate and planted his spear firmly in the dirt. After surveying the crowd, he selected the oldest among them.

"You." Longinus said calmly, gesturing for the man to step forward. "Come forward, grandfather."

Erik helped the defiant woman to her feet and noted she was staring at Longinus in a kind of dumb-founded silence. Then he turned to see an elderly man in the back of the mob step forward as the crowd made way for him. Erik frowned. They were curiously obedient after such a disturbance and simply stared at Longinus.

As the man stepped forward, Longinus had the remaining guard frisk him for any concealed weapons. The guard looked back at Longinus and shook his head. He saluted and returned to his post.

"State your name."

"Joseph, sir." The man was thin and weak.

Erik blinked. The Nazarene, the crucified man he spoke to on Golgotha, appeared in his mind suddenly. He was washing this old man's feet. He shook his head and tried to focus on the present.

"Tell me," said Longinus in even tones. "Why have you done this? Why are you disturbing the peace?"

The elderly man hesitated in the silence of the crowd, looking blearily from Erik to Longinus and finally spoke in a weak, raspy voice.

"Well, you see, sir," he began, "we are..." He looked back at the small crowd, many of whom lowered their heads and seemed to carry some measure of guilt about them. The man looked back at Longinus. "We are...err, friends of a man imprisoned unfairly within the walls. He is a law abiding man and the soldiers have made a mistake."

Longinus considered this. "What reason did the soldiers give for his incarceration?"

"They said he was a..." The man looked around again but no one looked at him. He turned back to face Longinus again. "They said he was a Christian."

Longinus stared at the old man for a moment. Many in the crowd looked around nervously. He knew very well what the term Christian meant. At the moment it meant *enemy of Herod* and some parts of the Jewish clergy.

Erik surveyed the scene beside his friend as flash-visions continued to invade his mind. Then he leaned over to Longinus and whispered. "They will be satisfied with your promise of a fair investigation. Don't ask me why."

Longinus hesitated. He glanced at Erik questioningly then back to the man before him. *Christian* didn't necessarily mean *enemy of the Republic* yet and Longinus held the republic in the highest respect.

"Very well. Listen to me, all of you." Longinus said loudly. The crowd fell silent once more. "I will look into the matter. For now, please return to your domiciles peacefully. You have my assurance this matter will be dealt with fairly." He waited for a reaction.

Erik noted the mob looked almost mesmerized and dumbstruck as they blinked up at Longinus. Seemingly at peace but somewhat confused, they dissipated and wandered off.

Eventually, Erik and Longinus were standing alone in front of the gates to Pilates compound.

"Well then. So much for our hunting and fishing day-off." Longinus sighed and gestured to the gate. "C'mon Erik, let's see this prisoner."

Erik nodded and gestured to the gate soldier who saluted and shouted for the gates to be opened. Erik and Longinus swept inside as the massive doors swung open.

They crossed the spacious courtyard beyond the gates and headed to the Officer's barracks, a small building beside Pilate's impressive compound. The evening watch was just leaving and guards saluted Longinus smartly as he swept past them and turned into his own, spacious office. Erik closed the door and leaned against it watching his friend silently.

Longinus unbuckled his cuirass and flung it onto his desk with a 'clang'. It scattered various, unfinished scrolls of his administrative duties and some fell to the floor. "What in Pluto's pits was that?" Longinus gestured to the general direction of the gates.

Erik shrugged. "The Nazarene had influence on some of the people. Perhaps one or more have filled his place."

"Oh, wonderful!" Said Longinus, throwing his hands up in the air. "That's all we need right now - *Messiah part II*. Pilate will find a way to blame this on me, mark my words."

Erik grinned humorlessly and nodded. He knew whenever Pilate needed something done, the Commander often had to do the dirty work. It was no secret the two men despised each other. This made Erik nervous because Pilate was becoming less candid with his hatred of Longinus' station.

"Have you ever seen such a thing? I mean people just showing up with women and elderly." Longinus shook his head.

"No, I haven't. It wasn't a threatening mob, I have to admit." Said Erik. "Did you see him observing?"

"Who?"

"Pilate. He was watching from his balcony when we arrived."

Longinus hesitated. "Did he see it all?"

Erik shrugged. "Who cares? Just deal with this matter the way your father would. You're not going to be here much longer anyway."

"My guess is he'll want to make an example out of the one of they arrested." Longinus sighed and looked out the window. The orange light of dawn silhouetted a sparrow perched on a metal torch ring outside the window. It chirped happily and flew off.

Erik nodded. "Well, what now?"

"Alright. Let's go see our prisoner." Said Longinus, re-fastening his cuirass. "If he's got a wreath of thorns around his head, I'm quitting and walking back to Rome. C'mon." They left the room and Erik followed his Commander across the courtyard to the dungeons.

The prisons of Pilate's compound were underground. Dank and smelly, the brown air reeked of bile and sorrow. Grid iron doors and small, dirt hewn compartments separated the prisoners. Even during the day there was little if any light so the guards fastened torches to the walls and kept them lit at all times. The jail keeper, squat and ape-like, stood up from his small table of cheap wine and bread to throw a sloppy salute as Longinus descended the stone stairs. He shambled over to the inner gate with a jangle of keys to unlock it as they walked down the narrow dirt hall. The iron gate creaked open and then shut again with an echoing clang as the two officers entered the squalid hallway.

"He's the only lucky one t'day." Said the keeper through the metal grid and he returned to his meager dinner.

The prisoner Erik and Longinus came down to see was lucky enough to have been thrown into the one cell with a small window cut into the wall where it met the ceiling. It was too small to be a security risk but just large enough for the cell's occupant to enjoy a bit of fresh air. The cell's occupant sat huddled in a corner covered completely with brown, ragged robes.

Erik and Longinus approached the door and stared into the cell. The heap of brown rags raised and fell ever so slightly, indicating the person therein was sleeping peacefully.

Longinus raised an eyebrow and looked at Erik. "Wish I had the peace of mind to sleep like that." Then he rattled his knuckles on the iron grid. "Hey you!"

The figure stirred and after moment peered blearily out from under the rags.

Erik gaped at the man in recognition. It was the man he met on the hill. *Blessed are the meek* echoed in Erik's ears. A flash of memory, not his own, seared across Erik's mind. For a split second he was sitting down to dinner with the Nazarene.

"Stand up and come over here." Longinus commanded.

The man stood, brushed some dirt off his already tattered robes. He caught Erik' eye and stared for a moment. Then he bowed slightly at them and smiled in a calm manner. "M'lords." He said courteously.

"What have you done? Why have you been thrown down here."

The man looked from Longinus to Erik. "Didn't the soldier's tell you?"

"I want you to tell me." Said Longinus.

"I am a Christian." The man smiled.

"How did you come to be here? Were you protesting the Nazarene's crucifixion?"

"I was simply at the wrong place at the wrong time."

"Answer with more detail, citizen."

The man seemed to consider something for a moment. "Alright." He said at last. "I was teaching children."

Longinus sighed. "What?"

"He was teaching the lessons of his master." Interrupted Erik. "He was a disciple of the Nazarene."

"Look, Nick, let me do the –" started Longinus.

"He's right." Said the man.

Longinus hesitated. "Come again?"

"Your friend has a gift for...intuition."

"Nick's gotta gift? Yes, isn't that nice. He's my friend, yes. Now, explain how you came to be arrested."

"Yes. As I said, I was arrested for teacher. For example, 'Blessed are the meek, for they shall inherit the earth'."

"Blessed are the meek?" Longinus looked at Erik.

Erik managed to shrug but his eyes remained fixed on the prisoner.

"Right." Said Longinus. "So you were teaching gibberish to kids. Well, wouldn't be the first time. My teachers in Rome weren't exactly Thales. What else? Were you disturbing the peace in any way."

"It is possible I incited a riot."

"Now we are getting somewhere." Longinus frowned again at the man.

"I instructed the children to obey their parents at all times."

"What? Not exactly a crime there, unless you're an Emperor. Go on."

"The Christians here in Jerusalem, few as they are, raided the temples yesterday and assaulted one of the members of its clergy."

"Bad move. Now you have angry Jewish community on your hands. Did you join the raid?

"No."

"Did you hurt anyone?"

"Not exactly."

"Not exactly?"

"One of the children," said the man in measured tones, "followed the words of his parents down to the last detail and assaulted a cleric. The cleric died. When asked about the crime, the child said his father told him to do it. Just before the father of the child fell under an officer's blade, he told the soldiers about me. I'm guessing they wanted to round everyone up."

"Let me get this straight," Longinus now leaned on the iron grid-work and stared intently at the man, "you taught some children a valuable lesson and have been arrested for the misgivings of a parent?

"Yes. That sounds about right." Said the man, lowering his head.

Longinus looked at Erik who shook his head and turned around. He snapped his fingers loudly at the jail keeper beyond the inner gate. The man hobbled towards them and after a moment the gate was swung open.

"Yes my lord?"

"Release this man and escort him off the premises."

"Sir?"

"You heard me." Longinus stared at the jail keeper.

The man shrugged and hobbled forward. After wrestling with the ring of keys, cell lock clicked and the iron-grid door swung open.

The prisoner stepped forward. "Thank you sir." He bowed.

Longinus gestured for him to leave. "As long as you weren't teaching Greek tragedy, you're fine by me. That stuff could seriously injure an impressionable mind. Now, get out of here and stay out of trouble please."

The man chuckled and nodded to Erik.

"Till we meet again." And he hurried down the hall towards an ushering warden.

Longinus suddenly froze and Erik could sense the air become cold. "Wait!" He shouted after the retreating man and walked swiftly up to him. He was slightly flushed in the face and looked at the man sternly.

"The father of the child!" He said, grabbing the man by the arm.

"The who?" The man asked, somewhat surprised.

"You said he was killed. Who performed the summary execution?" Longinus asked with measured anger.

"A large officer. He had dark eyes, a legion brand on his right arm and looked kind of like - "

"- like a pig." Finished Longinus, nodding. His face turned a shade of purple.

The man nodded silently.

Erik knew what was about to happen.

Centurion Cornelius, the *pig* in question, had a reputation around the city for sadistic punishments and blood-thirsty interrogations. He was one of Longinus' centurions. Longinus had him thrown out of the city on one occasion but Pilate had the brute reinstated just to spite him. Longinus hated the man and wanted him thrown out of the service but Pilate rather liked Cornelius' style and used him for *sensitive* interrogations.

"That son of a hog's ass end! That stupid, blood thirsty, mother -…"

Longinus threw his spear to the ground and paced down the dirt hall. He shouted a variety of colorful metaphors involving the soldier's mother, surgical accidents and large amounts of feces.

"How many bloody times does that sadist need to be told that no more summary executions will be tolerated in my bloody city? How many f – !"

Erik just stood looking at the former prisoner and tried to mime that it'll end in a moment and that he should leave.

Longinus breathed and collected his composure. He picked up his spear and pointed at the former prisoner.

"You. Get out of here. Be a good teacher. Don't break the law."

"You." He pointed at the cringing jail keeper. "Go back to your desk. Do the paperwork."

"Erik." Longinus turned to his younger friend. "We're going to see Corporal Corn but first we're paying a visit to Pilate." Then he stormed down the small hallway and began to climb the stone steps to the surface of the compound.

Erik paused as if to say something but a soft voice entered his mind.

We will meet again soon. Follow this path.

Erik stared at the man in shock for a second. The man had spoken but his lips did not move.

"Erik, come on!" Roared Longinus from the top of the stairs.

Startled, Erik nodded to the man. "As you were citizen." Then he hastened after his Commander.

****Jingle*Jingle*Jingle****

Pilate was sitting down to a nice evening meal with a few of his female *guests* when he was rudely interrupted. He had just begun to break bread when a loud hammering on his lavish doors disturbed the peaceful mood of his domicile. He cringed and threw the bread viciously at a servant.

"Get that." He ordered and stood straightening the robes of his office. His *guests* put on some more clothes and retreated to his sleeping area.

Two guards escorted Longinus into Pilates spacious, private domicile. It was a huge palace room on the third floor of the compound with all of the amenities that a Roman prefect could enjoy. Braziers of varying sizes lit the domicile with soft orange light and complimented the air with sweet incense. On a large, circular marble dais near the balcony were strewn an assortments of pillows and blankets. Spread before the dais on ornate tables were a variety of savory meats, fruits and cheeses on polished silver platters. A servant placed a large decanter of wine and several goblets on the table before retreating hastily as Longinus approached. Pilate sat behind the low table and stared passively at Longinus as he pored himself a goblet of wine. He did not offer any to Longinus.

Longinus stood at attention before Pilate and saluted smartly. "Hail Caesar." He said stiffly.

"Yes, Yes. Hail Caesar." Pilate replied as he stood up and walked around his dinner buffet. He looked over Longinus' shoulder to the guards by the double doors.

"Leave us." He ordered. They hastily left the domicile.

"Well now, Longinus." Said Pilate, chewing on an olive as he absently waved his goblet. "Why are you hammering on my doors at this hour?"

"Sir." Said Longinus curtly. "Corn has disobeyed me once more."

"Indeed? How troubling." Said Pilate, indicating with every syllable that he wasn't the least bit troubled. He took a sip of wine and sighed. "Regarding what exactly?"

"These Christians," started Longinus, "they are not yet an enemy of the Republic. They deserve the same liberties as the Jews to practice their faith and –"

" – What has Corn done?" Pilate interrupted coldly.

"He summarily executed a man today and arrested several others for their faith."

"And what is their faith?"

"They claim to be Christians. Followers of the one you murd -" Longinus stopped as Pilate gave him a swift and vicious glance. "- the *man* you crucified." He finished flatly.

"Well now," said Pilate as he turned to pour himself more wine. "I ordered all Christians to be brought in as of this morning. They are disturbers of the peace. Didn't you get the memo?"

"Sir, that is my jurisdiction. They can't possibly be a threat to peace and–"

"My order is law, Longinus. Do we have a problem with that?" Pilate's voice was biting.

"No sir." Longinus straightened. "What of Cornelius? I want him gone. He's not an officer. He's a menace."

"I shall worry about Cornelius."

"Sir, I must insist - " Longinus tried to continued.

"Must you? You will do as you are told." Replied Pilate casually, spitting an olive pit on the marble floor.

Longinus gaped at Pilate for a moment then saluted. "As you wish." He turned and stormed from the room, slamming the doors behind him.

He descended the wide spiral stairway and headed to the courtyard where Erik waited.

"What happened?"

Longinus face was red. "Nick. Assemble a group of men. Have them meet me in the courtyard in five minutes."

"Yes sir." Erik nodded. "What are we going to do?"

"We're going to go out and find Corn."

Erik looked worried. He knew his friend had a temper when it came to Corn. "And then what?"

"I'm a peacekeeper Erik." Said Longinus resolutely as he put on his plumed helm. and fastened his cloak. "That's my job. I'm bloody well going to go out and keep some damn peace. We're going to arrest the bastard for murder."

Chapter 4: Black-Eyed Peace

If it weren't for the fact that Corporal Cornelius was bipedal and wore Roman armor, many of the pigs in

Jerusalem would have found him rather attractive. This pretty much sums up the appearance of the man.

In addition to his unfortunate likeness to swine, Corn (as he was known about the city) was a simple man. He simply liked to hurt things. This simple fact pleased his *benefactor* but it often brought complications into his life as well. The most immediate complication at the moment was being locked up in a dirt cell underneath Pilate's compound. This was a complication he hadn't expected. Earlier that evening, the Commander and his side-kick arrested him in the wine house and thus made his simple life quite complicated indeed.

He spat and leaned against the iron bars of the cell as he replayed the previous evening in his head. The Commander was about to meet his end at the point of a boot-dirk when Erik smashed Corn in side of the face with a wine jug. He frowned and just as his slow mind worked up enough momentum for a more detailed recollection, the iron door at the end of the hall creaked open. He heard footsteps coming down the hall.

Corn stood up quickly and moved closer to the gate of his cell. *Must be precise with the timing!* He thought. *I can reach out and strangle the Commander or the jail keeper in two seconds….now!*

Cornelius sprang against the cell door and thrust a beefy arm through the gate, grasping the neck of Pontius Pilate. Corn's eyes widened and he released the Prefect immediately.

Pilate hadn't even flinched but grinned mirthlessly.

"Err...sorry master." Corn said gruffly. "I was just –

" - wanting to strangle someone? Well, who could blame you?" Pilate finished coyly. He surveyed Corn and nodded to as if to satisfy some inner calculation.

"Very well, soldier. You'll get your chance indeed." He turned and shouted. "Jailor!" The jail keeper hobbled down the hall, jangling keys and stumbling.

"Open this gate and release this soldier." Said Pilate, stepping back.

"Yes sir." The jail keeper complied. There was a rustle of keys and the grid-iron door swung open.

Corn stepped forward into freedom and grinned.

"Now" said Pilate, putting his hand on the large man's shoulder guiding him down the hall. "I have a letter here. Can you read?"

"No master." Corn looked down at the finely made paper Pilate held out. He stared at it with confused curiosity as they made their way out of the dungeon.

"Well then, if you could read, this letter would please you as much as it pleases me." Pilate turned it over to reveal the seal of the Senate of Rome.

"I recognize *that.*" Said Corn, transfixed on the seal.

Pilate grinned and slipped the letter back into the folds of his robe. "Yes, I'm sure you do." They began to ascend the stairs. "Let's chat about the meaning of this letter and how much money I - err - *we* are entitled to. Perhaps some wine with some concubines? You *do* like women don't you?"

Corn drooled and a grinned.

Pilate watched Corn and nodded sagely as they ascended the dungeon stairs. "I'll take that as a *yes*".

****Jingle*Jingle*Jingle****

Erik drained his mug in one shot and slammed the cup on the makeshift table. An old patron to his left, who looked as though he had slammed a few too many cups down over several decades, chuckled and nodded encouragingly.

"Wooh! Slow down there barbarian!" Longinus punched him on the shoulder from across the table. "You gonna save some wine for the rest of the city?"

"Yeah." He grinned blearily and nodded.

Erik and Longinus decided to return to the wine house they disrupted earlier that day to give the patron a bit of business. Since it was one of their favorite drinking establishments, it was an easy decision.

As most drinking establishments go, this one had all the qualities of humble pubs around the modern world. The lighting was dim, the beverages were warm and the food was simple. No one had to look for a shadowy corner because all of them were. At present, the wine house was filled with a mixture of merchants and fisherman. Those who didn't know Longinus, were trying very hard not to notice his eagle-crested war sword and what he could legally do with it. Considering this was the modern equivalent of a weeknight, however, most customers were quietly focused on drinking themselves into oblivion before they realized it. Longinus and Erik, on the other hand, felt they deserved a few jugs of oblivion after a hard day's work.

Erik looked around the wine house and replayed the previous evening in his mind. After leaving the compound, they finally caught up with him Corn here and it took several guards to subdue him. In the commotion, Erik saw Corn break a hand free and reach into his boot for a hidden dirk. If Erik hadn't sensed the danger and smashed the man over the head with a clay pot, Longinus could have been badly injured. Or worse. For some reason, Erik was troubled by the whole business with Corn but he couldn't say exactly why. *A* drink didn't help much so it was followed by fifteen more.

"Why the concern?" Longinus echoed his thoughts.

"Dunno. Maybe he'sh gonna get out."

"So what if does? That bastard is done in my service." Longinus waved a hand dismissively. "He's gonna be shipped off to Egypt. His men have already been reassigned. I took care of that personally this evening. My father has a special place for brainless brutes like him and if Pilate tries to interfere, there's gonna be hell to pay." Longinus drained his own mug and snickered.

"S-all fine and dandy but Pilate like's him. He *is* the Prefect of Judea you know. How much can your family do if…?" Erik trailed off as he stared into his empty mug and tried to remember how it became that way.

"You're drunk and paranoid." Laughed Longinus. "Let me worry about Pilate. You just worry about that fetching wife of yours." He grinned and gave the proprietor the silent and universal gesture indicating *we've had enough to drink and will go home now.*

"C'mon Nick. Let's getcha home." Longinus drained his cup. "Right after I visit mother Gaia."

He got up, dropped some coins in the expectant hand of the proprietor and headed out the back door. Like most wine houses around the Empire at this time in history, the location of the privy was *not inside.*

"I'll wait for ya' out front." Erik mumbled. After a moment, he managed to smile at several proprietors and attempted to stand. In his own mind, he stood up, bid the patrons a pleasant evening and walked briskly out the front door.

In reality, he stood up, swayed threateningly over a few customers at a nearby table who grabbed their mugs and food, waved at a surprised serving girl he thought was his wife for a brief moment and staggered towards a window. This didn't work as intended, so the proprietor helped him out the front door. A chorus of good-byes from the tavern customers followed after him as he vanished into the blue evening street.

"Alright fella's," said Erik to a group of soldiers standing watch in front of the tavern. "Long and I are off. Here," he fumbled with a purse of coins at his side and nearly dropped it. "Take this coin boys - a job well done tonight. Enjoy it."

He handed the purse over to one of the men. On seeing the generous amount of coin the men saluted and chorused 'thank-you's as they dispersed into the night.

Alone in the street, Erik swayed and stumbled around in front of the wine house waiting for his friend. Inside, he could hear Longinus saying goodbye to everyone. He peered upward and smiled. The stars were out again. The night air cleared his head and his thoughts drifted to his wife.

The night sky suddenly flashed as if a rogue lightning bolt got lost on its way down and decided to hit Erik. He closed his eyes and staggered as a vision of Aurelia appeared in his mind. He could see her struggling with someone. She was pinned to a floor but it wasn't their house. It was polished marble, like the stuff used in Pilate's personal chambers. Large, beefy hands held both of Aura's wrists and Corn drooled on her as he attempted to open her robes.

That bastard! I'll kill him! Erik thought as the vision faded. He swayed for a moment in the street as the evening came back into focus. All thoughts of Longinus were politely pushed aside by darker thoughts of vengeance. In a drunken stupor Erik stumbled off in the direction of Pilate's compound with wine-lacquered resolve. He rounded a corner just as Longinus came out of the winery.

"Erik?" Longinus looked around, peering down an alley beside the tavern. "Alright, c'mon Erik." He waited, peering into the darkness of the alley.

Longinus frowned and walked up the street towards their neighborhood. The alcohol coursing through his veins seemed to thin and he sobered slightly as concern took over his senses. The streets were dark and the occasional cat mewed at him from various shadows.

That wasn't like Erik to just wander off like that. He thought to himself. He was drunk but not that –

"Spare some coin for a young pilgrim, officer?"

Longinus jumped sideways as a slim, handsome young man with a simple white walking stick emerged from the shadows. He had long, black hair and wore a simple linen robe.

"Jupiter's lightning! You scared the hell out of me!" Started Longinus. He sighed and absently searched the pocket within his cuirass as he continued to look around up and down adjacent streets. He gave the young man some coins who took them with both hands bowed.

"Erik! Where the hell are you?" Said Longinus to the empty streets at large as he walked away from the beggar.

"Are you looking for someone sir?"

Longinus turned. "Yes. My friend was out here not three minutes ago. Did you see him? He's tall, fair haired and well…" he paused, "quite intoxicated."

"Ah, yes, yes." Whispered the young man. "He's gone that way, towards Antonia." A slender arm pointed in the general direction of Pilate's compound.

Longinus sighed. "Thank you citizen." He nodded to the man and hurried up the street.

The young man turned his head slightly and watched Longinus vanish around a corner.

"You're welcome, Commander." He whispered.

He waited for a few moments and then looked at the coins in his hand. Scanning the dark street, he spotted a humble house with slightly open shutters. Walking quietly over to it, he carefully placed the coins inside the windowsill. Then he turned and meandered quietly into the night at a pace normally associated with someone taking a leisurely stroll on a beach.

Some distance from the inn, the young man stopped as he was confronted by another beggar. This one was old and decrepit. This one had cheap linen robes splattered with blood and other unnamable stains. His teeth were yellow and his face was matted with hair and dirt. He smelled of alcohol, sweat and blood.

"Can I help you sir?" Said the young man, with casual politeness.

"Oh, well..." said the ancient, bedraggled man. He drooled and looked longingly at the young man as he licked his cracked, pale lips. "Indeed, you can my beautiful young boy." He cackled maliciously.

No one heard the young man's walking stick clatter to the stone cobbles.

****Jingle*Jingle*Jingle****

The jail keeper smiled stupidly, his head half submerged in a bowl of stew. Normally when someone is bathing in their food they don't smile like this but when one is black-jacked from behind, a bowl of stew is a nice warm pillow.

Erik dropped the blackjack and wrested the keys from the prone keeper's belt. He paused to look up the dirt stairs in case his infiltration was detected. No sounds. Good. As quietly as possible, Erik negotiated the lock with the ring of keys. This was not an easy a task under the influence of alcohol but he managed to unlock the gate with little noise. Slowly, the inner gate opened. Half way open, it creaked alarmingly and the jailer stirred in his stew.

Erik froze again and listened. Nothing. Good.

He stepped into the dark passageway and drew the iron spike from a pocket inside his cuirass. He looked down at its blood-caked shaft and sighed, shaking his head. He thought about the vision he had of Corn pinning his wife to the ground and it burned his stomach. In the last few days, Erik had come to realize the peculiar visions and feelings he experienced were not literal. He knew they were just amplifications of his own worries and senses but he had no idea what was causing them to occur. Somehow, he knew that Aura was safe at home but he just had to see if Corn was in the cell. He just wanted to scare the man a little. He wasn't about to commit murderer or anything.

Erik hesitated in the darkness. He realized the alcohol-laden vision summoned a desire for false vengeance against Corn. Now, his better nature was rousing from the confines inebriation and asking what the hell he was doing. He also realized Longinus was probably wandering around the city looking for him and felt terribly guilty.

Tired and feeling nauseous, Erik pocketed the spike and decided to go home. He turned in the passageway and followed the subtle candlelight of the warden's table as a beacon to fresh air. As he did so, he realized something was very wrong in the cell block. He stopped and listened. Nothing. No sounds of breathing or snoring. Absolute silence.

He walked hastily to the cell where Corn had been incarcerated. His heart skipped a beat as he gaped at the vacant cell. Most of his alcohol-soaked blood was suddenly laced with a strong dose of adrenaline. This made his head throb as the evening of euphoric drunkenness made way for the dawn of a hangover. He tried to remain calm. Pilate may have let Corn out but if he did, there will be hell to pay.

He decided to leave and tell Longinus provided he could find him. He headed back down the passage to the stairs, pausing to place the keys back on the belt of the slumbering jail keeper. As he stood he sensed something.

Danger was upon him!

Too late, on the way to the dirt floor he noticed the blackjack was not where he tossed it. Too bad he hadn't his own pillow of stew to rest his head in.

****Jingle*Jingle*Jingle****

Longinus jogged through the empty city streets towards Pilate's compound. He tried to calculate *how drunk Erik was* and attempted to factor in *how stupid he could be*. The resulting estimation made him hasten his step.

He rounded the last corner near the compound and bounded towards the gates. The guards on duty raised their spears in alarm at the charging figure but seeing their Commander enter the torchlight they saluted.

"Did Erik come by here?" He breathed.

"Yes sir. He came in about fifteen minutes ago."

"Did he leave?"

"No sir. No one has come or gone from the compound since then."

Longinus frowned and motioned for the gates to be opened. The guards saluted and called inside. As the gates swung open and Longinus swept inside he glanced up and to his surprise the demesne of Pilate was alight. A figure stood on the balcony. It was Pilate. Longinus cursed under his breath and stopped to salute. Pilate returned the salute and turned around, retreating to his domicile. Strange sounds echoed down about the courtyard from the third floor. Someone was being beaten. Longinus scowled at the thought of Pilate's abuse of power but focused his attention on finding Erik.

He hastened across the courtyard to the officer's barracks. Lamp light flooded the dark hall as Longinus entered the building. He sighed in relief as he flung the door open.

"Where in Pluto's pastures have you… - " He stopped.

A young officer, one of Pilate's private guards, stood up from the chair Erik normally occupied and saluted the Commander. Longinus recognized him as a new recruit from neighboring Syria.

"What are you doing here?" Longinus gaped at the man.

The young man saluted again. "Commander Longinus, sir. I have been sent here to await your arrival. Pontius Pilate awaits your presence. It is of the uttermost importance that you present yourself to him immediately." The guard hastily exited the office while Longinus continued to gape at him.

After a moment of confusion, Longinus gathered himself and hastily buckled his cuirass. He grabbed his plumed helm and decided to let Erik be for now. Regardless of his rising dislike for Pilate, Longinus would do his duty. He paused in the doorway and glanced at his spear, gleaming in the corner on a weapons rack. Then he closed the door and headed towards Pilate's palace room.

A guard on duty at the top of stairs saluted and stepped aside as Longinus approached. "He is waiting for you sir." Said the guard. But there was something in his face and his voice. The guard looked down at the Commander's sword and nodded silently.

Longinus paused for a moment and looked down then knocked loudly on large, double doors.

"Enter." He heard Pilate from the room beyond.

As Longinus entered, the first thing he noticed was a figure lying atop the central dais of Pilate's main room. Instead of pillows, tables of food and concubines lounging about it lazily, there lay a single prone figure. The figure was passed out, face down. Longinus noted the light spatter of blood near the man and realized he was not unconscious due to excessive wine. Then he froze as the hammer of realization clanged on the anvil of his wits.

Jupiter's mother! He thought. *It's Erik!*

Without thinking or looking around, he raced toward the dais to see if Erik was alive. Half way there, however, he was smashed in the face by the by a spear shaft. His head snapped back and he fell backwards to the ground, head spinning from the blow. His plumed helm clanged loudly on the floor and rolled away. "Welcome Commander." Said a quiet, polite voice. "We have much to discuss."

Chapter 5: Lamb Chops

Longinus blinked. His mouth filled with blood and his lip swelled. He looked up from the cold marble floor and tried to focus. He raised his head and began to sit up as Cornelius and Pilate emerged from the shadows. Cornelius casually shouldered a spear. He spat at Longinus' feet and leered.

"How dare you accost me! Have you lost what little mind you have, Pilate!" Longinus bellowed from the floor.

Pilate raised an index finger to his lips to shush Longinus and walked softly to a large desk near the balcony window.

On it were a multitude of scrolls, parchments and piles of money. He sat down behind it on a lush, high backed chair and looked at Longinus with calm smugness. His purple and white robes were spotted with blood. Longinus watched Cornelius follow his master like a feral but loyal hog. He stood behind the prefect and gave Longinus a mirthless grin. His fists were bloody.

An empty chair had been placed in front of the desk.

"Well?" Said Pilate at last. "Won't you join us?" He gestured dramatically to the empty chair.

Longinus looked at the prone figure of Erik and then back to Pilate. His mind raced. Memories of conversations with his father came to him instinctively. "*When the game is afoot,*" he recalled his father say, "*pretend you have a limp.*"

Longinus thought about the situation and quickly gathered himself. As powerful and influential as he was, Pilate would not risk such behavior without having certain guarantees. But what were they?

Pilate sensed Longinus' calculation. "Yes Commander. Let us be civil."

Longinus got to his feet and shook his head. Blood was beginning to cake his thoroughly swollen lip. His hand strayed to his war sword as he locked eyes with Cornelius.

"That," said Pilate quietly, "would be unwise." He glanced at Cornelius who quickly dropped his spear and pulled out a cross-bow from under the table.

Longinus hesitated. His cuirass, strong and polished, would not stop a war bolt of that size. More likely, it would leave a rather large hole in his chest and skewer the double doors behind him. His hand dropped.

"On the floor, Commander." Cornelius pointed to Longinus' sword.

Reluctantly, he unbuckled his eagle-crested sword and slowly placed it on the ground near the prone body of Erik.

"Now." Said Pilate. "Please sit down."

Erik stirred on the dais. He looked grim but not too badly beaten. This did little to ease Longinus' anger but he maintained composure in front of Pilate. The beating of Erik was obviously meant to get a rise out of him so he endeavored to be calm. Wiping some blood from his chin, Longinus walked over to the chair and sat down heavily.

Pilate stared at Longinus for a moment as if to contemplate something. Shrugging his shoulders he looked around his desk for something as Longinus glared at him.

"Ah, yes. Here it is." He picked up a letter with a gold and purple seal. "I opened this letter, thinking it was for me but it seems it was meant for you. Here you go."

Mocking austere politeness, he held out the parchment for Longinus who leaned forward slowly took it hesitantly.

Longinus looked at two seals on the back of the letter. One was the seal of the Roman Senate. The other was the seal of a magistrate - his father's seal! He hastily opened the parchment and read the letter:

Longinus,

I regret to inform you that on the XXII day of Antioch your father, Magistrate Gracchus Massimiliano, was found treasonous to the Empire of Rome by his eminence, Emperor Tiberius Caesar. On the XXIII day of Antioch your father was executed for his alleged crimes and all assets of your family have confiscated by the Empire. Your brothers and their respective families have escaped the city, choosing exile in Britannia.

I wish to extend my deepest apologies to you and your family at this time for Gracchus was a treasured friend. As many of our numbers fall to the increasing bloodlust of our mad king, I strongly urge you to find refuge far from the empire. May Jupiter find you well, there and forever after.

Destroy this letter as soon as you receive its message.

"**:P**" *(A friend.)*

Longinus read the letter calmly. He didn't know who **:P** was or why the monogram looked so odd. Over and over in his mind the words repeated themselves until he was overcome by an abstract symphony of spirit crushing silence. He dropped the paper and bowed his head. Time seemed to slow down. His mind raced and he calculated the necessary political reaction. To show his grief at this time would be a triumph for Pilate, who was watching him carefully. He tried to silence the words *your father was executed* repeating over and over in his mind but could not silence them.

"My deepest condolences Commander." Said Pilate calmly.

Longinus ignored the empty comment.

"My men are with me. They respect me. You will have a hard time convincing them to betray their Commander."

"Ah, yes. You're men have been well trained Longinus." Said Pilate quietly. "Yes, well trained to serve the Empire and by no small part of yours. In fact, you have trained them so well they would gladly dismiss any loyalties to you to serve the needs of the Empire. You are a criminal."

Longinus considered this. Gods be damned, the bastard was right. He trained the men to serve the Republic and now *he* was an enemy of it.

"And," continued Pilate as if he was listening to Longinus internal calculations, "you're family's disgrace in Rome has been posted on every barracks in every city and town from here to Syria." Then he raised both hands feigning innocence. "Not my doing. Rome did all that." Pilate lowered his hands and sat back in his chair.

Longinus knew all too well the fickle nature of public opinion. He could not combat such propaganda. His family was ruined so he had to think carefully about his next move. He had to think politically to save his friend's life and his own. He nodded his head and looked at Pilate who waited patiently. It took all of his self discipline to remain calm knowing that his father was dead and his family name destroyed.

"Alright. Well done Pilate. So what now? What of him?" He gestured to Erik who was stirring on the dais.

"I am not a heartless man, Longinus, despite what you may think. But I am forced to carry out the orders given to me by Rome." Said Pilate, glancing at Erik prone body. "You will both be sent to the front lines in Germania and your wives and holdings will be confiscated by the state."

Cornelius followed Pilate's gaze as they looked at Erik. That's all Longinus needed. *Fuck politics!*

He sprang across the table and swiped at the crossbow with his large hand. Cornelius, caught off guard, pulled the trigger too late and dropped the cross-bow. The war bolt rocketed across the room and shattered one of the double doors leading to the stairs. With his other arm, Longinus swung a vicious backhand which connected squarely with Pilate's jaw and sent the man careening off his plush chair.

Cornelius struggled with Longinus, who was now sprawling over the table and knocking wine, scrolls and money everywhere. Longinus was a large man but he was equally matched by Cornelius. In their struggle, the large desk was upended. A nearby brazier fell with a loud crash, sending up a cloud of bright orange sparks as smoldering embers rolled across the floor.

Behind the two struggling giants, Pilate staggered to his feet and swayed. He spotted a silver decanter nearby. Despite his spinning senses, he picked it up and swung it wildly at Longinus' head.

Seeing the flurry of movement in his periphery, Longinus turned and ducked just in time. The decanter smashed Cornelius in the face with a loud *clang*. The man grinned stupidly and fell to the floor leaving Longinus standing alone in momentary surprise. He turned and glared at Pilate whose face now drained of color.

Even if armed with heavy wine decanter, Pilate was no match for Longinus who was a much larger man and a highly trained soldier. The decanter fell to the floor from Pilates limp hand and he held out his hands to show he was unarmed. Unfortunately, his pride overwhelmed his sense of self-preservation and he glared at Longinus angrily.

"I was going to spare your life! This is how you repay my mercy?" He screamed.

"Your mercy would have Nick and I skewered at the front lines of Germania while our wives be enslaved in Rome." Spat Longinus, as he moved closer to Pilate. "I will not let that happen."

He bent down without taking his gaze off Pilate and grabbed Cornelius' cross-bow. He raised it and both men noticed there was one bolt left unfired.

"Guards!" Pilate screamed for help and backed away, staggering over stacks of his papers now strewn about the floor. His eyes chanced a look at the door but no help came.

"Perhaps the men have already chosen." Longinus breathed heavily and aimed the deadly end of the crossbow at Pilate.

Sweat beaded on Pilate's brow as he backed away. His eyes darted about as he vied for some advantage. "Well done, Commander. Well done indeed! You are not a murderer. Put the bow down and I will let you and your wives leave the city unharmed." His eyes spotted Longinus' sword lying not far from the marble dais on which Erik lay.

Longinus noticed Pilate's gaze and hastened his advance. Pilate stumbled backward in fright, sword forgotten and fell to the ground. He tried to get up but Longinus was on him, bringing the unfired bolt to rest just under Pilate's chin. Pilate was on his knees and froze as the cool metal tip of the bolt touched his neck.

"Ok, ok. Now look, Longinus, don't make your life more difficult than it already has become. Soon soldiers will be storming this place and Commander or not, they will cleave you down on my orders…err…" The crossbow bolt seemed to dig into his skin. "That's if I say so but, umm, I won't do that."

"Give me one good reason why I shouldn't blow your head clean off." Longinus breathed heavily.

Pilate noticed movement behind Longinus but kept his gaze steady. He raised his eyebrows and looked thoughtful, hoping to buy time. "Well, perhaps the whole Eastern legions on your trail would be a good reason. Come on Commander! You have a wife!" Pilate's eyes narrowed. "Take her and leave. You have my word you will not be harmed."

Longinus frowned as he thought of his wife. What could he do now? Alive or dead, Pilate or someone else would surely hunt them down.

"Looks like my options are few. Sorry, m'lord, but beating Erik was a wrong move." His finger tensed on the trigger of the weapon and the look on Pilate's face would keep Longinus warm on cold nights for many years to come.

The Prefect's eyes bulged. "Now you fool!" He shrieked.

Longinus swung around, dropped to the floor and fired the remaining bolt. An incoming bolt raced over his head and demolished a wooden shelf of exotic items, showering the sleeping area in an explosion of ceramic shards.

A guard stationed in the courtyard below, heard the commotion and came to Pilate's domicile. After surveying the scene he proceeded to stalk Longinus who, at that point, was pointing a crossbow at his Prefect's throat.

Now, the guard stood staring at Longinus in shock and dropped his crossbow. There was gaping hole where his chest should have been. He tried to mouth some words but fell backwards to the marble floor.

Longinus winced. *Damn* he thought. That was Marcus, a young kid from Tuscany. Longinus didn't want for that to happen but just as he was about return to the matter of Pilate, a cord slipped around his throat and pulled tight.

"Nice try Commander!" Breathed Pilate in his ear. "A fine hero of the people I'll make after I ring the life out of you!"

Longinus struggled to breath and gasped. He was much larger than the governor but the floor under him was spattered with wine, oil and blood, preventing him from getting his balance. His vision became starry as he twisted and gasped violently. The metal cord, used to stabilize the broken brazier to a nearby pillar bit into his skin and he felt blood trickle down his chest. He jerked violently and staggered backwards unable to breath.

Longinus was seeing stars when he heard a sound like a gong. A second later, Pilate's grip went limp. Gasping for breath and falling backward onto the chest of the prefect, Longinus relieved himself of the strangling wire. He blinked up at a figure towering over him as he gasped for air. The figure was holding a silver decanter.

"I thought you were out of it!" He said, then laughed.

Erik dropped the decanter and reached down to help Longinus to his feet.

"I'll live." Wheezed Erik. "We gotta get out of here. This mess is gonna attract attention."

They looked down at the unconscious bodies of Cornelius and Pilate. Erik reached down and ripped a large portion off of Pilate's white robe. He wrapped it around his head to keep it from throbbing and swayed a little. One of his eyes was swollen completely shut.

Longinus sighed as he looked about the disheveled room. "This is serious. What are we gonna do? Cass and I can't just pick up and leave. We have nowhere to go."

Erik tilted his head. "Pilate showed me the letter. I'm sorry about your family."

Longinus looked at Erik and shrugged nonchalantly. "Yeah. Well..." He looked around in an effort to conceal his grief. "Ok. We gotta go. As soon as this scene is discovered, all hell is gonna break - damn!"

A tapestry lining the balcony window had caught fire from the embers of a fallen brazier. The flames were spreading rapidly and black smoke was beginning to billow out of the balcony opening.

Erik turned from his friend and looked around. "Did you hear that?"

Longinus listened. He could hear gongs echoing across the courtyard. "The compound is awake. C'mon!""

The flames were growing larger and rising out of Pilate's balcony. Smoke was beginning to fill the room. As they passed Pilates' desk, Longinus grabbed the letter from Rome and stooped to retrieve his sword. Erik grabbed his own confiscated sword and hastily buckled it back on as they headed for the double doors.

As they headed down the stairs they noticed a large amount of blood splattered about the spiral stairway. Erik slowed to examine the blood and bumped into Longinus who had come to halt at the bottom of the stairs. He was staring at a body of a guard. The guard had apparently been shot in the back by the bolt which Longinus redirected from Cornelius' shot. It had gone right through the door and killed the guard instantly.

"I didn't know he was waiting at the door. He tried to warn me. Explains why no one came to back up Pilate." Said Longinus, shaking his head. "Good kid was only doing what he thought was right." He leaned down and produced two coins from a pocket inside his cuirass. He closed the young man's vacant eyes and placed the coins over them. "Damn Pilate for this!" Longinus spat.

"Come on, Long. We'll be swarming in guards soon."

Longinus stood and nodded to Erik. "Follow my lead."

They raced across the compound courtyard and were waylaid by soldiers and a water brigade.

"Pilate's been accosted!" Shouted Longinus, pointing up to the enflamed compound. "Get up there and douse the flames."

The soldiers hesitated and saluted. As far as they knew, Longinus was still the Commander.

"Post guards at every entrance and exit of the compound." He commanded.

They rushed to the barracks and gathered some belongings. Longinus grabbed his spear and a large backpack. On their way out, Longinus put his shoulder into the door of the tax office while Erik stood watch outside. In the confusion of the night there were screams of orders coming from everywhere and few if any soldiers looked at Erik. Longinus emerged, his backpack jingling with the sound of coins.

"What are you - ?" Erik started to protest.

"No time to argue. We need this if we are to survive outside the city."

Erik nodded and the two officers walked with purpose across the courtyard and out of the main gates. The guards posted outside the gates saluted and moved aside.

"I'm going to Herod. Do not let anyone in or out until the fires are contained." Longinus ordered the guards. They saluted as he and Erik departed down a street, out of view.

After dashing through the dark streets for a short time, they stopped near their respective homes.

"Right!" breathed Erik. "What..do…we do…now?"

Longinus winced as he tried to catch his breath. "OK. Go get Aura. We're going to the old stables near the south gate."

"The low Quarter? That place is a maze."

"Exactly. You know it's the only way out." Said Longinus sharply. "If we hurry I may be able to use my influence to get out of the gate. Get Aura and take was is only necessary to survive. Hurry!"

"OK." Erik swung his backpack over his shoulder. "Hopefully this is not the last time to salute you, sir." He saluted smartly. "See you down at the stables."

Longinus saluted back and watched his younger friend retreat. He turned, looked at his own house and groaned. He feared his wife was going to be a bit annoyed about having to leave the city so quickly.

Chapter 6: Stork Surprise

A short while later, Longinus, Erik, Aura and Cassie were navigating the dark but waking streets of Jerusalem. The two wives were anxious and worried but followed their husbands without question when pressed to leave the city. With only bare essentials in backpacks, the two couples managed to reached the stables undetected. They slipped inside and were pleased to find several well fed horses, ripe for the taking as it were.

There was one problem, however. The gates were closed and alarms were ringing out around the city. No gates were permitted to open as long as alarms were sounded. It was only a matter of time before they were cornered in the stables.

"Damn!" Longinus shook his head. "The gates cannot be opened as long as the gongs are being sounded. The guards up top have the keys. They've been trained."

"Long! What are we going to do?" Said Erik, holding his wife close.

"Perhaps hide in the carriages and go out later with the merchants?" Said Cassie lifting a canvas flap covering a wagon.

"That would be unwise, my lady." Said a voice from the shadows. "You must leave now, while you still have the advantage. Perhaps we can be of assistance?"

Longinus spun around so fast with his spear that he nearly clocked Erik in the side of the head. Erik ducked just in time.

"A moment friend." Said a calm voice.

Longinus and Erik stood in shock for a moment as four men emerged from the shadows at the back of the stables. They were bearded and heavily tanned with the haggard appearance of honest laborers. They were dressed in pale linen robes and carried of simple wooden staves. One carried a staff of white birch wood.

"You!" Exclaimed Erik, recognizing the man leading the others as he stepped closer.

"Yes. We meet again Erikssen Fisherman." He turned to Longinus. "And you, Commander."

"Teacher." Was all Longinus could say as he gaped at the man.

"Indeed. But this is not the time for pleasantries. You saved my life and now I shall endeavor to save yours. We must act quickly if you are to escape the city. Pilate was revived immediately sent orders for the gates to be sealed and for your arrests." He looked apologetically at Longinus. "I'm afraid you're influence over the guards is no more Commander."

"How did you know we were here and who the Hades – " Started Longinus.

The man raised his hand and nodded sympathetically. "There is little time Commander. I have been following your friend for a few days. I believe he witnessed some oddities on Golgotha but that is for him to discuss with you. As for now, you must trust me. I and some of my followers believe it is in our best interest to help you."

"Right. You have my attention." Said Longinus.

"The best plans are often quite simple." Said the man, coming closer." He patted the long snout of a horse in a stall and looked at Aura. "Find a safe, warm haven for this woman. She will begin the labor of birth soon."

Cassie, Longinus and Erik froze in shock and looked quickly at Aura who stared back in equal shock with her hand on her belly.

"How did you..." Erik trailed off and stared at the man. He recomposed himself. "Who *are* you?" He asked quietly.

The man shrugged. "I am a rock upon which you must now stand. We are Christians."

Longinus looked at Erik questioningly.

Erik nodded without taking his eyes from the man. "We can trust him."

"On my signal, ride hard. Don't stop until you are quite far from this city." He turned to leave with his followers but Longinus grabbed his arm.

"What signal?"

"The gates will open. As soon as you see them move, you will have little time.

Longinus let go of the man's arm. "Thank you, whoever you are."

"Pleasure is mine, Longinus. Blessed are the meek." And with that, the men vanished into the shadows at the back of the stables.

****Jingle*Jingle*Jingle****

Far above the stables, a watchman atop one of the gate towers frowned. Alarm gongs were still sounding and Longinus was just charged with treason. He crumpled up the message and sighed. Why did this have to happen on his watch? Across the city, he noted Pilate's compound had a little trail of smoke issuing from it but it didn't look that bad.

The watchman absently scratched his beard and belched as a sparrow landed beside him and chirped happily. He turned to look at the happy bird, thus completely missing the movement behind him. Then everything went peaceful and dark.

The *teacher* caught the watchman as he slumped to the ground. He looked across the gateway to the other tower and saw the other watchman was also neutralized.

Longinus and Erik monitored the take-over with open mouths. From behind the slightly opened stable doors Longinus peered out, looking this way and that to see if any of the populace witnessed the minor insurrection. After a moment of silence he grinning madly at Erik.

"How in blazes did they get up there? Do Christians fly or something?" Longinus shook his head in amazed disbelief.

Erik snorted and tensed. The horses were ready. Their wives were prepared. All they needed now was the signal.

Longinus and Cassie had one horse each while Erik rode with Aura. Longinus was particularly pleased to find one of Pilate's horses in the stable which he only rode while entertaining dignitaries from Rome. He grinned at Erik as he patted the horses snow-white mane. "She's a beauty!"

Longinus looked through the stable doors once more and squinted in the morning sunlight. The teacher was waving frantically from atop his tower. "That's it!" He turned to the others. "Gotta go! Girls come on!"

"Ride fast, babe." Erik heard his wife's urgent whisper in his ear. "Whatever trouble we are in is not over yet."

The Christians had managed to spring the gate mechanism which queued the escapees in the stables.

"Hya!" Shouted Longinus and his horse burst through the stable doors and galloped towards the city gates. Erik and Cassie trailed after him.

As they neared the gates Longinus noticed in his periphery that a squadron bearing short bows were entering the courtyard from an adjacent street. They were shouting and pointing at the galloping horses. Longinus spurred his horse harder, picking up speed and dust as the magnificent white steed stormed across the courtyard. Cassie, Erik and Aura were close behind him.

Erik shielded his wife with an arm wrapped behind him and held the reins of the sprinting horse with one arm.

A volley of arrows whizzed through the group as they raced across the courtyard. The horses, trained for military encounters, recognized the urgency and danger as arrows whizzed around them and sprinted even faster across the short distance to the gate.

Erik looked back at the pursuing soldiers and gulped as another volley was being aimed at them. His fear was not for himself but for his pregnant wife. Just one of those arrows could take out the horse. At this speed he and his wife wouldn't stand a chance of escaping major injury or worse.

A voice entered Erik' mind, crisp and clear, despite the rushing wind and tempest of dust. *Fly, brother, fly! Do not look back. Do not stop.* His senses were whipped into a panic. He dared not focus on anything but escaping the city with his wife unharmed.

They reached the gate just as the second volley of arrows were released but this time they thunked and clanged against wood and metal.

The Christians controlling the gate mechanism judged the speed and distance to the gate with amazing accuracy, triggering them to start closing as the four friends raced across the courtyard. Just as the horses were exiting the gates, they closed and the pursuing soldiers were left to deal with the Christians.

As he and his family raced across the open plain to the south, Erik chanced another look back and raised an arm.

The Christian on the tower, who helped Erik find the spike on Golgotha a few nights before, was now a shrinking figure as the horses sped on but he was able to make out a wave of goodbye.

Damn! Thought Erik. *They are trapped now! Would I have done the same for him? I shall never forget it.*

"Blessed are the meek, friend!" He shouted and waved.

Swallowing his guilt, he turned to continue his flight, taking his wife with his friends into the wilderness of Judea.

****Jingle*Jingle*Jingle****

An empty, silver wine decanter flew across the charbroiled domicile of Pilate's compound and clanged against a blackened marble pillar.

"They're gone?!" Pilate raged. He spat and blinked as a fresh trickle of blood spouted from under the white cloth he held to his head. The thin, red line traversed his jowl and dripped as he glared at the soldiers standing at attention before him. He still wore the white and purple robes of his station despite their soot-smudged and blood spattered appearance.

All of the forces in Jerusalem were summoned to the compound once word reached Pilate of Longinus' escape. To add further insult to injury, his steed was taken. This made Pilate, in the eyes of his servants, appear to have lightning bolts coming out of his eyes and horns growing out of a steaming brow. In reality, he was just really, really pissed off.

The assembled men stood at attention in Pilate's spacious but blackened room for some time while a doctor attended the prefect. When the doctor was finished, Pilate paced in front of them. He looked about the once white marble floor, now strewn with burned fabrics and other assorted flim-flam and stooped to pick up a broken, wooden desk leg. Once several hands long, it was now burned down to the size of a small club with a blackened stump. He eyed it with wild appreciation.

"They will be found." He said, his voice now calm but severing the air like a razor. "All of you will search for them without delay." He continued not taking his eyes from the blackened wood. "They will be brought back here to stand trial for their crimes."

He pivoted quickly, whirling the blackened club around and struck an officer across the face. The man fell to the floor unconscious, his plumed-helm clanged on the marble floor and rolled to a stop against the nearby dais. The other officers remained motionless and at attention. Pilate stared at each of them in turn then dropped the club. Some of the men flinched at the sound.

Pilate straightened himself and assumed a pious stature, flourishing his robes. "Is that clear?"

"Hail Caesar!" The officers saluted and chorused in general.

"Dismissed."

Moving in unison, the officers marched out of the room to and proceeded down the stairs. Moments later, they were screaming orders to their assembled men in the courtyard below.

Pilate beckoned to servants, who until now were huddling in terror in the corners of the ruined domicile. They came forward.

Pilate glowered at them. "Clean it." He commanded and left the room.

The servants looked at each other with fear and disbelief. Their expressions soon turned to dismay as they looked about the room, realizing just how much work lay before them.

****Jingle*Jingle*Jingle****

The three horses stormed south then veered east as Longinus led them over the morning lit plains of Judea. The companions covered a remarkable distance from the gates of Jerusalem that day because their horses were rested and the air outside the city refreshed their purpose. Every mile separating themselves from Pilate lifted their spirits. At least, as much as could be expected under such circumstances.

Erik knew there were deeper valleys and lushly forested areas far to the east of the city and that's exactly where Longinus was heading. For several hours they rode wordlessly, knowing full well that trackers and scouts would be sent to pursue them. Despite her condition, Aura fared well as the companions rode onward.

Finally, as Longinus crossed a small stream at the bottom of a shallow gully, he turned his horse and raised a hand for Cassie and Erik to halt. The companions and the horses were exhausted and fear made them all the more thirsty.

"How about a drink?" Longinus breathed heavily and wiped his brow. The noon sun, beaming in full strength, was taking its toll on the lot of them.

The others agreed. Cassie was already getting off her horse and tying her hair back.

"There's water on the side." Said Aura, licking her lips and blinking in the harsh brightness of the early afternoon sun. Erik tried to help her dismount but she shooed him off. "Go talk to Long. Here, take this." She handed him a water skin.

The companions stretched and Erik stood beside Longinus overlooking the edge of a long, deep valley. They took turns drinking from a water skin.

"Longinus, we can't tarry for long."

"I know. If I know Pilate, he's already got riders heading out of the city and tracking us." He continued to stare at the landscape as if trying to recall something.

Erik looked back and saw Cassie and Aura sitting on some mossy boulders under a tree. They exchanged quiet whispers and drank some water.

"You know, I think this is Runner's Walk. The smuggler's route my uncle cleared out years ago with his regiment." Said Longinus. "It runs straight to the coast but I don't think anyone ever ventures into it."

Erik shrugged as Cassie and Aura came up to the two men and looked down into the valley. "I've heard of it but had no idea we were close. Rumor has it demons and spirits dwell inside." He paused as if to consider something. "Good place to hide for a while I bet."

"Yeah." Said Longinus, looking back at Cassie and Aura. "If that teacher was right about Aura, we need to find a safe place to hold up." He gestured to the valley before them.

"This may be our chance. From what I heard, it's deep, dark and has lots of fresh water and game for food. What do you say?"

"I don't see any other option. Let's go." Cassie said.

"You got us this far Long. Let's try it."

"Agreed." Said Erik. He watched a sparrow flutter from branch to branch above them. Then it jumped out over fifty feet of open air and coasted down on swift wings into the valley below, disappearing into the foliage.

The decision turned out to be a successful one for the escapees during that time for there were no patrols checking the dark trails of Runner's Walk. Rumor had it there were dark things in the Judean wilderness that kept patrols from entering the valley but nothing ill befell of Erik, Longinus, Cassie and Aurelia.

After few days of traveling deep into the valley, they found a clearing of trees near a spring fed pool and decided to take a rest. The water was clear and fresh, the game was abundant and foliage was fruitful. They decided to stay for a while and let Aura rest. Hours became days, days became weeks and still Pilate was not able to find them. Therefore the companions decided to stay for a while longer.

Their time together was at first bittersweet. Longinus grieved for his father and family but he was not alone, for the others grieved as well. Cassie and Aurelia had families too and could only guess if they would ever be able to meet loved ones again. But grief soon changed to happiness, for during that time a new member of their company was born. The child of Erikssen Fisherman and Aurelia Floren was born beside a rocky pool somewhere in the wilderness south of Jerusalem. Thanks to the efforts of Cassie and the peaceful surroundings deep in the valley, the birth went smoothly and the baby was healthy. Longinus and Erik, uncle and father, celebrated with what little wine they managed to stuff into packs before escaping and provided what comfort they could in such an environment. Erik and Aurelia named the baby Nicholas, after his father's kin.

In later years, pilgrims (of a sort) would come to try and find the spot but the tranquil pool has long since been lost to drought and cratered by war. Regardless, every year someone manages to find the spot and, quite strangely, place a candy cane on the muddy ground where Nicholas was born.

Chapter 7: Goody Gum Dreams

From his pristine balcony, Pontius Pilate basked in the warmth of an orange sunset. Newly delivered tapestries heralding his office rippled in the evening's breeze. Braziers were lit and treated with incense and his new robes of state felt comfortable. All would have been well except for the matter of Erik and Longinus avoiding capture. By now they could be anywhere and it displeased him terribly.

He sipped some wine and chewed on some roasted chicken as he surveyed the lands south of Jerusalem. A small, jagged scar lining his temple wrinkled slightly as he squinted at the horizon. He knew they were out there somewhere, so he decided to hire the right sort of men who happened to know where *somewhere* was.

He tossed a chicken bone over the edge of the balcony and headed inside. Crossing the white marble floor to his buffet table, he poured himself another cup of wine as he surveyed a group of men waiting patiently for him. Well, waiting terrified was more like it.

Pilate sighed as he skewered each of them on the end of his gaze. He was rather vexed at his soldiers over the last few months for their inability to find the escapees somewhere out in the wilderness of Judea. As a result, he demoted Cornelius and sent him to Germania. He realized the man was every bit of a useless pig as his appearance lead one to believe. The present assembly of men knew this all too well so they seemed ill at ease as they waited for Pilate's orders.

Since he commanded a vast area, Pilate decided to conscript the finest trackers in the land to handle the mission instead. However, he wished to instill a sense of urgency upon the trackers. The matter of Longinus and Erik was an embarrassment to him so he wanted them found and brought to justice swiftly.

Pilate knew how to motivate men. He had always been rather skilled at it. Walking serenely to his administrative table he picked up a large bag of gold coins and upended it, spilling the contents so that all the men standing at attention before him could see the ample glitter. More than one of them looked at the pile of coins and smacked his lips.

"This," said Pilate, with a tone of a patient tutor, "is yours." Then he gathered the hem of his robes and walked slowly to the balcony, bidding the men to follow him. As one, the assembled trackers moved forward.

"And that," Pilate pointed to Golgotha. "is also yours." He smiled at them with grave assurance. "Your actions in the next few weeks will determine which of these gifts you will receive."

The men remained silent but if sudden perspiration made noise it would have echoed across the city.

"Now, listen carefully." He continued, leaving the balcony and returning to his desk. The men followed him. Pilate picked up a large parchment and placed it flat for all the men to see. They leaned forward to see it was a map of Judea.

"You are the best trackers in Judea." He said joyfully. "You will likely find the criminals somewhere in this area." He pointed to a general area on the map. "When you find them, bring them to me alive or dead. I care not which but alive would be preferable. There may be a child with them. Do not harm the child. I will not have it said the Eastern Empire is cruel. Understood?"

The trackers nodded silently.

"Oh! Wait, I almost forgot." Pilate set his cup down and clapped his hands.

The doors to his residence opened and an assortment of women and children were escorted inside. They were chained together and shackled at the legs. Some of the trackers gasped and cried out.

"Ah, yes. I see you recognize your wives and children. Good." Pilate nodded and faced the men. "Whatever befalls these lovely people," he thrust a thumb over his shoulder for emphasis, "will also depend on your actions."

"Should you fail to find the criminals and decide not to return to me," Pilate frowned and shook an admonishing finger at the assembled men, "I fear the penalty for such failure will be EXTRACTED", he screamed suddenly and the trackers trembled, "from these loved one's before you." He finished in smooth tones, recovering insanely quick from his outburst.

Returning to his table, Pilate picked up his wine cup and sighed. He drained the cup in one shot and slammed the cup to the marble floor. It clanged away and he glared at the trackers. After a moment he raised his hand, palm down. Each of the men stepped forward in turn and kissed Pilate's signet.

"Now go." Pilate commanded quietly when the men were finished.

The trackers, many of them exchanging looks of longing and fear with the women and children, hurried from the room and down the stairs.

Pilate turned after a few moments and looked at the women and children. They did not look at him and some of the children were crying.

"Centurion," He pointed at one guard in charge of the prisoners. "What is your name?"

"Lucesi, my lord." Said the man, stepping forward.

"Tomorrow morning, give each of these a few coins," he gestured vaguely at the women and children, "and send them home."

"Sir?" Said Lucesi, looking confused. "But you told the trackers these people – "

"Nonsense! I am not a monster, soldier." Pilate spat impatiently. "Send them home. They were only needed to motivate the trackers."

Centurion Lucesi nodded in approval. "Well done m'lord, as you wish." He turned to the soldiers escorting the prisoners. "Take them to the cells for now." He commanded.

Pilate watched impassively as the bewildered women and children were ushered out of his court. Centurion Lucesi saluted and retreated as well, closing the repaired double-doors behind him.

Returning to his balcony with another cup of wine, Pilate looked out over Jerusalem, lost in thought. He surveyed the rooftops as the orange horizon changed to purple and gave way to a deep, evening blue. *I am not a monster*, he thought.

*Jingle***Jingle***Jingle*

Erik stared into the glassy surface of the pool, lost in thought as baby Nicholas rested peacefully on his lap. Some months after escaping Jerusalem and finding sanctuary within the secluded valley, the companions were becoming restless. After all, they couldn't stay in the valley forever. Constant vigil and paranoia that trackers may discover their whereabouts was taking its toll. Aura and the baby faired quite well despite the rugged environment but Nicholas needed a real home. The matter of their criminal identities, however, was a dilemma. Longinus and Erik would be known to many soldiers in Rome and Judea by now so options were few. Therefore, they were considering exile in Britannia or perhaps Gaul.

"If you think too much, your hair will fall out before you're thirty." Longinus whispered loudly over his shoulder. "Just a tip."

Erik snorted but said nothing. Despite the warm beams of afternoon sunlight, breaking through the surrounding foliage, he felt ill at ease.

"Come on dad, let's eat." Said Longinus.

Cassie and Aura were busy beside a small fire where wild goose began to roast on a makeshift brochette. Erik's mouth watered at the smell. *Ill at ease* was temporarily eased.

He walked over and made himself comfortable near the small fire, trying not to wake Nicholas. To his mild surprise, Longinus passed Erik a large skin.

"Last of the wine." He sighed. "Took it from a cart near Pilate's horse back in the stables. Been saving it. Let's finish it tonight. "

"Special occasion?" Asked Erik, taking the skin.

"We're alive with our wives and children, eating roasted goose, drinking wine and we don't have to go to work tomorrow. Oh, and no one is presently trying to kill us."

Erik considered this. "Fair enough." He nodded and took a long draft from the wine skin.

As they ate and talked quietly, the newest member of the companions *cooed* and *gaa'ed* at uncle Longinus as he made the face of a monkey who had just run full speed into a door. But soon it was time for the baby to go to sleep and it was Cassie's turn to doddle over the child. Cassie had quite a pleasant voice and every evening she sang a quiet lullaby as Aura swaddled him in ample cloths.

After dinner, Longinus and Erik decided to engage in some discussion away from the fire. They looking up at the stars through the trees and passed the wine skin back and forth.

"Here, take a look." Erik drew forth the spike from within his shirt. He had fashioned a leather string to hold it and had cleansed any trace of blood from it.

Longinus frowned and took it from him, turning it over and over in his hands. He didn't say anything at this point but continued to stare at it as if considering something. He looked at his spear which rested against a nearby tree and glistened in the starlight. After some consideration, he looked at Erik once more.

"I think my spear is different." He said flatly.

Erik looked at the spear. "What do you mean?"

Longinus took a pull from the wine skin and shook his head. "Can't explain it really. I just feel empowered by having it. Like people do as I tell them just for having it in my hand. I noticed it at the gates of the compound with those Christians." He considered something for a moment. "These visions you've been having…they started after that night on Golgotha, right?"

Erik nodded, looking warily at his wife, who pretended not to listen.

Longinus lowered his voice as he handed the spike back and drained his makeshift cup of wine. "Do you think the Nazarene or his God may have something to do with this or my spear?"

"I really don't believe in that sort of stuff. You know me." Said Erik. He put the leather strap around his neck but the spike slipped from the loose leather knot and clanged loudly on a small, boulder near his feet.

The sound was eerie in the stillness of the valley. A chill made Longinus shudder as he watched Erik stoop to pick up the spike.

A raven squawked in a some branches above and flew away.

"Shh!" Whispered Aura. "You'll wake the baby."

"Sorry, bad tie." Erik said but Longinus said nothing. "Well. Where do you think we should head ? Gaul?" Said Erik as he retied the spike and slipped it into his robes.

Longinus nodded. "That's a start. I only hope that my brother's and their families are OK."

Erik felt a stab of sympathy for his elder friend but tried to lighten the mood.

"We could always take up fishing." He said suddenly optimistically. "I still know a lot about it." Erik grinned. He knew Longinus hated the water about as much as eating what was fished out if it.

Longinus took another gulp from the wine skin and passed it back to Erik. "Oh, yeah!" He whispered with mock eagerness. "Sure! What was I so worried about? Fishing sounds like an excellent plan." He glowered at Erik.

"OK, enough of the heavy talk." Erik looked at the girls. "We are boring the bosses."

Longinus turned and gave Cassie a wine soaked grin. "Yer right! Our women need us." He whispered loudly.

He staggered slightly as he strode back to the camp and then launched himself on top of his wife. Aurelia covered baby Erik, who continued to sleep despite the drama, and laughed quietly. Cassie giggled as she fought with her husband who tickled her mercilessly and began to nibble on her ear.

Erik drained a little more wine from the depleted skin and grinned at Aura as he sat down beside her. Despite their current situation, he felt as though a strange adventure was unfolding and all they had to do was keep hoping for the best in each other's company. That's precisely what too much wine achieves, said a small warning in his head.

Regardless, Erik leaned over and kissed his wife as Cassie silently screamed for help while her big, bad husband tickled her breathless. Soft laughter, rarely heard in that part of Judea, echoed out of the dark oasis.

An owl, trying to rest peacefully on a tree branch above the small camp fire twisted its head and fluffed its feathers. It looked down at the mild disturbance and blinked. *Humans!* it thought, and flew off to some other locale.

*Jingle***Jingle***Jingle*

Some leagues away, a tracker from Jerusalem sat under a tree at the edge of a valley. He hadn't made a fire, choosing instead to wrap himself in extra blankets and chew on some stale bread. As he listened to the wilderness and watched the stars in a moonless night sky, a raven broke the calm and landed beside him. It squawked and rustled black wings as it patted around the base of the tree. The tracker's dark eyes widened as he stared at the raven in disbelief. Then he grinned and looked down into the valley...

*Jingle***Jingle***Jingle*

Little to the tracker's knowledge, some leagues even further away, three hooded figures stopped in their tracks and glanced at each other. They leaned heavily on staves of white birch wood and hesitated. They were wandering in the twilight wilderness when a clear and ghostly ping of metal echoed across the tundra. Their fourth companion, a young man, paused behind them. He might have been handsome at some point but his long, black hair was matted and his simple linen robe was spattered with blood. Eyes, black as bottomless pits against pale and rotting skin, slowly turned towards the south as the metallic ping echoed around them...

*Jingle***Jingle***Jingle*

Little to the four wanderer's knowledge, still further away, three old men stopped what they were doing and looked at each other in amazement. They had apparently been arguing when a clear metallic ping sounded about their general vicinity. It sounded like a metal spike and caused the ancient men to hesitate. One was holding a dead chicken by the neck and another was holding up a small iron pot in a threatening manner. A third elderly man, much rounder than the other two, stood between them and grinned knowingly...

*Jingle***Jingle***Jingle*

Erik awakened. His wife and friends slept peacefully. A fog rolled in about the camp and in the dim light of the dawn he spotted an owl sitting in a branch above them. It blinked and flew away. He sat up, looked down at Aura and realized with sudden horror that his son was not there.

Erik looked around wildly hoping that Long and Cassie had awakened early and were giving the baby some attention. They were sleeping peacefully and there was no sign of Nicholas. He began to panic and tried to shout but his throat was parched from excessive alcohol the previous night. He could only croak and gasp.

A baby suddenly cried out in the darkness nearby. Erik stopped breathing and looked wide-eyed into the gloom. Despite the fog, he noticed a figure vanishing into the gloom with something clutched in its arms.

“Nicholas!” He tried to shout but again his voice cracked.

In a wild panic, he rose from his bedroll and thundered after the figure. Ignoring the sharp bramble biting into his skin, he tore through the foliage after the elusive figure. He dodged and ducked heavier branches as he leapt over logs, fighting his way toward the sounds of his crying child. Clearing after clearing, Erik bounded after the hooded kidnapper who was always just out of reach.

Erik screamed unintelligible curses as he continued to give chase. His lungs were bursting with pain and tears of rage creased his face. As they entered a larger clearing, the hooded figure stopped and turned as Erik came storming towards it. He skidded to a halt and looked down at his son, who stared calmly back at him from the clutches of the kidnapper.

Nicholas smiled at Erik who raised his hands imploringly. There were painful looking scratches and cuts on Erik's arms and legs from the overgrowth. Blood trickled down his limbs in a network of crimson lines.

"Take our gold." He waved fanatically back in the direction of the camp. "You can have all of our gold. Just give me back my son." He panted and sweat began to mingle with blood on his extremities.

The figure pulled its hood back. Erik was stunned.

"You!" Recognizing the teacher from Jerusalem. "How could it be?!? What are you doing?"

"It must be this way, brother." Said the teacher, panting. "But not forever. A darkness has taken interest in you and this child."

"What darkness?" Said Erik, stepping closer. "You are saying my child is not safe with me?"

The teacher began to speak but his face drained of color and his eyes opened wide. He was staring at something behind Erik and began to back away.

Erik was immobilized by the peculiar terror one feels when they know something dreadful is behind them by looks on the faces of those in front of them.

"Too late to explain." The teacher turned and dashed out of the clearing, taking the Nicholas with him.

Before Erik could react, he heard a thunderous crash in the trees and turned. A great, dark apparition carrying a dimly lit lantern advanced on him. It stood twenty feet tall and everything it touched withered to ash. It was humanoid but possessed no features, as if silhouette had taken form. Erik backed away.

"*Again you cross my path, primate.*" It said, towering over him. The voice was deep but sounded like it came across a vast distance.

A fear unlike anything he had even known paralyzed Erik. His son cried out in the distance but he could do nothing but tremble.

Chapter 8: Black Pudding

Erik gasped and awakened to swallows screaming and stomping around the camp. At least that's how little birds seemed through the foggy veil of an award-winning hangover. Longinus and Cassie snored quietly on the other side of the burned out fire.

He sat up, looked down at his son sleeping peacefully with Aurelia and sighed. *A nightmare.* He breathed in relief and briefly wondered if all new fathers felt like that. He squinted in the morning light which was heralded by a *coo* and *gaa* from his newborn son.

"Da!" Said Nicholas, from the depths of a small cocoon of skins and blankets. A tiny hand reached out and Nicholas leaned closer as Aura stirred.

"Daddy has a hangover little one."

As the little hand grabbed his nose, Erik marveled at his son's tranquil demeanor. He thought that newborns cried a lot no matter what steps were taken for their comfort. This made him feel strangely proud.

He got up and walked some distance from the camp to drain his bladder and clear his head. As his consciousness began the arduous climb to the summit of Mount Hangover, something occurred to him. The still of the morning was odd. No sparrows chirped in the trees above and the surrounding environment was curiously absent of the usual life that buzzed.

He turned around. Soldier's instincts awakened the rest of his slumbering senses. He looked to the watering hole where the horses were tethered the night before and caught his breath. He blinked in disbelief. The horses were gone!

He looked into the trees for any sign of movement in case the tether had loosened in the night and they wandered off. There was no sign of the horses anywhere nearby.

Adrenaline now did the pre-industrial equivalent of a nourishing breakfast and several pots of black coffee. Erik turned casually and walked back to their camp, keeping an eye out for any kind of movement in his periphery as he sat down. Pretending to be completely unaware of anything out of the ordinary, he stoked the embers of the small fire pit. He slowly picked up a date from a leather satchel nearby and lobbed it at his friend's forehead.

Longinus opened his eyes and looked blearily at his friend.

Erik smiled at him blankly.

Longinus' frowned for a second then froze. He recognized Erik's stare and looked around the clearing. Erik slowly picked up a water skin and took a drink from it. While making a dramatic display of the motion, his sandaled foot slowly hooked the scabbard of his war sword some feet way. As he dragged it closer, he noticed Longinus making similar attempts to prepare for the unknown.

Longinus eyed his spear. It was leaning on a rock a few feet away. It would take him only a second to grab it…but what of the women and the baby in that second? Aura and Cassie rested, totally oblivious to the impending danger. He looked worriedly at Erik and nodded to the baby with raised eyebrows.

Erik senior understood and was already picking up his son and placing him beneath some bushes. He pretended to play with the child while actually putting the babe in a safe place away from any violence that may befall them. He nestled his son down among the roots of some bushes and caressed the child's face for a moment.

"Shh, Nicholas." He soothed. "Daddy loves you." Then, without knowing exactly why, he took the spike from the leather strap around his neck and placed it within the blankets of his son.

He turned and grabbed the water skin once more while his other hand strayed close to the sword hilt at his feet. A twig snapped in the woods but Erik did nothing to indicate he heard. He glanced at Longinus.

With his eyes, Longinus indicated he was going for the spear and continuing in that direction.

Erik acknowledged it and tensed for the moment to come. He and Longinus hadn't experienced much combat but the two men were respectable brawlers in Jerusalem's city streets. They certainly knew how to hold their ground with gangs and street thugs but this was different. If there were trained soldiers waited in ambush, they had to act fast and be very, very lucky.

Longinus sprang up and grabbed his spear. Erik followed suit. grabbing his sword in one motion and leaping over a large rock behind him. Several ballistics whizzed through the air. One ricocheted off the stone he leapt over and spun off into the trees. Aura and Cassie wakened suddenly and called out but their husbands were busy.

Longinus was luckier than most people in a fight but in this case, luck was a debatable matter. After grabbing his spear and leaping into the foliage he just happened to slip on a rock that Erik *graced* some minutes before and lost his footing. He slipped backwards heavily and hit the ground with a thud. This proved an unexpected blessing because a volley of crossbow bolts rocketed over his head and pierced various tree trunks around him.

On the other side of the clearing, Erik rounded a tree and spotted a flash of crimson cloth two yards to his left. He leapt over a rotted log and slashed forward at a soldier who turned too late to fire a second bolt at Erik. The soldier's crossbow string was cloven by the slash. He backed away and frantically reached for his sheathed sword but Erik brought his own sword level with the man's neck. Erik was not a murderer but he was prepared to kill in defense of his friends and family.

"Don't move." A voice said behind him.

Erik reacted without thinking. He dropped and as soon as he heard the voice over his shoulder. With a vicious whirling slash, he cleaved the lower leg of a soldier pointing a crossbow at his back.

The stricken soldier pulled the trigger of his weapon as Erik pivoted but the bolt fired past Erik ear and plowed into the chest of the soldier Erik initially disarmed. The two soldiers were out of action. One was screaming in agony as he grasped for his lower leg and the other was pinned to a tree trunk from the blast of the misfired bolt. He was not making noise of any sort.

Back on the other side of the clearing, Longinus was in a struggle for his life. Two soldiers burst out the forest to attack him while he lay in a smelly puddle on his back. He defended their blows with the blunt end of his spear and managed to kick one soldier in the groin. The man let out an audible *hoo-ooh!* and as he keeled over slowly, Longinus whirled his spear around level and knocked the other off balance. While the two attackers slowly gathered themselves, Longinus quickly jumped to his feet. He brought the dangerous end of the spear level with the chin of the man he groined moments before. The color in the soldier's face slowly drained as he focused on the spear head. The other moved in to protect his comrade but faltered when Longinus raised his hand.

"Halt." He said and the two attackers froze. Their eyes were white and attentive.

Longinus examined them for a brief moment. The insignia on their uniforms indicated the ambushers were conscripts from Syria. "You will return to your units in Syria." He commanded pointing at each of them in turn. "You will bother us no more. Drop your weapons and run away. Do it now. Don't come back."

After a brief hesitation, the two men dropped what weapons they had and ran off into the forest.

"Longinus!"

Recognizing Cassie's voice, Longinus dashed back to the campsite. Erik had done the same but the two friends did not look at each other because they were temporarily mesmerized with fear.

In the center of the clearing, two Roman soldiers were holding swords against Cassie and Aura. A third man, a dark clad tracker, stood behind them. A raven squawked in a tree branch behind him. Storm clouds roiled in the skies above the valley and soft rumblings of thunder echoed down around them.

"That will be all." Said the tracker. "Drop your weapons."

Erik looked sideways at Longinus. His friend's face was red, threatening to become purple as he glared at the men in silent rage.

Erik didn't know what to do. He had neither the wit nor the experience to deal with such a dilemma but he was a good peacekeeper. That, after all , was his job in Jerusalem. He looked at Aura and nodded to her.

"It'll be alright babe." He soothed. "Don't struggle. Do what they say." His heart pounded at the site of his wife in the clutches of the soldier.

"Good advice." Said the tracker, nodding to Longinus.

Longinus slowly lowered his spear. "Wait." He said. His voice, although calm, seemed to echo throughout the clearing like a thunderclap. Even Erik was momentarily frozen.

At this point, several things happened.

First, Nicholas began to cry, which made the soldiers holding Cassie and Aura look around wildly and loosen their grips.

"Pilate said there might be a baby!" Said the one holding Aura as his eyes darted about the clearing. Aura took advantage of this momentary lapse of focus by slamming the ball of her foot onto the soldier's sandaled foot. There was a loud crack and the soldier's face went white. He dropped his sword and limped aside on one good foot, gasping in pain.

At the same time, mesmerized by Longinus' command and momentarily confused by the sudden sounds of a baby crying, the soldier holding Cassie also loosened his grip. Seizing her chance, quite literally, Cassie reached back and grabbed what parts of the soldier she could get her hands on.

The dark tracker hesitated. It had taken only a moment for both of his men to be neutralized. One was limping around in pain while the other's eyes crossed and his mouth opened in silent panic. He had become a physical extension of Cassie's hand and moved when she moved. After all, when a man is in the grip of a strong woman, there's nothing he can really do but go with flow, as it were. The tracker was suddenly alone but hadn't bothered to draw his weapon.

Longinus smiled and leaned casually on his spear. "They don't really need us, you know." He gestured to Cassie and Aura. "They just let us think that way to spare our manly feelings."

The tracker's hands strayed to his belt as Aura and Erik cared for baby Nicholas. Longinus stepped forward quickly and pointed his spear. "No." He warned. "Cassie, my dear. Let the nice centurion go. It's ok."

Cassie released her grip and stepped back from the men, standing next to her husband. The soldier fell sideways and rolled around the trackers feet, groaning.

"He has our families." Said the tracker, helping the centurion to his feet. "Pilate took our wives and children. If we don't return with you, they will be sold as slaves." The man sagged as Longinus exchanged looks with the others. "I'm sorry. We had no choice. Please let us leave."

"Bastard." Longinus spat in the dirt. "Pilate! Damn him." He sighed and looked at the ambushers with a sudden rush of sympathy. "I don't know how to help you. I'm sorry but -

Before he could finish the sentence, a lightning bolt struck a nearby tree which exploded. The force of the blast knocked everyone off their feet and baby Nicholas was launched out of his mother's arms. The bundled baby landed in bushes some distance from the clearing and, because he was a baby and unaware of perilous occurrences, laughed in delightful appreciation.

*Jingle***Jingle***Jingle*

Shadows lengthened. Storm cloud churned and flashed above the valley clearing. Four figures appeared out of the shadows and surveyed the scene. Three were hooded and one appeared to be a young man.

Cassie, Longinus and the three ambushers were lying on the dirt unconscious. They looked bruised and bloodied but not dead. Erik and Aura were in a similar state a few yards away.

"A well placed strike master." Said one of the hooded figures..

The young man looked around hungrily. "Find the key. It is here somewhere. It is a spike made of iron. Check the bodies." He licked cracked and bleeding lips. He spat out a tooth and breathed raggedly as the other rummaged around the bodies of the fallen.

"Disgusting meat sack." He gurgled. "Had I know what it was on Golgotha, we wouldn't have to use these vessels."

A sparrow landed in a tree branch and chirped at him angrily. The young man stared at it in alarm and waved a finger. The little bird suddenly burst into flames, its tiny feathers crackling in the heat. It squeaked in agony and fell to ash near his the young man's feet.

One of the hooded figures looked up. "Emissaries!" He whispered loudly as the remains of the sparrow scattered in the wind. "They herald the pilgrim's ilk. Master you are not whole and we are weakened. We mustn't tarry."

The young man snarled. "Very well. Send them to Enefka. These two," he pointed at Erik and Longinus.

"They were on Golgotha. And their wives. We will find the key later. One of them has it, I can feel it is close."

The others nodded silently and stood over the three companions.

Tendrils, inky black and snake-like, stretched forth from the surrounding shadows of the sanctuary and coiled about the bodies of Longinus, Cassie, Erik and Aura. Then, without any climactic exit, such as a flash or an explosion, they were simply gone.

The young man looked around the clearing once more. "If we find the key," he croaked to himself and spat blood," I will harrow Abanis and claim -" He stopped. Something caught his eye several yards from the clearing. A flash of metal in the darkness.

He stepped over to it and peered down. Longinus' spear lay in the grass next to a small tree. It gleamed in the flashes of the storm clouds above and looked like a sliver of sharp moonlight against dark green foliage. The young man's eyes widened. "It cannot be!" He exclaimed, staring down in disbelief. An inscription on the spear shaft began to glow which increased intensity as the young man reached down to pick it up. "The Aegis of Adamis! How is this possib - "

A flash of light erupted from the spear as the young man touched it. As bright as a lightning bolt, a charge of energy wrapped itself around the body of the young man who recoiled too late. Smoke and burning flesh caused a noxious vapor to issue from the young man's body as he was slowly consumed in the relentless current of energy. A ghostly scream, as if echoing across a vast distance, rose on the winds of the storm and then was suddenly ceased.

The young man was gone but spear remained.

*Jingle***Jingle***Jingle*

A short while later, the tracker who ambushed the companions regained consciousness. He stood up rather shakily and looked around. The two soldiers in his employ were charred and blackened bodies lying near a smoldering tree. The criminals he was tracking were gone. Only two things caught his attention. One, a baby cried out some distance away. Two, a magnificent spear lay in the grass some yards away. He walked unsteadily over to the spear and picked it up. It was the most impressive weapon he had ever seen.

He turned in the direction of the baby's cries but hesitated. He looked down at the spear and seemed to come to a decision.

"Sorry child." He whispered. Then he turned in the other direction and vanished into the trees.

Wildlife present in forest at this time slowly came to the fore. They hid among the trees during the disturbance but now ventured forth as the noisy human activity subsided.

A possum mother scampered forward with younglings close behind. It surveyed the scene, twitched it's nose in the air and squeaked. Then the younglings squeaked. Then swallows began chirping in the trees as some of them bounced down to lower tiers of branches to observe the scene. An owl landed on the ground beside baby Nicholas and hooted. Then a pheasant landed beside the owl and made some noise of its own. Then all manner of life around the area erupted. Animals of all sorts screeched, hissed and whined in a chorus of shock and sorrow. On and on, the strange cacophony of shock and sorrow rose in pitch. Then as suddenly as it rose, the noise stopped. The animals left the clearing and all was silent and still once more.

Then it began to rain. It was a trickle at first, followed by a more resonant pat-pat, followed quickly by a heavy and persistent shower. Baby Nicholas began to cry, his sorrow echoing about the forest clearing. A sparrow and her chicks nesting in a tree above the baby looked down and chirped. With all her fluttering heart she wished to ease the child's pain for there was a friendly aura about him. She knew the child would grow to befriend all manner of life in the world but there was very little that a tiny bird could do. She chirped merrily, therefore, hoping the happy sounds would comfort the child.

Alone in the emerald light of the forest deep lay young Nicholas swaddled in blankets, his cries echoing among the myriad of trees. As storm clouds rumbled and the rain fell heavier, baby Nicholas' cries died away to nothingness. He stared in fascination at the large drops of water piercing the forest canopy and falling lazily to the ground. The regular *plat* sounds made him laugh and he cooed in the din despite the storm...

Chapter 9: Whine and Cheese

Several hours later, as rain clouds and sunrays battled for dominion in the heavens above, three figures approached forest clearing. They were wrapped from head to foot in thick cloaks of varying styles and navigated slowly through the thickets. Bickering and aiming inaudible contradictions at each other, they hobbled through the undergrowth until finally reaching the edge of the forest clearing.

One figure, somewhat short and fat, wore a bright, orange cloak over orange robes now mud stained at the hem. Another beside him was tall, slim, and may have worn white robes at some point but they were now weathered grey. A third figure, bringing up the rear, was extremely short. He wore dark, brown robes so voluminous that he appeared to be an animated pile of laundry shambling after the other two. They were three old - very old - men and leaned heavily on staves of chestnut wood. Despite their natural infirmity, the voices of the three elderly pilgrims were young and full of vigor.

"No! No! No! The human body is not a machine! It can't be taken apart!" Yelled the grey pilgrim.

"Yes! It can. You just wait! They'll be cutting out bits, they will. Replacing this bit with that bit in no time to be sure." Said the brown pilgrim, sitting on a nearby boulder.

"Truly?" Asked the third, now stopping and pulling down his orange hood lower to block the rain. "You've never told me it would come to that."

"You didn't ask." Said the small, brown heap of robes. "It's your fault for not being querulous enough. Don't you learn anything meditating all the time?"

"Listen." Said the grey pilgrim, pointing an accusing finger at his brown clad companions. "Stop being so difficult. We have a long road ahead of us and your teaching days are over. At least out here. So clam up!"

"My teaching days are *over*?" Said the brown pilgrim, grinning. "Where have you been the last few *centuries*? You of all people should know that education is *our* best provision!"

"Indeed." Nodded the fat, orange pilgrim. He turned back to his grey clad companion in expectation, as if observing a sporting event.

"What?!?" The grey pilgrim rolled his eyes to the sky for assistance. "Right now, shelter and a decanter of wine is our best provision. What simpleton came up with that?"

"You did."

"Oh."

"It's OK, grasshopper." Said the brown pilgrim smoothly. "You've forgotten your own steaming pile of writings. Happens to the best of us. No need to be ashamed. At our age, the mind cracks sooner or later."

"Steaming pile of…? Now look!" The grey pilgrim was shaking a finger at both of his companions. "Don't start with the *grasshopper* bit! *My* boy conquered most of the known world under at one point and not just because he was a blond! I'm no spring chicken!"

"Ah, yes." Said the orange pilgrim, nodding sagely. "You're obviously an autumn chicken."

The grey pilgrim dropped his pointing finger and just stared at the orange pilgrim. After a moment he sat down on another boulder and mumbled to himself.

"Come, my old friend," said the orange pilgrim, sitting beside him. "Angry speech is painful. Let us enjoy the beauty of this natural oasis. You once told me there is something marvelous in all things natural. I believe you also wrote that."

As the storm clouds yielded to sunrays, the grey pilgrim looked up suddenly. "Shh!" He whispered loudly and looked around. His eyes widened and the others followed his gaze. "The key. It is near."

Just beyond the light of the clearing they saw the faintest hint of crimson cloth rippling in the wind. It was caught on a low branch some distance away. Whatever it was attached to was obscured by a large tree.

The grey pilgrim grabbed his staff with two hands and held it defensively as he meandered over to the tree. He peered cautiously around the trunk as the others crept up behind him and peeked out from under each of his elbows.

An arm reached up from the behind the tree, grabbing the air.

"Help!" Gasped a weak voice.

The three old men toppled over backward. Grunting and shouting, each struggled to get up by using the head of another but failed and slipped on the muddy forest floor. After several moments, the three pilgrims negotiated some method of disentanglement and were finally able to get to their feet. They argued with each other for a few seconds, then realizing what caused them to jump backwards in the first place, looked back at the tree in silence.

"What has happened? Oh. Oh dear, how awful." The orange pilgrim waddled over to get a better view behind the tree, his comrades close behind.

At the base of the tree, obscured by bushes and covered in blood lay a Roman soldier. His helm was nowhere to be seen. His eyes were wide, his breath was shallow and his left leg was alarmingly missing.

"He is near peace." Said the orange pilgrim, reaching down to hold the dying soldier's grasping hand and kneeling beside him.

The brown pilgrim poked his head around the tree trunk. "He is near passing." He sighed sadly.

The grey pilgrim poked his head around the tree trunk, looking down quizzically over the brown pilgrim's head. "He was a pawn in a game." He whispered gravely.

"Can anything be done?" Asked the orange pilgrim to the others.

The grey pilgrim examined the amount of pooled blood and touched the course skin of the fallen soldier's face for a few moments.

"No, too much blood loss." He did not elaborate. The soldier's leg was severed just below the knee. Major arteries were cut and blood had spayed all about the area. "However, I can see this one wasn't always naughty. He was nice, for the most part."

The other two nodded sadly and waited. The soldier, now so weak he could barely move his head, looked blankly at each of the men around him. He realized why their expressions were sober but he did not fear death. He was a soldier of Rome and would die as a citizen. This fact comforted him. His hand squeezed the orange pilgrim's hand.

"Thank you grandfathers...for your company. I go to Elysium."

The soldier closed his eyes and stopped breathing.

The pilgrims waited patiently for a moment and then stood, each of them retrieving their walking staffs. Silently, the grey pilgrim leaned down and placed a coin on either of the soldiers closed eyes.

"You *know* that's not necessary. Why would you do that brother?" Asked the brown pilgrim.

"There is something good in maintaining certain traditions even though they may be moot. He was a soldier and a citizen of a grand idea." He paused and looked down at the dead man, considering something. "The coins are for me. Not him."

The other two nodded silently. Engaging in debate had its time and place. This was neither.

"Well," said the grey pilgrim, now looking around and sniffing the air. "this is but one mystery." He squinted into the trees back to part of the clearing. Then, he looked up and examined the branches. Some sparrows chirped happily at him. Nodding to the birds he looked at his companions with a grave expression.

"There are more. Come let us see what tragedy has befallen this area."

They reached the clearing and surveyed the ground. In turn they winced at the sight of two charred and blackened bodies near a smoldering tree stump.

They brown pilgrim nodded.. "Yep. Something happened here."

Not a muscle moved on the grey pilgrim's face. Then he sighed and looked down at his companion. "Of course something happened here!" He exclaimed. "Tree's don't just randomly explode and kill Roman soldiers, I don't care how suicidal they are!" He finished wildly.

"Wait!" Said the brown pilgrim as he turned on the spot and looked about the area. His face contorted and he looked confused as the other two looked on. "There!" He whirled around and pointed. "There. Listen!"

To the casual observer, the old men might have been listening to crickets or birds. But what *they* could hear, what normal people could not hear, was life. The *beat* of life, to more precise. They heard the faint thumping of a heart beat.

As one, the crouching pilgrims turned and sniffed the air. They moved as a single unit and lumbered towards the burned out fire pit like a twelve-limbed toga-monster.

The orange pilgrim turned to his companions. "There's something – " But he was cut off.

Waaaaaa! Wa! Waaaaa!

If a dragon suddenly landed and roared deafeningly beside them, the look on the grey pilgrim's face would have been less terror-stricken as it now appeared.

The orange pilgrim smiled with excitement and tried to zero-in on the obvious sound of a baby crying. The brown pilgrim grinned happily. The Grey pilgrim's expression was similar to one who had just completed a thousand years of hard labor only to find it was the wrong job and had to start all over again.

Wa! Waa! Waaaa!

The orange pilgrim leaned down into some shrubbery beside the camp and stood up holding a small bundle in his arms. He turned and looked at his companions with glee.

"We have company brothers!" If it were joy incarnate the orange pilgrim carried, his face wouldn't have been more gleeful. He stepped over to the others, showing them the child.

Baby Nicholas looked up at the new faces with silent puzzlement. His tiny blue eyes darted from one old face to another as the three men leaned closer. Nicholas' eyes rested on the grey pilgrim scowling down at him and giggled. He reached up a tiny hand, grabbed the grey pilgrim's beard and pulled hard.

"Ouch!" The grey pilgrim grimaced and tried to free himself gently from the baby's clutch. "Easy on the beard! Easy on the beard!"

"You are always the one they like, brother." Said the orange pilgrim, smiling at him.

They grey pilgrim stopped struggling with his beard and just looked at the orange pilgrim with a blank expression. "That's what I'm worried about!" He whispered loudly.

Baby Nicholas agreed with an audible 'GA!' and a giggled.

"Alright he's cute and wonderful and all that. So what now?" He looked at the other two who raised their eyebrows at him. "Please don't say it. I know you're going to say it."

The orange pilgrim started to speak but something fell from the bundle in his arms and fell to the ground with a dull thud.

As one, the Pilgrim's looked down at the object. The brown pilgrim picked it up and displayed it openly for all to see. It was an iron spike wrapped in a leather strap.

"This," he said, not taking his eyes from the spike, "is quite interesting. It appears we have found the source of the sound brothers."

The other two leaned closer and examined the object. Baby Nicholas looked at it too and reached a little hand for it, saying "Da!" as he did so.

The brown pilgrim examined the spike so closely his eyes nearly crossed. Then he closed his eyes. After a few moments of concentration he gasped and looked at his companions with shock..

"Lords of Cupcakes!" He exclaimed.

"What? What?" Exclaimed the grey pilgrim, staring at the spike with horror.

"His name is Nicholas." Said the brown pilgrim. "Nicholas! What great name for a young boy, don't ya think?"

"Huh? The spike!" Said the grey pilgrim, pointing at it persistently.

"Oh yes. This is a key to Abanis." Said the brown pilgrim, frankly. "It would appear this child has been invited to our city, though I can't imagine why."

The grey pilgrim sighed.

"You might want to lead with that next time brother." Said the orange pilgrim. Then he looked down at Nicholas and shook his head. "It's not possible. We haven't had keys since before the Nazarene. They were used when The Pilgrim walked the earth with only very few of us. He made them for Hurum to find Abanis. But all the Hurum have been found."

They were silent for a time and baby Nicholas said *gaa!* to the world at large.

"Brother," said the grey pilgrim, "are you able to see who made this one? I ask only because," he shifted uneasily, "only few of us have the ability to craft such things. And, uh, we are near Jerusalem, so…." He faltered and sighed. "Was it him?"

The brown pilgrim closed his eyes for a moment and concentrated as he held the spike with two hands. He opened his eyes and looked at each of his companions and nodded sadly.

"He who left us made this key for the blood line of this child. There is no doubt." He said, looked thoughtfully at baby Nicholas.

The orange pilgrim stood and looked about the clearing. "Whatever the case, they were meant to meet us or find other means to Abanis. We must take the child." He grinned stupidly down at baby Nicholas who relished the new attention.

The others looked at each other and nodded.

"The provisions near camp confirms this was an ambush." Said the brown pilgrim, chewing on an olive and looking around. People were here for some time, possibly on the run from authorities.

"So where are they and why was this child left alone?" Said the grey pilgrim, looking at footprints for clues. The others didn't respond and shook their head, looking around the campsite.

"You are correct to wonder about such matters, masters." Said a voice from the trees. "I helped them escape Jerusalem."

The pilgrims would have jumped in surprise at the new voice but at their age, turning and raising an eyebrow served as well as a startled exclamation.

A younger man, clad in weather-stained robes stepped into the clearing. He carried a backpack and simple walking stick.

"Peter my boy!" Said the grey pilgrim, walking forward to greet the man with joyful enthusiasm.

The other pilgrims followed suit.

"You look healthy and full of vigor young one!" Said the brown pilgrim, smiling at Peter from under his voluminous hood.

Peter bowed low before the three pilgrims. "I heard you were in the neighborhood, elders. May I be of some assistance?"

"It's been a long time, young man. Come." The grey pilgrim escorted Peter to the nearby fire while the other pilgrim's followed. "Tell us how our favorite student is."

Peter looked around to the bodies of the fallen and his face drained slightly as he looked at Nicholas. "I have much to tell masters but allow me to attend to the fallen. We there others?"

"Only this bundle." The orange pilgrim shrugged and looked down at Nicholas.

"I think I may know this child and his parents but I can't be sure. Allow me to assist you bury these men. Then we can break bread and speak."

For the rest of the afternoon, Peter helped the elderly pilgrims buried the fallen soldiers. Nicholas whimpered slightly at the sight of the blackened tree stump so the orange pilgrim, sensing the child might be recalling some trauma, began to hum a peaceful melody. The cheerful melody rippled throughout the area like a cleansing wave and some animals came to sit beside the fire. Baby Nicholas had only been alive for a short time but even he was certain animals weren't supposed to do that. He stared in amazement at a mouse which sat comfortably on the shoulder of the brown pilgrim and chewed on a nut.

"It is done." Peter said wearily, sitting down in front of a small fire with the pilgrims.

"A good job m'lad and many thanks." Said the grey pilgrim, passing him a metal cup of mead.

Peter took it wine and drank deep. They passed him a wooden bowl filled with some sort of gruel and all began to eat. The brown pilgrim produced a fine white powder from his backpack and mixed it in a bowl with some water from the nearby spring. This produced a milky paste-like mixture which he then handed to the orange pilgrim. Soon everyone, even Baby Nicholas, were nourished.

"So then." Said the orange pilgrim to Nicholas as he laid the baby down into a cocoon of blankets. "Before we begin, allow me to introduce Harry," he gestured to the grey pilgrim, who rolled his eyes, "Fuzzy," he pointed to the brown pilgrim who leaned down to Nicholas and waved, "and I'm Buddy. This young man is Peter." He pointed to the bearded man who smiled down at Nicholas as he gulped down some gruel. Pleased to meet your little master."

"Brother, he's an infant." Sighed Harry.

"He'll remember." Buddy nodded, taking off his orange cloak and wrapping the baby in extra blankets.

"Well," Peter said, looking at each of the elderly pilgrims, "if you don't mind, I have much to tell. Matters in Judea are troubling."

*Jingle***Jingle***Jingle*

Pontius Pilate stretched blissfully. Golden, morning sun rays filtered into his room and warmed his enormous bed. Word reached him the previous evening of trackers returning to Jerusalem with Longinus' spear. He slept quite peacefully knowing the criminals had justice visited upon them and his reputation was left intact. Now he could focus his attention on governing Judaea.

He slid from his bed, yawned and walked lazily to a bronze basin atop a small marble pedestal. Slaves had it filled every morning with cool water and rose petals. After splashing his face he grabbed a towel and headed to his desk.

On his large, lacquered desk a silver plate was filled with a variety of cheeses, smoked meats, bread and fruit. Beside the plate were silver containers filled with fresh fruit juices, spring water and wine. As Pilate poured some juice into a silver goblet, he perused over his notes and nibbled on some cheese. He sighed with satisfaction as the salty creaminess of the cheese complimented the tangy sweetness of the juice. This was important because Pilate was the sort of man who made important decisions based on the mood his breakfast put him in.

After a few minutes, there was a soft knocking at his door but not the one for slaves. It was the *official* door.

"Not now!" He shouted.

There was a more persistent knocking now which angered Pilate. Irritated, he marched over and threw the door open with such force the it clanged into the wall and left a mark in the marble.

"How dare you - " He began to say but before he could start swearing, a ghastly image advanced on him. He jumped sideways just in time to avoid the man who burst into his room carrying a large spear. He gaped at the man then his eyes swiveled sideways to the spear.

Pilate, somewhat shaken by the intrusion, opened his mouth to shout for guards but stopped short. There was something odd about the man now looking at him, giving him reason to hesitate. It was the eyes. They were completely black.

The person, if that's what it was, looked like one of his trackers but he was terribly disheveled. His dark robes and leather vest, practical for travelling long distances in the arid regions of Judea, were splattered with blood and other unnamable stains. His face was matted with unkempt hair and dirt and he smelled of alcohol, sweat and blood.

The man staggered forward and fell to his knees on the marble dais at the center of Pilate's audience room. Morning light, streaming in from the balcony seemed to pain the man as he squinted and grimaced. His skin was wrinkled beyond belief and its pallor reminded Pilate of one of the numerous corpses he saw dragged from Golgotha.

"My lord," wheezed the tracker as he put the butt end of the spear on the marble floor and leaned it weakly towards Pilate, "I have done it. Release my family. I beg you."

Pilate stood in shock, looking down at the prostrate man. His eyes drifted to the massive spear once more. "The criminals are dead?" He asked eyeing the spear as he licked his lips.

"Oh yes, your reverence. Release his family. Take it. Take the spear. It is your trophy." The tracker cackled wildly and coughed, spitting blood onto Pilate's clean, white marble floor. "I found it and thought it must be given to one as supremely revered as you."

Pilate felt he was being mocked in some way but before he could respond, the man began to disintegrate. Pilate froze. This normally doesn't happen during conversation, he was sure. It was the sort of transformation that happens to corpses over a few years in a tomb.

Unfortunately for Pilate, he was front row and center stage, witnessing the miracle of decomposition at work in ultra-fast motion. The man's eyes turned up into his head and as Pilate watched in growing shock and revulsion, the sockets dissolved into hollow pits. Skin turned colorless and grey. Hair, black and greasy a moment ago, turned grey and grew long. Cracked and bloodless lips peeled back over blackening teeth and rotting gums. Pilate put his hand to his mouth as he watched the tracker decompose.

Pilate covered his mouth with a shaking hand as he watched the tracker decompose. He staggered back into a chair near his desk and stared at the still figure, now positively skeleton-like, near his marble dais. His mind tried to make sense of it all but gave up and allowed Pilate to stare a few more moments until more information became readily available. He looked to the doors and thought to call out for guards but couldn't build up the nerve to move or speak.

After a few moments, he stood up and walked over to the ashen horror on his dais. He eyed the corpse suspiciously as if expecting it to jump up and start swinging the spear around. He leaned closer and stared longingly at the spear. There was something strangely attractive about it. It seemed to emanate power, something which Pilate had always desired above all else in his life.

Take the spear!

"What? Who said –" Pilate stopped and looked around. He was sure he heard a voice. "Who's there? Show yourself!" He commanded with as much authority as he could muster. Unfortunately, his voice sounded weak, muffled and tinged with panic.

No response came. Pilate stared around his room and then back to the man and the spear. Until now, it had not occurred to him that whatever curse fell upon the unfortunate tracker might happen to him.

Do not worry old friend. There is only power to be gained.

The voice was unmistakable this time. It was as if someone was whispering in his ear, so very close. Pilate whirled about, half expecting to see an apparition give ownership to the voice but he was completely alone. Fear gripped him as he walked slowly around the dead beggar and looked around his room. A cold sweat formed on his brow and he raised the decanter of wine once more to drown whatever horror was growing in his mind.

"Who are you?" He said to the room at large after a healthy gulp of wine. "What manner of trickery is this?"

I am you.

Pilate paused frowned. "Me? You are me? Nonsense."

Why else would we call us old friend? Said the voice.

Pilate considered this. "If you are me then tell me how I came to hold this office." He said himself.

We murdered our former master in Rome and took his place.

Pilate froze. His face drained of color and his eyes widened. No one knew that! There were no witnesses! It was his own plan to usurp his former superior back in Rome. No one suspected Pilate could have been responsible. No one would have believed it, for they were such good friends...long ago.

"Are you a God?" Pilate whispered.

Yes and no! The voice echoed inside Pilate's head. *We are god-like because I am you. We are close to becoming so much more than! Take the spear Pontius Pilate! Take the spear and become a God! It is our destiny! It is our opportunity!*

"But I…" Pilate trailed off as the enormity of the promise sank into his mind.

Yes we can become god-like! The voice read Pilate's mind. *It is an opportunity. Just like when we erased our friend and master. The opportunity presented itself. And now, we have been blessed with another opportunity.*

Pilate listened and allowed his imagination to run wild with notions of divine power and what he could do with it. But Pilate was cunning. He did not become the Prefect of Judaea by trusting others. He did not even trust himself, especially now.

"And what is the price?" He asked, cold calculating confidence returning to him.

*Ah…*said the voice, every syllable whispering snake-like in Pilate's mind. *What god-like calculation we have. A mere trifle we must give. It is a trivial thing, a valueless thing to us.*

"And what would that be?" Asked Pilate, ready to bargain for even more power at the lowest cost.

Our soul.

Pilate frowned.

"And what is that? A soul? Does it cost money?"

No. We are lucky to give such a small thing for so much power. You cannot see it. You cannot touch it. It has no material value at all and it is certainly not as valuable as gold.

"And how is it that I can give that which I cannot touch, see or taste?" Asked Pilate. His excitement was growing at the prospect of profiteering so much for so little. He kneeled down beside the dead beggar and licked his lips as he looked at the spear.

It is easy. We need only take the spear and all will be exchanged. And we will become a God! The world will be ours to relish!

Pilate paused to evaluate the situation. If indeed he was not going mad, then he would receive more power than he ever imagined in this lifetime. If he was going mad, then he would take the spear and spend the rest of the day with his pretty slaves. It seemed like a win-win situation to him except for one thing.

"If I take the spear will this happen to me?" Asked Pilate as he looked at the mummified beggar.

Oh no! No, not at all! We will become so much more. This one was not worthy of such power and thus perished under it. We are special. We have special lineage. Our ancestors were...special. We are worthy!

"And no trickery or hidden contracts to sign?" Pilate asked, licking his lips.

Of course not. We have spoken truthfully. How can we lie to ourselves? I am you, old friend. But we must act quickly or another may be chosen amidst this palace to receive the power!

And that was the closing of the sale. Pilate's caution broke at the prospect of another benefiting from his opportunity.

Quickly now! Take the spear and become a God!

Caution now a fleeting memory, Pilate thrust his hand forward and grabbed the spear, wrenching it from the dead grasp of the tracker. As he did so the corpse shattered and crumbled to dust on the floor. All trace of the tracker's human form was lost in a pile of ash and dust as if it were the cremated remains of a funeral pyre.

Pilate stood up clutching the spear with both hands and waited expectantly. It was cold - as cold as anything Pilate had ever touched. He looked down and marveled at its luster and perfection. The spear of Longinus was his but at what cost? Was he truly going mad? Was the voice indeed his own? And if it were, did he truly believe that anything would happen?

"What is the meaning of this?" Pilate asked. He looked about the room and then looked outside his balcony window. There was something odd about the city but for now he wondered about his own sanity.

Pilate walked to the polished metal mirror near his bed. Nothing seemed odd about his reflection. He still had wrinkles. Perhaps –

Pilate gasped and froze. All of the hairs on his arms stood up and his heart nearly stopped beating.

In the reflection of the mirror, he could see himself lying on the marble floor, next to the ashen remains of the tracker.

Pilate spun around and stared at his own unconscious self on the floor. "What manner of trickery is this?!" He screamed.

The doors to his audience chamber burst open and an officer entered.

"Lucesi!" Said Pilate running over to him. "Thank the gods, get this imposter out of my - " He stopped. Lucesi ran right at him. Pilate closed his eyes and flinched but no impact came, only the sense of passing through a cold fountain of water. He opened his eyes and turned. Lucesi had ran straight through him and was leaning down next to his other self and calling out in alarm. Soon several servants entered the room and ran straight through the astonished Prefect to lean over Lucesi and his unconscious double.

"What is happening? What has happened?!?" Pilate was experiencing a terror that he had never known in his privileged life and verged on tears.

Then a deafening thunderclap peeled across the sky just outside Pilate's balcony. The sound of it shook Pilate to his knees and he clutched Longinus' spear as if it were a life line. His breath was shallow and he imagined his heart would soon explode from the shock of all that was transpiring. The light in the domicile darkened as brazier flames were extinguished. The sky darkened as a huge, black cloud moved in to cover the city.

Cursed are the Pious! For they shall inherit oblivion!

A voice echoed about Pilate as he looked around wildly. It was deeper than any voice he had ever heard and seemed to reverberate across the city. He expected to hear people screaming and closing up shutters around the city but all he could hear the ominous voice.

Cursed are the Pious! For they shall inherit oblivion!

Pilate shrieked as he backed away from his other self. A small part of him, buried deep where once he had been a good man, awakened and took stock of the situation. For the second time in his life, Pilate felt had done something truly terrible. That small part of Pilate's inner self, yet untainted by greed and lust, reminded Pilate of something. *A mere trifle we must give. It is a trivial thing, a valueless thing.* Perhaps the cost was too great.

From across the room, he glimpse his own reflection in the polished mirror and felt suddenly nauseous. As his doppleganger was being shaken by Lucesi, Pilate rushed back to the mirror and looked at himself once more. He was repulsive. Gone were his handsome features and noble Roman posture. What he saw was a retched, wrinkled, evil looking ghoul with pustule covered skin and rotting teeth. He raised a slimy hand to his face and gaped at his ugliness.

A lifetime of cruelty, lies and over-indulgent lust flooded his mind as memories of an unsavory life came crashing in. He realized that every act of malice, every choice in his life, no matter how big or small, sculpted the repulsive beast staring back at him in the mirror.

"No!" Pilate screamed, shaking his head as he stared down at the spear. "No! I don't want it! I don't need it! I don't want the spear!" He tried to throw it to the ground and saw the spear had changed too.

Pilate looked down at it and blinked in confusion. The spear appeared to have melted. The head slowly dropped and curved perpendicular to the shaft as if it were subjected to immense heat. Down it melted until the beautifully crafted spearhead was a large metallic arc projecting from the shaft, resembling a scythe.

He shook his hands violently and staggered around his chambers as more and more people entered the room and completely ignored him. Then he heard the voice once more.

We are unable to break the contract.

"No. I do not want this. Please let me go." Pilate pleaded.

But a gathering darkness closed in on him. Inky, black tendrils of smoke spewed forth from his grip on the scythe and spiraled around his body.

Do not be afraid. You are not alone.

Pilate hesitated. That was not the voice from before. It was another voice. It was soft and sounded almost caring.

Do not be afraid, Pontius Pilate. The soft voice continued. *You are caught in a struggle between forces beyond your understanding.*

"What? Who are you?"

We are you, as we have said before. Said the cunning voice. *Now, accept the blessed gift of immortality!*

It cannot hear us Pilate. Said the caring voice. *Accept and do what is asked of you for now.*

"And then what?"

We will become a god!

Your crimes will be forgiven. Said the caring voice. *You remember when once you were a good man, never cruel. But the unsavory life you have lived has left you vulnerable. Now you are infected with a virus that must be healed through selfless action.*

Pilate looked down at himself and felt nauseous. His pustule covered skin and decrepit form was loathsome.

"What have I done?" Was all he could whisper.

We are not foolish to accept such power! Said the cunning voice triumphantly.

You are human after all, Pontius Pilate. Said the caring voice. *Remember this well: blessed are the meek.*

Completely beyond the riptides of horror and swimming into a terrifying abyss, Pilate's mind decided that the universe had gone mad and decided to reboot. Before consciousness left him, a deep voice repeated a terrible litany in his head.

Cursed are the Pious. For they shall become Death!

Chapter 10: A Side of Ocean

"So let me get this straight." Said the Fuzzy from the depths of his brown robes. "The Nazarene is gone. You and your fellows have scattered. This one's father," he gestured to the baby sleeping in the orange pilgrim's arms, "who you say is named Erik, pulls a nail out of his foot, gets beaten by Pilate and runs out of the city with his best friend, who just happens to be the third son of a recently executed Roman magistrate, with their respective wives." He took a breath and continued. "They get ambushed out here, presumably by Pilate's men and are now missing, along with a spear you guess is an artifact of our ancient past. Correct so far?"

"Sounds about right." Said Peter smiling at Harry who was now draining his fourth cup of mead and mumbling inaudibly.

"Sounds like poorly written tragedy." Fuzzy threw his arms up in the air. "So when does everyone die?"

Peter snorted.

"I have just one question." Said Buddy, rocking gently with the baby. "Why would the Nazarene give such a key to Nicholas or his father? Surely he was able to see the officer and this child are human. Well, for the most part."

"His ways and means were strange, I agree. I have doubted him more than thrice but he never ceased to amaze me." Said Peter. "There is no doubt he wanted either the father or the son to make it to Abanis but the reason escapes me. The Nazarene was like The Pilgrim himself. They could see future events like one skipping ahead pages in a book. Such intuition is unfathomable."

"Well," Fuzzy sighed, "the Nazarene was one of our greatest and a loss beyond measure."

"Not a loss, brother." Peter interjected. "A temporary absence I'll wager."

"Be that as it may, I don't look forward to returning such tidings to our brethren if they don't already know. He was much loved and admired by many. A great light has faded, if not extinguished. And The Pilgrim is still absent. It's been nearly fifty years, as I recall."

Peter looked into the middle distance and said nothing but recalled the secret conversation on Golgotha. *I will be taking a pilgrimage of a sort and will not return for some time. Please tell no one of this meeting.*

"There are some who have taken Mary and the child away." Said Peter finally. "His line is safe for now but I fear those within it will be hunted in the future. Rome has little love for what he started."

"But there is hope in this one I think." Whispered the Buddy looking down at baby Nicholas. "The Nazarene would not have set such events in motion had he not seen the need for this child come to Abanis." He pulled the iron spike from his robes and stared at it thoughtfully. "We shall see what Pantilius, Aryu, and Gabriel think."

The others nodded, staring at the iron spike. It glinted in the subtle light of the campfire and everyone noted the dark stains on its surface.

The next morning the three pilgrims prepared to leave and cleared the camp as best they could. Baby Nicholas was awake and sitting happily in the haunch Buddy crafted around his chest.

As they made ready, Peter bowed before them.

"Come now." Said the Harry gruffly. "No need for that, young emissary." He stepped forward and straightened Peter's robe more comfortably under the man's backpack strap.

"I bow with respect to my teachers. Here our paths must part."

"But surely you need to return to Abanis." Said Fussy, raising his brown hood to peer closer at Peter. "Surely we must take council with Aryu."

"Nothing would make me happier than to return but I made a promise to do something for *him*." Peter sighed, smiling at each of the old men. "I need to care for some of his followers. Their faith is in peril and I will not abandon them to torture and death."

The elder nodded and each hugged him in turn.

"Take care Peter. Guide them well but be careful not to interfere. Remember the rules." Said the Buddy smiling. "You have only to request help and Abanis will answer."

Peter laughed and as he did so, the morning light in his eyes seemed all the brighter. "If I shall find myself hanging upside down from a tree then I shall certainly call!" With a wave he disappeared into the wilderness.

The pilgrims watched him as he departed but as Peter disappeared into the foliage baby Nicholas began to cry. Buddy looked down at Nicholas and jostled his ample belly. "It's ok little one, he will be fine. He will return to see

Abanis someday, just you wait and see." But that did little to comfort Nicholas, who whimpered at the shadowed trees where Peter bid farewell.

The elder pilgrims made their way through forested terrain, heading west towards the Mediterranean Sea. They stopped at some bleak villages along the way for supplies and carefully avoided any Roman patrols or stations. A few travelers passing the old men frowned in confusion at the sight of three extremely old men with an extremely young child.

Despite their extreme age, the pilgrims kept a steady pace and stopped only a few times during the day for brief rests. They took turns telling fantastic stories to Nicholas in the evenings, partly to amuse themselves and partly to amuse Nicholas. When Buddy put his arm around Harry's neck in an effort to demonstrate how the mighty hero defeated the mean monster, Nicholas giggled at the spectacle. He laughed even harder when Harry scowled at Buddy after the demonstration.

After a week of traveling thus, without any disruptions along the way, the four companions reached the ancient, port city of Gaza.

"Looks like it always has." Said the brown pilgrim, peering out from behind a bush atop a knoll outside of town.

The setting sun cast scarlet highlights on the ocean and the three men sighed audibly as they breathed in fresh, salty sea air. They could hear waves crashing lazily against the emerald tinted wharf, broken only by the shouts of deck hands on trading ships, rushing to unload their wares before sunset.

"Hello again, my dear." Said Harry to the coast in general. Aftera few moments of silent appreciation, he began a rhythmic whisper.

"From the Stars we came;
From the Earth we began;

Through oceans of rivers and rivers of sand.
As dusk looks back to admire the dawn,
E'er shall we as time flows on."

He stood silently for a moment, indulging in some long forgotten memory until he noticed the other two clapping quietly behind him.

"Well done brother. That was quite prophetic." Nodded Buddy.

"Did it take you several centuries to write that?" Grinned Fuzzy as he stuffed a pipe full of herbs.

"No." Said the Harry quietly. "I read it on a very old piece of parchment in the library of Twilenos." He turned to look at the ocean again. "It's an homage to oceans I think but I'm not sure what type it refers to. Regardless, I like it."

"Gaa!" Nicholas agreed and looked at the coast.

"Alright, it's almost dusk." Said Buddy wearily. "Once the sun sets we can flow to Abanis. Mrs. Bakersbee can care for the child, I'm sure."

The three men paused and looked at each other. Without speaking, they realized as one, a very important issue had been overlooked. It was perhaps the most important issue involved in traveling to Abanis. An uncomfortable silence ensued and they looked at the child. Then back to each other.

"I've never flowed with another - "

"What are we going to do about the bab –"

"We should teach the child before we go."

The others two looked at Fuzzy in amazement as he stared thoughtfully at Nicholas and puffed on his pipe.

"What in Hades haunches are you blathering about?" Exclaimed Harry. "Only trained acolytes are able to learn flowing. The key word, I might add, is *trained*, Fuzzy. *Trained.* This," he gestured dramatically at baby Nicholas, "is what we, in the real universe, call a *baby*."

"Oh c'mon." Said the Fuzzy, puffing more smoke into the air. "Just because he is a child doesn't mean he is not capable."

Harry gaped at him. "He's...he's a baby! He's not a student or part of our plan as of yet! He's doesn't even know what in blazes we're talking about!"

Nicholas watching them with wide-eyed wonder.

"Patience grasshopper," grinned Fuzzy, still looking at baby Nicholas. "Just because he is not able to communicate with us does not mean he is unable to communicate at all. We will speak," he paused for dramatic effect, "his language."

Harry sighed. He put a wrinkled hand to his forhead and closed his eyes. "I think I need to sit down for a minute or..." He began pacing in front ofk the other two.

Buddy grinned at Nicholas with astonished glee. "Did you just hear that little one? The brown pilgrim is gonna talk to you just the way he does to the grey pilgrim! Isn't that nice?"

After a quiet walk into the wharf district of Gaza, the pilgrims made their way to a local inn near the wharf. Subtle orange light cascaded out of an open window and illuminated a small portion of a wide boardwalk. Sounds of conversation, laughter and drinking could be heard.

"Alright." Said Harry to his companions. "Let me check the inn. Maybe the parents of this," he gestured to Nicholas, "bundle of mystery are miraculously alive. In which case, we will have words. You two head to the shore and start *speaking* to him or whatever you have planned. If you can get him to flow, I'm retiring." He glowered at them, opened the tavern door and vanished into the lively din.

Fuzzy and Buddy grinned as the inn door closed. "Ah, to be young and full of vigor." Said Buddy. Fuzzy nodded and chuckled as the two meandered away in the direction of the water.

Inside the inn, Harry noted it was a simple affair with few tables in what seemed to be a common area. The room was lit by here and there with oil lamps but left the innkeeper's desk remained in the shadows.

“Yes venerable one, a room for you?” Said the innkeeper, standing up from behind the desk. He was slim, handsome and had long black hair but reeked of fish and liquor. Harry didn’t look at him but kept an eye on a few fishermen drinking in the common room.

“A few supplies for the road if you have them young man.” Said the grey pilgrim as he rummaged around for some money within the confines of his robes.

“What will you be needing then sir? Food? Other supplies?”

“Blankets if you have them, lots of blankets.”

The innkeeper leaned closer over the small desk. “You going to some place cold? What you be needing blankets for?”

Harry looked up sharply. “That is none of your bus-.” He stopped and gaped. "Namtar? What are you doing here at - " Two hooded figures carrying staves of white birch wood emerged from shadowed corners to Harry's left.

"What would an emissary be doing here? Is it accompanying a child?" The innkeeper leaned forward even more, taking in the feeble-looking pilgrim. He leered and grinned again. “Going somewhere?” He asked. His voice had changed. It was low and whispery.

"You are not Namtar." Said Harry flatly, noting the others. "And you are not his brothers." He backed away and spotted a strangely unlit lantern on the desk which suddenly burst into life and flared blue.

Harry stared at the innkeeper in wonder and disbelief.

“Where are taking the chimp?” Said one of the hooded figures and stepped closer.

Harry moved suddenly. The small area near the door flashed with white light as he raised his staff.

“Certamen!” He yelled and everyone froze. A drunken fisherman, startled by the flash of light, sat frozen in place in the common room behind Harry. His mug and its contents were also frozen on their way to the floor.

The innkeeper was not frozen however. He looked around the room as if nothing had happened. "And what is it you hope to accomplish with this petty trick, youngling?" He asked.

"Youngling?" Harry frowned. "I...know of you! It cannot be…you… weren't you cast out or something? The Halaam were killed along with their cohorts." He reasoned with himself, eyes darting about the room. "That was so very long ago, before he found us…the histories tell us – "

"The histories are false, philosopher." The third figure drew nearer to the grey pilgrim. "Do you wish to hear our side of your so-called histories?"

Harry breathed heavily and stared in disbelief as the innkeeper walked around the desk. "Nothing to say? Well then I'll just take the child if you don't want to chat. I want that child or," and he smiled at the frozen people around the common room, "I shall kill everyone in this inn."

Harry's heart sank. It was his proud duty to protect these people if need be. However, if this being was what he suspected, a *Halaam* or *traitor* from his peoples' ancient past, there was no saving these people. If the histories were true, this being was beyond his skill to overcome. His best and apparently only option was to try and save himself and warn the others if possible.

"Nether!" Harry shouted. His frail body, robes and all, dispersed into a puff of mist which vanished out of an open window beside the door.

Run, fool! Said a voice in Harry's mind. *Run back to your Pilgrim and let him know we have risen.* The voice seared across Harry's mind as he materialized in the darkness near the wharf. He shook his head in an effort to block the voice but a flash of orange light made him look up.

The inn was on fire. Screams of agony, fear and panic echoed about the wharf. He could hear sounds of pottery being smashed and windows being broken.

Further down the wharf, Buddy was singing a lullaby to baby Nicholas while Fuzzy paced back and forth. The latter was muttering to himself about speech, syntax, development of thought and the mental capacities of babies.

Harry materialized out of the darkness and ran towards them.

"Did you get some blanke-" But Fuzzy stopped short. Sounds and screams of agony reached him and he turned towards the inn. He squinted at the bright, orange blaze and saw arms and legs sticking out of the small windows. Some people near the inn pulled at the front door and were trying to bash it in but the blaze was too powerful and the door was not opening. Other people grabbed buckets near the shore and began to assembled a water-chain.

"We must help them!" He rushed forward but Harry grabbed him roughly by the shoulder.

"Flow! We must flow now! We are in danger and so is the baby!" Harry shouted in his ear. He quickly told them of all that occured inside the inn.

"What? How?!?" They exclaimed, looking at each other in shock and surprise.

"No time to speak of insane Hurum! Namtar and his brothers are not who they appear to be. Now, we must flow now!" Harry looked at Nicholas and then to Fuzzy. "Whatever *goo-goo* and *gaa-gaa* you planned on speaking has to be done this instant!"

Fuzzy looked at baby Nicholas and breathed heavily. He looked at the other two pilgrims and nodded. "Give me the child." He said and Nicholas was handed to him. He covered the child in his voluminous robes and turned towards the shoreline.

"We are going to play a game little one…catch me if you can!" He stepped into the water and vanished instantly beneath the surface. The other two followed suit and soon the wharf shore was vacant.

Moments later, three figures materialized on the shore. The one posing as the innkeeper looked around as he paced the waters' edge.

"Flow away to your sanctuary." He smiled at the ocean in general. "Tell as many emissaries as you as you can. Riders are among you."

And with that, one by one, they stepped into the water and vanished.

*Jingle***Jingle***Jingle*

The vastness of oceans is somewhat unfathomable and quite fearsome to those unlucky enough to navigate them without the convenience of a ship. Yet somewhere beneath the immeasurable waves, traveling faster than an ship, the four companions sped onwards.

Baby Nicholas experienced two things the moment he hit the water with Fuzzy. One was wetness and the other was a desire not to breath. The latter was the most upsetting. He suddenly learned the full meaning of panic and whimpered little bubbles. Then he heard Fuzzy speaking to him.

Breathe little one. You breathed this way for eight months. You will remember how. It's ok. Try it. We will protect you. The voice was soothing and Nicholas knew what the voice was telling him. He breathed and coughed little bubbles and felt...perfectly fine.

That's it, yes. No time to lose now. It was friendly voice of Buddy now. *Let's play a game. It's called hide and seek. Come little one, come and find me!*

Nicholas understood the *feeling* of the words. They coaxed him with a playfulness he came to expect from the three elder pilgrims. He paused in the water for a brief instant and moved to the voice. He did not swim. He simply followed the voice in his mind.

Come little one, this way.

The voice was more distant now and Nicholas changed his direction.

A new feeling overcame Nicholas as he traversed the dark currents. He experienced *loneliness.* Fear gripped him again and he wanted to stop. He didn't like this game. It was scary and not fun at all. He felt lonely in the vast emptiness of the oceans and wanted to come out. The urge to breath air was suddenly overwhelming. He knew that breathing air was important.

Another voice broke the emptiness. This voice was weak and faded, as if coming from a vast distance. It was a woman's voice and sounded a lot like his mother.

Come to me, child, follow my voice.

Nicholas liked the voice very much. It was comforting, soft and nurturing.

Come to me. Follow this voice. You don't need to breath.

Baby Nicholas followed the voice in another direction and listened again.

You are here. Call to them. Call to Buddy.

"*Waaa*!" He cried in his mind and suddenly all wetness vanished and was replaced numbing cold. Nicholas fell onto ice and began to cry.

Almost immediately he was scooped up and smothered with thick, warm blankets. He was swept into the arms of Buddy and held close.

Harry looked at his companions and shook his head as Buddy rocked the baby in his arms. "Absolutely astonishing. Amazing!" He looked at Fuzzy. "You did it!" He considered this for a second and looked down at the baby. "*He* did it?"

Fuzzy shook his head. "No my friends. I tried to make it a game, which is the language of one as young as he," he gestured to the baby, "but I lost him half way. It's a miracle he arrived here. An absolute miracle." He sighed and shook his head.

"That's got to be some sort of record at least!" Said Buddy, looking down at baby Nicholas in awe. "No one can flow without at least some training. And he's human!" He shook his head.

Harry stepped past them. He looked out from the icy shore to vast, dark blue waters thoughtfully.

They were on the edge of a glacier with penguins chortling and squawking nearby. The stars were out in full force, gleaming and sparkling on the crests of lazy waves approaching the shallow ice shelf. Harry listened to the waves for a moment and looked back to his companions. Then his eyes fell to the baby. "He may have had help." He frowned thoughtfully.

Buddy looked down at Nicholas with a gleeful smile. "You see little one? The grey *meanie* lost his mind thinking we almost lost you! Isn't that sweet?"

Harry scowled and rolled his eyes. "Fine. Never mind then. Always with the jokes."

Fuzzy looked to the icy ocean thoughtfully. "Well, whatever the case may be, he made it. Let's get home before we freeze. Harry, would you do the honors?"

Harry looked at some penguins, who eyed the newcomers warily, then turned to Buddy. "Do you have the key?"

Buddy gripped Nicholas with one beefy arm and produced the spike from within his orange robes.

Harry took it and placed it in the snow. As one, they stepped back and waited.

After a moment, a hint of steam rose from the spike. Then a sudden stream of steam exploded from the spot like a geyser. Soon fog blanketed the area. As the clouds receded, the pilgrims could see a smooth, round tunnel melted into the ice beside the spike. Buddy leaned down and picked up the iron spike which hadn't melted into the glacier and returned remarkably fast to a cool state.

"Yep, it's the Nazarene's alright." He said, nodded to the others as they came in behind him. He looked down at the cylindrical tunnel. "Well. It's a strange gate but I always thought the Nazarene was a bit of a loony."

"I've seen many styles of gates for many newcomers." Said Fuzzy, grinning at the tunnel. "But this one looks like it's going to be the most fun I've had in centuries."

Then without ceremony, they each took a turn to leap in.

The last was Buddy. He looked down at baby Nicholas and smiled with excited anticipation. "This is called a *tube-slide*, little one. You're gonna love it!"

Then he leapt into the tube and vanished with a 'weeeeeeee!'.

A few moments later, the icy tunnel closed and the glacier was once again flat, pristine and quiet.

Chapter 11: One Order of Human, To Go

Pilate gasped and awakened in utter darkness. He couldn't feel his body and tried to remember how he came to this place. His eyes searched for a source of light but all was black. He breathed hard for a few moments and waited.

Good. We are the first to come so far. Many times we have tried to reach this place and failed. Pontius Pilate is strong.

"What is this? Where am I?" His voice trembled cold blackness but there was no reply. The sound of his voice did not echo as he expected but rather dissipated as soon as he mouthed it.

He struggled to his feet and reached out clumsily into the void to feel for a wall or anything at all. Although he sensed nothing physical, Pilate thought he could hear waves crashing into a shoreline.

"What is this?" He screamed at the void.

Now, now! Let's not be too rash my Lord.

"You!" Pilate yelled. "Where am I?" He tried to disguise the fear in his voice but the words quavered and he sounded like a frightened child.

My Lord, you are home.

"Home? I cannot see anyth - " He screamed but stopped short. A small twinkling of light overhead made Pilate look up. He could just make out some stars.

Laughter, twisted and maniacal, filled Pilate's mind. *You are in a space between spaces. It is where Gods walk. When you realize you no longer need to see nor hear nor feel, you will find you can experience any of your former sensations as often as you wish, oh yes indeed.*

"No longer need…?" He repeating the words and mulled over their meaning in his mind. Then the world opened to him. But what he saw and felt was quite shocking.

The first thing Pilate saw was a large fish looking back at him. This was only slightly less shocking than the fact he too was underwater.

Far to the north of what someday will be called Greenland, Pontius Pilate emerged from icy waters like a launched undersea missile. He collapsed sputtering and coughing on a twilight lit shoreline and tried to get air back into his lungs. He saw the gleaming scythe, formerly Longinus' spear, lying on the rocks near him. He picked it ip and leaned heavily on it as he staggered around and tried to get his berrings.

He was on an ice-covered, rocky shore and despite the quiet beauty of the local scenery, felt miserable and alone. He hated being cold, wet and especially hated being both at the same time. Shivering and dripping wet, he blinked and tried to focus on his surroundings.

"Where in blazes am I?"

It was night but he could see an array of floating ice chunks out in the dark water. They shifted lazily in the currents of the vacant bay like giant puzzle pieces seeking to reform. He turned inland and looked across a vast plain of flat ice, crested by a range of cliffs. The cliffs were tall and reached around to either side of the bay's shoreline, forming a kind of encircling wall. Above them, Pilate could see a majestic, snow-capped mountain peak but this is not what made him gape in wonder.

Far above the peak, stretching across the star filled sky, was a breathtaking array of streaking lights. Green, blue, pink and orange hues of streaking, pulsing lights danced in the night sky like ghostly remnants of a fire long since dead. Pilate stared in amazement at the spectacle and guessed he was observing the workings of the goddess Aurora. He heard of such celestial displays from Roman clergymen who served in northern campaigns for the Empire but he never believed such ramblings until now.

Yes, you understand it is a beautiful thing. This is good Pilate. Said the calm voice. *Acknowledging beauty in nature is another step you must take to heal yourself.*

Pilate sighed. He secretly wished the voices in his head were simply his own and that nice people in white robes would emerge from a rock, or something, and lead him to a safe and happy environment. Unfortunately this did not happen.

"Nature?" He asked, unable to take his eyes from the celestial display. "You mean the gods are not doing this?"

Yes. The Gods are trying to communicate with us. We have been acknowledged as one of their own. Said the cunning voice.

No. This is the beauty of nature Pilate. You must understand this. Said the calm voice.

Pilate shivered and registered the voices. He was getting used to their contradictions. As he guessed before, the soft voice truly cared for his well-being so he decided to heed it more than the other. The cunning voice, however, seemed to playing with his sense of pride and other base desires.

"What now?" Why am I here?"

Patience. Wait and we shall see. Said the cunning voice. *The Gods are sending a servant to greet us here.*

After a few minutes, Pilate spotted a small shape on the icy plain under the cresting cliffs. The shape was getting larger and he could just make out a small figure walking towards him. After some time he was able to see more detail. It was a small, humanoid looking creature, almost like a child. It wasn't hooded but heavily robed in white material of some kind and carried what appeared to be a square, black box in two hands. When it was closer he could see the creature was indeed childlike in stature but it's face was old. Very old. Even stranger was the creatures' large, upswept and pointed ears and vacant, opaque eyes. This unnerved Pilate and he gripped the scythe with two hands as it drew closer.

He recalled a creature like this from Norsemen mythos during studies back in Rome. It was supposed to be a benevolent being and servant of their Gods. This did little to ease Pilate as it approached in the flesh, as it were.

We must not be afraid. This is our servant bringing a gift from the Gods. Said the cunning voice.

Be wary. This being is not a divine messenger. Said the caring voice. *It is a slave.*

The small creature came to stand in front of an astonished Pilate and held out the box. Pilate hesitated and looked into the small, equine face and saw the deep, blue eyes were blank. It's hairless skin was tinted blue and clammy. It's face, encircled by an explosion of white hair, might have been oddly handsome at some point but was now drawn and gaunt. It simply held out the box to Pilate and waited patiently.

The box was a cube, eight inches all around. It was made of some dark metallic material that Pilate had never seen before. He leaned closer. It had the texture of iron or bronze but gleamed like the black crystal rocks he had once seen near the doomed cities around Pompeii. There were no intricacies or markings and just a simple metal latch kept it closed.

We must take the box. It is a gift for us. Said the cunning voice.

Pilate hesitated.

Why must we wait? Let's take the box and open it! A great gift is inside for us to have. It is a welcoming gift from the gods.

It is ok Pilate. Do what you will with this box and its contents. Follow this path for now. Later it will lead to the liberation of others.

Pilate nervously took the box from the creature, which then turned to stand beside Pilate like a tiny automaton. He stared down at it for a moment then looked at the box. He unlatched it and lifted the lid.

Inside, the box was lined with fine, ermine colored silk. And that was it. There was nothing in the box but a fine, grey metallic dust. The dust was dull but it sparkled ever so slightly in the starlight. Pilate tilted the box left and right, backward and forward, hoping some object would present itself but there was nothing else.

He frowned and looked at the creature standing immobile beside him. "What is this supposed to be?" He asked aloud but the creature remained expressionless and stared at nothing.

Pilate sensed mirth at his confusion.

"Alright," he sighed, "what's so funny?"

Patience. We must have more patience. Look closer at the dust. Said the cunning voice.

"It's just metallic dust. Slag of some sort"

Nothing is simply 'just' if it arrives in such a manner and in such a container. The cunning voice snapped angrily. *We must learn to see. Look closer at the dust.*

Pilate peered closer at the dust. It didn't seem any different.

We must look closer.

Pilate looked so closely at the dust he nearly put his face inside the box. He could see it was sparkling a little bit but it did not appear to be any different. It did, however, have an unusual smell. It smelled like oil but he was unable to figure what this had to do with anything.

We must look closer

"I've put my entire head in this box to look closer. What would you have me do? Said Pilate testily.

Pilate was suddenly struck with a kind of mortal reminder that he hadn't eaten, drank or rested for quite some time. He staggered on the icy shoreline and fell to his knees as hunger, thirst, bitter cold and fatigue assaulted his senses. He felt weak and helpless.

We must not be impatient, primate. We would not like to become human again. Not in this place.

On his knees, Pilate clutched his stomach and winced in agony. "No…we don't want that….," croaked Pilate. He breathed hard and dropped the box, spilling its contents on the ice. The tiny creature, standing resolute beside him, did not move.

Good, yes. We must learn to be patient.

Immediately Pilate regained his strength and the feeling of hunger, cold and exhaustion left him. He stood up and looked down at the dust and felt truly afraid for the first time in weeks.

Yes. Said the caring voice. *Yes, you understand now that you are at the mercy of a force which can hurt you. Be wary and follow my ministrations Pilate. We will heal your soul and you will be free...eventually.*

Pilate had the presence of mind not to respond.

"What now?" He asked, looking down despondently at the dust which was strewn about the ice at his feet.

We must look closer. Said the cunning voice.

"How? How do I look closer?"

What is it that we use to look at anything? Asked the cunning voice.

Pilate hesitated. "What do we use? Well, eyes of course."

Then use our eyes to look closer.

Pilate started to leaned down once again but hesitated.

Yes. Now you are beginning to see. Why should we make our eyes go closer to something when we can bring it to us?

Pilate looked at the dust. He focused on it and tried to see it more clearly without leaning down. He squinted at it and suddenly the dust was as close to him as if it were one inch in front of his face.

Good. Look closer.

Pilate focused on the fine dust particles once more. Suddenly they were as large as tiny stones. He focused further still they became like boulders. And they were strange to behold. The boulders were insect-like with numerous appendages but crafted of some sort of crystal. They were piled on top of one another like heaps of little statues. They appeared to be like little machines but much more complex than anything he had ever seen.

Good. We see them. They can help us.

"How?" Asked Pilate, still examining the incredible complexity of the tiny crystalline objects.

They're alive. They're sleeping. We must awaken them. We must say a magic word to them. But we already know what the word is.

Pilate blinked as he refocused on his surroundings once more and looked down at the dust. "A magic word to make them help me? Help me do what?"

What is it we require if not in Jerusalem?

Pilate looked around at the beautiful yet bleak shoreline and cliffs beyond. "A room for the night would be nice but – "

And they can help us.

"They can help us build a home?"

Not as such. They will help us find a home.

Pilate searched his memory. What kind of magic word could make such tiny things come awake?

Yes. We know the answer. What are these things? What is their size?

Pilate recalled his scholarly studies once more and a Greek word for something incredibly small stood apart in his mind.

"Nanos." He said.

Almost imperceptibly, there was a flicker of light from the dust.

Pilate focused on the dust once more. The little insect-like crystals were crawling over each other and moving about now with a myriad of lights and pulses dancing around them. Some of them found particles of rock and other material trapped in the snow. They scooped this material up and other units used tiny, blinding light at their appendage tips to crafted spawns of themselves. The fresh spawns would then assist crafting other crystals and so on and so forth until the small pile of metallic dust became a sparkling, living mound.

"They are making more of themselves!" Pilate blinked in amazement.

Yes. Yes they are very helpful indeed. We must now command them. They must find us a home in this desolate place.

"How do I do such a thing?"

What was the magic word?

"Nanos." Said Pilate, half expecting the mound to assemble itself into tiny rows of legions at his feet. They did not.

What would we command of them? What do we need to reside here? What do they need to find? Said the cunning voice and Pilate perceived it was filled with anticipation and excitement.

"Find me a home." Said Pilate.

Almost immediately, the dust rose from the box like a miniature thunder cloud and hovered in front of Pilate. Light flashed within the cloud and a generic human face formed within it.

"Daah!" Pilate jumped back and hesitated.

"*Hybrid life form.*" It said, sounding like a metallic echo. *Classification: Unknown Huru. We require more information, Huru.*"

"Find a home somewhere around here." Pilate waved his hand around wildly. He noted the words *hybrid* and *Huru* but couldn't guess their meaning.

"*Command accepted.*" It said and immediately flew towards the cliffs.

As it floated across the icy plain from the shoreline to the cliffs under the mountain, it grew larger and larger until it was an immense, dark cloud lined with bursts of cerulean colored lightning. It vanish as it hit the cliff face but as Pilate stared, a giant section of the cliff face suddenly fell away and landed with a deafening crash to the permafrost ground below. The sound echoed across the strand.

Yes. They have found a home for us. We must wait and see what this home is.

Pilate leaned on his staff and watched as portion after portion of the cliffs fell away and crashed into the icy plain below. Slowly, the facade of a massive building emerged from the ice and rock. After a short while, he could clearly see brown, rock walls supported by gigantic pillars at gargantuan intervals along the cliff face. He noted the architecture as ancient Persian in style but no structure he had ever heard of was built on such a massive scale except, perhaps, the pyramids of Egypt.

Pilate also suspected the structure was once occupied before and buried, perhaps for a good reason. He began to worry what his impending occupancy would entail.

Yes. Said the caring voice as the building emerged from its icy prison. *You are correct to be worried, Pilate. This place was the home of a dangerous being. It was buried for a reason and was not to be unearthed for many thousands of years. We may not be able to communicate once you are inside. Take heed.*

Pilate noted the caring voice in his head but remained silent. If there was *heed* somewhere, he was surely going to take ample amounts of it. For now, however, his academic curiosity was jumping with anticipation.

It was the most magnificent construction Pilate had ever seen since he visited the Parthenon of Greece so many years ago. As he walked closer and marvelled at the facades' sheer size, Pilate also noted it was similar to ruins he once visited in Cappadocia and northern Syria, reminding him of those ancient cultures.

Behind Pilate, the pointy-eared creature came to life once more. It picked up the box, and followed him. Pilate guessed it would take them some time to reach the colossal, stone gates embedded in the roots of the mountain. He also guessed the interior would hold many more things to be wary of.

Chapter 12: Guess Who Is Swimming to Dinner?

As historian of the ancient people called *Huru*, Usher Ravenscrawl is responsible for recording the history of *The Great Sphere,* where many of their offspring presently reside. To the dismay of countless acolytes over the centuries, he also endeavors to put his readers into an involuntary coma with every paragraph. He might spend three paragraphs carefully dissecting the color of a windowsill on some home in the outskirts of the city of Abanis, then frankly note in a single sentence who the home belonged to and why it was significant. Unfortunately, it was up to the students to find these precious sentences before succumbing to slumber amidst the rest of the paragraphs.

Here he is, offering some nearly harmless descriptions of Abanis from *The History of The Great Sphere: City of Abanis – Most Interesting Homes and Notable Architecture; Volume 1:*

"*The Great Sphere of Abanis was designed by The Pilgrim to resemble and celebrate the natural wonders of the Earth. If one were to hold The Great Sphere in the palm of one's hand and see its entirety, it would appear to contain a flat surface at the bottom, making 30% of the inner mass while the other 70% would consist of an artificial sky, complete with sun, stars, moon, and a wondrous variety of weather patterns. The meteorological cycles within the entire sphere are in a continuously breathtaking waltz. They were designed and crafted by The Pilgrim employing archaic technology and skills from our ancient past. (see Cronos Veritas or The Pilgrim's Watch for more information.)*

If one were to look directly down upon the lands surrounding the central city of Abanis at the heart of the sphere, it would appear to be sectioned like the pattern of an orange sliced in twain. Each section is resplendent with (for example) lush jungle and cascading waterfalls in one area, looming mountains in another, and snow covered tundra with deep fiords in yet another. Quite simply, The Pilgrim crafted each area in a magnificent homage to the natural beauty of planet Earth. At it's heart is the marvellous city of Abanis that many emissaries call home."

The only way to enter Abanis is to have a key or to be accompanied by a citizen. Each key has its own *style* of entrance. For example, one key might require the individual to answer riddles asked by a stone sphinx while another might invite the visitor to race a camel across the antarctic tundra. Whatever the entrance requirement, the visitor would soon find themselves transported into the heart of The Great Sphere. For Nicholas and the elderly pilgrims, the Nazarene had designed a much more exhilarating and deliberate entrance. After sliding down the ice tube, the four companions emerged over several meters of open air in a massive cavern, then plummeted into large pool of water.

Sputtering and splashing in the water, they were assisted out of the pool by four men who looked thoroughly astonished at their arrival. The pools' diameter was about six meters across and a perfect half-sphere cut into the ice and rock. One of the men stepped forward and bowed respectfully.

"Masters!" He exclaimed. "So good to see you return to us safe and sound!" He looked puzzled, however, when Buddy emerged from the pool carrying a baby.

"Blasted ice tube!" Spat Harry as he staggered around in wet, grey robes.

"Most fun I've had decades!" Exclaimed Fuzzy, shaking himself like a dog out of water.

"Heeheehee!" Laughed Nicholas who enjoyed the trip immensely.

Two of the other men brought them some steaming mugs from a table nearby. It was hot chocolate. By order of The Pilgrim, patron of Abanis, no one entered The Great Sphere without receiving a freshly brewed cup.

The guardians of the pool were significantly younger in appearance than the three pilgrims. Despite their obvious human appearance, their eyes were somewhat reptilian in shape and color. The armor they wore, made of some shimmering, pearl-like material, looked more ceremonial than protective and was crafted to resemble the scales of a fish. Their helms were designed in a similar way and had dorsal fins on the crown and two fins on each side. Their hooded robes were simple, dark blue and each carried sturdy staves of oak.

"Master's we were not expecting your arrival to be," he glanced at the ceiling, "so sudden." He grinned at them. "And, we were unaware you brought company."

He smiled down at baby Nicholas who goggled him with wide, astonished eyes. "And you," he said as Nicholas shook his finger, "I welcome to Abanis too, little one."

The elder pilgrims finished their cocoa and noticed their robes were bone dry. Even Nicholas was given a tiny sip. It is thought the hot beverage assisted in the drying process but The Pilgrim never commented on the matter if asked.

"We are off to have council, brother." Said Harry to the guard. He paused and looked back at the pool thoughtfully. "Bring more guards this day. Be watchful."

The guard looked startled for a moment then bowed. "As you wish, master."

The elderly pilgrims swept across the massive room, passed through the archway and climbed a wide, stone staircase that spiraled up for some time. Iridescent globes of turquoise and gold, placed in metal bowls and fastened to the walls, cast a mixture of soothing, prismatic hues around the stairwell as they climbed upward. When they they reached the top of the stairs and stepped out into artificial sunlight, Buddy looked down at Nicholas with another gleeful smile.

"Welcome to Abanis." He said.

They emerged from a set of double doors under a huge arch near the center of a vast and sprawling city. If one were to observe a drop of water falling onto the surface of a flat plane of liquid, and then froze the ensuing *crown-shaped* splash, it would be a fair model of the city. Great spires of twisting architecture spread out from the center of the city in concentric waves of rippled streets. Large areas of natural fauna, ponds, rivers, lakes, gardens and animals dotted the city. There seemed to be few right angles anywhere. Just when the eye thinks it may have seen a ninety degree angle, it vanishes amidst smoothly curved walls and twinkling window sills.

Most noticeable to Nicholas was the wondrous variety of color. There were lush green gardens with giant, bright red flowers. Sapphire pools of water with rainbow graced mists were home to a variety of orange and yellow fish. Beyond the city, Nicholas could see golden fields of flax and corn under azure skies with fluffy white clouds. Giant globes of turquoise and gold, similar to the ones in the staircase they climbed, sat in intricately designed silver bowls atop tall amethyst crystal poles. The buildings were as various in color as they were in shapes and all around the city a subtle twinkling of lights filled the air. It was if the spirits of fire flies came to this place to spend eternity. After a few moments Nicholas looked up at Buddy and smiled.

Buddy looked very serious and nodded in silent agreement. "His little majesty approves of Abanis but requests more purple." He said with mock seriousness.

Fuzzy and Harry snorted.

A crowd had gathered before the gates and surrounded the elder pilgrims. Numerous people of varying races and ages came forward to greet them. Most wore deep, blue robes but some of the younger people wore crimson or white. Everyone smiled and waved down at Nicholas who relished the attention.

"Welcome home brothers!" Said some. "Many greetings masters!" Said some others, who were quite young.

The elderly pilgrims greeted several people but found the artificial sun suddenly dim quite drastically. They looked up at the cause of the eclipse as other people wandered off.

Nicholas followed their gaze and looked up at the tallest man he had ever seen in his short life thus far. He was easily three meters tall and wore dark blue robes but under his collar was the unmistakable glint pearly scales. His brow was ringed with a simple, gold-circlet and his long hair was alternately streaked black and white like zebra skin. He appeared youthful and graceful but his eyes betrayed an eternity of experience. Much like the guardians of the gate pool, his eyes were reptilian in nature but seemed to shift hues depending on the angle one greeted him. He carried an oak staff which some might mistake for a tree trunk because of its size. Around his waist was a large, golden trumpet fastened to a silver waist cord.

He stepped forward to greet them and looked down at the baby in Buddy's arms. "Hello." His voice was deep and authoritative. "Welcome to Abanis."

"Well met Gabriel. We must have council as soon as possible." Said Fuzzy, grinning up at the giant man from under his brown hood.

Gabriel nodded. "Aryu is expecting you brothers. May I see the key?"

Buddy produced the blood-stained spike and held it aloft. Gabriel took it and examined it carefully, turning it over and over in his large hands. A hint of sadness flashed in his eyes but vanished as quick as it appeared. "It is true then. He is gone."

"I'm sorry old friend." Said Harry. "His departure is a loss beyond measure."

Gabriel looked up and nodded. "There will be time to reflect on that later. Come, I will escort you to The Pilgrim's home. Aryu is waiting."

They followed Gabriel across the plaza to the home of The Pilgrim, which was a most unusual building. It was a silver drop of bizarre simplicity amidst the splash of twisting architecture. Rising fifteen meters out of the central plaza, the dome rested at the heart of the city of Abanis like a giant drop of silver. It reflected the surrounding buildings and lights on its smooth surface, making the reflected architecture seem all the more bizarre if that was possible. At its base was a large wooden door with a small paned window in the center. Perhaps the most unusual thing about the building was a little, white sign hanging from a small nail under the tiny window. It read "*Out to Lunch. Back in 100 years.*" Under the hastily scrawled message was a monogram signature that looked like ' *:P* '.

Among all the wonderful colors and shapes in Abanis, Nicholas decided the big, silver ball-thingy they were approaching was the most interesting. He decided to stare at that.

They stopped outside the front door and looked at the sign.

"He has been gone for more than four decades, brothers." Said Gabriel, reading the sign as if he hoped it would say something different. "I expect he will keep his word and return to us after a few more have passed." Then he leaned forward and knocked hard on the simple, wooden door.

"Is Aryu taking care of things inside then?" Asked Buddy.

"Yes." Nodded Gabriel. "But I imagine the kitchen is a complete disaster."

Please come in. Said a voice in their heads.

Gabriel opened the door to reveal a wall of swirling smoke and flashes of color. He turned to the others and stepped aside. "After the evening festivities, we should have council. I am eager to hear about this child's story and other news. For now I must attend the Guardians. Ready?"

The three pilgrims nodded and stepped through the smoke, one after another.

They emerged in a massive, circular room. All along the walls were books, stacks and stacks of books. There were busts of apparently famous people, statues of grand craftsmanship and paintings of all sorts. There were small machines, big machines and medium sized machines. Some bleeped and blipped while others were content to simply collect dust. There beakers and bottles on a forest of shelves of such variety, sizes and contents, that baby Nicholas made a mental note of which ones he wanted to open.

Apparently the exterior dome was an illusion of some sort. The balconies of objects, accessible only by elevated platforms to the right and left of the door, climbed several stories high. At the very top, stretching across the length of the circular ceiling, was a painting of the sun. It was a friendly sun with a big smiling face. If baby Nicholas were somewhat cleverer and older, he would have remarked the sun had a light of its own. The light cascaded down to a gleaming, white marble floor, surrounded by a giant, circular seating arrangement. At its center, basking in the artificial ambience stood a dark-skinned, bald man with a tray full of cookies and a ridiculously over-sized pair of green oven mitts.

"Welcome home, dear brothers! I have been thoroughly enjoying The Pilgrim's kitchen!" He said walking over to them.

"Aryu Veda, you old cookie monster!" Exclaimed Harry. "How are things?"

"Oh you would not be believing me if I were to tell you, I'm sure!" Said Aryu. "The kitchen alone is a wonder of baking paradise, I tell you." His grin was so wide, Nicholas thought the man's ears would vanish.

Unlike Nicholas' companions, Aryu Veda was not quite so old in appearance. Although he was tall and lanky like Harry. His middle-aged face, however, did little to disguise the wisdom and experience etched in his deeply shadowed eyes. Unlike many of the others in Abanis, he chose to wear a simple, white linen robe tied at the waist with a bright, yellow sash.

"Now, before we do anything," Said Aryu happily, "please accompany me to the baking laboratory before my hands catch fire!"

Aryu turned and walked surprisingly brisk to a doorway on the other side of the massive circular room.

"I believe the term is 'kitchen', brother." Said Fuzzy, hurrying after him.

"Ahh yes, the colloquial terms of such wonderful things escapes me at times." Said Aryu, disappearing into the doorway.

They followed him into a kitchen that appeared to be under attack by a legion of pots and pans using flour and eggs as ammunition. In addition to these were stacks of over-cooked platters with blackened bits, all piled ungraciously in a basin too small to contain the mayhem. On one side of the kitchen was a huge oven that emanated heat as Aryu opened it up and took out another tray. At the center of the kitchen was a large, white marble table.

Aryu set the trays down on the table and gestured for the others to sit. As they each took a seat, Nicholas' curiosity radar zeroed-in on the rectangular platters of steaming *somethings.*

"So, what are – " Buddy began but Aryu raised a finger suddenly.

"Ahh!" He exclaimed. "Almost I be forgetting a most excellent companion to this snack." He stood once more and turned to the chaotic kitchen. He grabbed five glasses from a wooden cupboard next to the unfortunate sink and rejoined the bemused pilgrims. He placed them on the table, waved a hand over them almost nonchalantly, and the cups filled themselves with a cold, white liquid.

"Well that's an interesting trick, brother." Chuckled Fuzzy.

"Something The Pilgrim taught me long ago." Aryu nodded. Then he picked up a freshly baked cookie from a tray and held up a glass of milk with his other hand. "This may be the most astoundingly perfect combination," he said with a serious expression, "since oxygen met hydrogen and said *let's get liquid*!"

The pilgrims laughed and sampled the biscuits while Aryu grinned at them with a white-milk moustache. Even Nicholas munched on the subtle, sweet biscuit and was offered a sip of cool milk.

For a short time, they shared some small talk of Abanis and the world at large. When they finished the milk and cookies, Aryu rose and indicated serious matters were on the conversational horizon by taking off his bright, green oven mitts.

"I suppose it is time to deal with the sad and the serious. Come. Let's recline in the council room." Said Aryu, leading the elderly pilgrims out of the kitchen.

They emerged from the kitchen into the large, circular room and as the elder pilgrims sat down Aryu stood in the center of the white marble floor. Raising his hands to the ceiling, he spoke a few quiet words and the golden glow of artificial sunlight changed to a silvery hue.

Nicholas looked up and smiled in appreciation.

The painting of the smiling sun was replaced with an astonishingly accurate painting of a full moon against a deep, blue sky.

"Brothers, I will converse internally with our newcomer. It will make matters clearer to see." Said Aryu.

Now then, can you hear me little one? Said a voice in Nicholas' mind.

Nicholas looked up and said "Ehh?" to Buddy, who smiled down at him encouragingly.

"I believe so." Said Buddy.

Excellent. Welcome to Abanis little one. Let us be formally introduced. I am Aryu Veda. I am one of the first Hurum. This city is for those who are my family. These words I tell you now will be fully understood as you grow older, for they will be recorded in your mind. There was a pause and then he continued. *What is your name?*

Nicholas felt a searching sensation in his mind, a coaxing of information to be brought to the fore.

Nicholas, yes. Said Aryu. *I see, Nicholas it is then.*

Aryu looked at Fuzzy. *Do you have the key?*

Fuzzy handed Aryu the simple iron spike wrapped in a leather strap and returned to his seat.

There was a long silence as Aryu carefully examined the spike, turning it over and over in his dark skinned hands. As he stared at it, the other became aware that he was angered.

How cruel they can be at times. Aryu sighed. *How cruel to each other.*

Buddy sighed. *He was the best of us brother.*

We had to abandon him, said Aryu solemnly. *He abandoned our ways...but found a way to make them love one another without our interference. Which is our goal, after all, is it not?. Perhaps The Pilgrim's absence is related to his passing?* There was an extended pause and the others remained silent.

I must search the child's bloodline for information. Please give me a moment brothers.

Nicholas felt an apologetic intrusion in his mind and a series of events he did not understand flashed in his memory.

After a few moments, Aryu staggered and looked fearful as he stared on Nicholas. The others looked at each other worriedly.

Something wrong brother? Asked Harry.

Aryu turned to look at them. He looked afraid.

What is it brother? Asked Fuzzy, standing suddenly.

Aryu composed himself and nodded. *This one's parents are not among us anymore. As for the Nazarene, he may very well return to us with much to tell. He has passed into another place in the spirit of exploration. In doing so, he sacrificed his material body for humanity. It was something of a stroke of genius. We shall see what the future holds.*

Teacher. Asked Buddy, looking at his companions for support. *What is nature of beings who carry lanterns? Harry encountered one in Gaza. Is that what troubles you?*

Indeed. I was confronted by Namtar and his brothers but they were not themselves. They were interested in this this child. They called Nicholas a 'chimp' and referred to humans as 'primates'. Have you ever heard of such speech? And what malevolence could overwhelm an emissary as strong as Namtar?

Aryu remained silent looked troubled. Then he stared at the spike thoughtfully.

I could feel his age. Continued Harry. *Whatever spirit resided inside Namtar was immensely old. Older than you, Aryu. Although I'm not sure about Pantilius.*

Aryu didn't reply but remained focused on the spike.

Brother, are you ok? Asked Fuzzy. *I have never known you to harbor such fear.*

If my suspicions are correct as to the identity of those beings, said Aryu, finally, *then I hope The Pilgrim returns to us soon. We are not capable of dealing with this situation. Only The Pilgrim is their equal. Their age is so far beyond us, we are but infants to them. They must be seeking a way to enter Abanis. But why they would want this child? I have no idea.*

The others looked at each other in shocked silence.

What can we do about this matter? Is there anything we can do brother? Asked Buddy, bouncing Nicholas on his knee.

I will attempt to find the answer to that brother. Said Aryu. *Tonight the festival of Yule must be celebrated for the sake of our younglings, although it will be bittersweet. Later, we will speak of darker things. I must go to Twilenos and speak to Ravenscrawl. For now, go to Pantilius. He will care for the child and give him a home. He will be expecting you.*

"Good luck with that." Harry snorted, speaking audibly.

Aryu grinned and crossed the circular room to Nicholas and Buddy. He wrapped the leather strap around the iron spike and handed it to Buddy. *This is his for all time. Because he was invited by the Nazarene to enter Abanis and dwell here, he should take the name of Christopher Nicholas. What do you think little one?*

"Ga!" Agreed Nicholas in the language of infants everywhere.

Good. Nodded Aryu happily.

Buddy looked down at Nicholas and smiled gleefully yet again. *You are going to see the great giggler, Nick!*

Be careful of the sunflowers. Harry glowered. *They have deadly accuracy.*

"Ga?"

After leaving The Pilgrim's home the three companions decided to part company for a short rest. The sun was beginning its decent into afternoon which signaled to Fuzzy it was the perfect moment to yawn.

Fuzzy and Harry bid farewell with promises to meet later that evening and wandered off down a large street.

"Waa? Gaa?" Asked Nicholas.

"No. No." Said Buddy. "You will see them again soon. Now we are off to see Pantilius."

He turned and walked briskly down a large street which lead out of the city towards snow-capped mountainous. The road outside of the city was lined with coniferous trees. Beyond them, on either side, were rich green hills and snowy tundra spotted with lush pine forests. Further still, Nicholas could see icy fjords under majestic mountain peaks. Reindeer and similar animals grazed in the wild and Nicholas silently wondered when he would meet them. Soon the city boundary was far behind and they were heading towards a tall castle.

Nicholas stared at a magnificent, stone castle at the roots of a mountain. Its intricate, russet colored parapets and grand towers poked tantalizingly skyward and were rigned with light clouds. Along the way they met a few travellers on the road who waved at Buddy and Nicholas as they passed. Eventually they reached the base of the mountain.

The castle, constructed of large, grey stones and rich, brown wood, towered over them. It was only accessible by means of a narrow path in the snow branching off from the main road. As they started up the narrow path, Nicholas noticed brightly painted signs nailed to wooden posts near the junction. If Nicholas could read, he would have noted some signs were pointing to alternate locations outside of the city. Other, more colorful signs, had large and emphatic expressions like: "*Warning! Extreme Laughter Beyond This Point!*" and "*Stop! Thou must Giggle or go no further!*" and *"Last Chance to be in a Foul Mood for the next 5o Miles!"*

A short while later, as they approached the large, oak doors of the castle, Nicholas thought he heard a great throng of people laughing and talking inside. Buddy grabbed one of the large brass rings on one of the doors and knocked loudly.

"You must remember to laugh as much as possible in here. It's the rules." Said Buddy, looking down at Nicholas and nodding serenely.

"Daa!" Said Nicholas in agreement.

After a few moments, the doors of the castle opened and Nicholas gaped at the second-largest man he had ever seen. Standing an easy two-and-a-half meters tall, a giant, yellow bearded man leaned down and squinted at the newcomers. His grey-blue eyes twinkled in the morning light. Long blonde hair fell over his shoulders as he tried to get a good look at Buddy and Nicholas. Then his face creased into a smile and he laughed deep and long, patting his leather vest as he did so.

"Ho! Ho! Ho!!" The sound of the laugh echoed throughout the valley around the castle and a small avalanche poured off the mountainside nearby.

Nicholas gaped, uncertain whether the large man was friendly or simply loud.

Then the man reached out to Buddy's shoulder and hauled them inside.

"Greetings! Good to see you, brother!" He shook Buddy's hand so vigorously that Nicholas grabbed Buddy's sleeve in an effort to keep from falling out of the man's arms.

"Indeed, well met Himtall. It has been too long." Said Buddy smiling up at the giant Norseman.

"Have you returned to us for good? Or just the festival? Is Harry still in a foul mood?" Asked Himtall, while his blonde eyebrows formed a bridge over his eyes. "Is he in need of some laughter?"

Buddy hesitated. "No. Yes." He paused. "Yes and yes." He nodded happily.

Himtall let out another thunderous laugh and clapped Buddy so hard on the shoulder, Nicholas heard his companion let out a small 'oomph'.

"Well then," said Himtall nodding enthusiastically, "you tell Harry to get his skinny, little Greek-behind over to this castle and we shall pound some mirth into him!"

"I'm sure he would just love to do that." Said Buddy without an iota of sarcasm.

"Well now." Said Himtall, looking down at Nicholas with a giant smile and a wink. "And who are you?"

Nicholas, still gaping at the giant man, decided to speak. "Ni!" He said.

"Nick is it?" Himtall looked at Buddy, who nodded.

"His name is Nicholas. He has met Aryu already."

Nicholas decided he liked the happy giant and his wonderful ability to cause avalanches with laughter.

"Welcome to Mirthmyst Castle Nicholas! I'm Himtall." The man shouted, beaming down at him. "Pantilius is in his study with the children. Come this way."

He turned and stomped down the hall which led to another room with a spiraling staircase apparently built for elephants and not people. The walls of the castle interior were lined with pictures *of* children, pictures *by* children, and pictures *of* children *by* children. Ornate globes, such as the ones found all over the City of Abanis, lit the halls with a mixture of subtle blue and golden light. Buddy and Nicholas followed Himtall up the stairs and through a series of large halls to a smaller doorway. The doorway was covered with big, golden sunflowers. They move and swayed dreamily as Himtall turned to Buddy and Nicholas.

"These flowers are dangerous, Nick." Himtall whispered. "Let's see what happens today."

He attempted to tip-toe closer while reaching for the handle. The bizarre sight of the giant man tip-toeing towards a small, flower-covered door made Nicholas wonder all the more what possibly could await beyond. As Himtall was about to grab the brass door handle, the flowers suddenly pointed directly at his face and sprayed him with pink, watery liquid.

"Oomph! Aak! Damn!" He stood and looked blankly at Buddy and Nicholas who were safely out of range.

"Alright, alright," sighed Himtall, trying to wipe pink out of his beard and face, 'Very funny, ha-ha."

They entered a large room. Behind them, Himtall was forced on his hands and knees as he squeezed through the door frame. Nicholas heard one person talking and caught the last sentence.

"...and the peanut said to the elephant, 'Nuts!'" To which an applause of laughter ensued.

The large, circular room had tall windows and rich wood décor. Crimson tapestries depicting strange battles scenes lined the walls and the ceiling was made entirely of glass panels. It was domed and the metal frames were crafted to look like a smiling sun. All around the room were shelves of books, small tables and boxes containing what appeared to be toys. Children, ranging in age from toddler to about seven years old sat in a central, circular rug. They were laughing at a very strange looking man sitting in a plush, cushioned chair.

He appeared to be quite short because his legs dangled from the plush chair. He wore a red housecoat overtop bright, blue pajamas and on his feet were huge, fluffy rabbit slippers. But this is not what caused Nicholas to gape in wonder. The man had pale, blue skin and the biggest, pointiest ears Nicholas had ever seen on a person. (Nicholas hadn't met many people in his short life thus far but he was pretty sure that they weren't supposed to have big, pointy ears or blue skin.) He was bald except for a ring of white hair which pointed straight out from his head in such a way that would make even the most hardcore, punk-rocker weep in appreciation. When he turned to the newcomers at the door, he peered at them through some strange looking glass circles fastened to a metal frame. They rested on his disproportionately huge nose and the effect of the glass circles made the his eyes appear four times larger than normal. Nicholas laughed the sight and reached a little hand towards the man in the fascinated manner of toddlers everywhere.

At once, the strange man sprang up from his cushioned chair to greet the newcomers.

"Welcomehome! Sogoodofyou tocomevisit Brother!" The small man smiled. His great, white teeth, too large for his head, gleamed in the afternoon sun which filled the room. He hastened to them and nodded to Nicholas.

"Well, hellothere lil'one! Haveyou beenboredtodeath withalltheseolder people about?" His manner of speaking was twice as fast as everyone else Nicholas met thus far.

"Gaa?" He wondered.

"Indeed." Said Buddy, looking down at Nicholas. "Allow me to introduce Professor Pantilius."

Pantilius bowed gracefully.

"Welcome.. to… Mirthmyst.. Castle." Said Pantilius, pronouncing each word with the kind of volume normally reserved for people over a hundred years old. "You.. will.. be.. our.. guest.. until.. you.. are.. old.. enough.. to.. laugh.. elsewhere. Ha.. Ha.. Ha!" He said carefully and grinned broadly. Then he looked at Buddy. "Aryu sentword justafewminutes beforeyourarrival."

"Excellent." Said Buddy, striding around the room and smiling at the children. "Come my little sisters and brothers. Meet your new classmate."

As one, the children sitting on the circular rug stood up and came forward to wave and smile at Nicholas who relished the attention.

Suddenly, the light from the large windows was eclipsed by the largest ball of white Nicholas had yet seen. Actually, it was a woman who had been sitting quietly behind the children on a large, padded chair. Several of her jolly chins beamed down at Nicholas. She had a lily, white bonnet on her head and her dress was actually an immense cooking apron which reached all the way to the floor and nearly covered her shiny, white leather shoes.

"Oh hello my beautiful boy!" She chimed. Her voice sounded like it was about to break into song at any moment. "I'm- Mrs. Bakersbee-but-you-can-call-me-Marjorie. Scrumptiousness-and-thoughtfulness-is-all-you-need-to-make-of-me. In-my-kitchens-you-can-eat-ANYTHING-but-chicken-feet." Her voice was like a piano being played by a militarized squadron of bees. "What's-he-called-and-where's-he-from? Where-is-home, my-little-one?" She asked

Nicholas, who was mesmerized by the sheer circumference of the woman.

"His name", said Buddy, looking about the room, "is Nicholas. And he comes from Jerusalem."

A little girl with long brown hair and auburn eyes, who until now had been sitting alone, stared at Nicholas as she folded something. She walked up beside Buddy and gave Nicholas a little swan made of folded paper.

"Talented girl." Whispered Pantilius to Buddy. "Toymaker, I think. Rare manifestation of Huru lineage."

"What's your name?" Said Buddy leaning down and taking the paper swan.

"C-lr." She said shyly, lowering her head.

"She's Claire." Whispered Himtall, bending down and scooping up the little girl. She hid her face behind his blond beard. "Recently lost her mother and father to the Romans. I found her in the Black Forest. She's one of us." He looked at her and grinned. "She's a bit sad and timid for an angel, though."

Claire blushed and looked away.

"Thank you Claire, that was very thoughtful." Said Buddy. Nicholas giggled in appreciation at the paper swan Buddy showed it to him. To further show his gratitude, Nicholas decided to do what every child at his age does when receiving a gift, so he ate it.

Nicholas spent the remainder of the day with Buddy, Himtall, Mrs. Bakersbee and Pantilius in Mirthmyst Castle. After introducing him to an assortment of people and children around the castle, they left Nicholas in the care of Mrs. Bakersbee's legion of spherical caretakers. Quite exhausted from a day filled with wondrous, new experiences, Nicholas slept more peacefully than he had in several months.

That evening, Mrs. Bakersbee accompanied Pantilius, Himtall and Buddy to the city of Abanis where many citizens had gathered for a feast and celebration. The festival lasted well into the night but this did little to disturb the very young children of Abanis, sleeping peacefully in Mirthmyst Castle.

Among the sleeping children, Nicholas too was resting undisturbed in his little crib. For now, he was safe, happy and healthy but something ever present in his mind would never change. No matter how much he experienced or how much he laughed since meeting Harry, Fuzzy and Buddy, the loss of his mother and father would never be forgotten. As he tossed, turned, and whimpered in his sleep, Nicholas dreamed of dark apparitions, lanterns and scythes. Despite the darkness of his dreams, Nicholas would be safe for a time in the strange realm of Abanis, far from Judea.

Chapter 13: Sin and Bones

Pilate stood before the colossal, stone gates and admired their craftsmanship. Ten meters high and wrought of a stone seemingly alien to the area, he guessed not even paper could slide between the seams. On the gates were carvings of strange symbols and images that he likened to Egyptian or Sumerian.

He looked down at the expressionless creature beside him and wondered briefly if it's sole purpose was to hold the box. As if reading his mind, it opened the box and looked up expectantly. A grey, sparkling swirl of cloud issued forth from cracks and crevices around Pilate and was sucked into the open box. The creature closed the lid and put the latch in place.

Yes. Now, we must enter this home of ours.

The cunning voice trailed off in Pilates' mind as he looked up at the enormous gates once more. It occurred to him there was no obvious means of opening the gates so he decided to get the obvious approach out of the way.

"Open." He said, hoping this simple command would be enough to move the stone gates. It was not.

The small, blue skinned creature blinked and turned its head up to look at him. The eyes were not entirely vacant and there seemed a glimmer of recognition there. Its mouth opened and it appeared to be struggling to use its voice. The mouth closed and opened once more until finally it was able to croak one word at Pilate in a nasal, high pitched voice. "Sin." It said.

A sudden sound of grinding stone made Pilate jump. He took a step back as the giant gates shivered. A sliver of black appeared where the sealed doors met and it grew larger as the sound of grinding stone increased.

The stone gates stopped and Pilate looked inside the tall, narrow shaft of darkness. A series of subtle lights and lines on the stone floor could be seen just inside the entrance. Holding the scythe with two hands, he stepped cautiously into the darkness.

Pilate waited for his eyes to adjust as he looked around. The air was surprisingly fresh and he guessed there must be ventilation shafts built into the peculiar construction. He was standing inside a massive hallway which descended slightly into the roots of the mountain. After his eyes adjusted some more, he noticed the lights and lines on the floor were a reflective substance embedded in the stone. They made an intricate latticework of designs which linked with other designs on the walls and ceiling. He guessed they were not purely cosmetic but did not dwell on them. For now, he would do as the caring voice asked and continue on.

After descending a little ways into the darkness, he stopped suddenly at the sound of grinding stone once more. Turning back, he nodded despondently to himself and sighed as he watched the gates close.

"Of course." He said, looking down to his pointy-eared companion. "They just had to close, didn't they."

"Nuru." Squeaked a little voice beside him.

There was a subtle flash of light and Pilate looked around. Beginning at the entrance, the lines in the floor, walls and ceiling began to glow. They emitted a mixture of sapphire and orange hues descending down the hall and deeper into structure. It was a beautiful scene and he stared in appreciation for a moment. The intricate lacing of blue and orange lines revealed passageways branching off the main hall further down.

Now we must go. Said the cunning voice. *Now we must find our throne. A god must have a throne, yes.*

Pilate he turned and began walking down the hallway with his little, pointy-eared companion falling in behind. He secretly hoped the caring voice would speak up as he ventured further in but felt its tangible absence in his mind.

Continuing further in, he glanced right and left at archways of smaller hallways leading elsewhere. The lights down these alternate halls curved away into darkness but he ignored them for now. Finally, he could see a large hallway and an archway further ahead. He hastened his step until the luminescent patterns came to an end by weaving themselves into one another over the archway.

Pilate's attention was drawn to a vacant chair at the center of a huge, circular room beyond the archway. He stepped through and as he looked around, his mouth decided to fall open.

He was in a massive, domed chamber. Similar to the hallway, illuminated patterns on the floor delineated archways to the left and right but Pilate's gaze was drawn to curious lights on the ceiling. Some spots were large and bright and some were so small that in groups they appeared to be cloud-like.

Pilate stared at the domed ceiling, realizing the spots of lights made patterns which looked familiar. He focused on one grouping of lights and frowned as he walked further into the dome to get a better look.

"I know what that is." He whispered quietly. "Could that be...?" He paused, allowing his mouth to catch up with what his brain just realized. "Urania!" Exclaimed Pilate as he turned on the spot and looked around the ceiling with amazement.

No, the muse is not here. We did this, yes. Here, we can watch the heavens and all of creation.

"Urania be praised!" Exclaimed Pilate once more, ignoring the cunning voice as he recognized the map of all the constellations spread across the domed ceiling. It the most accurate representation of the cosmos he had ever seen beyond the real thing. It appeared to represent all seasons at the same time. The only exception was a single shaft of light descending to the chair from a heavenly body Pilate did not recognize. Pilate wasn't an astronomer by any means but he felt the star was a rogue and didn't belong with the rest of eternity. He frowned, unable to associate it with any celestial cluster and followed the shaft of light down to the chair.

The chair was on a raised dais at the center of the domed chamber. It was a simple, stone design and etched with the similar markings Pilate noted in the structure. In front of the chair was a pool of sapphire colored water, three meters across. The water was still and reflected the subtle starlight cast by the ceiling above.

He walked closer to the pool and peered into it. It didn't appear to have any depth but emitted a very soft light of its own. The light was so faint, however, that Pilate was still able to make out the constellations reflected on its surface.

That is a gateway.

"A gateway to where?" Asked Pilate aloud, staring into the depths of the water.

To wherever we want to go.

Mesmerized by the pool of water and the constellations mirrored on its still surface, Pilate waited patiently for the other voice but it did not register an opinion.

Pilate looked up to the odd light at the center of the domed ceiling. "I don't recognize that star. What constellation does it belong to?"

We can't recognize it because it is only visible to Gods. It is….a boat. A Ship.

"A ship?"

It is a ship like that of Charon.

"Charon?" Asked Pilate, knowing the implication all too well. "You mean it is a ferry for the dead?"

Yes. It is somewhat like that.

"What is it called?"

We call it…

Pilate registered the hesitation and wondered why the cunning voice was trying to conceal a mixture of cautious elation while talking about the ship.

It is called the Enefka Babellux. It was and is our home.

Pilate let the name roll over his tongue and decided it was too alien to understand. Although he was enthralled by all these discoveries, most pressing in Pilate's mind was his purpose for being there. Then something occurred to him.

"Was our home? Don't you mean 'is' our home?" He asked and looked up to the constellations once more.

Yes. Our home. The Enefka Babellux has remained vacant for us. It is where gods reside.

"So this," Pilate swept one hand around the vast room, "is not our home?"

No, this is a place for mortals. It is a… The voice paused again. *It is a processing place. A gateway for us, nothing more.*

Pilate looked up at the odd light at the center of the dome. "Our home." He said, frowning.

Then he looked down at the creature standing quietly beside him. "What is this creature?" He asked, realizing he hadn't enquired until now.

We call them Nelfilem. They are our…toys. They are our servants. We use them.

"Nelfilem." Said Pilate, leaning down to look closer at its little body. "He's not from Germania or Norse lands?"

He was our servant. We made him.

"We made him?"

As an artisan sculpts images from marble.

Pilate thought about this and decided the cunning voice was lying. He didn't know many artists who liked to treated their own work with sujch obvious callousness. But he did know many farmers who raised sheep for more than just wooly blankets.

"Then why is he enslaved? He looks to be more than just an automaton."

Clever we are to notice such things. We have many more servants like this one. Indeed they are plentiful.

Pilate looked around. "They are here?" He asked, looking at the archways leading away from the great domed chamber.

No. They are aboard our celestial ship.

Pilate was beginning to feel nervous about the welling excitement he sensed in the cunning voice. It was expecting something but Pilate was beyond his depth trying make sense of everything. He was an educated man with an above-average intellect but still a man. Or so, he hoped he was.

"Perhaps we need to be on our ship?" Asked Pilate. But he already knew the answer. He knew the cunning voice was setting the path for him to be curious about the chair.

Yes. The ship. We must take our place among the gods.

"How do I get to the ship?"

Ah, but we are clever. We know the answer. It is before us.

Pilate looked at the vacant chair and walked slowly around the pool. He imagined anyone sitting in it would have to place their feet in the water or on its mirrored surface. He approached it cautiously, knowing full well the cunning voice did not have his best interests in mind. The absence of the caring voice made him worry but he guessed it would want him to follow instructions.

"The chair. I must sit in the chair?"

Yes, how godlike our intellect is. We should sit in the chair and go to the place where no mortals can go. We should take our place among the constellations.

Pilate stood behind the chair and stared down at it. He recalled the words of the caring voice. *Repair what damage you have done over a lifetime of cruelty, malice and greed...* But he hesitated.

Time is running short. Said the cunning voice with a slight tinge of desperation. *The sun will rise soon. We cannot take our place among the constellations if it is approaching the horizon. We must sit now.*

Pilate knew the cunning voice was manipulating him. He suspected his chances of transforming into a God were about as high as his chances of transforming into a bowl of tropical fruit. He had little choice but to go along with things for now, as the caring voice advised before. Pilate decided to leave his fate with whatever benevolent beings there were left in the mad universe. If any.

"Very well." He whispered.

Pilate straddled the chair and sat down, placing his sandaled feet in the water. He found the surface of the water to be resistant and the weight of his legs and feet rested comfortably on it as he sat upright and waited.

Excellent. We are wise to accept such godly promotion. Said the cunning voice but this time there was a shrill laughter in Pilate's mind and a peculiar numbness spread to his limbs.

Pilate was afraid and attempted to rise from the chair but found he couldn't move. Although frozen in place by some unseen force, his eyes were free. He looked down into the pool and saw a funnel of darkness form at its center. Pilate stared transfixed at the abysmal maelstrom in the center of the pool and began to panic. The cunning voice laughed in his head as he was swuddenly and violently sucked into the water.

For a moment Pilate could feel the coldness of the water. He did not feel the need to breath and felt in control of his body once more. Blinking under the surface, he looked up. Above him, sitting peacefully on the chair he saw himself holding the scythe.

He tried to breach the surface of the water but it resisted and he was trapped beneath it. He stared at his other self on the chair and saw a wry smile appear on his own face. Pilate watched himself look around the chamber and then look down into the pool.

"Thank you Pontius Pilate." It said. "Long have I waited for someone with the strength to draw me completely from my ship. Of course, you needed this." The new Pilate held up the scythe. "Think of this weapon as a lighthouse for mariners navigating difficult waters." Then he stood, stretched and looked down at his hands. He inspected the fingers and clenched a fist.

"Most primates do not have the constitution to last longer than a few days in my company." Then he smiled and held the scythe in two hands, caressing the shaft admiringly. "However, once the spear of Longinus was blessed by the blood of The Pilgrims pup, all I had to do was wait for a monkey cruel and greedy enough to let me in."

The new Pilate looked down into the pool and sneered. "Enjoy your well deserved sleep, monkey. I *know* I will."

Pilate watched in horror as his alternate self walked away from the pool and out of sight. The tiny creature remained for a moment and stared down impassively. Then it walked out of sight.

Pilate cried out in anguish as the figure disappeared from view but as most sounds under liquid pressures, they were trifle and muffled. All light in the cavern suddenly froze for an instance in time and the universe exploded around him. Every pinpoint of light in his field of vision and every part of his body was stretched to infinity and violently sucked into a black vortex at the center of the pool. Then all was still and silent once more in the chamber of stars.

*Jingle***Jingle***Jingle*

Many years would pass in the city of Abanis after Nicholas' arrival. During this time, the world within and the world without would change. At this particular time in history, the Roman Empire controlled most of the lands surrounding the Mediterranean Sea and large parts of Arabia and northern Europe. In Asia, dynasties would rise and fall like grass amidst the changing seasons. Dwelling among the people of these various kingdoms, empires and dynasties, were emissaries of Abanis.

Emissaries from the city of Abanis were not the regular sort we know of today. They didn't show up with cultural gifts or mediate disputes or even have nice dinners with leaders of state. On the contrary, they were simply spectators of humanity, choosing to become beggars, pilgrims or quiet servants whispering counsel to people whom they think could use it.

During this time, the fears of the elder citizens of Abanis were coming to fruition as well. War, disease and pestilence was on the rise all around the world. This convinced Pantilius, Gabriel and Aryu that an entity of malcontent was present in the world and working against them. Regardless, citizens of Abanis were forbidden to interfere with the natural progression of human civilization on a large scale but were permitted to assist people in smaller ways. A man being attacked by a lion, for example, might suddenly find himself being assaulted by a confused duckling. Those kinds of miracles were considered acceptable. According to The Pilgrim, the patron of Abanis despite his absence, *small ripples don't interrupt the flow of a river.* For this reason, emissaries were quite adept at distinguishing *natural* disasters from *planned* disasters. High instances of war, pestilence and famine around the world cautioned them to consider it was being designed. This worried the elders of Abanis greatly and many silently yearned for The Pilgrim to return.

Furthermore, some emissaries were being *outed* in several places around the globe and accused by human authorities for being demons or other malevolent creatures. Considering emissaries from Abanis were trained to blend in with civilizations around the world, this indicated that *someone* or *something* was working to break their camouflage.

Away from all of the troubles of the world, under the care of Pantilius and Mrs. Bakersbee in Mirthmyst Castle, Christopher Nicholas would grow to be a young man. Well, at least a young man in Abanis. He was tall, fair haired and robustly jubilant much of time which made Himtall feel Nicholas was the little brother he never had. His icy blue eyes and friendly countenance made him a well liked personality among his classmates and educators alike.

Children at Mirthmyst were often audience to Pantilius' peculiar improvisations as they grew to adulthood under his tutelage. Nicholas especially liked Pantilius's attempt to demonstrate how Harry would perform Chinese opera. He and many other students were rolling around the floor laughing at the spectacle, especially the bit where a brass pot fell in love with a buttered yam. Harry, on the other hand, was ill-pleased at being the constant object of the professor's antics, which earned him the title of 'Grouchius Maximus' whenever he visited the castle.

A young man at the tender age of fifty-one, Nicholas was still living at Mirthmyst Castle. Thus far, he studied a plethora of subjects including history, aestheticism, world culture, social anthropology, and languages. He was told that he would study until such a time that he was old enough to learn more about the *big picture*, as Buddy put it. Whatever that *picture* was, Nicholas felt he was being prepared to see it. He often wondered if the *big picture* was too frightening or confusing to understand without sufficient education.

Professor Pantilius (as he was called by many young citizens in Abanis) was an exceptional educator and used the entirety of the sphere as his classroom. Harry often referred to his lessons as 'dangerously enthusiastic' but so far, his methods were considered very effective. When the students studied geography, for example, they were less likely to need a book for class and more likely to need hiking boots and a parachute. When Pantilius and a number of his pupils decided to use fireworks as a way to observe the explosive power of lightning strikes, Harry was less than pleased they chose to do so around his house at 3:00 am.

Such an educational environment was never dull and Nicholas excelled in most subjects, especially world cultures and languages. Unfortunately, he did not enjoy *Numbers* nor was he able to understand much of it, considering it to be the coldest language of all. But Pantilius was clever and realized Nicholas had a weakness for food, especially baked goods. He simply had Nicholas imagine every number from zero to nine as a kind of pastry, and *Numbers* didn't seem so bad after that. Yes, Nicholas chose a donut for zero.

One day, as he was approaching his 52nd birthday, Nicholas decided to venture forth into lands representing (what would later be called) Norway. It was a gorgeous, spring morning when he left the castle and he looked forward to hiking in the Nordic wilderness. At one point, he came across some reindeer at the crest of a valley which dropped into an icy fjord far below. They did not run from him as they would in the natural world but rather sniffed the air around him, hoping he would have some delicious grass on hand.

As Nicholas admired the scenery and breathed the salty, moist updraft of air from the fjord below, something caught his eye. He frowned and focused on the spot near some trees down in the valley. There was a streak of red in the snow. He knew there weren't any red plants of any sort in this area and wondered if it might be the grisly work of predators indigenous to the region. After all, The Pilgrim left nothing out when designing the lands and life forms living in the sphere.

Whatever it was, Nicholas decided to investigate and carefully navigated down the slope. After trudging through the deep snow and peering around a large tree, he realized it was a small reindeer lying on its side. He hastened his approach and looked down at the small animal, noting that it was badly wounded. He took off his eye-watering, orange scarf, a gift from Buddy for his last birthday and leaned down to wrap the wounded reindeer. Judging by the blood evidence, he guessed it had fallen from the crest of the valley and gashed open its side on a jagged rock sticking out of the snow nearby. He didn't know how to help the little animal so he decided to take it back to Mirthmyst.

He picked up the little reindeer, which mewed weakly in his arms and began to walk quickly up the slope. When he reached the top of the valley's edge, he started a mild jog back to the castle, swearing to himself he would not eat another jelly donut after 9:00 pm ever again. Well, ok 10:00pm. But that was it! After 11:00pm, no jelly donuts at all... unless it was an absolute emergency.

After a short while, Niholas rounded a knoll near the back of the castle and nearly ran headlong into Gabriel. The giant man was tending some sheep and smoking from a long pipe.

"Ahh good morning young Nicholas, what's this you have?"

"A….reindeer….wounded….in the wilderness." Nicholas panted.

"Indeed." Said Gabriel, looking down at the wounded deer. Nicholas was a big man for his age, almost two meters tall now but Gabriel towered over him still. His zebra-colored hair fell over his shoulders as he leaned down to inspect the deer.

"Give him to me." Said Gabriel, gingerly relieving Nicholas of the wounded animal.

Gabriel carefully unwrapped the reindeer and put aside Nicholas' scarf as he inspected the wound. The deep gash in the reindeer's side continued to bleed. He passed his hands over the bleeding wound and within moments, the bleeding stopped. Nicholas watched in fascination as the wound closed and skin began to grow around it. After a few more moments, patches of thin fur began to grow on the reindeer's side. Soon all trace of the wound was gone but the animal remained still. Then Gabriel leaned forward and whispered something in its tiny ear. A few moments later the deer sprang to its feet, blinked at Gabriel and Nicholas for a few seconds and dashed off into the wilderness in the direction of the valley.

"Wow!" Nicholas was absolutely amazed. He watched the young deer prance among the trees and then vanish over a snow drift with all the energy and playfulness that younglings have. It was as if no wound had ever befell the creature. Nicholas turned to Gabriel, spurred on by curious excitement.

"Will I be able to do that someday?" He asked.

Gabriel watched the animal run away and frowned as it vanished over a snowdrift.

"Gabriel?"

"Eh? What's that Nick?"

"Will I be able to do that some day?"

Gabriel picked up his pipe and stood up. He stared at a small patch of blood where the tiny deer was placed and then blinked at Nicholas. "Yes. I imagine you will be able to learn that someday Nicholas. It is a rare skill to manifest but you have the characteristics of someone who can heal others. That, however, remains to be seen."

"That was truly magical. I have no idea what you just did."

“Magic?” Gabriel chuckled and rekindled his pipe by making a small flame leap from his thumb into the bowl. “No. No. Magic is a word made my humans to explain skills they do not understand. When you are able to do such a thing, it will not be magic, it will be skillful.”

Nicholas shook his head. “I don’t understand." He said, noting that Gabriel's thumb was also doing something physically impossible.

“You will come to understand eventually young Nicholas." Said Gabriel, satisfied his pipe was smoking again. "You will come to see that the physical world is composed of things you cannot see just yet. Things so small you can barely imagine the size. As you are now able to write a poem in multiple languages or grow a plant from a seedling, things you can see and feel, so will you be able to control elements in nature that you cannot see. The only magic in Abanis or the world without is limited to what we allow ourselves to believe. The nature of things will become more *visible* to you as you grow older.” He smiled at Nicholas in such a way as to suggest the topic was not available for further discussion.

Nicholas nodded hesitantly and watched the tiny deer disappear into far off pastures.

“However, it was wise of you to seek help for the deer.” Gabriel put a hand on Nicholas’ shoulder and leaned closer. “Death is not unwelcome or uncommon in Abanis but charity is strongly encouraged.” He nodded in satisfaction at Nicholas then turned to tend his sheep.

Nicholas nodded but rallied again. “I do not understand death, Gabriel. I do not like it. It seems…” He paused, shaking his head in thought, “it seems wrong.”

Gabriel turned and looked bemused at Nicholas as he smoked his pipe and scratched an inquisitive sheep behind its ear. “Then you simply need to understand a little more about life, brother. They are two sides of the same coin.” Said Gabriel, his opaque eyes twinkling in the late morning sunlight.

Satisfied with this cryptic response, Nicholas nodded. "Thank you Gabriel, I will go back to the castle for some brunch now. I look forward to speaking with you again when I understand a little more."

"I shall look forward to that. Off you go now and have mercy on the pastries!" He chuckled and turned to tend his sheep once more.

Nicholas hastened to the gates of the castle and decided he would do a lot of research on death by learning all the more about life. This, of course, would begin with a four course luncheon. After all, food is one of the life's many treasures.

As Nicholas rounded a corner near the front of the castle, a peculiar sound made him stop to listen. He could see his own breath despite the mild, late morning air and he tried to quiet himself to get a fix on the odd noise. He looked towards the pine grove leading to the city and listened carefully. It was very faint and sounded like a chorus of mixed voices singing some kind of lament. It pulsed like a tangible wave coming up from the road and he felt compelled to follow it. Apparently it was coming from the city.

The song was mesmerizing and Nicholas found himself walking through the pine grove towards the city. He stopped suddenly, remembering that he had responsibilities in the castle, lessons to attend and most importantly, lunch to eat. Shaking his head, Nicholas turned back to Mirthmyst castle and saw Pantilius coming down the road with Himtall eclipsing the sun beside him.

"Oy! Nicholas m'lad, where you off to then?" Himtall asked as they approached.

"Nicholas? Aren't you supposed to be having lunch by now?" Asked Pantilius, poking Nicholas in the chest and grinning up at him through giant, copper-rimmed glasses.

"Yes, Professor. I – " Nicholas started but he turned again to the rhythmic sounds coming from the road and Abanis. The song was almost physical in nature and Nicholas felt compelled to find the source. It was so beautiful and sad at the same time. Forcing himself to concentrate, he shook his head and looked back at Pantilius. "Yes. Yes, brother, sorry. I just…" He trailed off.

"Wait!" Pantilius grabbed Nicholas arm. "You hear it!" Pantilius looked into Nicholas eyes and nodded, still grinning at him. Then he turned to look up at Himtall who leaned closer to look into Nicholas dumbfounded face.

"Aye! He hears it!" Said the giant man.

Nicholas blinked at Pantilius and Himtall. "Umm. Yeah. Don't you?"

"Oh, indeed we do." Said Pantilius, releasing Nicholas' arm and stepping back to look at his student up and down. "Someone has moved on. We must go to say goodbye. This also means that someone has arrived. In your case, I believe *you* are that someone."

"Uh, I arrived years ago, Professor. What do you mean?"

"This is the *big picture* we spoke of before. Come," Pantilius gestured for Nicholas to join them, "let's see where this path takes us."

As one, they turned and proceeded down the tree lined road towards the city. After some time, listening to the beautiful song as they walked together in silence, something else occurred to Nicholas.

"Pantilius?"

"Hmm?"

"Uh. Why are you speaking…" He paused, not knowing how to phrase the next part of his question without sounding indelicate. "Why are you speaking slowly and, uh, clearly?"

Pantilius grinned at Himtall as they continued their way towards the city. The two exchanged some silent understanding. Himtall slapped a shoulder-crushing hand on Nicholas but didn't say anything.

"I'm sure I have no idea what you mean brother." Said Pantilius, with that annoying *I know something you don't know* tone Nicholas had come to recognize quite well.

After a time, the song became louder as the three entered the city. Nicholas could see a great throng of citizens gathered in front of the Pilgrim's silvery home. Everyone seemed to be humming or singing the song quietly to themselves with heads bowed. This was the source of the sound but Nicholas couldn't figure out how he heard it from so far away. As they approached the central plaza, many citizens bowed to Himtall and Pantilius, stepping aside to let them through. Nicholas saw sadness in many of the faces which greeted him. Pantilius grabbed Nicholas by the arm once more and led him through the crowd until finally they came to the core of the event.

A body of a man, covered in dry, caked blood, lay on a stone altar near The Pilgrim's home. Nicholas couldn't recall ever seeing the stone table before and guessed it was brought there for this purpose. Even more strange were the man's arms and legs. There seemed to be holes in them. The simple, linen cloth covering the man's body was stained with blood in various areas. Aryu Veda, Buddy, Fuzzy and Harry stood on the opposite side of the table. Their heads were bowed and Buddy had a hand on Harry's shoulder, whose ancient face was streaked with tears.

The mood was understandably somber in the plaza and one of the first times Nicholas ever felt truly sad in Abanis. Oh, of course he remembered being sad when pudding was canceled from the lunch menu back at the castle, or when he was given extra *Numbers* homework but this was different. It was the kind of sadness that made all of his youthful stresses seem insignificant.

Pantilius put his hand on Nicholas arm and patted it. "We have lost a brother today lad." He whispered to Nicholas.

"Who was he?"

"He was called Simon by some." Whispered Pantilius. "But we knew him as Peter. What you are hearing is a lament for the fallen, Nicholas. Only those of us who have reached a certain understanding can hear the song of others."

"What does it all mean?" Asked Nicholas.

"That's a rather large question Nick. Care to be a tad more specific?"

"I meant," said Nicholas, leaning down to whisper closer to Pantilius' altitude, "will I eventually become an emissary like Buddy and have the ability to communicate with others across great distances and the like?"

Pantilius, dragged Nicholas away by the arm to an open spot under a maple tree. "You are wondering if eventually you will become one with the hive mind of the citizens of Abanis," he whispered conspicuously, "with the ability to communicate across the farthest reaches of the universe while wielding the power to manipulate the very nature of space and time around us?" He finished with an expansive whisper.

"Umm, yes?"

"No. Not really." Finished Pantilius abruptly and he returned his attention to Peter. After a few moments of torturous confusion, he looked up and gave Nicholas a sympathetic grin.

"Well," he said waving a small arm expansively, "you know what we do here. We are children of a different people looking out for humanity here and there. Some of us manifest skills stranger than others but we all have the same lineage. We are all human...ish. Some more or less than others. The fact that you heard the song from so far away, means that you have reached a kind of understanding with the rest of us. It is a natural progression m'lad." Pantilius pointy ears bobbed as he nodded up at Nicholas.

Nicholas looked at the mass of people around the body of Peter and considered something. "Can I have to become an emissary?" He asked.

Pantilius pulled a pipe out of his bright, purple jacket. He packed it with some cherry leaf and lit it with a small flame that sprouted from his thumb. “Oh yes, I believe you can m’lad." He winked. "But we will speak of that later. Peter will be ushered. It is important that you see the ceremony."

Aryu Veda who stood at the head of the stone table. It was a strange ceremony that seemed to end as quickly as it had begun. According to what little information Nicholas gathered over the years, *ushering* was not unlike a burial or a funeral pyre in the world outside. In other words, the recipient of an ushering would never return and is considered gone forever. Where they were ushered *to* was another matter altogether. Whenever he raised the subject, Pantilius would remind him the act of ushering was a rare and difficult skill to perform. It was rumored among the students at Mirthmyst Castle that only Aryu Veda, Gabriel and The Pilgrim himself could perform an ushering but Nicholas suspected Pantilius could too.

After saying a few simple words in a language Nicholas could not understand or identify, Aryu placed his hand on Peter’s forehead. A moment later the body was simply gone.

Nicholas gasped and stared at the empty slab for a moment, wondering if there had been a flash of light or something he missed while blinking but there was nothing. Veda was already bowing in thanks to the crowd in general and people were dispersing. Some went to sit at nearby tables laden with food and drink for the day’s event and some fell into small groups to have quiet conversation.

Chapter 14: Prison Plague Party

Pilate…awaken. You must awaken.

Pontius Pilate's mind stirred in a bodiless void. He was aware of himself but he could not feel anything.

Where am I? Am I dead? He thought.

You are in the Enefka Babellux. And dead is something of a perspective.

Pilate recognized the calm voice from before.

Why can't I feel anything? Will I be like this forever? He felt suddenly horrified at the thought of being a disembodied consciousness for all time in a void he could not fathom.

No, you can awaken but you must concentrate. You cannot do it alone. I must help you.

Pilate concentrated and tried to remember what it was like to have hands, legs, feet and a body. Something tingled his senses in the abstract disembodiment and he imagined his hands before his face.

Yes. Think of your hands. What have they done before? Concentrate on that memory.

If Pilate had a face he would have cringed. The only thing that sprung to mind was throttling the life out of his superior back in Rome. At that moment, Pilate could feel his hands. They were clenched so tight he felt his palms were bleeding from the nails digging into them.

Good. Now your feet and legs. A memory is all you need. Concentrate on it.

Again Pilate concentrated on memories that came to his mind. He repeated the process over and over until finally all that remained was his eyes.

Now the hardest part. Concentrate on the most beautiful thing you have ever seen. It must be a virtuous vision that fills you with happiness. Think carefully. What is beauty to one who has lived such a cruel life?

Pilate hesitated and realized that *not* thinking about something was opening the door to *actually* thinking about it. But it was so easy, for the most beautiful thing he ever saw in his life was his newborn son looking back at him.

Well done. Open your eyes Pontius Pilate and do not be afraid.

Pilate opened his eyes. He was immediately stunned by sudden brightness and squinted as his eyes adjusted. He was lying on a stone slab two and a half meters long by one and a half meters wide. The stone was exceptionally smooth and reminded Pilate of polished marble.

He looked at his hand and made a fist then opened it. Satisfied he was whole again, Pilate ran his palm over the smooth surface of the stone and realized he was naked but partially covered by a white cloth of peculiar weave. It sparkled slightly in the dim light of the area. When he ran his hand over it, Pilate realized that *he* was the source of the light. He looked at the back of his hand and turned it, looking at the palm and marveling at his innate glow. Then he looked around.

He was startled to find another stone slab of identical shape and size next to his. On it was an elderly woman with long grey hair and covered in a white cloth like his own. He looked behind him and, swinging his feet over the side, stood up. He turned on the spot in shock realizing he was standing amidst hundreds, possibly thousands of stone slabs, each with a different person. Some were old and others were young. People of all shapes, sizes and races were sleeping peacefully around him. He was a single beacon of light amidst a sprawling array of sleeping figures stretching far off in every direction.

He sat once more. Although the light which emanated from his body was dim, the utter darkness otherwise amplified it. Feeling somewhat conscious of his nakedness, he wrapped the cloth around his body and felt it hold shape as if made to do so. Feeling rested but neither hungry nor thirsty, he decided to explore his surroundings. Just as he was about to stand up again, the calm voice returned.

Impressive. Most would be terribly afraid of waking in such a place but you have done so with a calm demeanor.

"What has happened to me?" Asked Pilate aloud, looking around in every direction. "Is this the underworld?"

No but you could say this is not a pleasant place. You have been ushered here untimely. It is a kind of prison.

"Ushered?" Asked Pilate, again choosing to speak rather than use his mind. It made him feel human. "Is there a way out of this prison?"

I was hoping you would ask that. Said the calm voice.

Pilate was growing tired of things he could barely comprehend. He didn't know if this was heaven, hell or some warehouse in Rome.

"Who in blazes are you?" He asked rather testily.

I am a prisoner too. And I am right behind you.

Pilate froze. Despite the benevolent nature of the calm voice in his head, he didn't want any surprises. Especially in here, the biggest bedroom in the universe.

He slowly turned, expecting to see some new insanity leap out at him.

At the foot of Pilates stone slab stood the oldest man he had ever seen. He would have been as tall as a giant at some point in his life but now he was so hunched over, he looked like a capital 'C'. He leaned heavily on a staff of lacquered, white wood and wore a white cloth around his body the same as Pilate's. His hair, long and white, fell across his shoulders and down his back. His face was so affected by the cruelty of gravity that his chin was nearly smothered by his cheeks. These sank so low on his face he appeared to be partially canine. He had wrinkles within wrinkles and Pilate could easily make out bone structure and veins on the man's exposed skin. Most notable of all was the man's eyes. They were not white with cataracts as Pilate expected but utterly white with no pupils or iris'. The man also emitted his own luminescence and the overall affect made him look godlike despite his geriatric state.

"You are the – "

"Yep that's me. The idiot inside your head. Heh!" The man's voice sounded so ragged and coarse it could have sand-blasted the air smooth. "Let's have a look at you then."

He stepped around the stone slab and a shaking, ancient hand grabbed Pilates chin before he could back away. Pilate stood still as the man turned his head side to side and examined him closely.

"Good, ya look fit to me. Gonna come in handy around here."

"Where did you come from? Have you been inside my head the whole time? Are we alone here? What is this place exactly?" Pilate blurted the questions at the man and felt immediately like a school boy. In fact, his grandfather would have felt like a school boy in the presence of this man.

The old man raised an eye brow and sighed. "Over there. Yes. No. A prison." Then he turned and hobbled off.

"What? Wait, where are you – "

"Come with me child. We have much work to do."

Pilate stood silently for a moment and watched the old man hobble away. Standing amidst thousands of sleeping strangers in a place that could only be likened to hell's foyer, he decided company would be better than none at all. He hastened after the old man.

"How long have you been here?" He asked, walking alongside the old man.

"Since before you were born, sonny. And quite a boring place, I might add. Not even a chess board."

Despite his age, the old man moved deftly between sleeping people, zigzagging his way in one direction. At times he stopped, looked around to get his bearings and then continued. This confused Pilate because no matter which way he looked, there seemed to be the same, endless array of sleeping people in every direction. He guessed the old man was looking at the people themselves to navigate towards some location.

Pilate stopped suddenly and looked down at one man in particular. It was Corn, his henchman.

"I knew this man!" He exclaimed, coming to a stop beside the stone slab and looking down in amazement.

The old man stopped and did a slow, twelve-step turn. "Eh? Speak up lad, my ears are used mostly for ringing these days."

"This man." He said, pointing down at Corn. "He was under my command in Jerusalem."

Centurion Cornelius was sleeping peacefully on his own stone bed. His hands were folded on his chest and a white blanket was draped across his body. Pilate looked at the holes in the man's chest and cringed as a feeling of guilt swept over him.

"Yes. You should feel guilty." Said the old man, coming over to look down at Corn.

Pilate looked bemused. "What? I err – "

"You sent him to the front lines." The old man glanced as Pilate for only a moment. The eye contact was so penetrating, Pilate realized there was no point feigning ignorance.

"Yes." Pilate sighed. "I did but he was an evil man. He would have ended up dead or worse in any case." He concluded but his guilt wasn't so easily white-washed by the explanation.

"He was a simpleton. He only needed some guidance in the right direction and would have been just fine."

Pilate felt like a mosquito in a sunbeam whenever the man looked at him so he looked away. The man's white eyes bore into him, regardless.

"I suppose so, yes." He said quietly. "Why is he here?"

"Everyone here has damaged the universe in some way and drew unwanted attention to themselves by doing so. Like I said before, this is a prison. And the warden is ever watchful of those he can bring here." He said, then he turned and hobbled away.

"Wait," said Pilate walking beside the old man again, "what do you mean?"

"Whenever someone is dishonest, unfaithful or kills another in any way, there is discord in the fabric of the universe."

Pilate tried to wrap his mind around this but failed due to lack of materials.

"I know," said the old man, hobbling along at a steady pace. "it's a hard idea to grasp for you at this time. Do you like music?"

Pilate was yanked from his mental acrobatics. "Huh? Music?"

"Yes. Sounds put together to make more pleasant sounds. Do you like music?"

"Uh, yes, well, everyone likes mu – "

The man stopped and looked at Pilate. "What's your favorite song?"

Pilate halted and blinked at the old man. He couldn't imagine a stranger question at this time and place.

"C'mon lad, everyone likes music, even if they say they don't. What's your favorite song?" The old man grinned at him.

Pilate recalled a nursery melody his mother used to hum when he was a small boy. It brought back memories of a happier time when lust for power hadn't taken hold of him.

"Good, now sing it." Said the old man, staring at Pilate intently.

"How did you know wh–"

"Go on, give it a go."

Pilate looked like a person expected to do something childish. Which, in fact, he was.

"Hmm, hmm, hmm-hmm, hmmmmm! Hmmm, hmm, hmm-hmm, hmm. Hmmm.

The old man grinned and bobbed his head to the melody Pilate hummed. Then suddenly, he grabbed Pilate's nose when he was about to finish the chorus.

"HONK!" He shouted in Pilates face. Then he let go.

"What the – " Said Pilate, grabbing his nose tenderly and scowling at the old man.

"That's what murder does to the universe." Then he turned and walked away.

Pilate stood silently for a moment and nodded to himself grudgingly as he touched his nose. After a few moments, he caught up with the old man as they continued to zigzag through the array of sleeping sinners.

"Uh, who exactly are you, grandfather?"

"Oh, I'm just a pilgrim, lad. Treading along life's bumpy road." Said the old man flatly. He turned abruptly down another aisle and caused Pilate to trip up.

"How did you find yourself here?"

"I find myself wherever I go, my young Prefect. That's what happens when people go places. Wherever they go, that's where they are."

He stopped suddenly. "Here we are then."

Pilate was still trying to figure out if there was an answer or two to his questions when the old man stopped. He followed the man's gaze down.

Pilate's eyes opened wide and he backed away, stumbling into a stone bed behind him. He turned and found the stone slab he stumbled into was even more distressing. He backed away from it too. He turned and a third to his left was still more shocking and Pilate's mouth hung open as he recognized a fourth person to his right.

"I see you know them." Said the old man calmly.

"Yes." Whispered Pilate, fearing the admission would open a very uncomfortable door to his immediate future.

"They are not supposed to be here." Said the old man, coming closer to Pilate, his staff tapping the floor softly as he advanced.

"What do you want me to do?" Asked Pilate, dreading the answer.

"You have to waken them, Pontius Pilate. You have to waken them and get them out of here."

Pilate stood silently looking at the sleeping figures around him. The old man stared at him expectantly. The dim light of his luminescence did little to shadow the obvious features on the people he recognized so well.

"They hate me." He said softly. "If they awaken, they will kill me. What can I do?"

"You must face your fears in this place Pilate." Said the old man, standing very close to Pilate now. "The discord you committed during your cruel life can be repaired by following this path. Is that not what you want?"

"I do but – "

"Have faith. Without faith, we have only what we know. That is usually not enough in the grand scheme of things."

"You know," Pilate sighed, "you are like a passerby providing a drowning man with a rock to float with. Are you trying to confuse me with every sentence?"

"Humor. Good." The old man grinned and winked at him. "A little dry but the bouquet is nice. Keep your tongue in your cheek, I always say."

He stepped aside and indicated to one of the sleeping people. "Start with this one. I gather you know all too well where that scar on his forehead came from."

Pilate had the look of a condemned man being led to the gallows. He stepped forward in that peculiar way that made him appear to be wishing he were going backwards. He leaned over the sleeping man then looked up at his elderly companion.

"What do I do?"

"Whisper to him. Tell him to wake up. Only the one responsible for his being here can do that." Said the old man, watching Pilate with those searchlight eyes once more.

Pilate nodded and looked back at the sleeping man. Then something occurred to him.

"Hang on, if I'm responsible for *him* being here, that means *you* are responsible for me..." He trailed off as the old man grinned at him.

"You're getting the hang of this stuff, boy. A little slow on the uptake but you'll get there soon enough. Now," the old man pointed to the sleeping man, "get him up so we can get down to business."

Pilate shook his head as he looked at the sleeping figure. "This is going to be uncomfortable, old man."

Deciding this was the only option he could see for his penance, Pilate leaned closer to the man's ear and whispered to him.

"Erik. It is time to wake up."

Jingle*Jingle*Jingle

In a small jungle village in present-day Africa, a small girl lay wheezing among the bodies of her dead family. Scattered about the village, corpses were rotting in the unforgiving heat of the sun. Many of the bodies were emaciated and thin lines of dry, caked blood were streaked across the faces of the fallen villagers as if they had wept tears of blood before they died. The little girl had just enough strength to lift her head and look out from her hut to see that she was the only survivor of her community. She was weak, dehydrated and bled trickles of crimson tears down her face. She knew the end was near because her family died this way and now she was totally alone.

She heard footsteps outside the hut and saw a figure approach. She tried to call out but didn't have the strength. The figure stopped and crouched as it entered her hut and came closer to her. It was a man dressed in deep blue robes of the nicest cloth she had ever seen but this is not what made her stare in disbelief. His eyes were angular like small fish and his skin was not brown like her own but yellowish like papaya. His long, silky black hair was tied into a topknot but despite his alien appearance, she felt safe in his presence.

"Water." She pleaded.

"Yes child. I have water for you." He said and raised a clay cup she knew to be empty before but was now filled with clear, cool water. The man held it to her lips and she drank some, spilling a little on her pillow of leaves and animals skins.

"I will take you from this place, child." He picked her up gingerly and carried her out of the thatched hut.

She felt tiny and weak in his arms and her head fell back as he began to walk towards the pond beside her village.

"Do you disapprove of my cleansing of this monkey pit?" Said a voice behind them.

The man stopped in front of the pond and spun around quickly.

The girl felt herself losing consciousness but she was able to make out a terrible figure behind them and strained her head to see. It was a walking skeleton with large, black rags thrown over it so that the skull appeared to leer from beneath a hood. It carried a staff like her father used to have only this one had a long blade curving out from its tip. She recognized it to be a farm implement for harvesting crops. Seeing the skeleton walking upright was terrible to behold and she wept weakly in fear.

"I have reaped innumerable villages across this little globe over the last few decades but this one was particularly entertaining. They tried to bribe me with an offering of fruit and fresh swine meat." There was a terrible hissing sound as the skeletal figure laughed.

The man carrying the young girl whispered in her ear. "Shh. Shh." He soothed. "Do not fear little one." He held her close but tiny streaks of crimson tears fell across her face as she stared in horror at the apparition approaching them.

"This is murder, Halaam. Whoever or whatever you are, we are aware of your presence."

"Halaam…Halaam..." Said the skeletal figure, saying the name over and over. Its voice was like a razor sharp whisper. "Yes, I do recall the meaning of that. *Traitor*, I believe. How unjust it is for you to brand *me* in such a way, the most loyal of the Huru." The skeleton stepped closer. "You are a hurum pawn. Your ancestry stinks of primate and it seems The Pilgrim has not told you about me."

"We have been warned and I am proud to have such a heritage, Halaam. I may be only one fraction Huru but I'm a thousand times more human than you can possibly understand."

"Ah, you are a child of the three kingdoms." Said the skeletal figure. "I can see your story woven about you like the strands of a web."

"I am honored to be one among them now. They will become a great people." Said the man flatly, taking a careful step backward towards the little pond.

The little girl whimpered in fear as the skeletal apparition came closer but the man held her tightly and soothed her.

"You are old for a hurum. I know you, Saja. That is your name isn't it?"

The girl felt the blue-robed man tense but he said nothing.

"Join me and we can…" the skeleton paused, "start fresh."

"Never. You are a traitor to our cause, child of man." Said Saja as he held the child closer. "I am old enough to know certain truths of the Huru. You are not deserving of the great gifts given to your race."

"Child of man!" Hissed the skeleton. "Not deserving? You will learn something this day, Saja. I have become Death." It stopped moving and tilted its head looking at the child in the man's arms.

"Why do you protect this little monkey?" Said the skeleton passively. "Give her a banana and let her be on her way. I have no quarrel with you."

"You will not have her."

The scythe sliced through the air towards Saja's head but he was ready for it. Leaning almost level with the ground as the scythe passed over his ear, he pirouetted from the deadly strike and flipped over into the pond as he clutched the little girl to his chest. As soon as he hit the surface of the water, he shouted one word.

"Flow!" And he vanished with the child.

Death loomed over the pond for a moment, watching the concentric ripples radiating from the flow point. It leaned forward and pondered the reflection of Pontius Pilate on the rippled surface, turning its head left and right. Then it turned and walked towards the village once more, carrying the scythe at its side.

After a few yards, Death stopped turned back to the pond once more. Among the weeds, on the muddied bank of the pond, a small, magenta flower bloomed. Despite the surrounding pestilence and death, natural or otherwise, this tiny thing dared to bloom. Death approached the tiny spot of crisp magenta in the sea of green and brown and kneeled beside it. The flower was leaning away from the other weeds, desperately positioning itself despite all physical disadvantages for the maximum amount sunlight. A skeletal hand reached out and caressed the underside of the petals for a moment and in the reflection of the pond, the face of Pontius Pilate was filled with great anguish.

Seeing it's reflection, Death swiped at the still water and with a hissing snarl headed back into the village.

Jingle*Jingle*Jingle

A day that would later be known as December 25th to some and *Christmas* to many others, is a day of celebration in Abanis. To the citizens, however, the celebration is called *The Festival of Jolly*.

To Nicholas, the festival was important for two reasons. One, it was a time of remembrance for fallen emissaries and citizens of Abanis throughout the centuries. Two, it was his birthday. Most children in the universe feel that having a birthday on or near the same day as a major holiday is not unlike winning the lottery only to find out later the jackpot is a sweater. Nicholas didn't mind, however. To him, everyday in Abanis felt like a holiday. And besides, he liked sweaters. This year, however, the celebration was overcast by dark rumors of an unknown enemy.

Saja Goryo, an emissary for Asia, returned to Abanis some weeks prior to the celebration with news of his interaction with the enemy. After holding counsel with Pantilius, Aryu Veda and Gabriel, he returned to the outside world to inform others. Although Nicholas was not an emissary yet, he was told by Buddy that Pantilius and the other elders were deeply concerned by the news.

The enemy was being called the *The Greyman*, a name coined by Aryu in the following weeks. The reason for the name was a bit of a mystery to old and young citizens alike but stories of *him* were a common discussion because no one knew his true nature and origins. To modern observers, *The Greyman* was not unlike saying *The Boogeyman*. Nicholas recalled Himtall scolding him as a young man when he didn't clean up his room, saying that 'the Greyman will steal your jelly donuts if you don't!' Although having his jelly donuts disappear was enough for Nicholas to clean his room with the kind of perfection normally associated with military barracks, he knew *The Greyman* was just a myth. Now, it was being used like the myth was out there walking around for real. And that worried Nicholas greatly. Especially for his jelly donuts. In any case, emissaries were forbidden to engage in open conflict with him but encouraged to get as much information as possible until such time that The Pilgrim returned.

As for The Pilgrim, since he was *Out to Lunch*, there had been no word or sign. No one knew where he had gone or what he was doing but every citizen had faith their patron would return in his own time. The unerring faith of the populace of Abanis was further symbolized by a plate of milk and cookies, the Pilgrim's favorite snack, being set at the head of any table for any communal dinner.

The Festival of Jolly was held every year in Abanis. Emissaries and other citizens would gather in the city's central plaza to eat, drink, and let the woes of their struggles be temporarily set aside. The festival had been held for years beyond counting and everyone pitched in where they could.

Considering it was his favorite time of the year, Nicholas was no slouch and eagerly volunteered to help set up tables and chairs in the city plaza. It was a day before the celebration and he had ample time on his hands. As he was helping some younger pupils set up a particularly uncooperative table, he heard Pantilius talking to some newly arriving emissaries from the Afrikaans continent. He just caught the last sentence.

"...and the coconut said to the spider, *we're dropping like flies!*"

The emissaries laughed and Pantilius beamed at them. "OK, off you go Maurice, nice to see you again old friend." One tall and heavily built emissary bowed respectfully to Pantilius and led the others away.

Nicholas waved and smiled at Pantilius. The old Professor spotted him and, to Nicholas' astonishment, vanished.

Nicholas stared at the spot and looked around.

"Oy, down here big fella!"

Nicholas nearly jumped realizing Pantilius was standing beside him. "Wow! That was fast."

"Uhuh. I'm fast." He grinned up at Nicholas and grabbed a handful of peanuts and raisins from a nearby table. "So, got all of your homework done?"

"Yes. But rongo-rongo is kind of hard. I can't get the accent right."

"Some languages require practical field training." Pantilius nodded and winked at him. "But enough about that, tomorrow is Jolly and you should be enjoying yourself but," he paused and frowned, "Jolly isn't the only significant event to be held." Pantilius put his hand on his chin and tapped it as he looked up into the sky dramatically. "I knew there was something else. Something vaguely important...."

Nicholas smirked and looked down shyly.

"Pajamas!" Pantilius snapped his blue fingers. "It's also your birthday!"

Nicholas nodded sheepishly.

"Now run along to the castle and get your new robe on. Vee have to make you rook smashing for ze festival!"

Nicholas stared at the table leg he was about to set up. It was the kind of look most people make when backtracking to analyze Pantilius' chaotic narratives. In his mind, *get your new robe on* jumped up and down with its hand in the air saying oh! oh! like an overzealous student in class.

A raisin hit him on the forehead.

"Yes. Yes." Pantilius waved a peanut and raisin-loaded hand, showering some surprised passersby with them. He guessed what Nicholas was thinking. "I think it's time you changed into something a little more suitable for your studies. Now run along before you grow out of them."

Nicholas grinned and ran off excitedly. *New robe* meant he would become an apprenticed to an emissary. He raced towards the road leading Mirthmyst and vanished into the pine grove.

Pantilius watched Nicholas retreat and chewed on some peanuts. After a few moments, he became suddenly aware of the sun being eclipsed but didn't bother to turn around.

"Brother," sighed Pantilius, "it occurs to me that *Himalaya* might have been a better name for you than *Himtall.*"

"Ho-ho-ho!" Laughed Himtall as he sat down on grass beside the tiny professor. "So. Is he ready old friend?"

Pantilius squinted at the small figure of Nicholas as he disappeared into the pine grove. "Yes, there are some truths he should know and his lessons are going well."

But Pantilius' ever present grin faded again as his gaze ventured over to the dark and vacant looking silver dome at the heart of the city. "But if *he* doesn't return soon, we may need to take uncertain steps."

Back at the castle, Nicholas raced past a number of fellow acolytes. He acknowledged them as politely as he could and sped up the spiral stairways to his room in one of the castle towers. Like most acolytes living in Castle Mirthmyst, Nicholas' room was a simple one. On one side of the room was a bed with a small table beside it, a wooden closet for his robes and a large octagonal shaped window allowing ample daylight in to fill the room. On the other side was a writing desk. This was presently covered with paper, ink quills and curiously, with the remains of an evening snack which must have consisted of multiple dishes and a variety of different toppings. Perhaps evening 'four-course-meal' would have best described it. Above the desk was a simple shelf with a small mountain of books piled on top of it. Some of the books had titles like *How to Read Egyptian Without Serious Injury* and *The Humor Behind Positional Notation* and *One + Two = Banana.*

Nicholas burst into his room panting and found a new robe placed at the foot of his bed. Crossing the small room he picked it up and marveled at its craftsmanship. It was deep crimson color, which starkly contrasted with his light brown adolescent robes. How nice it will be, he thought, to wear something other than brown. He also mused it would make tomato stains much easier to conceal from Mrs. Bakersbee's tyrannical henchmen, *the Launderers*. He examined the robe more closely, marveling at the fabric's curious weave. He knew it would be warm in cold and cool in the heat, a signature of many of the fabrics made in the city. His thumb traced over a small embroidered name inside the back of the robe and he squinted at it.

"Weatherweave." Said Nicholas, who had never heard the name before.

He shrugged, took off his acolyte robes and put it on. He adjusted it and looked down his sleeves with satisfaction. Until this moment Nicholas couldn't believe the day had finally arrived that he would become an acolyte of Abanis. Crimson was the color of the acolytes in training to become emissaries. Today, he knew, would mark a new point in his education and his mind raced with all kinds of marvelous things he was about to find out. He sat down on his bed and looked out the window towards the city and the sounds of celebration already under way.

Nicholas hadn't dreamed of becoming anything other than a full emissary, someone out there in the world. He thought about becoming one of the *Legion*, as Mrs. Bakersbee's bakers and chefs were called. They didn't just make food for Abanis, they were artists and doctors of a peculiar sort.

Nicholas once saw an emissary come back to Mirthmyst Castle after being away for nearly ten years. He was sad and gaunt, as if all the life had been drained from him in his grief. After spending three days in the care of Mrs. Bakersbee, however, the man was well enough to return to the world and continue his missions. Nicholas always wondered what special powers baked goods could have over a person but never pursued the matter. He was content eating the finished products and never missed an opportunity to thank Mrs. Bakersbee and her legions for their masterful creations.

Nicholas also considered a life as a Guardian, a militant sect lead by Gabriel. They were masters of combat and other skills of a physical nature but Nicholas had never seen them do anything other than stand like statues for long lengths of time. They were tasked primarily with guarding the Gate pool beneath the plaza, currently brimming with home-comers. They trained inside a building called simply the *Temple*, a ziggurat-like structure in a mountainous region not far from Castle Mirthmyst. The area's high, jagged peaks and lack of smooth, grassy pastures prevented Nicholas and other acolytes from venturing close and he suspected the guardians liked it that way.

The Gate pool they guarded was the only way in to the great sphere and only those with a special key made by only the most powerful citizens. The key itself was a physical manifestation of a binding contract with the owner. If the key were lost or the owner was under duress, the contract would break and the entrance could not be found. Personally, Nicholas enquired numerous times about his entrance to Abanis. Although he knew it involved being orphaned and discovered by Harry, Buddy and Fuzzy, he was asked to wait until he was ready to hear the full story. He secretly hoped that day was fast approaching.

There were other vocations such as artisans, engineers, weathermen and chroniclers but Nicholas, like many other acolytes, was always drawn to the emissary class. They were the ones sent out in the world disguised as regular people to watch and occasionally nudge the ebb and flow of human cultures around the world. They were not permitted to interfer but here and there, a little assistance to prevent disaster was acceptable. For the most part, they were meant to help people learn to help themselves. That was all. But Nicholas had other insentives. He dreamed of standing before the great pyramid tombs of Egypt or sailing the middle oceans with Phoenician captain. He wanted to climb high mountain peaks of mountains far east of the Roman Empire or eat fruit straight from a tree in the jungles of the western world.

The great sphere of Abanis was Nicholas' home and sanctuary for those whose heritage could be traced to The Pilgrim's ancient people. Nicholas loved his home but strongly desired to see the world beyond. Therefore, he buried himself in studies neccessary to become an emissary. He was particularly interested in culture, communication and history. He was now fluent in over thirty-seven languages and dialects worldwide. He could select any point on a world map and describe the indigenous people living there and their history. As impressive as this may sound, it was only the very basic level of knowledge one needed to move on to becoming an apprenticed emissary.

Nicholas shook his head and stood up, admiring his new crimson robes. *Yes. This is what I want*, he thought to himself. He looked into a small, silver mirror on the back of his door and smiled at himself. Satisfied with the robe, despite it being a little snug around the waist, he sat down at his desk and opened a book called *Careful with that Rongo, Rongo* and studied late into the night.

Chapter 15: Rising Battered Jolly Pudding

Erikssen Fisherman awakened suddenly and gasped for air. He closed his eyes and grimaced in pain at the blinding lights. He curled up, shielded his face with his hands and felt cold stone beneath him as senses took hold.

"Talk to him." Said a voice nearby.

"What? Me?" Said another.

"No. The young fella three slabs down." Erik heard a crackly, old voice whisper loudly. "Yes, you!"

"Uh…"

Erik heard a familiar voice closer to him as he tested the light with his eyes. They still hurt but the pain was receding. He kept them closed. "Who's there? What is this? Where am I?"

"Friends. A prison. On a ship." Answered the old voice.

"Uh, friends, a prison, on a – "

"What?" Sighed Erik.

"Your sight will return soon, give it a few moments." Said the second voice. It was a familiar voice but he couldn't place it. He couldn't recall *anyone* he knew at the moment.

Erik ran his hands along the stone beneath him and then his body. Although he was naked, blind and apparently incarcerated with two strangers for reasons he couldn't begin to guess, Erik didn't feel cold, warm, hungry or tired. In fact, he felt rested and comfortable but ill at ease at the loss of his memory. He just hoped those in his vicinity were telling the truth about being his 'friends'.

"I'm in a prison? Why, what have I done?" He asked, opening his eyes a slight bit while shielding his face.

"You were…" He heard the familiar voice hesitate. "You were captured by a slaver."

There was another pause in which Erik heard some whispering from the other voice. Then the man continued.

"I awakened you so that we can help each other escape."

"Then I am in your debt, whoever you are." Erik said.

He winced and looked around, realizing there were three sources of light. One was a person standing to his immediate left, the second stood at the foot of the stone bed slab and he third, he realized, was himself. He sat up and looked around.

In front of him was the oldest man he had ever seen. He carried a staff and was wrapped in a white toga, similar to the cloth Erik had. To his left he squinted at a younger man, moderately built with a dark complexion. He had the air of someone used to command but seemed rather nervous and...somewhat familiar.

"Who are you?" Asked Erik. He squinted at them as his eyes continued to recover.

"His memory will return soon, boy." Said the ancient man to the younger. "Better get on with it or there might be drama. And I'm not talking about the silly Greek kind."

Erik sensed the man to his left was cautious and looked up at him.

"Uh, well..." Said Pilate nervously. He had the look of a man who was conflicted about either running away at full speed or informing someone of something unpleasant. "OK.

I am Pontius Pilate. And I am responsible for you being here."

"And..." Said the older man, nodding his head as if coaxing an incontinent student to come clean after stealing someone else's pencil.

"And...um, I'm fairly sure I did terrible, uh, things..." Pilate stammered.

Erik stared into the middle distance and frowned as he quietly repeated the name *Pontius Pilate.* As memories of his life began to emerge from deep recesses in his mind, Erik was suddenly struck by the impossiblility of his surroundings.

"What the Hades is this!" He exclaimed, standing up so suddenly even the old pilgrim raised an eyebrow.

Pilate stepped back and watched Erik nervously, who turned on the spot and stared at the array of bodies spreading out into oblivion.

"What kind of a boat is this? It must be massive! Is it Carthaginian? Egyptian?"

Pilate looked nervously at the old man for support but was faced with a bemused smile. It was as if the old man was trying to say *this is your show, I wouldn't dream of interfering.*

Erik saw the exchange but decided to ignore it for now. His eyes passed over a young woman sleeping on a stone slab to his right. Despite the insanity of his surroundings, he was drawn to her. He walked slowly over to her and leaned down, unable to shake the feeling that he knew her quite well. She was remarkably pretty. Her long, dark brown hair cascaded down and over her shoulders like rivers of smoothest silk. He leaned closer and watched her chest raise and lower slightly as she slept. His eyes took in every feature of her face and followed the bridge of her nose to her lips and....

Erik stood and staggered back as a lifetime of memories came crashing through the floodgates of amnesia. Flashes of Jerusalem, Longinus, Cassie, Aurelia, their escape from Pilate and his son being born in the wilderness seared across his mind. He gripped his head in pain and heard a familiar voice to his right.

"Erik. I am sorry. Please forgi-"

But Pilate didn't have time to finish the sentence. Erik launched himself at the man and the two went sprawling onto the stone floor.

Erik was a trained soldier so he easily overcame Pilate. He quickly straddled his opponent and had his hands over the man's throat.

"You!" He seethed. "You did this to me. To us!"

"Please." Gasped Pilate. The pitch of his voice was raised in that peculiar way when someone else was choking the life out of it. "Erik. Let me explain."

"Explain? Explain how you ruined our lives and tried to murder my wife, my best friend, his wife?" Erik roared. His face was a grimace of hatred and rage. "Where is my son?!"

"I- I did. I was...wrong." Pilate gasped and looked at the old man with pleading eyes.

The old man was standing behind the two, watching intently. He gestured for Pilate to continue.

"Yes!" Screamed Erik. "You are evil and cruel so I am going to choke it completely out of you!"

"Please...Erik-" Pilate gasped for air as his face changed into an unpleasant shade of purple. "Please forgive me." He spat and his eyes began to bulge. "Please ..forgive me. I ...am here to help you. Save...them." He gestured weakly to the other stone slabs.

"Save me? Save me!" Erik raged. "What nonsense! I could have killed you but I didn't."

"And why not?" Said the old man, nonchalantly leaning on his staff.

Pilate's bulging eyes moved to the old man in confusion.

Erik subsided slightly and looked up at the old man.

"He was unarmed. Longinus and I had already knocked him out cold." Then he blinked as if trying to remember something.

"Indeed. And now you wish to choke the life out of a person who has pleaded guilty and asked for forgiveness?" The old man nodded as if to confirm all the facts. "Revenge it is then. Understandable, of course. Very well, choke away."

Faced with the realization that he had never killed a man in cold blood but now had a chance to kill someone who truly deserved it, Erik's hesitated.

"That's the craziest thing about good people." Said the old man, examining his fingernails. "When vengeance seems righteous, they don't take it and feel better for knowing that they could. One of humanity's greatest virtues but at the same time bloody confusing, if you ask me."

Erik lessened his grip on Pilate's throat and stared at his hands but his face was still full of anger.

As Pilate gasped for air, the old man leaned down and whispered in Erik's ear. "A wise man once said that anger ventilated leads to forgiveness. Anger concealed hardens to revenge. Let it out and be done with it."

Erik looked up at the old man as if seeing him for the first time. Then he looked down at Pilate who was massaging his throat, coughing and still a disturbing shade of purple. Then he looked at his wife, sleeping peacefully beside them.

The old man stood up and nodded at Erik with satisfaction.

"Ahh, good. Blessed are the meek, I see."

"What?" Erik tore his gaze from his wife and looked up in confusion once more. "What did you say?" He asked, almost whispering.

"Blessed are the meek." Snorted the old man with the manner of someone saying something completely obvious.

"Yes." Said Erik, looking down at his hands and whispering the phrase almost to himself. "I know that. I never understood exactly what it meant." He rolled off of Pilate and sat agaisnt his wife's stone slab.

"Well," said the old man, waving a hand absently, "it's like saying *no worries*. Applies to pretty much everything in the universe."

"Huh?"

"Never mind. That's a few hundred conversations away." Said the old man, leaning down to help Pilate to his feet.

Pilate got to his feet panting and massaging his throat. He looked at Erik dejectedly but said nothing.

"Alright." Said Erik getting to his feet. He looked out to the endless array of sleeping people, then glared at Pilate. "You are alive because she wouldn't want me to kill you." He said flatly. "Now, I want answers. One - who in Hades is he?" He pointed at the bemused old man without taking his eyes off Pilate. "Two - where are we really? Three -" He pointed to Aurelia, "is she alive?"

Pilate looked at the old man who gestured for him to take the stage. He sighed and nodded. "Erik." He said, with the air of someone preparing for a two hour, marathon lecture on the nature of madness. "Yes she is and I will tell you everything I know."

*Jingle*Jingle*Jingle*

The Greyman surveyed the three men before him. They were standing on a snowy mountain summit, far above vast, fertile lands stretching away as far as the eye could see. The sun was setting in the west and long shadows stretched before the three, motionless figures. They were of different races and ages but each wore dark blue robes identifying them as emissaries of Abanis. To the casual observer it would appear the men were in poor health but closer inspection would reveal them to have a more *terminal* condition. Their skin had the kind of pallor that a coffee gets after sitting neglected on some desk for about three weeks. The skin on their hands was peeled and appeared to be rotting. Despite this obvious lack of a pulse, the men stood and stared blankly into nothingness.

"You did well to erase the anomaly on Golgotha brothers." The Greyman hissed. "But there is more work to be done before we proceed."

He raised a skeletal hand and showed the three men a snowball. For a moment he didn't move but empty eye sockets flared beneath the black cowl. The ball of snow suddenly crystallized and became a perfect, reflective sphere. A moment later, a rotating, profile image of a young man appeared within the globe.

"Do you see this youngling?" He hissed.

The men looked into the globe and focused on the image. "Yes master." They chimed.

"Have you seen him in the city?"

"Yes master."

The Greyman paused as if to consider something.

"When did he arrive and at what age?" He asked, stepping closer. "You." He pointed his scythe at one. "Answer."

"Fifty years ago. He was an infant." Said the man.

"Where was he found and by whom?" He pointed the scythe at the same man. "Answer."

"He was found in the Judean wilderness by the three magi, otherwise known as Harry, Buddy and Fuz- "

"Enough." Said the Greyman. He threw the globe aside and paced before the men.

"So, the Nazarene's pet monkey is among them now." He said after a while. "You say his father was on Golgotha and a Hurum. But his lineage must be weak for the others to miss it...and if the child is human, why did the Nazarene chose him?

His hissing introspection trailed off and he stopped pacing. He glared at the men once more and pointed his scythe at one.

"You. Who was your teacher?"

“This vessel was apprenticed to Aryu Veda.” His eyes didn’t flicker and his face was white.

“And what did he teach you?”

“He trained this vessel in the arts of understanding the biology of human beings. Medicine, physiology and –“

“Good. Contact your infiltrators at the festival. Abanis Elders already know this vessel, Namtar and his brothers are possessed but they may not know of the acolytes. Tell them to prepare the gatepool.” Hissed the Greyman.

The Greyman turned and looked out across the lands beneath the mountain. “Veda, the meat bag, was one of the first of them, I hear. The Hurum love him oh so dearly, I imagine. He shall fall first.”

The men remained still and didn't respond.

Thet Greyman turned to them once more. “War, Pestilence, Famine." He pointed the scythe at each of them. "You have done well sewing your arts and keeping yourselves hidden within these vessels all these years. You will be rewarded for your loyalty. We *will* ride again."

“Yes master.” They chimed.

The Greyman stared at the snowy ground between them and pointed at it. A bolt of flame erupted from his bony finger and smote the ice and rock so hard it created a small crater three feet in diameter. The edges of it made tiny *glinka-glinka-glinka* sounds as the rock cooled in the icy wind of the mountain's summit. He kicked some snow into it which quickly melted and turned into a puddle of crystal clear water.

“Flow.” He pointed to the puddle in the small crater. "I have business elsewhere."

Gathering black robes and leaning on the scythe to assist his fragile frame, The Greyman slouched away. As the men watched, he navigated down the rocky, snow covered slopes of the mountain and vanished from view.

Sometime later, one by one, the three men stepped into the pool and vanished.

*Jingle*Jingle*Jingle*

The Festival of Jolly had finally arrived. Nicholas jumped out of bed with the kind of enthusiasm that most people require several espressos to achieve. Not only was it his birthday, it was also a time when emissaries would return to Abanis for a brief rest. They brought home tales from the outside world and Nicholas never tired of hearing them. And of course, there were endless platters of cakes, cookies, pies, puddings and food of all kinds for citizens pouring into the city. Nicholas convinced himself it would be the height of bad form to not appreciate the skills and talents of Mrs. Bakersbee and her legion of busy bakers. He therefore promised himself to make a concerted effort to sample healthy amounts of everything available. Just to be polite, of course.

Nicholas put on his new crimson robes but froze while looking in the mirror. Something in it's relfection made him tilt the mirror and peer closer into it. Then he turned to look at his door. A small mountain of brightly wrapped gifts blocked it.

"Wow!" He scooped the presents up and sat down on his bed. They were wrapped in variously colored papers and had labeled cards attached to them with messages like *To Nicholas* or *For my young friend Nicholas* written on them.

Nicholas grabbed one from the top of the small pile. It was small, rectangular and wrapped in blue paper. He read the label aloud. "To my young friend Nicholas, Protector of Reindeer. -Your friend, Gabriel."

Nicholas tore open the blue paper to reveal a small, black, polished wooden box. On the side was a silver latch. He flipped the latch and opened it. The inside was lined with a soft, red fabric Nicholas had never seen before and in the center was a pipe that appeared to be made of bone. He picked it up and examined it. It looked hand-carved and was seven inches long, smooth and white. Etched into the bone along the side of it was inscribed the word *Solace.*

There was a small note inside the box as well. It read: *Happy Birthday Nicholas. You may be interested to know that a stag left a horn on my doorstep last night. I believe it was meant as an offering of thanks to you for your charitable actions. I used it to make this pipe. - G.*

Nicholas had never owned such a nice pipe before. Come to think of it, he never owned a pipe at all. He never picked up the habit of enjoying cherry leaf but intended to try some at the festival now that he had a spectacular pipe.

He put the pipe back in the black box, set it aside and grabbed another gift. This one was somewhat soft under the paper and labeled *To a Diligent Cookie Inspector.* There was no signature but Nicholas immediately recognized Pantilius' playful script.

He tore open the present and held up some crimson material. He had to stand to see its entirety and realized it was a cloak. It had white fur lining the large hood and cuffs.

A tiny note fell to the floor as he rustled the fabric. He picked it up and read it: *The weather in Abanis, providing the Weathermen are not having a fit insanity, is usually quite stable. However, as an apprentice, you will be venturing out into the real world from time to time. This will keep you extra warm or extra cool as needed. Besides, the color matches your crimson robes and you don't want to clash when you study. - P.*

PS: Batteries not included.

Nicholas shook his head in wonder and snorted. He hadn't the faintest idea what a *battery* was or why it wouldn't be *included.* Even more amusing, he thought *you don't want to clash* was remarkable advice coming from Pantilius, who often wore eye-watering orange pajamas and purple bunny slippers almost every evening.

He put the letter down and closely examined the cloak. It matched the color of his crimson robes perfectly. Nodding in satisfaction, he looked at another gift wrapped in purple paper. This one was from Himtall and Mrs. Bakersbee.

Nicholas tore open the purple wrapping and held up a thick, black belt and a matching pair of black boots. They were made of the thickest, hardest leather Nicholas had even seen. They had a scaled pattern he couldn't recognize but then again, he wasn't very good at zoology. Perhaps it was from an animal he had yet to discover in his studies. Despite its thickness and strength, the leathery material was remarkably light. Silver buckles clinked as he held up the belt and boots.

As he expected, a tiny note fell out of one of the boots and landed on his lap. It read: *The boots are treated with oils from bone. Wherever you go, you're always home. Never stay away too long, this land is home and makes us strong. - H. & B.*

Nicholas silently thanked Himtall and Mrs. Bakersbee as he inspected the boots. He wondered if they *were* dragon scale or something similar. He knew that dragons, or something like them, existed in prehistoric earth. Pantilius called them *Bigassaurus* and *Teethaplentius* but Nicholas strongly suspected the names were just made up.

Nicholas set the boots and belt aside and grabbed a small, circular shaped gift wrapped in white paper. It was labeled, *To my younger brother. - A.V.*

Nicholas delicately unwrapped the white paper and held up the most peculiar item thus far. As far as he could tell, it was a compass device. It was brass, about one inch thick and small enough to sit in the palm of his hand. The face was protected by clear glass and a red dial spun lazily around a white disc-face inside as he moved it about. He was familiar with the physics of compass devices and had just finished studying how sooner or later, humans would be making them. What confused Nicholas was that there were no directional points such as north, east, south, and west. There were only two points. One point at the bottom of the dial was labeled *Naughty* and it's polar opposite on the top was labeled *Nice.*

Nicholas looked around his bed for a note and found a message written on the underside of the wrapping paper. It read: *Are magnetic poles the only things in the world capable of sending out readable information on such a device? I think not. This tool will assist you if you ever need to truly know the motives of others. - AV.*

Nicholas looked down at the compass once more and found the dial resolutely pointing to 'nice'. He looked around his empty room and found himself staring from the small mirror.

"It appears I am in good company then." He said aloud and chuckled in spite of himself.

Nicholas marveled at the peculiar compass which came with a small, brown leather pouch. He put the compass in the pouch and pulled the string taught. He added it to the birthday pile and grabbed another gift.

This one was wrapped in orange, silver and dark brown paper. He would have wagered a serious pile of donuts it was from Harry, Buddy and Fuzzy. Unwrapping the tri-colored paper Nicholas was surprised to see three books fall into his lap. He picked one up. It was bound in soft leather and on the front, etched into the leather was the word *Hortensius.* Another, bound in a similar nature was titled *Imhotep: How we did it.* There was a small diagram of a pyramid on the cover. The last was called *Poems by Lee Moonlit River.*

An envelope fell out of the wrapping paper. Nicholas opened it and found a note inside. It read: *We saved these from extinction, Nick. We know you like to read so please enjoy these masterpieces.*

Nicholas looked at the books once more, realizing they were written by humans. He continued reading the letter.

Someday, you will understand why such treasures from the world without need to be saved. You are a treasure keeper now. Take care of these books until they are ready to return to the world. You will know when it is time. - Three Wise Fools

Nicholas ran his hand over the leather covers of the books and grinned. He placed them carefully beside the small pile of presents and looked down at the last gift.

After doing some mental arithmetic, he was puzzled and wondered who the gift was from. *Saja Goryo perhaps?* He thought to himself. *Maurice maybe?* But he didn't know those emissaries well. He was puzzled.

He picked it up the last gift and examined it. He could tell it was hard and cold beneath black cloth wrapping. The cloth was fastened with a gold seal that looked like **:P** which seemed familiar somehow but Nicholas couldn't recall. He unlatched the gold clasp and unrolled it from the black cloth until a round object fell into his palm. It was once a spike or nail of (what he assumed) to be iron but was bent into a circle. The thick, iron hoop had gold chain links fastened to it so that one could wear it like a pendant. It was beautiful in its simplicity but Nicholas was uncertain of the dark stains on the iron hoop.

Shrugging, Nicholas put it on. As the chains touched his neck and the iron hoop rested against his chest, something happened to the room. It was as if his peripheral vision faded and he suddenly felt a strong desire to flee his room and run as far away as he could. He breathed faster now and as the feeling faded, he heard a voice in his head. It was a calm, male voice and sounded strangely distant.

Dear Brother. It said. *If you are hearing this message, then I am still out to lunch and did not have the pleasure of presenting this key to you myself. I am known by many as The Pilgrim. Do not dismay of your instinctual fears at this moment. As a newborn child leaving his mother's womb, so are you taking a fearful step into a new life.* There was a pause, then the voice continued. *I asked Aryu Veda to seed the key with this message and craft it so that you can always wear it. It is an heirloom to your house and family. Welcome to Abanis. I sincerely hope our paths cross soon. Be safe, happy and healthy. Blessed are the meek.*

The message ended and the room came back into focus as Nicholas breathed hard.

"Wow!" He said aloud and looked down at the pendant. Nicholas didn't exactly understand the message but it seemed to make sense in some obscure way. "I have taken a step?" He asked aloud.

"Indeed you have." Said a voice from his doorway. Nicholas was startled and looked up. Pantilius was standing in his doorway grinning and smoking a pipe. "That is your key."

He crossed the room and pointed to the hoop resting against Nicholas' chest. "It is a key to this city. You must never lose it." He nodded at Nicholas. "It is possible The Greyman desires one of these keys Nicholas, that is why we make all emissaries who venture forth from this sphere, guard their keys closely until we know his motives. It is very difficult to enter Abanis without one."

Nicholas had heard The Greyman mentioned numerous times lately but didn't understand why he would wish to do anyone in Abanis harm.

"Why is he evil?" He asked quietly. "I don't understand it."

"Why do sharks eat anything that is unfortunate enough to be in open water? You might as well ask that, Nick." Pantilius snorted. "Some beings just *are* a certain way. If The Greyman is who I think he is, I know he wasn't always evil. Long ago, he cared about things but he fell from that grace for reasons too hard to explain. He is old beyond measure and may be considerably weaker than he was long ago." Pantilius sighed, almost to himself.

Nicholas caught the undertone of regret in Pantilius' voice and felt like a child who heard something he wasn't supposed to. He looked down at the pendant again. It was beautiful and made him feel strong though he couldn't reason why.

"I know this thing." Said Nicholas, his fingers tracing the peculiar stains on the metal. "It feels familiar to me." He looked up questioningly at Pantilius.

"Well." Started the old professor. "It's like this, Nick. Harry, Buddy and Fuzzy found you with this spike. The Pilgrim felt it was special and sent word to Aryu for it to be presented to you in this manner. That's about all I know."

"Thanks you professor. For everything." Said Nicholas blushing. "I won't let you down. I'll study well."

"You're welcome, young apprentice." Said Pantilius. "Off I go. There are many old students and many old friends I must tend to. See you down at the celebration." He patted Nicholas on the shoulder then with a wink and a nod, left the room.

After a few minutes, Nicholas put on his new attire and scrutinized himself in the small mirror near his desk. The long, crimson cloak, black belt and matching black boots shone in the subtle, lamplight from the hall. He stuck the stag horn pipe in his mouth and looked at the iron hoop pendant on his chest. His cheeks were rosy red from hours spent outside and his long, bushy blond hair fell over wide shoulders. His blue eyes twinkled in beams of sunlight streaming in from a tiny window next to his bed. Thoroughly satisfied with his image, he grinned at himself.

"Hello." He said to the mirror.

He frowned and cleared his throat.

"Hi, you look lovely this evening." He said again, his voice significantly deeper. Then he snorted. "Ho-ho-ho!' He laughed and realized he sounded like Himtall. Shrugging, he left the room and headed down to the Festival of Jolly.

Nicholas entered the and found it bustling with all kinds of seasonal activity. It was mid-morning and many children around the plaza were playing games while their respective caretakers assisted with final preparations for the festivities.

Chefs were bringing out snacks of all sorts and placing them on tables so long that yardage would be required to measure their length. These tables were already under siege by hungry home-comers eager to sample the wares of the city's legion of chefs.

Some people were stringing up lines of what appeared to be rope and on which sparkled an assortment of colorful lights. Nicholas knew the lights were actually 'fyreflies', little insects indigenous only to Abanis, or so he heard. They were known to emanate a peculiar light on this day only and some speculated that they were created by The Pilgrim himself. The ropes on which they perched were saturated with nectar so the little flies would sit and sparkle happily as they fed.

Nicholas watched in fascination as an artisan spoke to a family of owls living in a park near the plaza. He noted the woman was using sounds and clicks rather than words. After a few moments, the owls flew to a nearby box filled with the nectar-saturated rope and were flying back and forth across the plaza. After a short time, fyreflies came to savor the sweet juices on the lines of rope. The resulting spectacle of lights overhead looked like hundreds of thousands of yellow, green, red, orange, blue, violet and white twinkling stars.

Nicholas looked on with rising anticipation and noticed a group of three elders huddled around a spot in front of The Pilgrim's silver domed home. It was Harry, Buddy and Fuzzy, his patrons and educators. As Nicholas approached them, he saw Buddy and Fuzzy raise their hands and step back.

Nicholas gasped as a tree of significant girth thrust up through the cobblestones like a knife through butter. It was a full, green coniferous tree and stood over thirty feet tall. Everyone in the plaza stopped what they were doing and burst into thunderous applause at the astonishing appearance of the *Jolly tree.* Emerging from under the tree, coughing and sputtering, was Harry who appeared to be spitting out needles and covered in sap. He immediately engaged in an argument with his partners-in-tree-making as Nicholas crossed the courtyard to greet them.

"You said go after three!"

"No brother, I said *on* three." Said Buddy, looking to Fuzzy for support.

"That's what I mean!" Snorted Harry, who struggled to remove his hand which was now glued to the side of his robe. "One-two-three. And then go."

"No, no, sorry brother." Said Fuzzy who was trying very hard not to smirk as he consoled his sticky companion. "I meant, one-two-and three. Like that. You see?"

Harry glared at his two companions who were trying very hard to win a *do not laugh whatsoever contest*, and coming in last.

"How many more centuries are you two – " Harry began but he caught sight of Nicholas and stopped short. "Nicholas m' lad!"

The other two turned and Nicholas flushed with pride as he approached the three wise men.

"Look-y here." Said Fuzzy, reaching up and fidgeting with Nicholas' new robe with the keenness of a professional tailor. "Crimson robes." He grinned at Nicholas who could only nod sheepishly.

"The books were an amazing gift, thank you professors." Said Nicholas bowing to them.

Harry and Buddy beamed with pride beside Fuzzy.

"You're welcome." Said Harry. "Pantilius told us last night. An apprentice emissary already." He shook his head in happy disbelief.

"We are very proud of you, boy." Nodded Buddy, his eyes betraying some moistness as he admired Nicholas' new robes.

"Shush," said Fuzzy stepping back from Nick and looking up at Buddy, "he isn't a boy anymore, he's a man. Fifty-two years old but looking not a day over twenty."

The other two nodded with satisfaction.

"I can't wait to start my training. Is there anything I can help you with today?"

"No, no, no, we'll hear nothing of it." Said Buddy. "Today is your birthday. Go see your friends. Eat, drink, play, laugh, and most of all, remember."

"Indeed," nodded Harry, "we will have ample time to talk later. Enjoy yourself, Nick."

"Go say goodbye to Robin, Nick." Said Fuzzy. "He's leaving tomorrow for Britannia, or whatever the Romans are calling it these days. You may not get a chance later."

"Very well fathers. I'll be sure to see him." Nicholas looked up behind the three elders and nodded at the tree. "Will you teach me how to do that someday?"

As one, the elder men looked at the tree and Harry realized a fyrefly was stuck to some sap on his shoulder and blinking purple.

"Oh," said Buddy, waving a hand absently at the tree, "I think you'll find that out on your own."

With a final nod, Nicholas wandered off into the crowds. Behind him, he could hear Harry continue an argument with the other two over a blinking bug on his shoulder. He chuckled and wondered how the three ancient men had remained so close for so long.

Nicholas crossed the courtyard and spotted adolescents carrying boxes of colored balls and other such things towards the giant tree. He felt a pang of regret that the fun of decorating the tree was now behind him. The Jolly tree was fun to decorate every year but he was a little too old for that now. He sighed and wondered who came up with the rule of *being too old* for anything.

After some mingling, Nicholas found Robin among some older apprentices who also lived at Mirthmyst. Robin was a handsome, dark-haired man who coined the nick-name *Bear* for Nicholas. They greeted each other with congratulations and after some small talk, Robin bid Nicholas *not to be a stranger* and disappeared into the crowds.

Nicholas liked Robin for they both shared a playful disregard for rules (to the chagrin of a beleaguered Himtall, caretaker of Mirthmyst Castle). In addition, Nicholas recently discovered he and Robin shared the same interest in the *fairer gender*, as Robin described them. They both liked *shapely* women and would occasionally exchange the voiceless communication that all young men have when seeing the same *woman of interest* walk by.

Nicholas was no stranger to the concept of love or relationships but he rarely had time to pursue such things because of his arduous studies. He kissed a girl once when he was only thirty-nine but felt awkward about it and strongly suspected she did too. He wasn't afraid of girls as some of his adolescent friends were but was more curious than anything. Women, he had to admit, were stranger and more wonderful than anything he experienced thus far in Abanis.

For the rest of the day, Nicholas mingled with emissaries and talked to other apprentices about what kind of training was on their educational horizons. In the afternoon, emissaries from all over the world demonstrated and performed an immense variety of music, dance and artistic forms from their respective cultures. Nicholas enjoyed visual arts most of all. He watched one emissary paint a vision of present-day Rome from memory and used only his finger to render the image on a bit of stretched canvas. The resulting picture even managed to capture throngs of citizens in the Roman capital city and the newly constructed Coliseum.

Nicholas.

As the afternoon turned to dusk, many citizens retreated to the massive array of tables in the central plaza. As Nicholas headed towards them, he stopped suddenly. He could have sworn he just heard a woman's voice in his head.

Nicholas.

There it was again. The woman's voice was familiar somehowand he associated it with...swimming.

Nicholas stood still and smiled at passersby. He contrived to look as if he *did not* just hear something in his head. This strategy didn't work because it only made him appear look lost and confused.

He is coming. When the time comes, find me Nicholas. Said the pleasant, female voice.

Nicholas blinked and his eyes crossed a little bit as he tried to understand who was speaking to him. This made a young girl passing by Nicholas laugh so hard she staggered into a chef, who was rushing to the tables with some pastries. The chef staggered backwards and launched the contents of the laden tray towards the head of one of the tables. Nicholas watched as missiles of freshly baked cupcakes arced towards the tables and disappeared in the crowd. After a few moments, Nicholas decided to get some fresh air outside of the city.

He passed near one of the head tables on his way back to Mirthmyst and was mildly surprised to see Harry with a cupcake stuck upside-down on top of his bald head like a tiny baked hat. He was pointing an accusing finger at both Fuzzy and Buddy who were protesting their innocence over the icing-coated projectile.

Nicholas chuckled on his way back to the castle and wondered what was in store for him there. After all, it was his birthday and Pantilius was the most generous joker in all the world, as far as Nicholas knew.

He headed towards the pine grove and saw some girls laughing and talking with each other in a small park nearby. They spotted Nicholas and waved at him, yelling out birthday wishes. One of the girls was Claire, a former resident of Mirthmyst and the girl Nicholas had kissed some years ago. His heart skipped a beat when he saw her wave enthusiastically at him. He returned the greetings by waving back shortly before walking into a lamp post near the road. The lamp post made an audible **clang** as he bumped his forehead and the young women laughed. He blushed and decided that was enough fresh air for now. He grinned at the girls and walked briskly back into the city plaza, seeking shelter from the burning embarassment among festival crowds.

Nicholas thoughts were often drawn to Claire. They studied together with the other young orphans in Mirthmyst Castle under the tutelage of Pantilius. She had long, silken brown hair and a delicate gleam in her auburn eyes that always made Nicholas feel as though she knew what he was thinking. And her laugh was as strong as Himtall's.

Nicholas shook his head as he meandered back into the plaza once more. Lamp posts and mystery voices weren't about to ruin his day. The huge Jolly tree was alight with multi–colored globes and children were playing a variety of games beneath it. Everywhere Nicholas looked was music, dancing, story-telling and exhibitions brought by emissaries from cultures all around the world. Culinary dishes of all kinds assaulted his senses. His mouth water as he scanned sprawling array of tables laden with food. He heard Pantilius some distance away and just made out the last line.

"...and the Walrus said to the Oyster, '*Aww, Shucks!*'"

Nicholas heard several people laugh and decided to join them but could barely walk five paces without seeing something he wanted to sample or experience. Stepping as carefully as he could through the crowd, he bumped into some dancers and while backing away apologetically, bumped into someone else behind him.

"Nick?"

Chapter 16: Homecoming Punch

Nicholas turned to apologize and found himself rather speechless. His mouth opened but nothing came out of it.

Claire, an orphan like himself and someone Nicholas was looking forward to seeing, stood smiling at him with red wine dripping from her hand. Her long, silky brown hair was pulled back into a tail which made her natural beauty all the more apparent. He had never seen her hair pulled back and realized she was more beautiful than he remembered. Her amber eyes drilled into his own and her snug, crimson robes did little to conceal the fact that she was, indeed, a woman.

Claire and Nicholas grew up together in Mirthmyst but she was a little older. She became apprenticed to Fuzzy two years ago and although he was happy for her, he was also sad to see her leave Mirthmyst. She originally came from the large island the Romans called Britannia, where Robin was to be stationed. Rumor had it she was discovered hiding in a forest by Himtall after her parents were butchered by a Roman soldiers for unknown reasons. After Himtall realized she was distantly related to The Pilgrim's ancient brethren, she was brought to Abanis.

"Pardon me." Was all Nicholas could say and he grabbed the hem of his own robe and wiped the spilled wine from her hand. "Won't stain." He said, smiling at her as he dabbed her hand.

Nicholas wondered for a moment if he would be able to speak more than two word sentences but was suddenly more focused on the softness of her skin. In his periphery, he could see her ginning at him and the subtle evening breeze caused his senses to be further assaulted by how good she smelled.

"Uhh, sorry. Claire, I was just – you know. Good time?" *Great.* He thought to himself. *More than two words. Perfect. Now if I can just start to make sense.*

"Wow, I didn't notice!" She exclaimed, looking at Nicholas up and down. "Oh dear, congratulations Nick! You got the crimson robes!"

She flung her arms around Nicholas and patted him on the back. "That's incredible, I'm so happy for you!" She said in his ear.

For a moment Nicholas was stunned and unable to respond. He seemed to be having a difficult time talking to Claire and wondered if he was making a fool of himself.

She stepped back to look at him once more.

"Who is your trainer Nick? Do you have one yet?"

"Tomorrow." Nicholas nodded, feeling that intelligent speech was now only a few miles away.

"Tomorrow? So today you got the robes?" She asked.

"Umm, last night. Tomorrow I will meet Pantilius and begin. Not sure who my trainer is yet. It all happened so fast though. I had no idea I was so close."

"I know, they just drop it on you suddenly." Claire nodded. "But forget that, it's your birthday! Happy birthday Nick!"

"Thanks." Nicholas grinned stupidly. "How did you know?"

"Oh come on," she punched him playfully on the shoulder. "Growing up in Mirthmyst, it's kinda hard to forget the only boy whose birthday is the same day as Jolly."

She said *boy* Nicholas thought. She didn't say *kid* or *child* or *orphan* or *resident...*

"So what did you get?" She asked, grabbing another silver goblet of wine from a nearby table. "Anything interesting?"

"Loads of stuff." He displayed his new gifts to Claire who was particularly interested in the odd compass Aryu gave him.

"Bizarre. I imagine this could really come in useful outside."

Nicholas nodded with pride but then realized he was breaking one of the fundamental rules for men when talking to a woman. A rule that Robin shared with him some years before. Talk about *her*.

"But enough about me. How is your training?" He blurted, somewhat loudly. Some younger girls passing by giggled at the two.

Claire smiled at Nicholas. If he were made of glass, it would have shattered him into a bazillion tiny fragments.

"So far, I've been traveling among the Norse people." She said, taking a sip of wine. "Given my natural appearance, Fuzzy decided they were a good start."

Nicholas nodded. He understood emissaries in training usually started with people close to their original ancestry. Changing one's appearance to blend in with a local populace was a skill learned much later in apprenticeship.

"So for now, Fuzzy keeps me close." She tilted her head and stared at him, as if realizing something.

"Here, let me show you something I learned recently." She set her wine glass down. "Put your hands out."

Nicholas obeyed and held out his hands. She grabbed them and made his hands form a cup.

"There. Hold still." She said. She reached in her robes and placed a tiny gold statuette in the cup of Nicholas' hands. Nicholas recognized it was crafted to resemble a tiny Valkyrie, a being from Nordic mythology.

Claire covered Nicholas' hands with her own and closed her eyes.

For a moment, Nicholas thought the universe stopped. The sounds of merrymaking around them faded to nothing, the motion of dancing in his periphery ceased and even the wings of flickering fyreflies stopped. Then as soon as the sensation began, it ended and all senses returned to normal.

Claire opened her eyes and grinned. "OK Nicholas. There you go."

Nicholas looked down at the tiny Valkyrie in his hands and was startled to see it's little gold wings stretch. It stood up, blinked at Nicholas then flew up from his hands. It buzzed around his head a few times like a gold-plated hummingbird then landed on his shoulder.

"Amazing!" Nicholas exclaimed, looking at the Valkyrie on his shoulder and patting it gently. The little, gold Valkyrie seemed to enjoy the attention and nestled closer to his hand.

Claire, beaming with pride, patted the tiny Valkyrie and inspected her work. "But I can only do that with tiny objects. Anything bigger than a cup won't animate."

"Did Fuzzy teach you how to do that?"

"Yes and no." She shrugged, turning to pick up her wine glass once more. "To animate something, we have to understand the makeup of it and manifest the skill naturally. Sometimes he says things I don't fully understand but from what I gather." She paused to sip some wine. "He's helping to release something already inside me." She waved a dismissive hand. "Or something like that."

Nicholas nodded. He knew that Harry, Buddy and Fuzzy, were renown for being trainers of the emissaries. It was rumored that Buddy and Gabriel trained the Nazarene for a short time before the student became far more knowledgeable than his masters.

"Anyways, happy birthday Nicholas. That's my gift to you." Claire blushed at him. "You have to name her though," she said, patting the tiny, gold Valkyrie. "Without a name they fade and never develop a persona."

Nicholas recognized the need to create a name. One name came to him suddenly from his studies of the Nordic people.

"I will name her *Kara.*" Nicholas patted the Valkyrie some more. "Hello Kara."

The tiny Valkyrie buzzed aerial loops over Nicholas shoulder and he felt the name was appreciated. She flew around Nicholas' head for a moment and then, tucking her wings back, dived straight into his breast pocket and curled up to sleep.

"Incredible. Thank you, Claire. I will take good care of her." He patted his breast pocket. Nicholas was very aware that they shared a kiss a over a decade earlier when they were still acolytes. He always wondered if a second chance would present itself. Unfortunately, her apprenticeship to Fuzzy and subsequent absence from Mirthmyst prevented this from happening.

"So, umm," he mumbled, clearing his throat. "would you like to, uhh - "

"Would I like to enjoy dancing, playing games, eating new food, seeing new art and talking to emissaries from all over the world with you this evening?" Claire said quickly, stepping beside him and locking her arm under his. "Why certainly, Nick."

"Yes. That." Said Nicholas, flatly. He felt silly for being so nervous. She was the kind of woman you could talk to about anything, like *one of the guys*, as it were. Yet she maintained an aura of femininity that drove Nicholas to new heights of fumbling idiocy. He rather felt she realized this and enjoyed it.

"Way ahead of you Nick, got to try and keep up." She laughed. She walked beside him into the throng of people and put her head on his shoulder.

"You know," said Nicholas as they waled through the crowds, "it does seem like a bit of a coincidence I *bumped* into you back there."

"I have no idea what you mean, Nick." She said coyly, grinning up at him.

The aroma of a thousand different dishes assailed them and Nicholas' mouth watered. He was absolutely famished.

"Come on." Said Claire, pulling Nicholas in an alternate trajectory through the crowds. "Let's go eat some eastern food. I've never had it before and Aryu Veda told me I have to try it."

Never dreaming his birthday could be so perfect, Nicholas walked proudly with Claire towards the eastern emissaries. Being with her would have made even Numbers class exciting. Over the course of the evening they spoke with emissaries of all sorts, played strange games with children, listened to music and sampled cuisine from all over the world. The city plaza was filled with a plethora of cultural experiences for all tastes.

A most intensely, interesting sample was some meat smothered in a kind of reddish-brown gravy from Aryu Veda's people. It was quite delicious but made Nicholas' face red, his brow sweat and burned the inside of his mouth. After thanking the emissary for such delicious tasting fire, he turned away and drank his mead down in one gulp. Then he took Claire's and drank hers. Judging by the grin on her face, Nicholas guessed she knew this was going to happen.

One of the more memorable experiences of the evening was watching Pantilius serenade a lamp post with a mask pasted to it that looked vaguely like a woman. He was singing in perfect Greek and drew quite a crowd to the spot in the plaza. Swinging a wine goblet and spilling most of its contents as he stepped poignantly around the lamp post presented a comical image. Some of the onlookers wondered if he was mocking Greek culture but despite the ridiculous performance, Nicholas knew better than to think of Pantilius mocking any human culture. Judging by the dampness of Harry's eyes, he guessed it was a sincere homage to a culture the old man dearly missed. Claire, having a little more experience with the outside world, explained to Nicholas that the song was actually a form of dramatic poetry and this particular one was about tragedy, love lost and sacrifice. To the surprise of many onlookers, Harry enthusiastically joined the thunderous applause when Pantilius finished and bowed deeply to the little professor.

The festival lasted all evening and continued deep into the early morning hours. The citizens of Abanis ate, drank, danced, talked, laughed, played and sang to celebrate the sacrifices of fallen emissaries and all that humanity had to offer. As dawn approached, many people trailed off to their respective lands within the great sphere for a well deserved rest. Soon Nicholas and Claire found themselves facing the end of a tremendously enjoyable evening.

"Thank you Nick." Said Claire, holding Nicholas and facing him in the center of the city plaza. She looked up into his blue eyes and playfully tossed his eternally disheveled blond hair. Her face was flushed from too much wine and she smiled at him.

"No, thank you Claire. Best day ever." Nicholas smiled down at her and held her close. Her long, dark brown hair fell over her shoulders and Nicholas thought he was the luckiest apprentice in all the world.

Dawn broke the horizon and crisp colors cascaded about the nearly empty plaza. Some retreating couples smiled at them as people wandered off to their homes. After some time passed, Claire grabbed Nicholas' ears, pulled his head down, and kissed him. It was the best thing he experienced thus far.

"Have you ever seen an ocean sunrise?" She whispered to him.

He shook his head slightly.

"Then come with me." And she led him away towards a landscape filled with tall, green-crested cliffs and dawn lit strands that seemed to stretch into eternity.

As citizens departed the city center, some emissaries lay down on benches in the plaza to sleep or wandered off here and there. The city of Abanis gradually fell quiet and no one noticed three acolytes slip quietly into the doorway leading down to the gate pool.

Jingle*Jingle*Jingle

"Let me get this straight." Said Erik, pacing in front of Pontius Pilate and the grinning ancient man. "I, along with my wife and friends, were brought here by means unknown."

"Correct." Said the old man cheerfully.

"And this ship or boat is some kind of prison."

"Indeed."

"And we are not dead, and this is not Elysium or some other such place."

"Not even a little."

"And we can go back?"

"Naturally."

"And Pilate is now one of my allies?" Erik waved a hand vaguely at Pontius Pilate who looked grim.

"You betcha."

Erik looked around once more to the endless array of stone slabs.

"And what about them?" He gestured with a sweeping hand. "Are they not worthy of returning?"

The cheerful manner of the old man's face went wooden for a moment. Then he sighed. "Some are and some aren't but what we will accomplish here will free them all. In a manner of speaking." He paused and looked at Erik as if to consider something. "Even now, you think of others. I rather like that in a person." The old man snickered and elbowed Pilate in the ribs. "Keep an eye on this boy, kiddo. Follow his lead and your soul will be just fine."

Erik walked over to a stone slab and kneeled down beside Aurelia. Then he looked at Longinus and Cassie on either side of her. "How do we awaken them?" He asked, caressing his wife's cheek.

"Just whisper in their ear, tell them to get up." Said the old man wistfully.

Pilate gaped at him. "He nearly choked the life out of me!" He squealed, pointing to Erik. "You intend to wake them all?"

"Well," the old man look nonplussed, "of course. We need them. Besides, it will speed up your healing process. Better than a high fiber diet and early morning jog, heh-heh." He slapped Pilate on the shoulder.

The former prefect looked down at Longinus. The man seemed larger and more dangerous to him than ever before, despite being unconscious. Pilate had the look of a man who just had just *volunteered* to participate in games at the Coliseum

"However," the old man whispered in Pilate's ear, "when *he* awakens, the healing process is going to be quite interesting to see."

Pilate groaned...

Sometime later, pain happened to Pilate. He remembered a lot of soft sounding confusion at first, quickly followed by shouting mixed with sounds of the old man cackling with laughter. In just under one hour he was threatened repeatedly, slapped, nearly kicked in the nether regions, choked, held upside down, pulled around by his hair, pulled around by one of his ears, deafened somewhat and generally beaten. But not so much that he was seriously injured. The healing process, it turns out, was not unlike going to a wine house regularly patronized by soldiers and wearing a toga that says "Centurions are Sissy's" written on it.

Pilate sat leaning against a stone slab and put a hand to the side of his head. One of his eyes were slightly blackened and his lower lip was swollen. He groaned as the old man leaned down to sit beside him. Across the narrow space between the stone slabs, Erik and Aurelia were looking at each other in the way that couples do when no one else in the universe matters. To their right, Longinus and Cassiopeia were holding each other and whispering about their situation as they looked around in disbelief.

"Ahh." Whispered the old man, looking at Pilate and rolling his eyes, "l'amore. Craziest thing in the universe and something of a mystery even to one as old as I."

"What is your name?" Whispered Pilate. It was softly asked but there was an edge to it. "I want," whispered clearly, holding the side of his head but not looking at the old man, "to know your name. Who are you?"

The last question was spoken considerably louder which made Erik and the others look at Pilate. Then they looked to the old man expectantly.

The old man looked around and nodded. He stood up and walked a little ways out into the sea of sleeping people. "I have had many names." He said quietly. "But the one I was given, very long ago in a place you may not understand, is Enlil."

Pilate stared at the old man and frowned. He was still holding a hand to the side of his head but had the look of someone who was trying to recall something important. "Enlil. Enlil." He said, repeating the name as if to clarify something in his mind. "Enlil?" He looked at Nicholas and the others then back to the old man. "Enlil? I know that name."

"Yes, I thought you might." Said the old man. "You are educated in some manner."

"But...." Pilate paused as if what he was about to say couldn't possibly be true. "Enlil is a very old name." He looked at the old man as if he was going to sprout wings or become something other than an ancient person leaning on a staff.

"Yes well," the old man waved a hand vaguely, "people always like to make things up and uh, it's all just made up stuff... " He seemed to shrink under their gazes. "I am but a wanderer." He finished lamely.

"Our son. Where is our son? Does he live?" Erik asked, glancing at Pilate.

Pilate shrugged slightly but Enlil seemed to brighten when she said this.

"Oh indeed!" He said happily. "He is safe, for the most part. I am led to believe he was found by pilgrims and kept well."

Aurelia looked at Erik with relief and sighed, grabbed her husband's hand. "Thank you Enlil." She Said. "For saving us."

The old man looked at her and his eyes softened considerably. "You are welcome my dear." He stared at her for a moment and looked genuinely touched. "You would be surprised how many people don't say that. He," said Enlil, pointing at Pilate, "played a part in your freedom too."

Then Longinus stood up. He was a giant among them and Pilate looked at him nervously. Longinus had been the most *interesting* part of his *healing process.*

He walked over to Pilate and looked down, towering above the mildly concussed former-prefect like a titan of retribution. Then he extended a hand.

Pilate looked at the hand as if it were the jaws of a shark. He took it gingerly and was yanked to his feet by Longinus.

They stared at each other for a moment then Longinus slapped Pilate on the shoulder which made the slightly built man stagger a little. "Glad to see there's a man inside of you after all Pilate."

Pilate looked at Longinus as if he had just said he liked wearing women's clothing. "Thank you, Commander." He said quietly, hoping the military honorific would soften any incoming healing processes.

"Enlil, or whatever your name is," said Longinus stepping around Pilate and facing the old man, "thank you for freeing us from whatever nightmares this place held in store. Let's get out of here."

"Indeed," said Enlil nodding to all of them. "If we are going to get out of here, we are going to need some help. Follow me." He turned and hobbled away into the sea of stone slabs.

Pilate groaned as the others stood up. It was that peculiar groan when someone thinks it may be lunchtime but is only just 10:30 and there was no more coffee. He looked balefully at the others and slouched after the old man.

Longinus turned to Erik. "Well, here we go. This should be interesting."

The four companions followed Pilate into the endless array of sleeping bodies on a ship far beyond the depth of their understanding.

Chapter 17: One for the Road

Nicholas awakened. It was the kind of sudden thrust into consciousness that is invariably followed by asking oneself *what happened last night?* He was in his room at Mirthmyst Castle and Claire was sleeping soundly beside him.

Ahh. He thought. *Right.*

Any other time he would have smiled at the memory of a spectacular evening and morning but something else had awakened him. He felt instinctively around his neck to the iron spike. It was cold as he expected. Confused as to why his heart was pounding, he quickly scanned the room but saw nothing unusual. A bright sliver of late afternoon sun streamed in through slightly opened curtains. There were no unusual sounds except the soft breathing of Claire sleeping beside him.

The little gold Valkyrie Claire had created the night before suddenly landed on his lap. If Nicholas were a cat, he would have hit the ceiling claws first. Instead, his heart decided to stop for a microsecond. The tiny figurine was gesturing frantically as if it were in some sort of panic. Although she was incapable of making any sounds, Kara made up for this by jumping up and down and pointing energetically towards the door.

"What is it Kara?" Said Nicholas quietly.

The Valkyrie continued to point in the direction of the door. Then she started to pull the covers off the bed, which was surprising considering the creature had the approximate mass of a salt shaker.

Nicholas slid from the bed softly, careful not to wake Claire and followed the Valkyrie to his door. She was flying around his head now, pointing a needle-like spear at the door and beckoning him to open it. Curious about the strange panic of his little companion, Nicholas decided to obey.

He put on his robes and gently pulled a blanket up to cover Claire . She smiled softly in her sleep as Nicholas touched her cheek with his hand but did not waken. He returned to the door and opened it, venturing forth into the Castle with the fluttering gold Valkyrie near his shoulder. The Castle was quiet and there seemed to be no one around.

Although the citizens of Abanis do not require the same amount of sleep as humans, they do enjoy rest after a long periods of celebration. Most of the emissaries returning to city for the Jolly celebrations were probably awake for two or three weeks prior to the festival. For this reason, the day following Jolly has always been decidedly quiet within the great sphere.

Nicholas listened carefully. He thought he could hear the famously, earth-shaking snores of Himtall in some other part of the Castle. Despite the eerie calm, there seemed little else to give credibility to a feeling of dread Nicholas felt as he walked down the hallway.

Dread was a strange emotion to Nicholas. Having been sheltered in Abanis for his entire life, the great sphere under the Antarctic was not unlike a paradise compared to the outside world. There was no discord, disease, and hardly anyone died unless it was their time to be ushered.

Kara flew down the hallway a short ways and pointed to a window. She did some aerial acrobatics in front of it as Nicholas approached. He looked outside and immediately noticed something peculiar about the light of the day. It was not the bright, golden afternoon light or the overcast, grey light of a rainy day. It was somehow *less* light outside. He looked across the vast, rolling plains off the southern edge of the Castle and spotted something rather strange. Some animals, deer in particular, were running this way and that as if in a state of confusion or panic. He never saw such a thing before. He stared at the stags and fawns as they galloped about, in no apparent direction, darting in and out of forested areas.

Then he looked up into the sky and caught his breath. The sun was indeed shining today but it was black. Nicholas looked away quickly and realized it was an eclipse of some sort. He learned of such celestial rarities in his studies but never in his life did he see one. Certainly not in Abanis. The great sphere, built by The Pilgrim was like a miniature version of the Earth, or so he recalled from his lessons. He knew the celestial network of the sun, moon, planets and stars were exact replicas, despite being wrought in some artificial manner. But a lunar eclipse was something he *knew* never happened. It couldn't happen. At least not within the sphere.

He chanced another glimpse at the sun and looked away, fearful it would damage his eyes. He realized the sun wasn't eclipsed as he first thought. It was blotched with black patches, as if it were somehow infected with darkness.

Nicholas listened to the Castle once more and realized there were voices coming from outside. Turning to look out the window at a different angle, he noticed some emissaries far off near the city pointing to the sky and talking with one another in groups. Some were standing in groups on grassy knolls and pointing to the sun.

Nicholas wasn't about to stand there and be dumbfounded. He knew more important people than himself would want to know about this if they didn't know already. He decided to try something that he hadn't realized was possible until a few days ago.

He closed his eyes and concentrated. *Pantilius? Professor, can you hear me?*

Nicholas reached out with his mind and waited. There was no immediate response so he repeated himself.

Professor? Are you there? Can you hear me?

No answer and then…

Yes Nick. I can hear you. We are aware of the situation. In all his life, he never knew Pantilius was capable of worrying about anything. But Nicholas sensed the professor was worried. And that worried him.

Nick, come to the Learningarten at once. Quickly, grab your birthday gifts and come now.

Nicholas left the window and went back to his room. Claire was still sleeping but she woke when he entered.

"Nicholas, come here." She smiled at him but it quickly faded when she saw the expression on his face. "What's wrong?" She sat up slightly and looked about the room.

"I don't know Claire. Something is wrong with the sun." He gestured to his window. "And now Pantilius wants me to grab my things and meet him in the Learningarten."

Claire jumped up quickly and looked at Nicholas. "He asked you to grab your things? He said those words exactly?"

Nicholas nodded.

Claire looked into Nicholas' eyes for a second then closed her own. A few moments later she opened them and tried unsuccessfully to conceal her concern. "Fuzzy is there and he wants me to come too. Quickly, Nick get your things."

She jumped out of bed and grabbed her robes and put them on while Nicholas scrambled to grab his possessions. He paused and looked around. What was he supposed to do? Bring his entire room down to the Learningarten?

Claire noticed Nicholas' hesitation and climbed over the bed as Nicholas was trying to squeeze his entire bookshelf into a leather back pack.

"No Nick," She smiled at him, "just the essentials. The gifts you received last night were not just birthday gifts, they were meant for you to use as an apprentice. Take them and leave everything else."

Nicholas nodded. He tried to appear calm but his eyes betrayed him. In addition, he was suffering from the inevitable after-effects of overindulging in mead the night before.

Claire spotted the panic in his eyes as she put her crimson robe on. She put her hands on his cheeks and kissed him tenderly. The leather sack dropped out of his hands and hit the wooden floor with a *thunk*.

Claire looked closely at him. "It's ok Nick. There are some truths you haven't learned yet. Don't worry. Nothing bad is going to happen." She patted his cheek and turned to grab her own backpack.

After a few minutes, they left Nicholas' room and headed down the staircases to the Learningarten. In the hallway, Nicholas was afraid the sunflowers would spray them both but he saw the door was open and there were people talking in hushed voices within.

"He must leave my old friend. I have seen it. The fallen Huru wants him for his hu – " Aryu Veda stopped as Nicholas entered the room.

Claire stepped in behind Nicholas. Aryu, Himtall, Mrs. Bakersbee, Gabriel and Pantilius were talking near the old professors desk. Harry, Buddy and Fuzzy were nearby but staying out of the conversation.

"Nicholas, come here lad." Said Harry softly.

"Claire, come m'dear," said Fuzzy. He smiled at Nicholas as she walked over. He looked at Claire and then looked to Nicholas again. His smile went wooden for a moment. Looking away, he coughed and grimaced at Buddy, who was beaming at the young couple.

"Ah. To be young once more and -oomph!" Buddy started to say but Harry elbowed him in the ribs. As one, the three pilgrims grinned at Claire who blushed and said nothing.

The others finished their hushed conversation and turned to them.

Pantilius walked over to Nicholas and to everyone's surprise, his eyes were slightly moist despite his famous grin making a triumphant reappearance.

"Nicholas. You are to become *my* apprentice this day but something is occurring in Abanis we are unsure of. For now, I want you to leave with Gabriel. He is going to take you from here."

"What is happening professor?" Nicholas' heart was beating with anticipation and fear.

Before the old professor could answer, Aryu Veda intervened.

"Claire, you must return to Britannia with Fuzzy at once. Robin and some others flowed there already. Fuzzy will watch over you both until such a time the great sphere is safe."

Claire and Nicholas glanced at each other. She touched his hand.

Pantilius noticed the exchange and stepped closer to the two, looking at each of them in turn.

"All in due time." He said quietly. Then looked at Claire. "He must not be near any of us. Please understand."

For a moment Nicholas suspected Pantilius was telling Claire something with his mind.

"Yes professor." She nodded and said nothing further but now held Nicholas' hand tightly. Her eyes were watering but her face was impassive.

Nicholas' frustration at knowing little of what was going on forced him to interrupt Gabriel who was talking to Harry now about gathering other apprentices and retreating to the Mediterranean.

"Professor!" He said loudly.

Everyone stopped and looked at Nicholas.

He didn't mean to shout but his panic and dread hit a boiling point when he saw tears in Claire's eyes.

"I'm sorry. I didn't mean to…. I just don't know what is going – "

Pantilius stepped closer to Nicholas and looked up at him. He smiled and patted the iron hoop on Nicholas chest with a wrinkled, blue skinned hand.

"It 's ok Nick. It's ok." He continued to pat Nicholas chest reassuringly. "I'm going to let you in on a little bit of truth."

"Harry lost his apprentice, Nicholas. His name was Peter. The one who was ushered yesterday. He died defending the beliefs of the most powerful citizen to ever come from this city."

Nicholas knew Pantilius was talking about the Nazarene and nodded silently.

"The Nazarene," continued Pantilius, "or The Pilgrim have set something in motion that we must follow to the end despite our inability to understand it." He paced in front of Nicholas with his hands behind his back as his brow furrowed. "The Nazarene discovered there was a link between apprentices and their teachers. You are my apprentice now and the link between us is almost living thing. In the same way, some of us who are older than you can imagine, are linked to the sphere of Abanis. The strongest, of course, is the link between Abanis and its creator."

"This place," Nicholas paused for a moment to consider what Pantilius was telling him, "is alive?"

"Yes." Said Aryu Veda. "The great sphere is a living thing Nicholas. The Pilgrim is linked to it. Consequently, what happens to him out there," he gestured vaguely above his head, "has been known to manifest here. Some of us are aware of its condition more so than others. In the same way that teachers and their apprentices are linked, so is The Pilgrim linked to this paradise he built for us."

Mrs. Bakersbee, Himtall and Gabriel nodded.

"Then why is the sun black?" Nicholas asked, looking at all of them in turn and realizing the answer wasn't one he wished to hear.

"Because," said Pantilius softly. "wherever he is, The Pilgrim is dying. And so is Abanis."

The Learningarten was silent for a brief time as Claire and Nicholas absorbed the enormity of the words.

"Nicholas." Said Pantilius. "You must leave with Gabriel as soon as possible. We will meet again soon. I promise."

Nicholas nodded and tried to smile at his old patron.

"Mrs. Bakersbee," Pantilius said, turning to the ageless, spherical woman. "Gather the children and meet us in front of the Castle. We are going on vacation. Somewhere tropical." He grinned at her as she nodded and hurried to the side entrance leading to the kitchens.

"Come now." Said Gabriel as everyone began to file out of the Learningarten. "We must make haste."

Nicholas held Claire's hand tightly as they made their way through the Castle. He tried to remember every detail of their brief time together. She held his hand tightly in return, silently conveying to him that their fast approaching separation was inevitable.

As they reached the Castle's foyer the building was suddenly struck with something that must have been huge. Everyone lost their balance as the very foundations shook.

"It's worse than we thought brothers." Said Pantilius, pulling a blue cloak off a nearby wall and heading quickly out of the Castle entrance.

Pantilius ran outside and looked up into the sky. His eyes went wide for a second and he suddenly raised his hands. He stood concentrating on something above the Castle for a few moments and grimaced.

Nicholas and the others came out of the castle behind him. Claire looked up suddenly screamed in terror. A gigantic slab of ice, forty feet long and several meters thick, was plummeting to the ground and about to crush the very spot where Pantilius stood. Without thinking, Nicholas made to run out to the professor but Gabriel held him back.

"Professor! No!" He yelled from within the iron grip of Gabriel's hands.

Pantilius looked up and raised his hand. Just as the ice sheet approached and darkened the spot where the tiny professor stood, it exploded into a giant cloud of yellow, black and orange specs. Pantilius was lost in the cloud. Like a billowing wave with a mind of its own, a swarming cloud of a million butterflies swept up from the spot and followed thermals towards the city. Pantilius emerged from it smiling at them as the butterflies dispersed.

Claire and Nicholas stood gaping at Pantilius as he walked briskly back to them.

"All in the wrist, lad. Chin up, now." He patted Nicholas on the elbow and walked past him to speak quietly to Aryu Veda.

Nicholas felt Gabriel's hand release him. He looked at the spot where the ice sheet should have flattened a large area of the castle courtyard.

He looked at Claire, who returned his awestruck expression.

"Wow." Was all she could manage, shaking her head in disbelief.

Nicholas looked up into the sky and saw more and more pieces of the sky falling towards distant lands. He looked towards the city as sounds of crashes and screams echoed through the pine groves. He could see smoke rising from it and went to head in that direction with Claire in tow.

"No!" Shouted Pantilius as he turned from Aryu Veda. "Do what I have told you. Go with Gabriel."

"But Professor, I won't leave you here with – " Started Nicholas.

"It's ok," Pantilius chanced a wink at him. "We can take care of ourselves. Right now, you must leave and do it now. Go!"

Claire pulled Nicholas hand towards Gabriel, who was now heading towards the pine grove and beckoning for them to follow. “Come on Nicholas, he is right.” She said.

"One moment, brother." Said Aryu Veda quietly.

Standing in the Castle entrance, Aryu closed his eyes in concentration. His lips were moving but Nicholas couldn’t hear anything. Finally, he heard Aryu’s voice in his mind and knew every soul in Abanis could hear it as well.

Brothers and Sisters. The great sphere is compromised. Please leave at once. Go to your assigned retreats in the world without and await The Pilgrim’s return. Blessed are the meek. Keep yourselves safe.

And as soon as the message ended, Aryu opened his eyes and stepped towards Nicholas. Sweat beaded on his bald head he appeared to be fatigued by the announcement. He ripped something from his chest and thrust it in Nicholas’ hands. “Take it and keep it safe.” He said, not unkindly. “Go now brother.”

Nicholas didn’t look at it but thrust the object into his pocket and nodded. Claire was pulling Nicholas hand and Gabriel was shouting for them to follow him.

"This is my home!" Shouted Nicholas. It sounded silly, childish and trivial but he didn't know what else to say.

Himtall eclipsed the afternoon sun and leaned down to Nicholas. His giant, blond beard bristled with encouragement. "The whole world is your home, Nicholas." He nodded encouragingly. "The whole world. Never forget that."

With one last look at Mirthmyst and the people he had come to love dearly, Nicholas turned and raced with Claire in hand along the pine groves towards the city. Gabriel was jogging ahead of them, taking gigantic strides with his black and white striped hair flowing out behind him. Harry, Buddy and Fuzzy, were with them too. For three old men, Nicholas was mildly surprised they sprinted quite easily beside them.

They reached the city and found citizens of all vocations jumping into pools, ponds, fountains and any other surface of water to flow away from Abanis. Several buildings were already destroyed by falling debris and Nicholas glanced up to see the sun was darker than before. Black spots covered more of its surface and debris could be seen falling from the heavens to various regions around the great sphere.

Gabriel looked around and spotted a pond near the pine grove exit and headed for it.

As they reached the edge, he turned. "Claire. Flow now." He said.

Claire looked at Nicholas and he saw fear in her eyes for the first time. It was now Nicholas' time to comfort her.

"I will find you. I promise." He smiled and kissed her as tears ran down her face.

"Come dear! Now!" Fuzzy was beside Gabriel beckoning her over. With one last look at Nicholas she turned and ran past Fuzzy. She leapt into the pond and vanished as soon as she hit the water.

Fuzzy turned to Nicholas after he was certain Claire was safe. Harry and Buddy stood on either side of him.

Nicholas was also on the verge of tears but he was determined to be strong on the first day of his apprenticeship.

They each put a hand on his shoulders. "You'll be fine with Gabriel lad." Said Harry. "I'm going to Greece."

"And I will join my ancestors people in the middle kingdoms," said Buddy.

"Already you know I will go to Britannia with Claire," said Fuzzy, "to meet Robin and some others apprentices. She'll be fine Nicholas."

"Thank you. I will – " Nicholas couldn't finish but looked at them.

"Brothers!" Shouted Gabriel as a slab of ice the size of a building crushed an actual building some distance from them.

As one, they pushed Nicholas towards the pool. Gabriel grabbed Nicholas shoulders and looked at him.

"Nicholas, you have never flowed as a man but you did as a child. You are a natural."

Nicholas looked at the pool and then to Gabriel. "But Gabriel, I – " he started but Gabriel cut him off.

"No time. Listen. It is the way we travel about the world. Water is the source. It can be used as a conduit. I am going to give you a push and your instincts will lead you the rest of the way. Do you understand?"

Nicholas nodded uncertainly.

"Good, did Aryu give you something?"

"Yes, I have it right – " Nicholas started to pull the object from his pocket but Gabriel stopped him.

"No, it is for your safekeeping. It is a device you'll learn to use eventually but not at this moment."

"Yes Gabriel." Was all Nicholas could say.

"Good, close your eyes. When I say go, you must jump into this pond and flow. I will give you the needed push to start. You must go to north and then west. Picture a small island alone in the great ocean. It is triangular with lush, green fauna and a small volcano near it's center. You will not miss it for I am pushing you near it. Imagine it in your mind. Keep focused. Go there."

Nicholas nodded again but looked at the pool with fear. He heard of flowing but was told he would learn the way of using it after studying as an apprentice for a short time.

"Do not be afraid." Gabriel said, guessing Nicholas thoughts precisely. "Just find the island. It is alone in the great ocean. Are you ready?"

Nicholas looked at his elders and tried to smile. Before he could answer, Gabriel shouted something in a language he didn't recognized and pushed Nicholas into the pond. As he hit the surface of the water, everything went white for a brief instant and then all was dark.

*Jingle*Jingle*Jingle*

Gabriel turned to look around the city of Abanis and his eyes flared bright blue. After making sure Harry, Buddy and

Fuzzy were safely away, he headed towards the Gate Pool entrance. While keeping an eye on his surroundings to avoid any falling debris, he pulled the golden trumpet from his side and blew it. The trumpet blast echoed for miles around, signaling to any nearby citizens that they should leave the great sphere immediately if they hadn't already done so. Nothing stirred in light of his warning. He whispered to Pantilius and the others in his mind as he crossed the abandoned city plaza.

Good. They are safely away. He thought.

As he marched towards the double doors leading to the Chamber of the Gate Pool, he ripped his dark blue robes from his body with one hand. Walking naked across the plaza towards he looked around and listened carefully. The city was quiet except for the sounds of falling slabs of ice hitting it from the heavens above. No one responded to his trumpet blast and he guessed the great sphere had been evacuated quickly.

Gabriel reached the entrance doors to the gate pool and paused. He sniffed, recognizing something familiar in the air. His eyes flared in anger once more. Grabbing the handles, he ripped the doors off their metal hinges and threw them half way across the courtyard behind him. They crashed into the cobblestones where less than a day earlier, people were celebrating Jolly festivities. His enormous strength and temper was now unchecked. Rage compelled him to seek out the manner in which his beloved realm was crumbling. And he suspected he knew exactly where the source was.

He descended down the wide staircase to the bottom and saw the door to the Gate Pool chamber was broken and hanging off its hinges. It was as if something had smote it from within. The door was covered with blood and a guardian lay near it, just inside.

He hastened to the body of one of his pupils and roared in sadness. He passed a hand over the vacant, open eyes of the man and closed them. Standing once more, he looked about the cavernous chamber. He saw three other guardians strewn about the room. They were torn and hacked to pieces. Their silver armor was covered in blood which stained the icy floor about them. All were killed by something with the strength equal to his own.

As he inspected the dead guardians, small horns appeared on Gabriel's brow. They broke through his skin and sent tiny trails of blood down his cheeks. Spiked scales erupted from his shoulders as he stood and walked towards the Gate Pool.

There were three more figures lying around the pool but they were not garbed in guardian attire. They were robed in the simple manner of acolytes. Steam rose from him and as he sniffed the air and looked around. Spikes of bone and cartilage erupted from his back now as he drew closer to the gate pool. His size seemed to increase commensurately with his rising anger.

As he came closer to the pool, he was able to see the younglings were covered in blood and quite still. He recognized the acolytes belonging to the weathermen faction, not from Mirthmyst.

Gabriel frowned and his nostrils steamed as he sniffed again. There was something familiar in the air, a scent which pulled at his thoughts. He looked around the cavern once more as if to remember something.

He looked down at the fallen men once more. Each had an arm outstretched and submerged in the glimmering pool but why and how, he could not guess. The gate pool was only *one way*. Opening it from within Abanis would take incredible strength of will and knowledge of the peculiar engineering of The Pilgrim. He did not know any being as powerful and as old as...Gabriel froze.

He recognized the familiar scent.

"Good. You are angry." Said a voice from the darkness beyond the pool's light. "Why not let your glorious form come forth. Why do you wear that disgusting meat sack for clothing?"

Gabriel's eyes opened wide. Despite his shock, he continued to grow in size. His skin was stretching and ripping as if it were being shed. Bloody lines streaked down his body to the floor where it pooled at his feet. He continued to stare in amazement at a dark robed figure just beyond the pool's light.

The Greyman swung his scythe about as he emerged from the shadows. Using it as a walking stick, he jammed it into in the ice-hewn floor, cracking it slightly as he stepped around the pool's edge. He glared at Gabriel with the face of Pontius Pilate beneath a black cowl. His black robes, tattered and worn, were streaked with blood. Gabriel envisioned this man gleefully hacking his guardians to death. His olive skin and handsome features were those of Pontius Pilate but the eyes were unmistakable. They were black, fathomless and completely opaque with no iris' or pupils. They were quite similar to Gabriel's own azure eyes and he could see himself transforming within them.

"I would ask you the same." Said Gabriel, still shocked and beginning to back away.

As The Greyman approached the pool, he looked down and caressed his chin as he admired his own reflection.

"I do so like what this little oasis does for my complexion." Then he looked at Gabriel. "Out there, I am but bones and sinew to the apes running about but here," he grinned, "I look marvelous!" He put his hands on his hips and struck a pose.

Talon-tipped claws ripped through tendon laced fragments of skin and flesh on each of Gabriel's hands. His face was completely covered in blood now as skin cracked and his head slowly elongated. His teeth lengthened and new horns sprouted from his brow. They began to curl around lengthening ears, growing pointedly outward from the side of his head.

"I'm rather impressed my brother was able to make this sanctuary come to fruition." The Greyman said casually as he tapped the ice with the end of the scythe. He looked around the cavern and nodded approvingly. "It appears he followed my designs to the letter. Is he here? Or has he sent his lap dog to greet me?" He looked around the cavern expectantly.

"Traitor." Snarled Gabriel. "I have bested you before and brought you to justice. The Pilgrim tends to his flock above us." Gabriel lied. His voice was deep and harsh now and he stepped slyly back into the shadows as his body further enlarged.

"You only did so after I was blown half way round the world and lying in a state of twilight and misery." Said the Greyman sharply. "Our home was destroyed and my body was broken. It took me centuries to recover."

"How did you escape?" Grumbled Gabriel.

"Escape? Oh, I escaped that prison my brother built the moment he underestimated me." He nodded as if Gabriel knew what he was about to say next. "I became it's warden. And made it a prison for thousands of others. But I am disappointed that you, little whelpling, betrayed me. That, I did not expect."

"I am as you made me. Father." Said Gabriel, hatred and anger forcing his body to transform further.

The Greyman continued to step around the large pool and leered into the shadows.

"Aww, such a good boy you are to acknowledge me as such. Maybe we can call the emissaries back for milk and cookies with the maggot, Pantilius. Tell me, does he still live?" He asked, tilting his head and nodding with theatrical concern.

"Master Pantilius is alive, no thanks to your efforts to betray and enslave his people. If they still live at all." Said Gabriel, his silhouetted form growing immense in the shadows. "And he is far more powerful now. His age is unmatched in Abanis, besides The Pilgrim himself. Or have you forgotten?"

"Not older than I, I'm afraid." Said the Greyman flatly. "Ahh, but of course," he continued, pursing his lips and looking skyward as if to remember something. "He would have become the leader of our little playthings when his brother vanished. Quite a court jester his brother was to me."

"They were your friends. They were your creations!" Gabriel snarled from the darkness. "And you betrayed them. Your selfish arrogance not only risked the human race but nearly destroyed us all."

"Friendship." The Greyman snorted and chuckled. "What does that have to do with the price of feet?" He paused and stared into the shadows. "I was trying to save us!" He screamed and spat suddenly.

Then, regaining his composure, he frowned at Gabriel's silhouette as if he was scolding a child. "And you didn't punish Pantilius for his part." He shook a finger in Gabriel's direction. "Naughty boy. I'm guessing my brother found him up north and gave him a chance to prove his worth to the primates above us, hmm?"

"Enough!" Roared Gabriel. His voice sounded like gravel rolling off a cliff. "You opened the gate. You fed him lies and false promises. And for what?!? Mother is dead and gone, along with our island home and all of its people. You betrayed the promises made to your makers. Your crimes are unforgivable!"

"I would have done anything for her." Said the Greyman flatly. "The risk to Adamis was nothing to me because my brethren worshiped them, the suckling beasts above us. The humans of this time are cannibals who feast on each other's misfortunes. They do not deserve this paradise!" The Greyman screamed again. "Why do they deserve such and we, the Huru, do not? They made us to survive! They made us to rule, you simple minded whelp! Pantilius and his Nelfilem maggots were not. They were a mistake! Rule or go home! Those were my only options."

"You are still blinded by arrogance. I never understood it father but you will not interfere anymore. As for Pantilius," Gabriel paused, "he would give his life for any human. His loyalty to our cause was never in question. He is far more Huru than you could ever be!"

"I grow tired of this old argument." The Greyman sighed. "I shall put that theory to the test. I will flay Pantilius alive before his cherished primates and see if he wishes to pick one to die for." He inspected his fingernails and sucked his teeth as he looked down at the dead emissaries. "As for you, my son – "

But he didn't have time to finish the sentence.

Gabriel jumped from the shadows and landed less than ten feet from The Greyman. Great leathery wings unfolded from his back and buffeted the area around the pool. During the brief conversation Gabriel had transformed into dragon. The icy floor shattered beneath his giant talons and his tail cracked the air as it whipped around behind him. His red, scaled body was fifty feet in length and sparkled in the sapphire light of the cavern. A river of fire exploded from his mouth and engulfed The Greyman as he landed.

Gabriel roared and found his unleashed rage a delicious freedom that he yearned for these many years. Ice melted around the spot where The Greyman stood. The ceiling of the cavern shook causing slabs of ice and rock to fall crashing to the floor as he breathed deeply for another blast.

Yet, The Greyman was untouched by the flames and held the scythe before him amidst the fire.

"The blood of my nephew protects me, my son. And now," he drew the scythe back and sneered as Gabriel let forth another wave of fire, "I shall have to punish you, boy."

Chapter 18: Welcoming Goodbyes

Pontius Pilate and the others stopped behind Enlil. The old man staggered and fell to one knee.

"Sir!" Erik came running forward to help Enlil who rose unsteadily to his feet. "We have been walking for hours. Do you require rest?"

"I am fine, thank you lad." Enlil whispered. He sighed and looked at the others. "Come, it is not much farther."

The old man had lead them deep into the ship or far, they could not tell. It was difficult to tell time or distance in this place because it appeared to be endlessly similar.

They continued onward. After what seemed like a few more hours of walking, they came to a wall. Or at least that's what the others perceived it to be. A wall generally requires there to be a floor or a ceiling which makes it appear to be or have 'wallness'. But this was not really the case. It appeared that the floor and the endless array of sleeping figures on stone slabs around them simply came to an end. There was no more floor and there were no more stone slabs. There was simply an impenetrable blackness before them. It was as if the designer of this madness hit the age of sixteen, went *gothic*, and decided everything was going to be black here on out.

The old man turned to look at his companions and frowned. Then he looked back at the blackness and started mumbling to himself. He tried to walk into it but was repelled by some unseen force and staggered back. He pointed his staff at it, mumbled something but nothing happened. After a while, he looked back at the companions and gestured for everyone to gather around.

"OK. We have, as you might have guessed, come to an impasse." Enlil said roughly. He jerked a thumb over his shoulder at the wall. "Any of you take a guess what that is?"

Erik looked at the blackness as if there might be something different about it than a moment before. "Not really. There seems to be nothing there."

"Precisely." Said the old man, his eyes twinkling madly. "But I know, there is more there than simply nothing. In fact, I'm one hundred percent sure there's a whole lot of something beyond it."

"Is it a special part of this...prison or something?" Cassie said looking around behind them.

"Oh yes." Said Enlil, nodding to her. "Very special. The beings beyond this spot are our allies."

Longinus looked, over the old man's shoulder at the wall of blackness and raised an eyebrow. Then he looked back at Enlil. "Say that again, gov'ner? What is beyond the wall?"

Enlil looked at him and frowned. "Allies, young man. Allies. They are beyond the blackness. Trapped in some clever nightmare I suspect."

Longinus looked at the wall as the others kept staring at Enlil.

"Uh," Longinus paused, looking back to the old man. "Allies. OK. Tell me about them. Who are these allies?"

"Oh, they are ancient creatures to you. Friends of mine, they were, so very long ago."

Longinus glanced over the old man's shoulder again and nodded. "Ancient friends. OK good." He said. "And, uh, can you describe them to me? Who are they and where to they come from?"

Enlil sighed and looked into some middle distance as he tried to recall something. "They are my kin. Small creatures, they were. Some treated them poorly because they were considered aberrations from a failed experiment. But I did not see them as such for they are very special creatures. Nelfilem they were called. And they were our friends."

Longinus looked over the old man's shoulder and grinned slightly. "Uh, Enlil - " But he was interrupted by the old man.

"Not now, young man. Now, this seemingly impenetrable wall might be opened by a variety of clever strategies....

"Uh, Enlil, I think you - "

But the old man was lost in deep consideration. "We may have to split up and look for key markers on the floor, yes that may be it."

Erik and Aurelia looked over the old man's shoulder now and gaped.

"Umm, Enlil. You may want to - " Said Aurelia.

"Then at those key points we may have to hum a special chant to break the code of the blackness." Enlil continued, lost in deep problem solving mode. "Or perhaps there is an audible key code!" He continued. "Yes. That might work. The correct phrase may warp the barrier just enough to let us pass through and - "

"Enlil!" Shouted Longinus. "Were these allies shorter than humans, as dwarves, with pointy ears and mildly blue-tinted skin?"

The old man looked at Longinus with surprise. "My goodness, dear child how did you know th-" He stopped. Longinus was pointing behind him. He turned.

"Ahh." Said Enlil, looking at the scene spread before the companions. "It appears we simply needed to know what lay beyond the blackness to actually perceive it." Then he turned back to Longinus. "Well done young man. That was positively quantum."

Before them we're hundreds of tiny figures standing in formation like rows of legions. They were quite small compared to Longinus and Erik and wore simple white robes. Much like the companions, the tiny creatures appeared to emit an innate light so their proximity to one another illuminated the area brightly. Some were bald and aged, some were young and had long hair but each of them had an unusually large set of ears which pointed out of their heads rather comically. All of them were standing in some kind of hypnotic state and did not react as the companions came closer.

"My dear friends." Said Enlil as he stepped into the rows of figures and looked around. "It has been long since I have seen them. How cruel it was for the warden of this prison to enslave them. I suspected was responsible for their disappearance but never knew for sure until now."

"This is incredible." Said Erik, looking around at all of the figures. "Do they exist outside the Roman Empire? I have never seen or heard of their like before. Are they human?"

"Oh yes, they are the blood of humanity, no doubt Erikssen." Said Enlil, looking around at each of the figures as he stepped carefully through them. He stopped and touched the cheek of one unresponsive Nelfilem. "But they are, in some ways, more human than we are."

"They seem to be in some sort of trance." Said Pilate leaning down and looking closer in the face of one. "What must we do to help them Enlil?"

The old man looked up and around. "Ahh. Yes, we must find the leader. He is the key to unlocking them from this trance. I may be able to help him as I did you Pilate."

"There are so many and they are so cute!" Said Cassie looking around smiling. "Which one is the leader?"

"He will be marked by a brand on the palm of his hand. It is the mark of the warden." He said looking at each of the tiny figures. "Look for an eight-sided star."

Pilate looked up from the face of the Nelfilem he was examining and frowned. "The Symbol of Saturn? Are you sure?"

"Yes, my educated prefect." Said Enlil, sighing. "An eight-sided star was not originally the symbol of Saturn nor is the warden of this prison Saturn himself. But he would like you to think of him as such. I'm sure you understand that symbols, religions and dogma all get mumbled and jumbled in the fullness of time. Most of the world religions are simply re-mastered ideals of previous civilizations. It is the way of things."

Pilate nodded as he stepped through the tiny figures and looked for an eight-sided brand on their palms. He knew the Roman pantheon was adopted from Greek dogma and he was pretty sure the Greeks took theirs from elsewhere in turn. He never had much time for religion until now however. If Enlil was not a God of some sort, then Pilate was a fluffy, bunny rabbit.

"Found him! I think." Said Erik from some direction to his left.

The companions converged on Erik and the old man looked down excitedly at the figure whose hand he upheld. There was an eight-sided star branded into the flesh of the old Nelfilem's palm.

"Yes. That is him!" Enlil exclaimed. He dropped the white, birch wood staff and placed his hands on the side of the creature's face. "Hello again, Arkilius." He whispered.

The old Nelfilem was built sturdier and looked sterner than the others. He had huge, snowy eyebrows and long, braided white hair which fell over muscular shoulders. A bald head rose from the explosion of white locks so that the overall effect made him appear to be an enraged dandelion. His large, flat nose and round face might have been pleasant at some point but was now scarred and mildly misshapen. Longinus guessed that the creature had seen many battles but he could not fathom what kind of fights this small creature could uphold.

Enlil closed his eyes and put a second hand on the side of the old Nelfilem's head. "Arkilius. Awaken. We are in need of your help." He said.

A few moments passed and the milky white eyes of the old Nelfilem slowly began to change hue. The companions stepped closer, except Pilate, who had an instinctual urge to be at a safe distance when newcomers threatened to appear.

A few more moments passed. Enlil opened his eyes and stepped back. He looked down at the old Nelfilem expectantly.

The creatures lips moved slightly and it blinked. Then it's lips curled into an evil grin. "Pantilius! You bleeding heart, butterfly chaser!" It shouted in a voice that sounded like a seasoned sailor after too many whiskeys and not nearly enough coffees. He swayed and blinked at the five companions.

"Pantilius!" He shouted again. "You little whippersnapper! Where did you get off to? Get 'ur little pansy, blue-skinned butt in formation!"

Then, blinking again at the five companions, he swayed a little and fell flat on his face.

*Jingle*Jingle*Jingle*

After being pushed into the pond by Gabriel, Nicholas' universe went white and then black. Alone in deep water somewhere in the Pacific ocean, he and held his breath for a time and noted the water wasn't icy at all. In fact, despite a painful desire to breath, he felt rather comfortable. Unable to bear the pain in his lungs any longer, he coughed and could feel soft bubbles of spent air pass lazily over his head. He drew water into his lungs and began to panic but the sensation lessened as the last bubbles of air escaped his lungs. He breathed in a lungful of seawater and although this comforted his oxygen deprived system, it was a terribly strange sensation nonetheless.

Ok. I'm somewhere in the pacific ocean and I need to find a triangular island west of the southern continent with green grass and a volcano. Not a problem. He thought, the last sentence not entirely without sarcasm.

He recalled Gabriel's last words and wondered how he would go north and then west in this utter blackness. Even as he thought about his desired destination, he felt himself move.

Mildly elated at this movement, he thought about the island once more. He imagined an island with green grass on it and he moved again without even trying. He thought about the island once more and this time, he tried to imagine its shape with a small volcanic rise at the center. As anticipated, he began to move faster. In addition to the movement, he felt a strong current of water pushing against his left side, as if his movement were going against natural flows.

He recalled a lesson Pantilius taught him some years ago about the oceans and meteorology. Pantilius mentioned that ocean currents were like 'rivers within rivers'. He recognized at the time the old professor was talking about great currents under the surface. Judging by the push to his side, he was crossing one such current now and felt he heading in the right direction.

As Nicholas flowed onward, the target-island in his mind became clearer and more detailed. He could see vegetation, cliffs, and shores materialize in his mind's eye until finally the darkness yielded to a slightly brighter darkness. Eventually his surroundings turned into a rich variety of blues. He was startled to see a large sea creature with entirely too many teeth pass by so fast he could barely make out what it was. Rocks, coral and other sea life appeared and blurred under him as the water became more and more shallow. Sunlight filtered through the rapidly approaching surface and gleamed off colorful sea life as he rushed past them.

Finally, Nicholas exploded from the water. He plowed face first up a sandy beach and came to a stop at some brown-skinned feet. After coughing and sputtering the water from his lungs, he moaned in agony and wondered briefly if plowing the shore with his face was not entirely the way emissaries were supposed to stop flowing. Once he recovered and started breathing air again, he noted the tanned feet. After blinking at them for a moment, he realized they were attached to a person.

Nicholas looked up.

A man, whose body was covered with so many tattoos that it would make even the most enthusiastic tatoo artist shed a tear in appreciation, looked down at Nicholas. His mouth was open and eyes were bulging out of their sockets. Holding a fish in two hands and shaking slightly, Nicholas had the brief impression that the man's eyes were not unlike those of his recent catch, which also stared down at him with that mad panic that all fish have out of water.

Realizing it was highly unethical for a citizen of Abanis to appear to a human in such a way, Nicholas tried to grin up at the man. Before he could say anything, the man screamed, dropped the fish and ran away as fast as his legs could carry him. Nicholas watched him disappear over a small embankment and could hear the man's screams trail off into the distance.

"Hello." Said Nicholas grimly, and his head sank into the sand once more.

After a brief, mental check to make sure he was in one piece, he sat up and wiped sand off his soaked robes. Seeing the fish flapping on the shore beside him, he realized it too was probably trying to flee in terror. Nicholas picked it up, tossed the creature back into its home and looked around.

He was alone on a sandy, gravel strewn beach. A brisk wind chilled him as he stood up to get a better view. Lush, green grass sprawled across flat plains and rose near the center of the island to a seemingly extinct volcano. Despite its natural beauty and the first glimpse of the 'outside world' he had ever seen, Nicholas was surprised to find the island was not unlike tropical locales within Abanis. It was the sort of island that, in Pantilius' words, 'required fruity alcoholic drinks with little straw umbrellas' to truly appreciate the natural splendor.

Nicholas breathed deeply and listened to waves crashing into the shore. Clouds sprawled across the sky, highlighted golden yellow by a swift sunrise. The world outside Abanis was truly a beauty to behold and he barely noticed shivering in the cool wind on his wet robes. He looked up and down the shoreline and saw the beach extended as far as the eye could see. He suddenly recalled studying this island as part of his geography lessons and remembered Pantilius called it *Rongo-rongo.* He couldn't believe he was standing here now and breathing air as fresh as anything he breathed in Abanis.

Despite the morning sun warming the shoreline, Nicholas shivered and decided to pay attention to more human comforts. He took off his robes and after a brief, one-legged hop dance, freed one foot from his new boots. It came off suddenly, making a 'thook' sound. After placing his boots and robes on some rocks nearby to dry in the sun he checked his backpack to make sure everything wasn't wet.

He opened his backpack and before he could reach inside, a golden object buzzed out of it. Kara performed aerial dance around Nicholas as she looked up and down the shoreline. Satisfied the universe hadn't gone insane, she landed on Nicholas shoulder and saluted him smartly.

"Hello again," said Nicholas, patting the little figurine. "Looks like it's just you and I for now."

Nicholas was glad to have his companion more than ever. As he stared at the little Valkyrie, thoughts of Claire and Abanis threatened to cloud his mood but he was determined to remain positive. Whatever was happening, things would work out soon enough.

He checked his backpack and was relieved to find everything bone dry. Deciding it was as good a time as ever, he took out his new stag horn pipe and decided to try some smoke. The pipe box came with a little compartment of cherry leaf and the sweet fragrance was not completely lost on the wind as Nicholas packed the pipe.

Nicholas soon realized he didn't have a source of fire. He looked at his thumb and remembered how Gabriel and Pantilius lit their own pipes. Out of sheer curiosity, he flicked his thumb experimentally. Nothing happened. Although his thumb didn't catch fire, he mused that perhaps this was not a bad thing.

Nicholas frowned and looked inside the pipe box again. Just under the fabric, barely noticeable against the wood, was a single piece of flint stone and Nicholas smiled to himself. Gabriel certainly thought of everything.

After a while, Nicholas was enjoying a smoke of cherry leaf in the morning sun and thoughts of his friends came back to him like a speeding storm cloud. He wondered when Gabriel would come exactly. He was under the impression that he was to wait just a short while for Gabriel but sensed something was wrong. To make matters more worrisome, he was beginning to feel hungry and all attempts to contact Pantilius with his mind were met with emptiness.

He looked into the water again and found the fish he tossed there had died. Realizing there was dry, drift wood on the beach nearby, fresh meat and source of fire, Nicholas decided to put them all together and make some lunch.

For fifty years, Nicholas learned a plethora of subjects in Abanis. One of the things he learned was how to survive in the wilderness. After all, Mrs. Bakersbee's legions didn't do deliveries thousands of miles from the south pole. Nor could they cater to emissaries out in the real world. Nicholas knew it was a harsh life so learning how to survive in primitive ways was essential for all potential emissaries.

He searched inside his backpack and rummaged through his survival equipment. After finding a small knife Pantilius had given him years before, he began to prepare lunch.

Sometime later, as the morning sun drew closer to noon, Nicholas found himself amply warm and full of barbequed fish. His robes dried quickly and he soon found them comfortable to put back on.

Deciding sun-sickness was not a good thing to catch on his first day outside of Abanis, he retreated to a shaded area under a shallow cliff and decided to take a rest. Using his backpack as a pillow, he leaned back, put his feet up on a rock and watched the waves crashing into the shore.

As Kara nestled into his shoulder and curled up to sleep, his thoughts drifted to Claire and Abanis. The damage it had sustained under mysterious circumstances was unlike anything he imagined could happen there. Where was The Pilgrim? How was he 'dying' and how could the citizens save him?

Despite all his worries and concerns over Abanis, his thoughts drifted inexorably to Claire and they way she looked at him before vanishing into the pond. It was love, fear, panic and resolute duty all rolled into one look. He remembered the night they shared together. He remembered kissing her and tried to let his thoughts drift into greener pastures as the sun warmed the shoreline and incoming waves…

Nicholas woke suddenly. Realizing he had drifted off to sleep, he looked around the beach and squinted in the afternoon light of the sun. Some sound had awakened him but he couldn't hear it now. He looked up and down the shoreline and then inland. There were no people he could see or any sounds out of the ordinary. The incoming waves were gentler now and the wind had died down. Kara woke as well and fluttered about in Nicholas' periphery as he continued to look around and listen.

There it was again. It was like a growl but it sounded like it was inside his head. He looked around quickly, thinking a beast of some sort had wandered into his vicinity. There were no prowling beasts he could see. Kara looked at Nicholas questioningly, and joined his scan of the beach.

Looking out at the incoming surf, Nicholas scanned the ocean for anything out of the ordinary. He noticed a dark patch far out in the water and squinted at it, thinking it was shadowed waves beginning to form.

Nicholas. Help me please.

As clear as if he were standing beside him, Nicholas heard Gabriel's voice in his mind. He stared at the surf once more and realized there was a large shape in the water.

Realizing something was wrong he started towards the water, pulling his robes and boots off.

Yes. It's me. Do not be afraid.

Nicholas dove into the water and swam against the incoming currents. It was not Gabriel but somehow he knew it was him. He loved the water and felt at ease in it as he took broad strokes far out into the surf. When he reached the dark shaped drifting towards the beach, he stopped and stared as a giant, talon-tipped claw reached out of the water. It pawed at the water in an effort to swim but the bulk of the body attached to the claw did not respond to its efforts.

Nicholas reached out with his mind. *Gabriel. Is that you?*

Yes, I am unable to return to a more suitable form. I am injured.

A large head broke the surface of the water. It's reptilian shape was horned and wet, red scales flashed in the sunlight.

It is I. Do not be afraid. Help me reach the beach brother.

A golden eye fixed on Nicholas' own as he tread water in front of the huge beast. Despite his mouth hanging open at a the fact this drowning dragon was Gabriel, Nicholas found his eyes lock in place. He was transfixed by the stare and suddenly envisioned himself dragging the enormous beast to shore. Besides the fact Nicholas was small in the vision, he was succeeding nonetheless. As soon as it came, the vision passed.

Without thinking, Nicholas grabbed the giant claw and, slinging it over his shoulder in the water, he began treading to shore.

Good. Said Gabriel in Nicholas' mind. *We are making headway. Humans are capable of much more than their senses allow them to believe. It is called inspiration. Remember what I have just shown you.*

Nicholas panted and struggled against the great bulk of Gabriel's body but sensed they were making progress. After a while, as they approached shallow waters, he found the struggle ease.

Well done brother. I can take it from here.

Nicholas could sense Gabriel's weakness in his own mind and it filled him with concern. The great claw slipped from his shoulder and plunged into the water beside him. His mouth fell open again as he turned to see Gabriel stand on all fours in the shallow water and begin to lumber uneasily towards shore. Nicholas had read about dragons by studying legends and folklore in Abanis. There were great, reptilian beasts in almost every culture but he had no idea they were real.

Nicholas noted Gabriel was injured. One of his wings was completely gone. It looked as though it was hacked off and the open wound bled, leaving a trail of crimson curling in the ebb and flow of the incoming waves. One side of Gabriel's face was lacerated and one of his horns was broken. An eye was grotesquely mutilated, leaving a pulpy mass where it had once been. Looking at his injured friend, a surge of sympathy and anger welled inside Nicholas. He felt helpless watching Gabriel move, bleeding as he did so from more wounds on his torso and tail. As he reached the shore, Gabriel collapsed sideways and his enormous body shook the ground under Nicholas' feet as it crashed onto the sand.

Nicholas stood in shock for a moment, not knowing what to do. He ran over and kneeled beside Gabriel, whose chest heaved in an effort to breath.

Wait a moment Nicholas. Stand back.

Nicholas obeyed and as he backed away, Gabriel's form seemed to shift and warp. The remaining wing and spiked tail shortened as talons retracted and claws became smaller. Horns retreated and scales vanished as Gabriel's face reformed to become recognizable once more. Gabriel's entire body continued to shift and morph until finally, the elder Nicholas had known all his life was lying naked and bleeding on the sand.

Kara flew past Nicholas with a large banana leaf and dragged it over the man's body. After a few trips, Kara had successfully covered the man with a green blanket of local fauna and returned to her spot on Nicholas' shoulder.

"Thank you little one." Gabriel coughed and spat blood on the ginger colored sand where it clotted and almost instantly. Nicholas grabbed his own robes and started towards Gabriel.

"No." Gabriel coughed and wheezed again. "No, warm yourself and put your robes on Nicholas. Do as I say."

Deciding not to protest, Nicholas put his robes back on and knelt beside Gabriel. His worry heightened as he took in all of the man's injuries once more.

"Gabriel what can I do, I wish to help you but I don't know – "

"Hush. It's ok Nicholas. Give me a moment." Gabriel closed his one good eye.

Seeing Gabriel as weak as he was made Nicholas ever more fearful of the path he could see manifesting in his future. He waited quietly and watched Gabriel's wounds close. Then his eye opened and looked at Nicholas once more.

"Inspiration. It is one of the first abilities most emissaries manifest in the open world." He said. "I know you have it because I felt it in you the day you brought me the wounded deer."

Nicholas nodded and began to speak but Gabriel cut him off.

"Do not concern yourself with me. Remember what I did to you out in the water. With practice and concentration, you can do it to humans. Remember that."

"The vision? Of dragging you to shore?"

Gabriel nodded. "In time, you will learn to force such feelings on others."

"I will remember Gabriel. I promise." Nicholas was amazed. Not that Gabriel was a dragon, that was beyond incredible. He was amazed that Gabriel felt obliged to be a mentor even now in his condition.

Nicholas stared at the partially closed wounds on Gabriel's face. They continued to seep blood but not as much as before. Gabriel's eye was not fully repaired either. It was as if he was born with a fleshy eye-patch at birth because skin had grown over where his eye should have been.

"Come. I have little time." Gabriel croaked as he beckoned Nicholas closer.

"Gabriel y-you're a d-dragon!" Exclaimed Nicholas, nearly incoherent as he stammered in amazement.

"There are few of us left. The blood of the Huru affects us all in different ways Nicholas. Know that."

He sighed and looked around the island. Satisfied they were alone, he looked back at Nicholas who sat quietly. "For me, the manifestation of my heritage was much more… physical."

Nicholas nodded. He knew that the citizens of Abanis were all human, in varying degrees but also carried the blood of Huru. Pantilius described the manifestation of such heritage like fingerprints on the soul, each one having a different design and make up.

"Can we go back to Abanis and repair the damage done there? Help you?"

Gabriel shook his head. "No. The Greyman has taken Abanis."

"The Greyman is there?!? But what of The Pilgrim? And Pantilius, surely he-"

"The Pilgrim may not be aware. And Pantilius has safely escaped with the inhabitants of Mirthmyst to some place I cannot see." Gabriel coughed again and his lips were stained with blood. "I battled him for several hours and barely escaped." He croaked. "He is more powerful than I and carries a strange scythe that protects him from physical harm. I do not understand it."

Gabriel moved a little to his left and pulled some driftwood closer so that he could lay his head on it. "Listen to me Nicholas. You must activate the pendant and watch it as you venture forth. Do you still have it?"

Nicholas remembered the strange pendant Aryu gave him. He reached inside his robes quickly, thinking it may have been lost on the journey. It was still there.

He pulled it out and looked at it. It was an seven sided pendant with onyx jewels set into a silvery metal frame. At the center was a strange looking, heptagonal diamond. It was flat and didn't sparkle. He turned it in the sun because two of the onyx jewels we're sparkling significantly brighter than the others. One was tinted blue and the other yellow.

"Good." Said Gabriel, seeing Nicholas ponder over the pendant. "This is a device, Nicholas. It is not a piece of jewelry. You must never lose it."

"This is all well and good," said Nicholas, pulling his eyes away from it, "but we have to get you somewhere safe so you can mend. Where is Aryu, I'm sure he –"

"No. Under no circumstances must you come into contact with others from Abanis Nicholas." He said sternly, sitting up a little and looking at Nicholas intently. "Not even Claire."

Nicholas went silent and bowed his head. The enormity of Gabriel's commands sank in as he absently turned the pendant over and over in his hands.

"I'm going to make this simple and clear Nicholas." Said Gabriel after a moment. "They Greyman wants you Nicholas. We, of the Huru are drawn to each other. If you are not in contact with us in any way he cannot find you."

"He wants me? But – "

"Listen." Said Gabriel sternly. "I know the reason why. I didn't see it before but I suspect Pantilius did. You are human."

Nicholas looked up and frowned at Gabriel. "Of course, we are all human to some degree but –"

"No, Nicholas." Gabriel cut him off again. "You are one hundred percent, pure-blooded human. Your mother was Aurelia Floren and your father was Erikssen Fisherman, a Roman officer. They escaped Jerusalem after the Nazarene was crucified. You were born in the Judean wilderness and sometime later, your parents vanished. Do not yield to false hope, though. We presume they were murdered by servants of The Greyman."

Nicholas was stunned. He stared at Gabriel for a time and tears welled in his eyes as he tried to grasp what he had just heard. He had never known about his parents, or where he came from. He was promised to learn of such things when he was ready but didn't expect to hear it now.

"Better to have missed a good father than to have a terrible one, lad." Gabriel patted his forearm and looked away.

"What do you mean I am human? How is it possible? Don't they age and die? Pantilius always said it was a great gift to humankind from the universe but I never understood his meaning."

"Yes. Nicholas, for some reason, you are manifesting the traits of the Hurum but you are not one of us by blood. Your body must have acclimated to our ways. You can flow. You can understand and respond to speech in the mind. You speak to toys." Gabriel indicated Kara on Nicholas shoulder.

Nicholas looked at the little golden statue standing on his shoulder. Kara pointed a thumb at Gabriel and nodded to Nicholas, as if to verify the truth of this.

"Do not let yourself believe that your home is not Abanis, however." Said Gabriel, wheezing more now. "You are one of us in any case."

"Why does The Greyman want me?"

Gabriel looked reluctant to continue. "The Greyman's true physical form is bound to a prison but he has learned how to escape without it. His consciousness has traversed an unimaginable distance from the prison to this world to find a host body. However, he can only inhabit those who have Huru heritage, like those of The Pilgrim's people, even if it is very small. When he does so, they wither quickly under his infection so he must change hosts frequently. Humans, however, do not wither as such but there is a catch. Humans can repel him for some inexplicable reason."

Nicholas shook his head. "I don't understand."

"Nor do I." Said Gabriel, shifting his weight and wincing in pain as he did so. "The Greyman is a kind of virus."

Nicholas didn't recognize the word exactly. "A…disease?"

"Yes but humanity repels him and they are not capable of hosting his mind unless they are Hurum. He can inflict bodily harm to them and whisper evils to them in dreams but he cannot possess them fully. He knows you are completely human yet manifesting the traits of our ancient people. That is why he wants you. I was able to get The Greyman to reveal to me his assumptions. He thinks with your body, his consciousness can survive indefinitely." Gabriel sighed. "In other words, being full human and still accessible, makes you the perfect host."

"So, The Greyman can't inhabit other humans but you think he may be able to control me because I'm able to manifest Hurum traits?"

Gabriel nodded. "He shouldn't be able to control you but we fear he may be able to because you're manifesting the traits of our people. You are 52 years old but have the body of a young man. You have stopped aging. This is an anomaly we haven't seen before. Only The Pilgrim could understand the full nature of it but I do not."

Nicholas nodded.

Gabriel winced and blood formed at his wounds once more which trickled down his chin. Nicholas dabbed the blood with the hem of his robe and listened to Gabriel intently.

"The body he infects now is failing." Gabriel continued. "He tricked the poor man and uses the body but it will disintegrate soon. Already he walks about the world in skeletal form. If he has you, he can live for millennia and you will cease to be."

"Pantilius knew didn't he."

Gabriel waved an arm absently. "Pantilius is far older than you might guess. I am guessing he did." He paused for a moment and continued. "He found me wounded and near death nearly seven thousand years ago but nursed me back to health with skills that only the very ancient of us possess. He was my teacher and a damn good one. Whatever he knew or suspected, Pantilius had good reasons to keep you misinformed all these years. He loves you dearly Nicholas, never doubt that."

Nicholas nodded. He felt mentally drained trying to absorb all that Gabriel was revealing.

"What do we do now?"

Gabriel looked up at Nicholas with one eye. It was a look Nicholas had seen before when someone was trying to convey bad news.

"I am broken Nicholas." Gabriel wheezed and his head laid back on the driftwood once more. He looked out across the ocean and his eye flashed in the setting sun. The sky was streaked with scarlet and mauve and the surf was picking up. Waves were crashing louder now and water crept closer to the two with every wave.

Nicholas realized what Gabriel was saying but he couldn't believe it and felt helpless.

"No! No Gabriel we must – "

"You must do what I say Nicholas. This vessel is broken and I would only be a burden to you. You must follow your instincts and keep hidden for now. I have means of keeping myself camouflaged in the outside world and as human, The Greyman cannot see you amidst the rest." Gabriel breathing was ragged and he closed his eye before continuing. "Pay attention to the pendant. If one of the jewels start to glow, you have learned something. Pantilius will figure out what to do about The Greyman and in time he will find you, have faith in that. Should you try to contact other Hurum now, you will only endanger yourself and any emissaries you come in contact with." Gabriel coughed and winced in pain again. "Do you understand?"

"Yes." Nicholas was unable to say anything else.

"Good. Now, there is something I need you to do for me."

"Anything Gabriel." Said Nicholas, sitting up and ready to go to North pole if he had to.

"It will help ease my pain." He said softly, his one eye barely able to open now.

"What do you want me to do brother?" Asked Nicholas, a feeling of dread creeping up on him.

"Put your hands on my forehead."

Nicholas started to do so but hesitated.

"It is ok lad, this will help with my pain."

Despite a feeling of uncertainty, Nicholas obeyed. He placed his left hand on Gabriel's forehead.

"Good." Gabriel closed his eye. "Now, close your eyes."

Nicholas obeyed and did not notice that several of the island natives had crept into their vicinity. They watched in fear from behind some trees some distance up the beach.

"Now imagine the most beautiful place you have ever seen in your life. Capture every detail. Every shadow. Every sound. Every color. Focus on it. Imagine you are there."

Nicholas kept his eyes closed and could only envision the fjords in Abanis. He pictured Claire's eyes and the way the morning sun shone on cresting waves far below rocky cliffs. He imagined the salty spray of sea water and the taste of her lips. He heard her laugh. He tasted rich fruit and watched fyreflies twinkle in a myriad of colors as they danced in the air above their heads.

Then a discord shocked his senses and he was brought out of his reverie. Something was wrong. He opened his eyes. His left hand was resting over thin air and Gabriel was gone.

Nicholas bowed his head and wept.

Chapter 19: Fish n' Chipped, To Go.

Nicholas remained kneeling on the beach for a long time. The sun had set and he watched the waves until it was too dark to see. After a while, he looked into the heavens. Despite his grief and loneliness, he could not help himself marveling at the beauty of the stars. They were innumerable and the skies in Abanis did not have such resplendent detail as the real thing. He noticed one cluster and recognized it from one of his astronomy classes.

He smiled slightly, remembering Pantilius was eating a muffin at the time of the lesson. At some point he threw crumbs over his head. Instead of showering everyone in the Learningarten, the crumbs scattered about the ceiling and began to sparkle in various clusters. He had called it a 'muffin map' and Nicholas suspected the old Professor made it up as he went along. He loved that about Pantilius. He could even make crumbs seem important.

Unbeknownst to Nicholas, a few island natives remained hiding behind a few trees some distance away. For several hours they watched Nicholas and whispered to each other.

Nicholas looked down at the banana leaves on the beach and his heart sank. Never before had he felt so sad and alone. He didn't understand where Gabriel had gone or where people go when they are ushered but it might as well be death. Ushered citizens of Abanis never return.

Nicholas didn't understand death or how it could be a 'gift', as Pantilius had said many times. He didn't like endings. He knew that he would never be able to talk to Gabriel again or here him laugh with Himtall. He wouldn't see him tending his flock in the far green pastures beyond the city of Abanis. He was gone forever and everything that was Gabriel, the Herald of Abanis, was over. He hated death and couldn't possibly understand how it was supposed to be a 'gift'.

Memories of Gabriel in Abanis crossed Nicholas' mind and his stomach ached. He choked back fresh tears as he tried to repress the images in his head. It hurt so bad and he wondered if all humans felt such pain of loss. The pain was an emptiness that seemed to feed off his memories and he nearly doubled over as he tried to control his emotions. It was a terrible feeling and only reminded him of his loneliness. Unable to relieve the ache in his chest at the loss of his friend and mentor, Nicholas sighed and decided to bear it. He would press on and do as he was told.

It was then he felt a hand tap his shoulder.

Nicholas spun around so fast he fell over in the sand and sprawled on his back. His heart pounded and he was surprised it hadn't leapt out of his chest and ran down the beach without him.

A woman stood looking at Nicholas with so much shock and fear in her eyes, she nearly dropped what she had been carrying. She was dark complexioned as were all of the native people of this part of the world. She trembled as Nicholas sat up to stare at her in disbelief.

Nicholas could hear men shout something in the darkness behind her. She turned and snapped something at them angrily. Satisfied they were quiet, she turned to look at Nicholas again.

She stepped closer and Nicholas could see she was middle aged. She carried a spear at the ready and a bundle of green leaves in the other hand. Lines of grey in her long, black hair and ample crow-feet around her eyes spoke volumes of information to Nicholas. He tried to think of what to do in this situation and recalled several sociology lessons. The woman's coral necklace and significant tattooing told Nicholas she was 'the boss' rather than 'just a kind woman offering a strange demon from the water some food'. He imagined they were a matriarchal tribe of some sort.

Nicholas realized that if the natives witnessed Gabriel's passing and draconic nature, he would probably be considered a dangerous enemy of some kind or worse, a God. Pantilius voice rang in his mind as another lesson was pulled from the archives of his memory: "If they think you're a god, it's time to act like lightning and bolt."

Nicholas laughed at the time but he was not laughing now. He was famished and grief had weakened his resolve to deal with this unexpected company. He looked around, fearful that Kara's presence might make the woman resort to the spear but his companion was nowhere to be seen.

The woman was very close now and she was looking at him strangely. It was sympathy and awe mixed into one look. Nicholas realized his face would be spotted with some of Gabriel's blood and streaked with dirt and tears. He sat up and started to wipe his face with his sleeve but the woman kneeled quickly and grabbed his hand.

"No." She said, and Nicholas recognized the word. Some male voices behind her shouted again. She turned and snapped angrily at them. "Away. Away."

She turned to Nicholas and the angry look was replaced by nervous sympathy. She dropped the spear and the bundle of leaves and knelt close to him. She grabbed one of her own locks of wizened hair and spat on it. Nicholas decided to sit still as she used it to wipe his face clean of blood and sand.

It was an uncomfortable moment. Nicholas remained still until the woman finished. Although he didn't realize it now, Nicholas would eventually understand that it was a tender, nurturing gesture. Only a woman would have the bravery to do such a thing to a creature such as he.

When she finished, she backed up and bowed to Nicholas, as if to be penitent. Nicholas immediately stopped her, realizing what she must think of him.

"No. Man." He said, pointing at his chest and grabbing her hand in an effort to raise her out of sublimation. Impersonating a God among humanity was only done by the Nazarene out of some desperate purpose. Nicholas knew it was forbidden to all others and wasn't about to break the rules on his first day out in the real world.

She looked at him and shook her head. "Water home." Then she pointed at the water. "Water God." She pointed at Nicholas.

Nicholas shook his head. Realizing he was going to lose this argument fast, he decided to use a different approach. One that could explain even the most shocking circumstances and events.

"Foreigner." He said pointing to himself.

Her eyebrows raised and she peered at him closer, grabbing his long, ragged blond hair. She smelled it. Then she put her hand on his chest and felt it for a moment. After feeling a heartbeat, she recoiled as if Nicholas was a beast.

"Man?" She said in disbelief.

"Foreigner. Man." Nicholas nodded and shrugged.

She wasn't convinced. She pointed to the banana leaves. "Friend. God?"

Nicholas hesitated. He wasn't sure how to explain Gabriel as a dragon to a person from Abanis much less a native of this island. He decided to go for broke.

"Pet." He said and looked away. "Pet died."

Some male voices shouted at them again from the darkness. Again, the woman turned around and snapped at them angrily. What she said sounded like 'just wait until I get back to the hut, you'll be in so much trouble' but Nicholas was unable to tell exactly.

She turned to Nicholas and sighed. It was the kind of sigh most mother's do when having to climb a mountain of testosterone to reach the summit of sensibility. Nicholas recognized it because he heard Mrs. Bakersbee sigh like that almost every day of his life.

The woman grabbed the bundle of leaves and opened it. Inside was some smoked fish and a few pieces of fruit.

"Eat." She said, then she grabbed her spear and stood.

Nicholas bowed in the universal gesture of "thanks" and stood as well. He wasn't sure if he should leave now or try to repair what the natives have seen.

"Sunrise. Go home." The woman pointed at the ocean. Then she pointed at the sand. "Our home. Not yours." She tried to look apologetic but Nicholas guessed her life was made difficult by his presence and would be made easier if he were gone.

Nicholas nodded. "Sunrise. I will milk a sheep." He said, hoping his *rongo-rongo* was not saying anything other than his promise to leave.

She looked at him strangely for a moment and frowned in confusion. Then she shrugged, turned and walked away. Holding his fish and fruit dinner, Nicholas watched her retreat into the darkness. By the sounds of the panic-filled voices that greeted the woman, the entire tribe must have watched the interaction from the darkness.

Nicholas looked down at the smoked fish and tropical fruit. It was a hearty portion and he was famished. He sat down to eat and mused about the situation as he sampled a mouthful of fish. It was a little salty but delicious. The meal dispelled any speculation Nicholas had about his safety. He knew all too well that most indigenous people around the world disliked foreigners but he felt rather safe here. For now.

As he listened to the voices continue out in the darkness, something occurred to Nicholas. He walked over to his backpack where it rested near the sandy embankment. After rummaging inside it, he pulled something out and pointed it in the direction of the voices.

The dial of his compass spun around *Naughty* and *Nice* several times and slowed to a stop. It pointed due *Nice*. Satisfied he was not in danger, he returned to his dinner.

Sometime later, Nicholas finished eating and made a small fire. He discovered Kara sleeping in his cherry leaf box and decided not to wake her. With a full belly of delicious fish and what he thought might have been papaya fruit, Nicholas leaned back and drifted off to sleep under the sandy embankment. The sound of ocean waves was soothing and he decided he liked sleeping near water.

The next morning, Nicholas awakened rested and comfortable. The early morning sun was bright and clear skies greeted him as he stood and stretched. A fresh, ocean breeze greeted him and he felt energized, dry and warm. He gathered his belongings and decided he would leave the natives and their island as soon as possible. He hadn't the foggiest idea where he would go but he promised the old woman he would leave. He just hoped he would be able to flow without anyone seeing him. He also wondered if he would be able to flow at all without Gabriel's assistance.

Thinking about his friend, Nicholas looked down at the place where his friend had vanished. The banana leaves were gone, taken by the tides. Kara buzzed around his head and guessing his thoughts, nestled close to his cheek.

"Just you and I, Kara." Nicholas sighed.

He continued to stare at the spot on the beach where Gabriel told him so many things. He wanted to do something for his elder friend. Something he had seen before while studying human cultures around the world. In some cultures, when someone died the people would leave a marker where the body lay, as if to remind themselves of the person they missed. Nicholas wanted to do this for Gabriel but he had little time.

He looked around the beach and up the sand embankment. Standing alone amidst tall grass and weeds, a stone jutted out of the earth. It was perfect. He walked over and examined its surface. His mind raced as he thought of various possibilities of marking it in some way but he was faced with a pressing desire to leave.

Kara flew in front of Nicholas face and made some gestures he didn't recognize. Her golden wings flashed in the morning sun, making him blink.

"Yes? What is it Kara?"

She pointed to the beach where Gabriel had died. Then she pointed to the stone and tilted her head in the universal gesture of a question mark.

"Yes. That's right." Said Nicholas, smiling at her. "I want to make a marker for Gabriel. I thought about using metal to etch an image in it but I've never done something like that."

Kara shook her head and waved a finger.

"Well, what would you propose Kara?" He looked around in case natives were watching them. "Is it against the rules? Should I not leave something behind?"

Kara shook her head. Then she pointed at herself and then to the stone.

"You?" Said Nicholas, wishing she could speak. "What about you?"

Kara frowned and looked around the sand. She spotted something and dragged the front of Nicholas' robe down to look at it.

"What's this?" Said Nicholas as he bent over to pick up a small piece of drift wood. "What about it?"

Kara held up a two hands and Nicholas guessed she wanted him to stand still.

"Ok. Stand still?"

She nodded. Then, carefully drawing her golden spear, she hacked at the drift wood. Again and again she chopped bits of it off, increasing in speed with every stroke. Soon she was a blur of golden energy, buzzing around the driftwood in Nicholas' hand like some sort of machine. Nicholas watched in amazement as bits and dust of driftwood flew out of his hand in every direction. Finally she stopped spinning around the wood and held out her hands as if to say *whallah!* She beamed at him.

In the palm of Nicholas' hand was a sculpture that looked remarkably like Claire. It was simplistic but Kara had captured all that was unique about Claire's face and rendered it from the wood. He looked at it closely and felt a desire to see her more than ever. He cradled the tiny, wooden sculpture in his hands, realizing she meant more to him than he expected despite their brief time together. It was a precious gift Kara made for him.

Kara sighed and bonked him on the forehead with the end of her spear. Nicholas looked up, nearly forgetting what he was trying to do. She was pointing to the stone and pointing to the face of Claire.

Realizing what she essayed, he smiled excitedly at her. "Yes! You can cut the stone?"

She crossed her arms in front of her chest and gestured vaguely as she looked away. Realizing this was the universal gesture of 'oh please! I can cut anything!', Nicholas nodded encouragingly.

"Good. Just a simple likeness of Gabriel is enough. I want him to be remembered."

Kara saluted and turned to the stone. She grabbed her spear in one hand and the held a thumb out in front of herself as she closed one eye. She fluttered around the stone and Nicholas guessed she was making some kind of measurements. He smiled to himself as she did so because he also guessed she was grandstanding.

After a few moments, she dove at the stone with her spear and sparks immediately flew. Buzzing around the stone, she hacked and sawed until it disappeared inside a small, white cloud with orange sparks flying out of it. Bits of sizzling stone flew out of the white cloud in every direction.

A short while later, Kara emerged from the cloud and flew over to Nicholas. Her tiny golden spear was glowing red-hot at the tip and she looked at it with annoyance. Licking her thumb and forefinger, she grabbed the spear tip which made a tiny 'tsss' sound and a little trail of smoke rose from it.

Nicholas stared at the stone as the smoke dissipated. A face bearing the likeness of Gabriel stared back at him in the morning sun. The long nose and pursed lips of the ageless face had sunken eyes which glowered at him under a heavy brow. It was a crude representation of Gabriel's features but Nicholas nodded in appreciation.

"A triumph Kara." He said, patting Kara gently as she landed on his shoulder.

She wiped a forearm across her brow and nodded at it. Then, as if to say she was done for the day, she flew into Nicholas' breast pocket and curled up to sleep.

Nicholas grinned at her and then to the stone face of Gabriel. "Here you can always see the ocean. Good bye." Then he turned and walked towards the ocean.

Making sure his backpack was closed, he sighed at he touched the curved, iron spike around his neck. It was mid-morning and the natives would be expecting him to leave. He breathed deeply as he approached the turquoise waters of the ocean. He decided to go west and find a secluded place to hide for now. He knew human settlements were less crowded there so it seemed a good place to lie low.

Focusing on flowing, as Gabriel instructed, Nicholas walked into the ocean. Satisfied that he was in a good amount of water, he concentrated all of his attention on one word. He focused all of his attention and spoke the word clearly.

"Flow."

And he vanished into the waves...

Later that afternoon, an island native returned to the beach he fled from the day before. Satisfied the usurper was gone, he prepared to do some serious fishing. He happily reclaimed his fishing spot after it was so rudely occupied by the *white demon* from the *great mother*.

Looking around the fire pit and the place where Nicholas had slept, he happened to spot the stone face of Gabriel. He dropped his fishing spear and ran up to it, running his hands over the stone and talking to himself. He was amazed at the smoothness of the features and the image appealed to him. He imagined the white demon left it here for some important reason.

Being a fisherman, he was prone to believe in things like luck, fate and continuous prayer. He quickly cleared the weeds and grass around the stone face so that it could clearly watch the ocean. Satisfied it was clear of foliage he leaned back and admired the stone face. The long nose and pursed lips of the ageless face appealed to him. The statue's sunken eyes which glowered back at him from under a heavy brow was exactly the way he imagined a god to look like. Surely it was a sign of good fortune for him and his people.

As he knelt beside it, he looked further inland to a huge stone with the same dimensions of Gabriel's monument, only quite a bit larger. The huge stone was ugly, shapeless and many of his kinsmen disliked it.

He looked at Gabriel's face. Then he looked at the huge stone further inland. Then he looked at Gabriel's face once more as ideas fired in his mind. He grinned, a toothless grin and ran back his village…

*Jingle*Jingle*Jingle*

The Greyman looked around the cavern that was once the Gate Pool of Abanis. The ceiling was cracked, the ice and rock hewn floor was blackened by dragon fire. The subtle, emerald hue of the gate pool was dim and the water was still. He looked at a long streak of blood mixed with ash leading to the pool and he wondered briefly where his offspring would have escaped to. He could have slew Gabriel before his escape but it mattered not. No doubt he would perish before long. He did not hold back punishing the whelp for his insolence.

He looked down at his reflection in the pool and turned his head to the side, admiring the handsome features of Pontius Pilate. He liked this suit. It...suited him, as it were. He grinned at his own reflection for a moment. No doubt the city was abandoned for he could hardly believe The Pilgrim would have allowed him to nearly destroy Gabriel and enter the city thus unchallenged. No doubt he was now the master of Abanis.

He leaned down and touched each one of the guardians on the cheek and closed his eyes.

"Yes." He whispered. "Yes, you have much more work to do my brothers."

He stood up and waited expectantly in the dim blue light of the pool.

The three bodies jerked suddenly. Then, one by one, as if controlled by marionette strings, they jerked alive and managed to rise before The Greyman. They were youthful acolyes but their eyes were black. He looked at each of them in turn and brought the scythe about to lean on it.
"Brothers." He nodded.

The three ghouls bowed.

"Thank you for inviting us in, master. We left the bodies of Namtar and his brothers safely elsewhere."

"You are but shadows of your former selves but you have done well." Said the Greyman quietly. "We four once rode against the host of Adamis and so we shall ride once more. Come!"

They passed under the archway and ascended the stairs. The four emerged from the large double doorway and The Greyman looked around the city plaza of Abanis. He glanced briefly at the doors obviously ripped from their metal hinges and thrown across the courtyard. Then looked around.

"Oh my, oh my, oh my!" He said quietly looking around at the city. "Dear brother you made this exactly to my specifications. How marvelously productive you have been."

The Greyman beamed at his three cohorts and then looked up to the sky of the great sphere. It was cracked at numerous points and the sun and moon, although in the sky at the same time, were dim and lifeless globes. It was as if the peculiar celestial clockwork of the heavens inside the great sphere had stopped working altogether. The sky was grey and dim. There was an odd smog cloud over the city and lightning flashed on several horizons, indicating violent weather systems in distant lands.

"Still," The Greyman nodded as he looked around, "the place needs a little work but I think with a little elbow grease and a loving touch, we can use it to destroy every spec of life on earth and start the whole nonsense all over with a fresh coat of amino acids. Aha!" The Greyman noticed the silver dome that was the home of The Pilgrim. "Here we go, that is the operation center of this," he waved a hand vaguely in the air, "monstrosity. If my brother followed my designs," he pointed the scythe at the silver dome at the heart of the city, "that is where we can get our business kick-started." He turned and walked across the city plaza. The three ghouls looked at each other then followed him.

The silver dome was curiously undamaged by the devastation of the buildings around it. In all directions, the spiraling architecture of the city was crumbling and numerous parts of buildings had covered parts of the dome but it gleamed as if impervious to everything that had occurred around it.

The Greyman, using the scythe as a walking stick, waved a hand in the direction of the dome as he approached. Giant slabs of ice and building debris were blasted off of it as if moved by a the biggest leaf-blower in the universe. The debris landed some distance away near peripheral buildings and left the doorway cleared.

The Greyman stopped in front of the dome and frowned at the ridiculous entrance. The wood framed doorway cut into the edge of the silver dome remained unchanged despite the devastation around it. He shook his head as he looked at the simple door with the tiny circular window. Then he looked down at the worn mat in front of the door, which read "Welcome" in large, friendly, yellow letters. He snorted and looked back to the approaching ghouls as if to share some inside joke.

"He may be my brother but there's no accounting for taste."

He turned back to the door and stepped forward to grasp the handle and then froze. The little white sign that had been on the door when Nicholas first came to Abanis was still there. It was somewhat wrinkled and aged but still clearly readable: "Out to lunch. Back in a hundred years."

The Greyman hesitated. He grasped the note and tore it off the door and read it over and over in disbelief. "No." He said flatly.

The three ghouls were very astute in gauging the mood of their master. As one they stepped back a little.

"No." Said the Greyman again. "No!" He screamed and the ghouls retreated even further. "No, no, no, no, no, no, no!" He raged and threw the scythe to the moss covered cobblestones and ripped the note into little pieces with his teeth. Then he turned to the door, grabbed the tiny brass handle with two hands. He yanked and pulled and kicked as he tried to open the door but it wouldn't budge.

"No!" He screamed again.

A stray lightning bolt, seemingly summoned in response to The Greyman's frustration, peeled across the sky above them. It struck the silver dome, ricocheted off to an adjacent building then made an arc across the plaza to an amethyst lamp post where it exploded. The ghouls froze while being showered in sizzling shards of purple crystal and, quite strangely, the smoldering remains of a paper mask painted to look like a female face.

The Greyman backed away from the simple wooden door and closed his eyes. The ghouls could feel rage pulse from their master like a palpable wave.

There were several long minutes of tenuous calm as The Greyman concentrated and the ghouls trembled behind him expectantly. Then he opened his eyes and sighed deeply as he pick up the scythe. He turned to them and smiled, shaking his head as if he had just spilled some coffee on his robes.

"I'm sorry brothers. I have a temper, as you might recall. It seems my brother may have expected this little insurrection. It vexed me but," He raised a hand theatrically, "I'm over it now."

One of the ghouls stepped forward and bowed. "What is the problem master? Perhaps we could assist you."

The Greyman looked at the door, then looked at his three colleagues. "He must have crafted a key. And I think I know what it is." He finished shaking his head. "I knew I should have pursued it but....it was too soon....I needed more time to finish my business with Pilate." He whispered to himself.

He held forth his hand and an image appeared over it, rotating slightly. The three ghouls stepped closer and looked at the image.

One ghoul examined the image closely and looked up to The Greyman. "I recall," he whispered, "that you were trying to take us home, long ago. Will we be able to go home finally?"

The Greyman nodded. "But that mission has changed and so have I. We have business to do here before we make that attempt once more."

"This key will propel us closer to that goal?" Asked another ghoul.

The Greyman nodded.

"A dream, it has been, for us at last to return home. We do not belong here." Said a third ghoul. "We will help you find this key, master."

"But it will be difficult to track." Said The Greyman. "Unlike those of our kin, humans are difficult to discern from a great distance. Their minds are, as yet, incapable of hosting a connection for long. My clever brother saw to it that this key was well hidden. For the one who carries it is human. You will find your mounts buried with your remains in Egypt. They will rise if you call them. Go there. Take to the skies. Find him."

The three ghouls nodded as they continued to stare at the ghostly image of a simple, iron spike.

Chapter 20: Shortstacks

Pantilius pulled his hand out of the river and stood up frowning. There was no word of Gabriel in the waters. Although Gabriel's mind was unresponsive he did *feel* that Nicholas was in the water and going somewhere. This, along with numerous other things, worried him greatly.

He was standing on the soft, muddy bank of a slow moving river. Above him, the branches of numerous trees that lined the bank made a green ceiling of foliage. It was morning and shafts of sunlight penetrating the canopy cast angled shafts of light around him. Birds chirped in the trees and everything else in a forest that could *bzzz*, did so. He breathed deeply and sighed.

Sounds of chirping made him glance at a large oak tree beside him. It was bigger than the other trees in the area and a family of robins were living in a hollowed out knot in the trunk. Pantilius watched the nested hatchlings for a few moments. They gaped, open mouthed, for the mother robin flying to and from the knot with several unlucky insects.

Pantilius watched the robins appreciatively and wondered what the old oak charged them for rent and if utilities were included.

He looked away and waited. It was here, so very long ago, that The Pilgrim had found he and Himtall sitting beside a campfire. Long after the destruction of Adamis, Pantilius assumed there were no more Huru so he hid among the Scandinavians for a time. It was then he discovered a youthful Himtall, who had been outcast from his home for simply being too large. Pantilius thought that was quite a stretch for Viking standards to banish someone for having *giant* blood or whatever nonsense Himtall's people used to get rid of him. It was also a time when he felt more shame than he had ever felt in his long years. Then, out of the forest, The Pilgrim had poked his head around the large oak tree Pantilius was presently admiring and asked Himtall if there was any mutton left. He grinned at the memory of seeing the young giant fall over backwards in shock and set fire to his own boot.

Pantilius sighed again and wondered about the fate of Nicholas once more. He knew The Pilgrim was not moving anywhere in the waters of the world or he would have felt it. He knew Nicholas was special to The Pilgrim and wished more than ever to make sure he remained safe. And where was Gabriel? He could not guess but he knew that Nicholas was on the move. He wanted to be there for the young man but it was far too dangerous. The Greyman would find them. As long as Nicholas stayed clear of Hurum, he would at least blend in with humanity. This fact considerably increased his chances of remaining safe.

"Getting old dear Professor?" Said a voice in the forest nearby. Or are you simply indulging the zeal of a young pupil?"

Pantilius smiled and turned around. "You know, I was just thinki-" He stopped. No one was there.

"Aha! The ol' 'what shape am I' game!" He exclaimed looking around excitedly. "Of course, it's a little less fun without large amounts of wine involved."

Pantilius scanned the area and grinned evilly. After retrieving some smoked venison from a pocket in his robes, he waved it around so that the meaty fragrance filled the air. Satisfied the odor was filling the immediate area, he kneeled, ripped off a piece and placed it on some leaves in front of him. Then he waited expectantly.

A few moments later, a fox poked it's head around the trunk of a nearby tree. With eyes that seemed unable to fixate on anything other than the delicious meat, it scampered forward and snatched up the venison.

The air blurred around the fox. Suddenly Claire was sitting in front of the old professor looking up at him rather guiltily with the strip of venison still clutched in her teeth.

"My word Claire!" Said Pantilius laughing. "You certainly got the hang of morphology alright! That was a magnificently beautiful fox!"

"That's not fair!" Claire exclaimed, faintly disheveled and taking the venison out of her mouth. "You cheated! I couldn't help myself." She said, a little reproachfully as she stood up and wiped mud off her crimson robes.

Pantilius grinned and nodded. "Indeed, a rather nice trick. Changing is one thing but controlling the instinctual urges of the target shape in question is a whole other matter. They can get you into all kinds of trouble if you don't concentrate enough."

"Any word Professor?" Claire asked as she stood up.

Pantilius knew what she meant and felt reluctant to share what he knew. It would only make this happy, talented young woman worry. "He is on the move, my dear." He patted her on the cheek and turned to sit down on a large rock beside the river. "And he is safe, for the time being.

Claire sat down beside him and waited for more information.

Pantilius looked at her and then sighed. "Gabriel is absent, my dear."

"What? Absent? What does that mean? He was supposed to be with Nick. Only he could shield them from the surveillance of The Greyman, didn't you say that? And what can we - "

Pantilius raised a blue tinted hand. His large, white eyebrows followed in suit as he stared at her.

"S-Sorry, professor." Claire stuttered and bowed her head. Her long brown hair fell over her face.

Pantilius could see her eyes mist over slightly. "Don't worry, my dear." He said soothingly. "We are not going to let anything happen to Nick. He is safe for now."

Claire nodded and looked at the mildly rippling waters of the river. She tried to think that Nicholas was alright. She tried not to think he was like a child in the world outside Abanis and that they were forced to abandon him for his own good. And that he was all alone.

"Where is The Pilgrim, professor?" She said suddenly.

"Well," Said Pantilius, sounding unsure of what he was about to say. "The ways of The Pilgrim are strange indeed. We have to have faith that he is aware of what is occurring, wherever he is."

Claire nodded and shifted position on the rock so that she could see her reflection in the river water.

"Did I ever tell you about how Himtall and I met The Pilgrim for the first time?" Said Pantilius, gearing up for a story.

"Professor. Everyone in Abanis knows that story. It was here right? We learned it in your class."

"Indeed, my girl." Nodded Pantilius. But his educational speech engines had geared up for a story that no 'heard it before' road block in the world could stop. "It was many years after the fall of Adamis, home of the Huru. A sad time indeed. Himtall and I were having mutton just over there when ...." He stopped suddenly.

Claire looked at him and waited. Pantilius had the expression of someone who had left home for a long vacation and wondered if they left the stove on.

"Claire..." He said quietly.

"Yes?"

"Do you recall this rock being here when we met some days ago?"

It was then the world turned upside down. The large rock heaved and Pantilius and Claire were thrown into the air. Claire landed in the water and splashed around trying to figure out what had just happened.

The rock readjusted itself into a familiar shape and stood up. Himtall looked at Claire and blinked blearily at her. "Oh my dear!" He bellowed, stepping a giant boot into the water and leaning down a tree branch sized arm to her.

"Himtall!" She laughed and clambered up his arm.

"Sorry about that my dear. I must have dozed off. I came here early yesterday to wait for you and Pantilius." He watched Claire scramble back onto the river bank, sopping wet, and sighed at her. "Where is the little rascal?"

"Umm," Said a voice above them. "I am wondering if you would be so kind as to give me a hand here."

Himtall and Claire looked up and saw Pantilius hanging from a branch 12 feet above the ground.

"C'mere Professor. Ho-ho-ho!" Laughed Himtall as he reached up and grabbed the little, blue-skinned figure in the branches.

"Good stone ol' boy! You had me completely fooled there." Said Pantilius grinning as Himtall set him to the ground.

"I was going for the strong, silent type." Grumbled Himtall, winking at Claire. "So what's the news, Professor?"

"Gabriel is absent but Nicholas is on the move." Said Pantilius flatly.

Himtall nodded. "Do you think he..." He let the question mark dangle in the air like a spider interrupting a tea party.

"I'm not sure," said Pantilius hurriedly, glancing at Claire, "but where is Fuzzy? Is he not with you?"

"No." Sighed Himtall as he sat down under the oak tree. The branches shook as he leaned his enormous back against the trunk. "He wanted to go and get the other two fools and come meet us. They feel that safety in numbers might be for the best right now."

"What about Aryu and Mrs. Bakersbee?" Said Claire, coming to sit beside Himtall.

"They've gone to some safe haven far to the east." Said Pantilius. He absently waved a hand and Claire's robes were suddenly bone dry. She gaped at her robes and then at him.

"Near Aryu's original home in fact." Pantilius continued. "They've taken the children of Mirthmyst for now. They should be quite safe for the time being."

"Ok. So what about The Pilgrim. Where is he?" Said Himtall, pulling some linen wrapped objects from a huge coat pocket.

"We don't know. For now everyone is safe as far as I can tell. But I'm not sure what action we should take at this t- "

"Excuse me." Said a tiny voice above them. Even Claire heard it and the three looked up.

On a branch a few feet above the old professor was a sparrow. Claire blinked at it and wondered if it was another emissary in disguise. She was pretty sure sparrows didn't speak but this one sounded just fine.

"Would you happen to be General Pantilius?" It said in a voice so high pitched it could have shattered glass with just a little more volume.

For the first time in her life, Claire saw confusion on Pantilius' face. It was a brief flash but quickly followed by the expression that he knew the answer to everything. This was his trademark expression.

"I certainly am, uhh, 'General' Pantilius, yes. And, uhh, who might you be?"

The little brown sparrow saluted smartly with a wing. "Corporal Twerp." It said in a manner which caused Claire to cover her hand with her mouth as she snickered. "First Airborne Company. Jerusalem."

Pantilius hesitated. "Let me get this straight." He said, glancing at Himtall who grinned and shook his head in confusion. "You are a talking sparrow." It was a rough statement that indicated a response was needed to polish it up.

"That is correct sir."

"And you are a corporal. A rank which, uh call me crazy, indicates there are a legion of you fellows."

"Yes sir." It chirped.

"And, you come from the city of Jerusalem?"

"Yes sir."

"Several hundred, if not thousands, of miles away."

"Yes sir."

"And you flew all the way to this spot at this time to find me?"

"Yes sir."

"Well then, certainly one of the more interesting things I've seen in my time, I have to admit. This has The Pilgrim's style written all over it. I'm sure of it." Pantilius beamed at the others and then looked at the sparrow. It was standing attention in such a way that it's feathers looked streamlined to defend a nation, if not only a well fortified nest.

"Very well, Corporal Twerp. What is it I can help you with?"

"Sir! I have come to read you a message, sir." It chirped. Then it contrived, as well as a sparrow could manage, to look as if it was reciting a message. "Please answer the following questions so I can correctly identify you as General Pantilius of Abanis."

"Uhh, ok but..." Pantilius started to say but the Corporal Twerp continued.

"What is green on the outside and yellow on the inside and hangs around in bunches?"

Claire's shoulders shook slightly.

Pantilius re-tuned his mind to the peculiar subject at hand and thought. "Bananas dressed up as cucumbers, naturally." He said, nodding to the others as if this was perfectly obvious.

"Correct sir. Sir, why did the banana go out with the prune?"

Pantilius raised his eyebrows. "Because he couldn't find a date?"

"Correct sir." Said Corporal Twerp.

Claire had to turn her back as this point.

"Sir," said the little sparrow, attempting to whisper to only Pantilius, "one of your officers is unwell, it seems. Shall I continue?"

"She's fine Corporal Twerp." Said Pantilius glaring at Claire. "Please continue."

"Sir," the little bird straightened up, "what's yellow and always points north?"

"A magnetic banana, of course." Said Pantilius, who was probably the only person in the known universe who could answer that question without hesitation.

"Very good sir. You are indeed General Pantilius of Abanis. Shall I recite the message to you sir?"

"Very well, let's hear it."

"Sir. I was told to inform you of a family reunion scheduled to occur in the very near future at the North Gate. Please bring fruit salad."

There was silence. Claire turned around still trying not to burst out laughing but the look on the faces of Pantilius and Himtall made her smile vanish immediately.

"Thank you, Corporal. That will be all." Said Pantilius quietly.

"Will you be heading home little one?" Asked Himtall, standing up and looking nervously at Pantilius.

"Indeed I will, sir." Said the sparrow.

Himtall handed the sparrow a small bit of bread he unfolded from some cloth. "Safe travels little friend. I hope we meet again."

"Thank you sir!" It snatched up a small bit of bread in its beak and flew up above the branches of the forest and high into the sky.

All three watched the little Corporal disappear from sight. Then Pantilius turned to the river.

Claire couldn't see Pantilius' face now but noticed a flicker of shock and fear in his eyes before he turned around. It was an uncomfortable moment so she decided to wait for him to speak. Himtall remained silent as well but looked at the old professor with curious concern.

Pantilius suddenly turned to Claire. Although he resumed the ever grinning, ever know-it-all expression of teachers everywhere, she thought he looked much, much older than before.

"We must gather an army." He said to her. Then he looked at Himtall. "We must go north to Sin." He turned back to the river and remained silent for some time.

Himtall nodded gravely and sighed. "Come Claire, help me make a campfire." He grumbled, not unkindly. "We have much to discuss and do before this day is over."

Chapter 21: Aged Enefka Babellux with Shortcakes

After being pulled to his feet by Longinus and Erik, Arkilius looked around blearily and stopped when he noticed Enlil. He blinked and squinted, trying to focus on the old man and then he grinned again. "Enlil!" He shouted and yanked his arms free. He staggered towards the old man and the two embraced.

"Good morning my old friend." Said Enlil, laughing. "I do apologize that there is no coffee. The room service here is atrocious."

Arkilius laughed and stepped back to get a better look at Enlil and then turned to look at the five companions. Pilate looked on nervously, wondering if any more 'healing process' was on his immediate horizon.

"Well, well, some genuine humans here, I see." Then he looked back at Enlil, who retrieved his staff from the floor and was nodding. "So, if you are here, then you know what happened to us." He said flatly.

"Yes." Said Enlil, his smile fading. "And I didn't know until recently. I am sorry old friend."

"Your progeny?" Said Arkilius, looking at Nicholas and the others as if this was understandably unbelievable. "I must have been sleeping for a long time. Where is the lil' rascal, Uncle Arkilius will show him how to throw a stone fifty miles and target a ghoul with it! Hah!" He said looking around as if there might be another person he missed.

Nicholas and the others noticed a slight crack appear in the Enlil's happy manner. The old man looked at Arkilius with the eyes of one who has lived through many centuries of toil. "He is lost, my old friend." He said quietly.

Arkilius looked at Enlil and sighed, shaking his head. "Did *he* do it?"

"No. He chose his own fate and left us...." Enlil paused for a moment, "hoping it would save humanity."

"The Nazarene." Said Erik suddenly, stepping forward. "For some reason, I know you speak of the Nazarene. I spoke to him on Golgotha." He said. It was not a question but rather a statement he hoped would be clarified by the old man.

Enlil looked at Erik and Longinus for a moment then his gaze fell on Pilate. Turning an even lighter shade of grey,

Pilate had the look of a man who had just cursed someone for stepping on his foot, only to find it was Tiberius Caesar.

"Yes. I thought you might have." Said Enlil quietly.

Longinus stepped forward. "His death was unjust." He said and pointed a finger at Pilate. "I told him but he insisted - "

"Pontius Pilate," said Enlil in a voice so strong it silenced the giant commander, "was politically motivated, cruel and greedy." He stepped forward and looking intently at Longinus. "But *that* man is dead. The man standing there behind you risked much to awaken you from this nightmare, took a beating or two and begged for your forgiveness. I daresay you might be even."

Longinus looked at Pilate who had lowered his head. Then he looked at Erik and shared a silent exchange. Whatever madness they experienced on Golgotha, seemingly so long ago, made sense in light of the fact the Nazarene was Enlil's *progeny*, whatever that was. "I am sorry. The empire is cruel at times." He said somewhat lamely.

"And yet they have officers who actually care." Said Enlil. "And that is an encouraging thing."

There was an uncomfortable silence broken by Arkilius clearing his throat. "Well, twinkle-fingers, seems you still like drama." Said Arkilius roughly.

Cassie leaned over to Aurelia and whispered. "Did he just call the old man 'twinkle-fingers'?"

Aurelia snorted and nodded.

"Indeed I do. Let's get the family awake shall we?"

Arkilius nodded and turned to the others. He focused on Longinus, walked over to him and looked up.

Longinus looked at the others and then looked down. "Uhh, hi. Sir."

Arkilius smiled. "Manners. Good." He nodded to Longinus. "You have the aura of a natural leader, long shanks. Your voice could inspire thousands. I'm going to need your help."

"Uhh, ok. Sir." Said Longinus, glaring a Erik who was trying not to laugh.

"Come with me." Said the old Nelfilem as he stepped around Longinus and strode away. The rest of the companions looked at Enlil who shrugged and fell in behind him.

Longinus walked alongside Nicholas and whispered to him loudly. "What the hell does 'long shanks' mean?"

Cassie and Aurelia snickered.

Arkilius led the companions to the front of the assembled host of entranced Nelfilem. He gestured Longinus to come forward.

"You're human." He said as Longinus stood where he indicated.

Not knowing to what context the statement referred, Longinus said, "Uh, thanks."

"It wasn't a compliment, Long shanks, it was an observation." Said the old Nelfilem as he scanned the mesmerized legion of his people. "You have the voice, young fella. You can inspire thousands on the field of battle. It's a kind of charisma. Oh, and the fact you are more human than I means you can awaken my people. Don't ask how or why, just nod."

Longinus shrugged and nodded.

"Good." Said Arkilius. "Now repeat after me: 'I'm a little teacup.'"

"I'm a little..." Longinus started then he stopped. "What?!?"

Arkilius looked around and winked at Cassie who had covered her mouth to keep from laughing at her husband.

"He nearly fell for it! Ha!" Arkilius slapped Longinus on the leg. "OK, ok."

Enlil looked on smiling and leaned heavily on his staff.

"Alright, Long shanks, just kidding. You're a good sport. Repeat after me: *Namses Igi-lib*. Say it."

"Namses..." Longinus paused , trying to pronounce the peculiar accent. "Namsus Igil ...ib." He stuttered.

Pilate, seeing this may be something he could actually contribute to, shook his head and strode forward. "Sir? May I help?" He said to Arkilius and gestured to Longinus.

Arkilius looked the former prefect up and down and shrugged. "He's all yours, olive-oil."

"Commander," said Pilate, coming to stand in front of Longinus, "I believe you are being asked to say some kind of ancient word. It is an old language. I don't know what it means but I'm familiar with the pronunciation. Now, repeat after me - namses."

"*Namses.*" Said Longinus.

"Good." Nodded Pilate with the air of a satisfied educator. He raised a finger to annunciate the sounds perfectly. "Now, *igi* and then *lib*, like this *'igi-lib'*."

"Nams...'ig'ilib." Said Longinus, frowning as he tried odd accent.

"No, no," said Pilate shaking his, slightly admonishing the large man, "you have to use the rhythm."

Longinus nodded.

"One-two, one-two-three. Like this, Commander, *Namses Igilib.*" He said loudly and clearly. "Now you give it a tr-" He stopped.

Longinus grinned as he looked over Pilates shoulder.

Pilate hesitated and then his face drained of color as he realized why Longinus was grinning. "They're awake aren't they." He said flatly.

Longinus nodded.

Pilate turned around in horror, expecting some new insanity to add to the long list of things he had witnessed recently. It was worse than he could ever have imagined.

Several hundred imp-like faces looked at him admiringly and quite awake. The closest of the Nelfilem looked at Pilate with unbridled hero-worship.

"Thank you for freeing us, brother human!" He said and rushed forward to hug Pontius Pilate who stood frozen in shock. He looked to the others for help.

Before he could say anything however, the entire host of Nelfilem suddenly rushed forward and began to hug him. Pilate was carried around, pushed, pulled and lost in a sea of hugs and thank-you's as the others looked on grinning.

"I'm afraid my brothers are a quite affectionate, Olive-Oil. You're the hero. Enjoy it!" Shouted Arkilius. Pilate screamed and disappeared in a sea of hugs and kisses by his new army of admirers. The companions watched as the throng of admiring Nelfilem passed Pilate among them like a rag doll.

"Arkilius," Said Enlil, "it would seem Pilate is also a natural leader. You know he was a prefect of Judea at one point. It's like being a kind of overlord."

"Is that so." Said Arkilius, laughing as he watched his brother Nelfilem thank the unfortunate former prefect.

"Do you think we should rescue him?" Said Cassie, without much enthusiasm. "No one deserves that much attention."

Longinus and Erik snickered as Pilate attempted to claw his way back to the rest of the companions. He almost made it but was pulled into the throng once more for a second round of hugs.

Sometime later, when the excitement passed, Pilate managed to find his way back to the others. He was disheveled and wide-eyed. "I'm just going to sit down." He giggled, not exactly in a happy way, and slumped to the ground.

Arkilius went to his people and spoke to them as the companions watched. He shook hands and greeted many warmly while talking officially to some elders. He pulled Enlil over and many of the Nelfilem bowed respectfully to him as if he were some patron. After a little discussion, they all seemed to come to an agreement and turned towards the companions.

"Right." Arkilius nodded to Nicholas and the others. "We have to get out of here and I know the way. Gather around." He gestured and the companions, along with a thousand Nelfilem, surrounded him. To the modern observer, it would have appeared to be the largest football huddle in history.

"Long ago," he said roughly, looking around the gigantic huddle, "we were enslaved. It may have seemed quite easy to release us from our trance but the warden of this prison did not expect anyone to be walking around up here. So I thank you." He paused, nodded to each of the companions and cleared his throat. "My brothers and I know the way off this nightmare. It's not going to be easy but - "

He stopped suddenly and frowned, focusing his attention on Pilate. Then he pointed a pale, blue finger at him. "You have the taint of evil on you. Why?"

Enlil leaned closer to Arkilius and whispered hurriedly in his ear. The old Nelfilem frowned and looked back at Pilate.

"I see. You were chosen by the warden for a reason. He was inside you at some point which means you know the way to the Procharioit." He said.

Pilate, whose face had already drained of any color it had left some hours ago, shuddered in confusion. "The pro-what?"

"The Procharioit is a pool of water." Said the old man over Arkilius' shoulder. "You do remember how you arrived here, right?"

Pilate seemed to shrink. "Yes. It was unpleasant."

"Good." Said Arkilius. "Lead the way and when we get to where we need to go, we'll be taking another step."

Several hundred sets of eyes looked at Pilate.

"Huh?" He said weakly.

"The pool of water you entered to come to this place is a gate." Said Enlil. "And I'm sorry to say 'part ' of you is being used at the moment by the warden. That means you have a connection to him."

"Umm, used? But -" Said Pilate but Enlil steamrolled over his confusion.

"You can focus on that connection to take us closer to where we need to go."

"Well, I don't know if I can - " He stopped and noticed several hundred admiring Nelfilem looking at him expectantly. "But, uh, I'll try." He said feebly, ready to run for his life if another hug was incoming.

"Good." Said Enlil, stepping around Arkilius and coming to stand in front of Pilate. "This is your moment, young man." He said barely audible to anyone around them. "Think about home and take us there."

Pilate looked at the ancient man and then to Erik, Longinus, Cassie and Aurelia. He bowed his head. "What if I fail?" He whispered.

The ancient man leaned closer and whispered in his ear. "Since when does Pontius Pilate ever fail?"

Pilate looked back into the opaque eyes and was curiously filled with an inexplicable urge to lead. He felt that failure would not occur but he couldn't explain how he was so sure. Suddenly, he looked away from the assembled companions across the endless expanse of slumbering people. He focused on which direction *home* would be and it simply came to him.

"That way." He said loudly and pointed into the vast array of stone slabs. Then he looked back to everyone else.

"Well done, olive oil. Lead the way." Said Arkilius, not unkindly.

The companions stopped. All of the stone slabs were empty.

"Where have they all gone?" Whispered Cassie, turning on the spot.

Erik and the others were speechless and looked to Enlil.

The old man sighed as he took in the terrible vacancy of their surroundings. "It has begun." He put a hand on Pilate's shoulder. "We must hurry. Onward please."

Pilate shrugged to the others and continued to walk. The assembled host of Nelfilem followed along with the perplexed companions deeper into the prison. Although noone voiced it, the absence of all the sleeping people somehow felt creepier than before. As if in response to the distressing erriness, a very young looking Nelfilem ran forward and held Pilate's hand. Pilate looked down at the little pointy-eared, blue-skinned creature and decided not to wrest his hand free. He sighed and held the younglings hand.

After a while, Longinus was walking beside Pilate with Cassie at his side. They acknowledged each other but didn't say anything. At least for Longinus part, there was no love lost between them.

Pilate suddenly leaned closer to the man he once wished dead and whispered. "I swear to Jupiter, if these little munchkins start whistling and singing, I shall go quite insane."

Longinus, taken by surprise, let out a bellow of a laugh. It was deep and echoed around the area despite there being very little in the way of sound to do so amidst the stone slabs.

Erik, who heard the comment, laughed as well. He was behind them holding his wife's hand and the small hand of one of the younger Nelfilem.

Arkilius, who was walking sturdily beside his ancient friend looked at the five companions and grinned too. "I miss that." He said suddenly.

"Eh?" Said Enlil, his walking stick clicking the stone floor as they hobbled along.

"The laughter. The sound of it." Said Arkilius solemnly. "They laugh so heartily, don't they. So rich and powerful, it is. A miracle of nature I say."

"Indeed." Said Enlil, nodding. "It may be there are very few beings in the universe that can laugh. As far as I was told, anyways." He looked down to his old friend. "For that reason alone they are so very precious."

"My brother made me laugh." Said Arkilius. "So long ago."

Enlil detected the baited query and decided to bite. "He is well. Pantilius lives and misses his older brother dearly." He patted the old Nelfilem on the shoulder. "And you will see him soon I expect."

There was the tiniest hint of moistness in the old Nelfilem's eyes and he remained silent for a time.

After walking for an indeterminate amount of time, Pilate stopped and everyone waited. He had already stopped several times up to this point but now he appeared to be stumped as to which direction he should go.

The companions and Nelfilem gathered around as Pilate concentrated on several different directions. Enlil and Arkilius came up beside him.

"What is it lad?" Said Arkilius.

"I'm sorry." Said Pilate, looking around in several directions into the blackness beyond the innate light of the companions. "It seems to end here. I cannot explain why I know it but," he shook his head, "there's nothing here."

Arkilius looked to the floor and then looked up. As with most people who do this, those nearby feel compelled to do the same. A thousand heads looked to the floor and then to the blackness above in confusion.

Enlil, on the other hand, was staring at Pilate. He seemed to consider something and then looked around at everyone else. "Step back." He said loudly.

Erik and the others did so but Arkilius remained standing beside the old man. "You sure this is the spot?" He leaned over and whispered loudly.

"Yes." Said Enlil. "You may also want to step back. I'm not sure what to expect in this place."

Arkilius nodded and hobbled over to the widening circle around the old man. He looked up at Pilate and elbowed the man in the ribs. "Good work kid."

Enlil raised his staff and looked into the darkness above them. "Sin!" He shouted. His voice was so loud it prompted many of onlookers to take a synchronized step back.

The old man waited in the vacant circle for a short time. Many of the companions looked up expectantly. After a short while there was a screeching sound from the blackness above their heads and many of the younger Nelfilem cowered at the sound. A few moments later a silver disc appeared out of the blackness above and grew larger as it descended.

Enlil stepped deftly into the crowd and watched as the disc came to a rest softly on the floor where he once stood. It was four meters in diameter and incredibly thin. Longinus looked closer at it, being somewhat familiar with metalwork and thought it was silver or some other kind of reflective, white metal.

"Well done Pilate!" Said Enlil, looking at the man whose mouth was threatening to hang open for the rest of his life.

"Good work kid." Said Arkilius. "This is the only way out and we could have wandered endlessly looking for this spot." He slapped Pilate on the back.

The man shrugged and contrived to look like 'it was nothing really' in case another session of hugs was on the immediate horizon. He glanced at the rest of the Nelfilem nervously.

Erik and Longinus stepped closer to the disc and shook their heads in disbelief that the thing didn't come crashing to the ground.

"How is this possible?" Asked Erik, waving his hands over the edge of the discs' surface. "No strings or ropes. It just glided down. Are you implying this is a lift?"

"Must be some kind of magic." Said the all-knowing Longinus, shaking his head.

Arkilius looked about to say something but was beat to it by a quick thinking Enlil.

"My dear boy." Said Enlil walking around the disc to stand in front of the two men. "Watch this." He held up his thumb and flicked it. Nothing happened.

The two men looked at the old man's thumb and then nodded as if they were sympathetically patronizing the worst magician in the universe.

Enlil stared at his thumb, quite surprised and then looked a little embarrassed. "Uh, one second." He flicked it again and, to their utter astonishment, the old man's thumb was on fire.

"It's a trick!" Exclaimed Longinus. He reached forward suddenly and recoiled, shaking his finger. "Ouch!"

"Careful lad, a trick is just a trick to some but a skill to others. But my point is this. Imagine my thumb is a candle flame." He held it out towards Nicholas.

Erik looked at the old man's thumb and imagined the tiny flickering flame on the end of it was as a candle flame. "Ok. It's a candle flame, now what?"

"Now, hold your hand several inches above it. Go on."

Erik did so and, as with a candle, even though the flame was not several inches high, he felt the heat of the flame and quickly pulled his hand away.

"Yes." Said Enlil, nodding. "You feel the heat there. There is heat above the flame but the flame does not appear to be eight inches high. It is only perceivable as a small flame." He shook his hand and the flame vanished. Then he pointed to the disc on the ground. "Just because you cannot *see* ropes and pulleys or some other form of engineering, doesn't mean they are not there."

Nicholas and Longinus nodded grudgingly and shrugged.

"So where does this lift take us then sir." Asked Longinus, looking warily at the disc and then up into the black depths above them.

"This lift will take us to The Prochariot, Long shanks." Said Arkilius gruffly as he stepped forward and examined the smooth, reflective surface of the disc. "In words you might recognize, right now we are in the hull of a ship and this lift will take us to the bridge."

Off to the side and unnoticed for the moment, Enlil was looking at his thumb with a look of genuine concern and worry on his old face.

****jingle***jingle***jingle****

The Greyman stared at the door to The Pilgrim's Silver dome. His ghoulish consorts had left in search of the iron spike, the key to opening the dome. He employed a number of different tactics to enter the dome, such as blasting it with fire and then ice, but the simple wooden door was impenetrable. He spoke many words in numerous languages, hoping they might trigger the door to open but that failed as well. Out of frustration, he slashed his scythe at the door but it didn't even leave a mark in the seemingly fragile wood.

He paced in front of it for a long while, lost in thought and muttering to himself. Then suddenly he straightened up and sniffed the air. It was a peculiar reaction that made him look as if he was lupine and about to howl at the moon. Turning around on the spot, his head jerked this way and that as if he was concentrating on something. Then he stopped and lowered his head. After several moments, the face of Pontius Pilate grinned.

"That is my domain, little monkey." He snarled and walked towards the very same pond that Nicholas used to escape Abanis. "Daddy, is coming."

Chapter 22: Ocean Salad Surprise

The oceans of the world are big. Really, really big. If one is unfortunate enough to find themselves in the middle of an ocean without a boat nearby or anything visible on any horizon, then *big* is something that is truly understood. However, when you can travel faster than anything that can travel through water (or on land, or in the air for that matter) and *still* get completely lost, then *big* doesn't even come close to an appropriate adjective.

As you might have guessed, Christopher Nicholas was completely lost in a seemingly endless expanse of blueness. Above him was a lighter tone of rich blue, below was a darker blue and all around his immediately surroundings was blue. You might even say that he *was* blue. *snare roll-symbol*

Since leaving the island, Nicholas traveled to many beaches around the world looking for a safe place to exit the water and take rest. However, every time he found a nice place to make camp, he found people had made camp there first. Since he was hesitant to make contact with humans, it was a deeply frustrating endeavor. If the entire world was an airport, then Nicholas would have been driving around the parking lot for days.

Since he was feeling neither tired, hungry nor thirsty, Nicholas decided to keep on the move. He concentrated on one direction and decided to go there. It was northwest. His favorite direction, although he could never understand why he felt that a direction merited being someone's favorite. After some time, he came to an immediate stop and felt as though he was repelled backwards by some unseen force. He looked around and realized that he had flowed into something quite big. After a moment of confusion, the largest eye he had ever seen came into view and squinted at him.

If Nicholas had a mouth in his present state of flowing through the ocean's, it would have gaped open. He moved himself back a little and realized he was looking at the largest creature he had ever seen in his life. It was a blue whale or 'blubberus maximus', as Pantilius called them.

The blue whale's eye stared at him as the enormous bulk of the creature swung lazily around in the water and confronted him. A head that could easily be mistaken for the front of a house faced Nicholas, who felt as though he was being scrutinized. Then he noticed something ebbing from the creature's side. It looked like blood.

Nicholas flowed around to get a better view of the source of crimson trails and noticed the creature had sustained some injury. There were lines of scars on the side of the whale and they were bleeding profusely. Nicholas tried not to imagine what oceanic horror could have done such a thing to a creature.

Nicholas remembered the injured deer and how Gabriel healed it. He wished he had the skill to help this creature. He knew whales were greatly respected by emissaries of Abanis although he didn't know why.

The creature turned its massive head and one eye stared at Nicholas as if it was pleading. Then, thinking that trying was better than wishing, Nicholas put his hands on the injured area of the creature's side and closed his eyes. He imagined the scars closing. He imagined the wounds cease to bleed and saw that the flesh mend. He repeated a word over and over in his mind, hoping it would help. Heal, heal, heal. He said inwardly.

He opened his eyes and was disappointed to see that the wounds were still there. He sighed inwardly and felt foolish for trying. Then something occurred to him. Although the wounds were still open, the bleeding had stopped completely. Despite his inability to properly heal the creature, he sensed that he was indeed able to lessen the creatures pain and prevent it from attracting predators. Satisfied that he did something completely blind of any lessons, he flowed back to the front of the creature and looked into its massive face once more.

After a few moments, Nicholas felt a strange sensation inside his head. It was a kind of pressure or mental itch that he could not understand. If his consciousness had a door, someone or something was knocking on it.

Nicholas decided to concentrate in the manner which allowed him to communicate with Pantilius the day he escaped from Abanis. It was like turning up his observation to maximum volume.

Suddenly, the door of his mind opened and a deep voice echoed inside his head.

"Thank you." Said a voice. "Friend?" It asked.

Nicholas hesitated. Anything or anyone concerned enough to ask if someone else was a 'friend' was probably qualified to be a good one in kind. He also realized that this whale, which would be cramped inside an aquarium the size of the coliseum, was speaking to him. He was pleasantly shocked and decided he could use a friend right now. Especially one that might be able to give him directions in this oceanic countryside.

"Yes." He said in his mind. "Who are you?"

The voice answered but instead of words, images formed in Nicholas mind. They were images of the whale gliding peacefully through the oceans with other whales. There were also images of scary creatures of numerous shapes and sizes in darkness, quickly followed by a pleasing image of a sunset on endless horizon of blue and gold. Nicholas didn't perceive a name, as such, but rather an identification of this whales experiences in the water.

Then he remembered Pantilius' talking about blue whales as if they were an alternate intelligence on this world, in case humans didn't work out. He spoke of them as if they were 'watchers' and taught Nicholas they were the largest creatures alive today and should be treated with respect.

Nicholas decided to offer a name to the whale. It was a human thing to do. "Can I call you Blue?" He asked. It was a simple name and he thought it might please the creature.

Nicholas felt the whale express pleasure at the name. After a few moments, he felt the whale inquire if he was an old person.

Nicholas hesitated again. He was sure Blue just asked if he was 'old' but he rather felt the question was more to do with his identity than an enquiry about his age. He suddenly realized this whale may have met others from Abanis.

"No." He said to Blue. "I am not an old one. I am a young one."

Nicholas felt his response was accepted. It was the mental equivalent of saying: 'Ahh. I see. That makes sense.'

Now he felt another question in his mind and translated the imagery and feelings. It was a strange question. The whale was asking if he was going to see the Hag. This confused Nicholas because 'hag', he always thought, was a rather rude reference to a disgruntled, old woman. But like the previous question, the whale was using the word in a specific kind of way. Nicholas didn't know how to respond.

"I don't know who or what the hag is." He said, hoping his assumptions on the matter were correct.

He felt surprise from the whale. Nicholas imagined the whale was saying "Wow! You don't know who the Hag is? What kind of ocean traveler are you?"

Nicholas responded mentally, confirming that he didn't, in fact , know who the hag was. "Does she live here in the oceans?" He asked.

Blue nodded inside Nicholas head. "Follow?" It asked Nicholas.

"I want to find a place to rest, Blue." Said Nicholas. "I am lost and I don't know where to go or what I should be doing."

The whale seemed to consider this for a short time. Then Nicholas felt it speak to him once more. "Follow me, child. The Hag of this ocean is kind and welcomes travelers."

Nicholas nodded and accepted the whale's suggestion. He honestly didn't know what he should be doing or where he should be going as long as it was not in the company of citizens of Abanis or near the Greyman. Whoever or whatever the 'Hag' was, he knew that Blue would not lead him into danger.

The whale swung lazily in the water and Nicholas half imagined one of its giant fins gesture, as if to say "C'mon kid."

He followed the whale easily. It was truly an immense creature and Nicholas wondered how old it could be. He knew that blue whales were long lived creatures and quite intelligent but he didn't know he could actually communicate with them. He felt he learned something new this day and made a mental note to tell Pantilius all about it whenever they met again.

Nicholas suddenly felt an ache in his imaginary stomach. His thoughts turned to Claire and he wondered if his friends were ok. The passing of Gabriel was heartbreaking for him as well but he still hadn't come to terms with the whole 'death' notion. The pain of losing his older friend was like a sliver that, when pulled out of his palm, would reappear some time later to hurt again. It was a distressing feeling to know that he would never speak to Gabriel again.

He flowed through the water for quite a long time behind the whale and felt they were going deeper and deeper into the depths of the ocean. After a while the deep blue of his surroundings became quite dark and he needed to use his instinctual compass to focus in the whale in front of him.

"Are we there yet?" He asked, in the spirit of every young person in existence on a trip.

"Yes." He felt the response. "Not much longer, young one."

A short while later, Nicholas perceived they were very deep in the ocean and saw something he didn't think was possible at this depth. There was light all around below him. It was a faint glow but seemed to be getting brighter and brighter as they descended. Deeper and deeper they glided through the currents until finally they rounded a hill on the floor of the ocean. Nicholas was astonished at what he saw.

A glorious myriad of colors, lights and oceanic splendor spread before him. He stopped behind the whale to take it all in. He was looking at a natural reef formed around a hollowed out dome-like structure that looked similar to the peculiar architecture of Abanis. Thousands of fish, crustaceans, and larger sea life swam lazily around the reef as if it were the center of a marine city and this was rush hour. At the heart of the spectacle was the hollowed out dome, which looked like the ruins of a ancient building. All of the rainbow colored lights of the area seemed to be coming from the heart of the dome.

"The Hag is there. In the heart of the reef." Said Blue. "Introduce yourself, youngling."

"Thank you Blue." Said Nicholas. "It was nice to meet a friend."

Nicholas felt the mental equivalent of "Aww, shucks." Inside his head and imagined the whale would have shrugged and grinned stupidly if it could.

"We will meet again, I think. Take care young human." Said Blue in his head and Nicholas watched as the giant creature swam away and joined some other whales.

Nicholas turned back to the glorious scenery and looked at the dome in the heart of the reef. The light emanating from within flashed and pulsed like nothing he had ever seen before. He mentally prepared himself for meeting this hag, whoever she was. If he wasn't in a state of flowing, he would have flattened his hair, straightened his robes and dusted off his boots. Instead, he simply flowed closer.

The closer he got to the dome, the more he felt the structure looked familiar. He could see more detail on its white marble construction and felt he had seen it before but could not imagine where or when. He continued onwards, flowing around groups of inquisitive squids and nervous crabs living amidst the ruins of many buildings that had collapsed around the dome. He wondered what city it had been and why it was at the bottom of the ocean but decided to investigate that oddity later.

Just as he was about to see the source of the light within the massive dome another knocking came at his mental door. This time it wasn't the kind of knock normally associated with a friend but rather the knock of authority demanding to come inside or the door was going to be bashed in.

Nicholas halted. That wasn't the friendly presence he was expecting. "Who is this?" He asked mentally.

A presence entered his mind and he felt it was demanding to see some form of identification.

"Who are blessed?!?" It demanded.

Nicholas felt the presence in his mind was female and quite old. Although he never knew his mother, Mrs. Bakersbee was more than capable of filling the role in his youth. And, like most matrons across the universe, her motherly radar could vaporize the veils of any deception like a stick of butter under a blowtorch. This was exactly how he felt now.

"Who are the blessed? Answer!" Said the voice once more in the mental equivalent of a shout.

Nicholas mind raced. He recalled Pantilius say something like that before. Then his imaginary hand went to his chest and he remembered the iron spike he received from The Pilgrim as a birthday gift. The recorded message attached to the broach came to mind.

"The meek?" He said sheepishly.

A feeling of relief and happiness suddenly entered his mind and he heard a voice accompany it. "My child. It is you. Come to me." It said.

Nicholas flowed into the dome over a slight rise in the ruins around it and looked inside. At the center of the hollowed out dome was a gigantic platform of white marble. It was elegant in its simplicity and he imagined this dome would have been a meeting hall of some sort. All along the remaining walls were images carved into the marble. They depicted beings with unusually tall and equine features offering assistance to humans. They depicted scenes of agricultural practices, architectural construction and banquets of grandiose scale. But Nicholas was entranced by the light at the heart of the dome, at the center of the platform.

At the center of the white marble platform was a strange construction. It was the frame of a door, without an actual door. It was magnificently carved with square shapes of varying sizes that didn't seem to depict anything that Nicholas could understand. It was as if the maker of the doorframe had taken the abstract, crisp angles of a crystalline rock and carefully replicated it to even the smallest resplendent detail. All around the frame were twinkling lights and shifting shapes as if simple objects were flashing in and out of existence.

In the center of the door, however, was the silhouette of a woman. Tendrils of light radiated from the silhouette and wrapped around the doorframe in a kind of lovers embrace or a desperate clutch for survival, Nicholas could not tell which. The light emanating from the woman was intense and Nicholas had to shield his eyes, despite being in a state of flowing.

"My dear child." Said the woman. "Come closer, let me have a look at you." It said in a voice so soothing that Nicholas felt himself gliding closer without thinking.

"Hello." He said. "I am Nicholas. I come from Abanis."

"Yes. I know you do. I am the Hag Nosis. I am pleased to meet you, Nicholas." She said in a voice so sultry, Nicholas found himself thinking of Claire and would have blushed if he could.

"The Hag, Nosis?" Said Nicholas in as friendly a manner as he could manage. "Hag is a rather unwarranted for one such as you, it seems."

Nicholas felt appreciated laughter in his mind and continued to find Claire more and more in his immediate thoughts.

"It is a kind of penance I impose on myself, Nicholas. I am a shadow of my former self. I am here but I am not here, at the same time."

Nicholas considered this. Apparently Nosis felt she was to be punished for something but he could not guess what such a beautiful creature could have done.

"But we met before, Nicholas. I have been waiting for you to return."

Nicholas hesitated. He suddenly wondered if he was speaking to something or someone who had lost their mind in isolation.

"Umm, I don't recall ever being here my lady - "

"You were a child, an infant." Said Nosis. "I guided you to the three wise men who essayed to bring you to Abanis. You were lost. I found you."

Nicholas was mildly stunned. He didn't know how he actually came to Abanis, only that Harry, Buddy and Fuzzy brought him. "You mean I ..." He paused for a second and continued. "You mean I flowed? As a baby?"

"Indeed you did, my child. It was a gamble the old men took to save you. The risk would have ended poorly had I not heard you."

"That's what Gabriel meant! I've flowed before." Nicholas blurted out. He felt a little ashamed for a moment. "Uhh, sorry, just thinking aloud."

He felt laughter inside his head once more. It was the kind of giggle one would expect from a young woman.

Nicholas looked around at the flashing doorframe and then at the silhouetted woman. "Well you have my thanks for saving my life." He bowed to the woman. "I owe you much, Nosis. But who are you?"

"Nicholas, I have been waiting for you. The one you know as The Pilgrim asked me to do something for you."

"The Pilgrim! You know him?" Said Nicholas excitedly. "He left before I came to Abanis. I have never met him but I have heard so many things and...." He stopped, feeling like a school boy who couldn't stop talking. Which, in fact, he was.

"Yes. I sense that I have little time here and have waited for you to come Nicholas. You are very special to us." She said. The tendrils of pulsating light around the door pulsed and flashed, then she continued. "Please open your mind to me. Allow me to take you on a trip to the past so that I may accurately convey what you must come to know."

Nicholas nodded and he felt his mind being opened in the way that awakening does to those who have slept deeply. He saw flashes of strange images at first. Then he saw a sprawling, white city on an island surrounded by a seemingly endless ocean. It was clear and crisp in his mind. He could see the details of lush gardens with huge trees, waterfalls, giant domes and pyramid-shaped buildings with immense obelisks rising from the constructions. It looked as if someone took all the best ideas from the Incans, the Egyptians, the Greeks and the Sumerians to make one city.

Then the scene changed. He zoomed in and he saw a woman whose beauty he had never seen an equal to. Her features, however, were quite strange to Nicholas. She had long black hair which fell over her shoulders to a slender waist and wore a white dress, the likes of which he had seen in pictures of Roman women. This was all well and good but the woman's body seemed odd. Her skin was grey. Not grey like someone who had died and shouldn't be walking about, but grey like that of unpolished silver. She was beautifully proportioned but her legs and arms seemed elongated and her almond shaped, dark eyes were twice as large as they should be. Nicholas wasn't sure but he estimated her to be at least three meters tall and doubted very much that she was human. At least, one that he had studied and knew existed in the world. She was standing on a balcony, looking at the horizon with a worried expression on her face.

Then the scene changed and he could see what the woman was looking at. It was four shapes coming closer to the city on the horizon. Nicholas focused on the airborne shapes and realized they were birds of some kind because he could see the flapping of wings. A moment passed and he could see that the winged shapes had riders. After few more moments, Nicholas gasped. He could clearly see the winged shapes were dragons! At least, they resembled what Gabriel had looked like when he washed up on the shore of Rongo-rongo. The reptilian beasts were green and on their backs, riding the dragons like horsemen, were four men who looked very similar to the woman in their peculiar appearance.

As the magnificent dragons came closer and circled the balcony, Nicholas was able to see more of the rider's features. The one seemingly in the lead had long golden-white hair and was quite handsome. He wore strange attire that Nicholas assumed was armor but the likes of which he had never seen before. It looked similar to the guardians of the gate pool of Abanis but was somewhat more detailed. All four riders wore black capes that billowed out behind them as they came closer and closer to the balcony.

A few moments later, the four immense dragons landed on the massive balcony. Nicholas felt an urge to step back a little as they did so, despite knowing he was envisioning a memory.

The riders dismounted and the leader met the woman who ran forward to embraced him. The other riders waited patiently behind the two. After a few moments, the woman began to speak to the golden haired leader in hurried whispers. Then the discussion became more heated and she yelled something at him. He yelled back at her and made a gesture with his hand that he would not tolerate any more discussion.

It was a language that Nicholas did not recognize but he was easily able to see it was a quarrel of some kind. The other riders looked uncomfortable but said nothing as they stood some distance away. Finally, the male leader slapped the woman across the face. As she fell to the ground, he spat at her and cursed. Nicholas' chivalric senses were jostled at this point. He suddenly felt an overwhelming desire to see if the golden-haired freak would like to try slapping him.

Then the image of the balcony scene faded and reformed. He was inside the city now and standing inside a huge dome. At the center of the dome was a platform with the very same crystalline doorframe that Nosis presently inhabited. He realized that the dome and everything in it was the same. The only differences seemed to be that it was whole, undamaged and quite noticeably *not* under several thousand feet of water. Standing on the platform was a humanoid that resembled the woman and the dragon riders. He had long, black hair and wore blue robes like those of the citizens of Abanis. He carried a long spear that looked as if it was crafted entirely of silver and stood as if he was guarding the doorframe. Behind him, the space inside the doorframe seemed to flash and pulse with light.

After a few moments, the golden-haired leader of the dragon riders entered the dome by means of a simple archway. Nicholas realized he was not in the best of shape and looked quite disheveled, as if he had just come from some battle. His black cloak was torn in several places and his shining armor was streaked and splattered with crimson stains Nicholas guessed was blood. He carried a scythe, also covered with blood, and used it as a walking stick as he limped slightly towards the platform.

The black haired humanoid stepped down from the platform to confront the newcomer. They shouted at each other in the language Nicholas heard before on the balcony. He assumed it was a severe argument because the black-haired humanoid was nearly in tears with frustration. Then suddenly, the dragon rider lashed out with the scythe. It was blocked by the other's silver spear.

A fight ensued and Nicholas watched in awe as each employed skill that he had only read about in world mythologies and fantasy fictions. Lightning flashed inside the giant dome, fires erupted out of nothing and were extinguished by icy blasts. The two danced around each other, the scythe and spear whirling about in a blur. Attacking and parrying each other amidst the elemental devastation around them, they flew up into the air and seemed to defy gravity as each vied for advantage. The building itself seemed to strain under the forces unleashed and the dome cracked. Huge chucks of marble crashed to the ground as the glittering flashes of scythe and spear cast sparks around the battle zone.

Then with one mighty swing, the golden-haired dragon rider shattered his opponent's silver spear into innumerable shards. There was a loud metallic sounding 'clang' followed by some kind of explosion as the spear was destroyed. The black-haired humanoid fell to the ground, deeply wounded, and unarmed.

The dragon rider looked down at his fallen opponent and looked about to finish him off when he stopped suddenly. He appeared to struggle inwardly and yelled something at the fallen guardian. Then his eyes fell on the doorframe and he seemed entranced by it. After a few moments, he laughed as one who had overcome much to be in this position. He stepped over the fallen guardian and walked towards the platform.

Out of the corner of his eye, Nicholas saw the woman from the balcony scene appear in the archway. She screamed, ran towards the fallen guardian and knelt beside him. The black-haired humanoid seemed to plead with her and gestured to the doorway. The woman looked up and rose at a run.

Several things happened at this point which made Nicholas blink mentally. The black-haired guardian rose to his knees, clutched his chest and shouted something. Then he simply vanished with a flash of light.

The victor, not noticing the newcomer, began to chant something in front of the doorframe. The flashing lights and swirling abstract shapes within it pulsed and shifted as if responding to the words. Before he had time to finish the chant, he turned in surprise as the woman ran full speed into him. Nicholas wasn't sure but it looked as if she was attempting to prevent some kind of procedure.

The rider moved quickly and tried to avoid the woman but the two collided and fell into doorway. The rider screamed in shock and horror. For a brief instant, the two seemed frozen inside the pulsing light of the doorway as if in a lover's embrace. The rider's face was frozen in terror. Then the world exploded and the entire image went white.

Then Nicholas found that he was looking down at the city and the island once more. There was a flash of light from within one of the domes. It was so bright that he felt the urge to look away. In slow motion he saw the entire island blasted apart with so much force that huge chunks of smoldering land and rock roared passed him and landed in the ocean miles from initial explosion. The blast radius of the island's devastation was so huge that some pieces of land were still on an upward trajectory and becoming smaller as the island sank beneath the waves. The skies flashed with lightning and turned orange and crimson as clouds formed over the doomed island. Massive waves, the size of which Nicholas only read about in apocalyptic texts, spread outwards from island, continuing long and far towards every horizon. Then all went black.

Nicholas found himself inside the dome once more. He looked up at Nosis and the doorframe she occupied. He felt her pain and anguish in his mind. He saw some images of objects blink in and out of existence around her and realized what he had just witnessed. He looked around the dome and realized why it had initially looked familiar. He was at ground zero of the destruction of Adamis, the first home of the ancient people called the Huru. It was a story he heard from Pantilius and Harry more than once about their origins and why they were different from humans.

"It was you, wasn't it?" Said Nicholas. "You were the woman."

"Yes." Said Nosis softly.

"Who was he, the one you loved? Am I right in assuming he was a companion of yours?"

The Hag Nosis was silent for a time and Nicholas guessed she was reluctant to reply. But she spoke eventually. "He was my husband."

"I'm, uhh, sorry."

"Do not be afraid to ask Nicholas. You're training as an emissary was not complete before Abanis was abandoned. You must understand this history before you can go further. Every emissary of Abanis comes here to see something of the road ahead of them. It is what I do."

"Very well." Said Nicholas, politely. "Who were the ones who fought? Why was it important for me to see that?"

"The fair haired, dragon-rider you saw was my husband. He has many names among humans, some less kind than others. Some of our people called him The Morning Star because he was the brightest and most beautiful of our people. Despite being the greatest of us, he was not immune to weariness and eventually fell into a deep depression which consumed him. He abandoned our ways and his actions in the latter days of Adamis were cruel and thoroughly evil."

"The Morning Star." Said Nicholas. "I recognize the meaning of the name but I have never heard of him."

"You know of him, Nicholas." Said Nosis. "In your mind, I sense that you refer to him by a different name. He is The Greyman."

Nicholas was shocked. "What? How can this be? Wasn't he killed in the explosion? Because he is back."

Nicholas suddenly realized he ran past another important point and backed up. "And how is it you are here?"

"That is a matter for a later discussion, child. There are forces in the universe that you will come to understand in time. I was destroyed but he survived. For now, try to think of us as shadows of our former selves. Trapped in a way. Only his shadow is longer and darker than mine."

"I see." Said Nicholas. Trying to make sense of everything. He felt he was in numbers class again and shuddered.

"Nicholas." Nosis continued. "You must know the players in the upcoming confrontation that must surely happen."

"Confrontation?" Said Nicholas with the air of one whose only confrontation had ever been with himself over a choice between chocolate or vanilla.

"Yes. The citizens of Abanis must find a way to overcome The Greyman. He has been using powerful skills to keep his consciousness alive."

Nicholas nodded but did a little backtracking. "Why was The Greyman trying to enter the doorway?"

"It may be difficult for you to understand the answer." Said Gnosis.

"Try me." Said Nicholas softly, trying not to imply that nothing at this point would surprise him.

"The doorways were a failed experiment. The Nelfilem made them in an effort to help us. They were supposed to lead to our home but the gates are unstable so we dared not use them lest they cause some kind destruction here on this world. We are lucky only the city of Adamis was destroyed when we entered the gate. It could have been much worse and the human race may have been lost."

Again Nicholas tried to understand what Nosis was saying. He tried to organize the growing pile of questions in his mind.

"The Nelfilem?"

"Yes, we presume Pantilius is the is last of his kind but once he had many brothers and sisters. They were cruelly mistreated by my husband but loved by others."

"Wow." Nicholas nodded. He knew Pantilius was not entirely human but not entirely like the others. The fact that he was another *kind* of human was something he knew but needed to hear from someone else for it all to make sense. "Who was the other? The one who had the spear and guarded the doorway?"

"That was The Greyman's twin brother. They were very close and loved each other dearly, long ago. But in the end, my husband's arrogance and pride overwhelmed reason."

"He fought his own brother!" Nicholas said in disbelief. He never had a brother but always wished he had. And if so, he could not imagine fighting him over anything. "What was his name?"

"You know the answer Nicholas. Think."

"The Pilgrim!" He gaped at Hag Nosis, knowing his assumption was correct. "The Greyman and The Pilgrim were twin brothers!"

The silhouette of Hag Nosis nodded silently.

Nicholas had never met The Pilgrim but he was regarded by Pantilius, Harry, Buddy, Fuzzy and all the others he had come to cherish as their legendary patron. He was the creator of Abanis and rumored to possess powers he only heard about in stories and books.

He stared at Nosis in disbelief as the puzzle pieces of some ancient drama began to slide into place. The origin of the Huru and who they actually were was troubling him.

"Wow." Was all he could say as his mind raced. He started to ask something but back-tracked to something else. Then he backtracked again and something truly confusing that was nagging at his mind like a bad hangover sprung up and demanded to be acknowledged. The Greyman was trying to *'go home'*. But where was *home*?

"Who are the Huru?" He asked. "Where do they come from?"

He suddenly felt the Hag Nosis scream in his mind. For a moment he wondered if his question was a little too intrusive. She was terrified and Nicholas felt every molecule in his flowing body freeze in horror at her sudden outburst.

"It's not a question of *where* we came from, primate." Said a soft but severe voice from behind him. "It's a question of *when*."

Chapter 23: Watery Tomb Ambrosia

Nicholas spun around. Behind him was either the strangest or the most horrid thing he had ever seen. A man, or what he thought was the remains of a man, floated behind him. It was a skeleton of a human, robed in black, tattered cloth and carrying a scythe. In the sockets where eyes should have been, two red sparks of light flashed as they focused on Nicholas.

"How easy it was to guess your route, child." Said the skeletal terror. "But come now, Nicholas is it? I only wish to speak at this time. Do not be afraid."

"Do not trust him. Flee, boy! Flee!" The Hag Nosis screamed in Nicholas head.

Nicholas made a sudden movement. He decided rather quickly that the ghost of a alien woman, long dead, was more trustworthy than a floating skeleton wielding a farm implement.

But the skeletal creature was inexplicably in front of him no matter what direction he turned. Then a cold, bony hand was around his throat and Nicholas felt he couldn't breathe. He was still in a state of flowing, not having a body exactly but he felt that didn't matter to the being now choking the life out of him.

Nicholas realized two things at this point. The first was that this creature was The Greyman although he could not explain why he just knew. He felt he had been in this situation before. This was the bogeyman, feared by Pantilius and the others in Abanis enough to abandon the city altogether. The second realization confused him. He felt the same urge to heal this creature as he did Blue just hours ago. The urge, however, was quickly overwhelmed by a more primal urge to stay alive.

"You are The Greyman." Nicholas said flatly.

"Oh, I have so many names." The creature hissed. "This is my domain, little monkey. Water is my kind of thing, you might say." Said an old, malicious voice in his head. "And now I have the key you carry and the vessel you inhabit." Nicholas saw the scythe raise in a skeletal hand and wondered what it was going to be like if he died at the hands of this creature.

"Leave him! Let him be, Halaam!" Screamed Nosis.

"Silence, woman!" Said the skeletal creature. "I should have known you were able to cling to some sort of consciousness all these millennia. I will tend to you next."

Nicholas mind raced. He realized this was a no-nonsense kind of evil creature. In the poems and epics he read from multiple civilizations around the world, he always wondered why the 'bad' hero and the 'good' hero had a two-hour long discussion before actually fighting to the death. But this creature looked about to strike and get everything done without any dialogue at all. He also realized that the 'good' hero won in most of the stories he read and wondered if he was that particular 'good' person this moment. Unable to move and unable to breathe, however, made him feel that this particular story would be quite short and end rather badly.

Then a name came to his mind. He didn't know why he thought about it but he raised the volume of his mind and screamed one name.

"Blue! Help!" He screamed to the ocean at large.

Just as the scythe was about to swing at his head, tendrils of light wrapped around its shaft and the body of The Greyman.

"Flow Nicholas! Find Michael! Find Michael!" Shouted Nosis. "Come my children, come to your mother's aid!"

Several things happened at this point. Nicholas saw the skeleton yanked away from him suddenly and wrapped in tangled web of illuminated tendrils that stretched from the doorway Nosis occupied. He saw the skeleton turn and slash the scythe at them, severing many of the strings of light. He heard The Hag Nosis scream in agony inside his head. Against all common sense, he wished to come to her aid but as he started towards her, he was suddenly aware of the light around him being eclipsed. Before Nicholas could understand what was happening, a mouth that could have engulfed a small village swallowed him up and began to swim away at great speed.

The last thing he saw before the gigantic mouth closed around him was the skeletal creature slashing and defending itself against legions of sea life coming to Nosis' aid. It was if the ancient reef itself, and all the life inhabiting it, attacked The Greyman in defense of The Hag Nosis and the ruins of Adamis. Then all went black.

A short while later, Nicholas decided to take a stab in the dark, as it were. Not literally, of course. "Uhh, Blue?"

He felt the familiar presence of Blue inside his head again. It confirmed his enquiry. "Yes."

"Umm. I'm inside your mouth aren't I."

"Yes."

"Thank you, Blue. I'm guessing I owe you my life."

"You are welcome, youngling."

"Where are we going?" Said Nicholas, who was trying not to feel uncomfortable talking to the largest mammal on earth from inside its mouth.

Once more, Nicholas sensed through imagery and feeling that Blue was taking him away from great danger.

"I can flow, Blue. If you can give me some directions to some coast where there are few humans, I may be able to - "

But Nicholas was interrupted. "We are flowing now." Said Blue.

Nicholas was startled. He knew that flowing was a means by which emissaries of Abanis moved about the world. He knew that humans could not do it, although apparently he could for some reason. He certainly did not know that animals could.

"You can flow? How?"

Nicholas felt the presence in his mind unable to convey an exact response but the image of a fair haired humanoid flashed in his mind. He saw it speaking to whales. It was the leader of the dragon riders Nicholas saw in the vision that The Hag Nosis showed him, The Greyman.

"He taught you how to flow?"

Nicholas felt an affirmation to this. "Long ago, he was a friend to our kind. He taught us much."

Nicholas mused about this. Then he remembered what the Hag Nosis shouted to him about finding Michael. He didn't know who 'Michael' was or where he would find him but he was certain that 'Michael' wouldn't be shopkeeper in Rome, or fishing at a lake somewhere in Britannia. He shuddered at the thought of leaving Nosis and wondered about her fate. He tried not to think of what may have become of her at the hands of The Greyman and wondered if she could actually die. He still didn't understand what she was or how she lived so long in such a strange state. Whatever the case, her situation with an enraged skeletal being was probably not good. Someday, he thought, he would make amends for all these beings risking so much for his protection.

"We have arrived, youngling." Said Blue.

His enormous mouth opened and Nicholas flowed out of it. He looked around and realized they were in another reef but this one was in considerably more shallow water than the one at the bottom of the ocean. Sunlight penetrated the sea's surface and shone down into the shallow waters. Nicholas surveyed the emerald tinted reef, filled with all the sea life that inhabits such places, and looked into the giant face of Blue.

"Again you have helped me Blue. Thank you."

You are welcome, youngling. Here you will find a shore presently uninhabited by humans."

"I owe you much. Umm, do you know who Michael is?"

"The Hag spoke to me when we escaped. She told me to take you here but I do not know who Michael is. Perhaps that creature is nearby."

Nicholas nodded to himself. The fact that Blue regarded Michael as 'that creature' did not go unnoticed. "Will we meet again Blue?"

"I am sure you will find yourself in the oceans again youngling. But I would be wary of flowing in the near future. Water is his domain and he will find you if you flow again. Take heed." And with that, the gigantic whale turned lazily in the waters and vanished into the depths. Nicholas half-imagined a massive fin wave to him in the kind of way that made him feel the whale was trying to say 'later kid.'

Great. Nicholas thought. *Can't flow and can't contact anyone I know.*

He turned to the look at the shoreline and flowed towards it. When he felt that the water was sufficiently shallow, he emerged from it and stood up. He was standing in waist-deep water at the center of a small lagoon. It stretched around behind him on either side in a kind of horseshoe. Just beyond the ring of sandy beach was a ring of trees that looked as though they could double as a fortress wall. Giant palm trees and ferns that didn't understand the meaning of 'large enough' lined the jungle wall. He imagined the immensely thick foliage would offer ample protection and privacy for a while. He also wondered if he would ever be able to get out of the lagoon without flowing.

He trudged through the water, up to the sandy beach and sighed. He breathed deeply and found the air to be crisp, salty and fresh. Judging by the sun, it looked to be morning and he decided to take a short rest and stock of his situation. Pleased that his backpack was still slung over his shoulder and curiously dry, he opened it up and sat down on the sand.

Before he could reach inside, a streak of gold flew out of it and buzzed around his head, sparkling in the morning sun.

"Kara!" He said, smiling at the little gold Valkyrie.

The animated figurine buzzed around his head happily, landed on his shoulder and saluted to him smartly. Then she gripped her spear in two hands and turned on the spot. She looked at the emerald lagoon, then the sandy beach and then the jungle over Nicholas shoulder. After taking in their surroundings she looked at Nicholas inquisitively, as if to say 'where the heck are we now?'

Nicholas looked around and shook his head. "I haven't the foggiest idea, Kara. But I'm sure we'll find out soon enough."

He took off his soaking wet robes, boots and cloak and laid them out on the sand. After some rummaging around, he found his pipe and was soon basking in the warmth of the morning sun smoking some sweet, cherry leaf. He was happy the peculiar backpack was always dry after flowing but he wished his robes had the same quality. He blew a few smoke rings and did some inner calculations.

He realized he was neither tired, hungry or thirsty but guessed he might become so now that he was out of the water. He basked in the morning sun and decided to take a nap while his robes dried. Then he would take a walk into the jungle... and see if this 'Michael' person was around somewhere.....perhaps he would have some fruit or whatever....might be available ....in the jungle.........

Nicholas opened his eyes and then closed them, cringing in the afternoon sun. He felt as though he slept for a long time. He heard purring sounds beside him and saw Kara curled up into a little ball of gold and sleeping on the sand beside his head. He grinned at her and sat up to inspect his clothes. They were dry and warm.

After putting his clothes back on, he rummaged around in his backpack for something to eat. It was empty except for a few crumbs of a cookie long since devoured. He sighed and looked back at the green wall of trees and ferns. There may be some fruit in there.

"Kara, c'mon." He said softly to the purring ball of gold in the sand beside him.

The little Valkyrie blinked at him, stretched her wings and buzzed up to his shoulder where she sat down heavily. She yawned and gave him a thumbs up, indicating she was ready to go.

Nicholas slung his backpack over his shoulder and waded into the thick jungle. The air was densely humid and Nicholas struggled with every step to navigate through the foliage. Despite a few beetles clicking in protest as he passed through the greenery, the jungle was curiously quiet. He stopped and looked around at one point just to make sure. It was eerily quiet despite some minor rustling in upper levels of the canopy. There were no birds but seemed to be a lot of spiders. One spider he deftly avoided was so big he wondered briefly if *it* ate all the birds.

He continued for some time until finally he could see some light up ahead. It appeared to be a clearing and he hoped this jungle business would come to an end. Hastening his step he pushed his was through some stubborn overgrowth and emerged panting from the jungle wall.

He stumbled around for a moment in the sand, trying to yank his backpack from the clutches of a fern that didn't want to let go then looked around. It was indeed a clearing.

Before him was a sandy path. On either side of the path were four meter high walls made of huge, sand colored, stone bricks. The path seemed to stretch straight into the roots of a forest covered mountain rising above the stone. On either side of the path, the walls continued and dug into the jungle.

There were no signs like "Welcome to Such and Such a Place" nor were there any statues forbidding entry or even mysterious markings on the stones. It was simply a path leading to somewhere. Nicholas decided that going somewhere down the sandy path was preferable to navigating through the jungle of giant spiders and no birds. He looked at Kara standing on his shoulder, ever on the lookout. She shrugged and nodded.

Nicholas sighed, tied his hair back into a pony tail and trudged forward. Despite the afternoon sun descending rapidly into dusk, the air was really hot and he was sweating heavily. He felt hungry and thirsty now but tried to ignore it as he walked down the simple sandy path towards the base of the mountain.

The stone walls on either side of him looked to be crafted with incredible skill and accuracy. He brushed his hand along a few seams as he walked and marveled at how perfectly they fit together. Nicholas guessed they were made by humans but he didn't know his exact geographical location. He knew, without actually knowing how, that he was in lands near Egypt or the Great Desert but he could not be certain.

He walked for what seemed to be hours and the mountain loomed over him. He was becoming increasingly aware of hunger and thirst as he continued onward and wondered if he should have looked for fruit in the jungle. It was getting darker now and there was only a mild scarlet hue in the sky above the stone walls. Despite the darkness setting in around him, he felt mildly pleased to see stars twinkling above as they came to life in the evening sky.

Finally, far ahead he thought he could see a flicker of orange light. It was faint but appeared to be getting clearer as he walked along. After some time he could clearly see it was a torch set into some framework beside a giant door. He quickened his step, hoping someone would appear soon with frosty mug of mead and a bowl of stew. The walls on either side of him branched off left and right, widening the sandy path as he hastened forward until finally he was standing in front of a huge metal door.

Above the door was a cliff so massive that it would bring a tear to eye of even the most insane rock climber. Although it was now silhouetted against a starry sky, Nicholas could see that the side of the mountain stretch far above him. It was if the mountain was cleaved in twain and then covered with greenery to mask the scene of the crime.

He looked down at the metal door and then to the torch beside it. He stopped and looked at the torch again. It wasn't a torch at all. It was some form of crystal carved into the shape of a flame and seemed to glow bright orange. He put his hand close to it and tested the air near it. It was cool. He touched it and found the crystal was cool to the touch but appeared to glow intensely yellow when he touched it. He pulled his hand away and the light faded somewhat to a warm orange hue. It reminded him of the amethyst lamps in the central plaza of Abanis, crafted by The Pilgrim, or so he was told.

"OK." He said aloud, nodding to Kara. "That's pretty amazing."

He would have spent more time studying the strange torch-like crystal but hunger and thirst demanded more attention. He looked at the door.

At least he thought it was a door. Most doors have a handle and an indication that there is something beyond it. That's what distinguishes doors from walls. But this door had no handle. It was about four meters in height and Nicholas imagined whomever made it were tall people indeed. It was made of a silvery metal, possibly steel, but other than the fact it appeared to lead inside the mountain, there nothing else about it indicating 'doorishness'.

Nicholas stepped closer to examine the weather stained metal. Other than patches of rust, there were no markings on it except for a strange indentation in the center. It was faint but he could just make out the shape as he leaned closer. It was the outline of a hand. He traced a finger along the lines and realized the indentation looked familiar.

He looked at his hand. Then he looked at the indentation.

"No, it can't be." He said to Kara. He placed his hand in the indentation and it fit absolutely perfectly, as if he made the indentation long ago.

Nicholas looked at Kara on his shoulder. "I've never been here bef-"

There was an earsplitting screech of metal and the door slid back on metal hinges.

"-ore." Finished Nicholas, catching himself from falling into the darkness beyond as the door opened. He stood holding his hand in mid-air and looked into the gloom.

Nicholas paused. He wasn't sure if "Uh Hello?" was appropriate but he didn't know what else to say.

"Uh, hello?" He said. The sound of his voice echoes into the gloom. He imagined a very large space beyond.

There was no response. Deciding the alternative to entering the darkness was to stand stupidly in front of it for gods know how long, he decided to venture in.

As Nicholas passed the threshold of the doorway a light flared beside his head and he closed his eyes.

"Ouch!" He exclaimed, cringing in the new light. He blinked a few times and found that a crystal, embedded inside the stone archway was not unlike the one outside the door. It glowed purple. As he stepped around it and ventured further inside, another crystal flared to life a few meters ahead. He realized his proximity was probably igniting them.

Nicholas was standing a large hallway that stretched deeper into the base of the mountain. Walking slowly forward, other crystals flared to life. Some were green, blue, orange and purple and all appeared to be natural crystal of varying shapes and sizes. After walking down the huge hallway, he passed through an archway and the world lit up like a thousand Jolly trees.

Nicholas covered his eyes with his hands as thousands of crystals flared to life. He blinked as blue, green, purple and orange crystals illuminated the immediate area.

After his eyes adjusted, Nicholas looked around. "Wow!"

He was standing at the base of a massive cylindrical chamber. It was bigger than any building he had ever seen from the inside. The mixture of crystal lights sparkled high up into the distance as he tried to understand the architecture. On his right was a stone carved staircase at least ten meters wide. It coiled up to the first level and he could see rows and rows of shelves in various rooms branching off from the stone stairs. He followed the coiling staircase as he stepped slowly into the center of the chamber. He counted at least seventeen different levels until his neck began to ache and his eyes began to water.

"What is this place?" He said aloud. He looked at Kara who shrugged and shook her head in disbelief as she gaped upwards.

"This is a Library, young human." Said a clinical sounding voice behind him. "And I would appreciate it if you would give me your name."

Nicholas spun around, his heart nearly stopping. The last time someone spoke unexpectedly behind him was quickly followed by extreme unpleasantness.

Nicholas gaped. "Gabriel." Was all he could say.

He said it because the voice belonged to a huge man whose long hair was streaked alternately white and black like the skin of a zebra. His eyes were opaque and his blue robes looked like they hid more than just a tall frame within. He was neither old nor young in appearance but his skin had the peculiar gold-yellow hue that Gabriel's had. He was holding a thin, rectangular piece of wood and on it were an assortment of parchments. He checked off something with an ink quill in his left hand and looked severely at Nicholas.

Then the man leaned down to Nicholas. "I ..highly doubt.. that your name... is Gabriel, young man. That... would be.. improbable."

Nicholas found himself staring at the man and noted the voice. It was a clear, severe voice that annunciated every vowel and syllable with the kind of precision normally associated with complex engineering.

"Uhh." Said Nicholas, still shocked.

The huge man swept the quill along the parchment once more and surgically checked off something.

"'Uhh' is not..a name, young human. It may have been popular 20,000 years ago in caves but I'm afraid these days most names have a little more substance." He stared at Nicholas severely.

Nicholas finally pulled himself together. "Sorry, not Gabriel. I mean, my name isn't Gabriel. My name is Nicholas. Christopher Nicholas."

"Christopher Nicholas." Said the man, his zebra-like hair falling over his shoulders as he peered closer to the parchment on his board. "Child-of-Erikssen. Yes. That name will do."

Again the quill swept across the parchment. The man checked something off so quickly that Nicholas was amazed it did not leave a small

thunderclap in its wake.

The man looked at Nicholas once more. "I am Ravenscrawl. You may call me Ravenscrawl. Why are you here?"

Nicholas hesitated. He wasn't sure if he was in the right place. "I'm looking for Michael."

There was briefest flicker or shock in the stone-like face but the man recovered quickly. He remained staring at

Nicholas with the kind of look a mathematician gives abstract art. "Why?"

Again Nicholas hesitated. He wasn't sure how to explain everything that happened while he was with The Hag Nosis.

"Well," he started, deciding to try to summarize his oceanic mishaps, "I was in the ocean and met a woman at the bottom of it. Long story short, I had to leave because a skeleton attacked me and she told me to come here and find Michael."

Again the quill swept towards the parchment and paused. It hovered over something written in a language Nicholas couldn't see clearly but nothing was checked off. Then the man looked up. He was troubled by something and began to speak but stopped. Then he nodded and returned to staring at Nicholas with measured severity.

"Very well. Come with me. But," He raised a finger so quickly between them, Nicholas thought it left a smoke trail, "you are malnourished. You will drink this." He produced a small, corked tonic bottle from within his robes. It was dark green and the liquid inside appeared to be viscous. He handed it to Nicholas.

Nicholas took it and uncorked the bottle. Despite his anticipation, it smelled quite pleasant. Like strawberries and cream.

"Drink." Said Ravenscrawl with the air of a doctor waiting for a patient to swallow his medicine.

Nicholas drank the liquid and immediately felt better. He was suddenly neither hungry or thirsty. "Fantastic." He smacked his lips. "Tastes delicious. What do you call it?"

"Ambrosia." Said Ravenscrawl, taking the empty bottle from Nicholas and placing it within his robes.

Then he turned and walked so swiftly up the giant staircase that Nicholas had to run to keep up.

After a short while, Nicholas was able to catch up to the tall man and was speed-walking beside him. "Did you say your name was Ravenscrawl?" He said, panting slightly as they climbed the massive staircase.

"Yes." Said the man. Then he veered left suddenly and walked into a huge room just off the stairs. They were on the third level of the library and Nicholas was relieved they were not climbing up to the 18th or whatever level of the place.

"I know that name..." Said Nicholas to himself. He stopped and looked at Kara on his shoulder. She nodded in agreement. "You know it too?"

Kara mimed writing and reading books. Then Nicholas realized. "Usher Ravenscrawl!" He shouted.

He turned to look at the tall man at the back of a huge, barren room and ran towards him. "You are Usher Ravenscrawl? You wrote the History of Abanis! And , and," Nicholas mind raced, looking inward for the most notable examples. "The Genius of the Pyramids of Egypt and, and.. The Rise of Primates. I read all of your books! But I was told you vanished long ago. What happened - "

"I am he." The tall man cut Nicholas off. He bowed slightly and gave Nicholas the most miniscule glimmer of a smile. Then he gestured to the portion of the wall.

Nicholas stopped and looked at the wall. He realized looking around quickly they were in a room with subtle lights, not as bright as elsewhere. Engraved in the stone was a large symbol of a dragon wrapped around a sword. Under it, a message was carved into the stone:

Here lies Michael, Champion of Adamis.
Beloved Son of Nosis.
Brother of Gabriel and Raphael.
Sire of Rudolph, Uriolph, Sariolph, Raguolph, Ramiolph, Chamuolph, Zadkiolph and Haniolph.
Slain defending the First Promise.

"As you requested." Said Ravenscrawl. "This is the Tomb of Michael. My brother."

Chapter 24: Bookworm Surprise

Nicholas stared at the stone wall and read the inscription over and over. Kara mimicked his actions and shook her head.

After a few moments, he sagged. "Oh." Was all he could say.

"Tell me," said Ravenscrawl folding his arms across his chest, "of this woman you met in the ocean."

"What?" Oh, yeah." Nicholas blinked in recollection as Ravenscrawl began to pace around him. "She was beautiful."

This was the first and most pertinent thing he could recall. He felt as though The Hag Nosis was hard to describe and....he paused and read the inscription again. Then he turned to Ravenscrawl.

"Michael was your brother? Gabriel too? Then which one are you? I do not see Ravenscr -"

"I am Raphael." He cut off Nicholas. "By now, I'm sure you realize the remaining Huru have multiple names belonging to different cultures. But please... continue. Tell me more about this woman." He had his back to Nicholas now.

Nicholas hesitated. Unless this was the biggest coincidence he had ever seen, the Hag Nosis was this man's mother. "As I said. She was beautiful. She was kind to me." His voice cracked and he suddenly wondered about his own mother and how he would feel if anyone told him about her. "She was trapped in a prison or something."

Ravenscrawl spun around. "Tell me exactly what you saw." He advanced on Nicholas and towered over him.

"She was wr-wrapped in light. Trapped in a doorway." Nicholas stuttered, taken off guard. "She was made of light but silhouetted somehow. I can't explain it. B-but she wanted me to come here. The Greyman found me and attacked us. I escaped because of her. She saved me and told me in my mind to find Michael."

Ravenscrawl looked into Nicholas eyes and said nothing for a few moments. Then he lowered his head and put a hand on Nicholas' shoulder and patted it.

"I see truth in your eyes young human. Did she show you a vision?"

"Yes but - "

"No need to tell me." She shows each visitor a different vision pertaining to the road ahead. It is your responsibility glean whatever knowledge you can from whatever she showed you."

Nicholas gaped at him, realizing something else. "Is The Greyman your father? And the father of Gabriel too?"

Ravenscrawl looked genuinely surprised. "Well then. It appears she showed you much, young human. More than others who visit her during training. Yes." He sighed. "Halaam we call him now. He is a traitor to all Hurum and humans. And he is the strongest of us, even if we all stood against him at the same time. Only the one you know as The Pilgrim is his equal and he was defeated once by my father."

"Yes." Said Nicholas. "I saw. Nosis let me see the past. I saw what happened to Adamis."

"Indeed?" Said Ravenscrawl. "Why would she show you such a thing?"

"I don't know but she wanted me to know the history. The reason why The Greyman must be stopped but he interrupted us and nearly killed me."

"He is back then." Said Ravenscrawl, glancing at the stone wall. "It may be time for humans after all."

"What?"

"How much of your training did Pantilius complete, young human?" Ravenscrawl said loudly, his voice thunderous.

"Uh. I don't really understand. I was made apprentice only recently."

"Then you are ready for basics. Come with me. We have much to do."

Nicholas shook his head in an effort to tread though the waves of history threatening to drown him. He sped after Ravenscrawl, who was already walking swiftly up the giant, coiling staircase.

"Sir, do you prefer me to call you Raphael or Raven - "

"Ravenscrawl will do, Nicholas. It is a name I have come to be proud of. I am glad my works did not go in one of your ears and out the other."

Nicholas nodded. They were walking quickly up the staircase and he was beginning to pant in an effort to keep up.

"Umm, what is this place?" He asked, trying to breath as he speed-walked.

"This is the Library of Twilenos." Said Ravenscrawl, waving a huge arm at the massive interior complex. "It is an archive of all the Hurum knowledge and history here and..." he paused, "elsewhere."

"I've never heard of it." Said Nicholas, marveling at the immense library once more and hoping he wasn't going to have to climb many more stairs.

"You weren't ready until now. This is the next step or 'big picture', if you prefer."

"So, why did my hand fit perfectly into the metal door outside? That can't be a coincidence."

"No." Said Ravenscrawl. "The door is fashioned in a way that only those who need to enter will find their hand perfectly fits and thus opens the locks. It is a safeguard."

"Ahh."

"I recognize this little friend though." Said Ravenscrawl, glancing sideways and patting Kara on the head.

"What? I've never been here before. How - "

"I recognize the skill." Ravenscrawl stopped suddenly and examined the little, gold Valkyrie on Nicholas' shoulder.

Nicholas was walking so fast, he blew by the huge man and had to back up.

"Yes. She is a remarkable woman." Said Ravenscrawl, smiling down at Kara who was truly loving the attention.

"Kara?" Said Nicholas, looking down at his shoulder and nodding. "Yeah she's one of a kind."

"No I meant the woman who made her. I recognize the skill. Very few of us manifest the ability to make familiars. My mother was one of them."

Nicholas frowned. "Wait? Claire. You know Claire?"

Ravenscrawl raised his zebra colored eyebrows and looked bemused at Nicholas. "Indeed, young human. She was here not long ago in training. Every emissary comes here but is sworn to secrecy thereafter. We like to keep the library as it should be. Quiet as possible."

"Wow." Nicholas said as he watched Ravenscrawl examine Kara.

"Surely Pantilius told you that the manifestation of Huru blood in humanity yields unpredictable skills and traits, yes?"

"Yes. He mentioned something like that." Nicholas nodded.

"Well, Claire's skills and traits are rather curious. She can create manifestations of her personality and imbue objects with them. A very rare skill indeed." He pointed to Kara and looked at Nicholas. "What you have standing on your shoulder is part of her, literally. You must have been very special to her."

Nicholas felt he was being interrogated and looked away. He wanted to remember that perfect, single day and night he shared with her but not share it with anyone else. "The feeling is mutual, sir."

For the first time since they met, Ravenscrawl smiled at him. Nicholas was immediately reminded of Gabriel and felt the ache of his passing return like a dark cloud. He wondered if Ravenscrawl knew if his brother was dead and if he should tell him.

"Indeed, you surprise me young human. She is a rare flower." Then he turned and walked hastily up the stairs once more.

Nicholas sighed and looked down at Kara. She snuggled up to his cheek and gave him a thumbs-up. Then he hastened up the steps to keep up with Ravenscrawl.

After sometime of walking in silence, Nicholas decided to ask something that had been nagging at him. "Sir, are you aware that Abanis has been abandoned?"

Ravenscrawl looked down at Nicholas and nodded. "Yes. And not a moment too soon. Aryu Veda came to me shortly after it happened. He was with Mrs. Bakersbee and many children."

"Are they ok? Do you know of Claire and the others?

"Yes, Claire is ok. She is among the Norsemen with Pantilius and Himtall. Aryu and the others have gone to some retreat in the Himalayas. They are quite safe, for time being."

Nicholas felt a wave of relief wash over him. He was afraid to ask what became of those he cared for.

"Here we are then." Ravenscrawl veered suddenly left and Nicholas nearly tripped up. They walked into a huge room filled with rows upon rows of leather-bound books of all shapes and sizes. Ravenscrawl walked down one of the rows and traced a finger along some of the books until he found what he was looking for. He pulled out a huge book that could have doubled as someone's kitchen table. He walked over to a round marble table with richly lacquered chairs around it and set the book down carefully. He opened it up and smiled slightly as the binding made a subtle cracking noise as he flipped through the papyrus pages. He stopped and nodded to himself. Then he looked up at Nicholas.

"Sit and read this." He said, not unkindly. "It is important you understand."

Nicholas sat down in a chair and pulled the book closer. The script was easy to read:

At the apex of her golden age, the elders among the Huru in Adamis became torn between two factions - those endeavoring to reach the stars and those who wished to remain among the humans. Darkness surrounds the motives behind such lofty desires but the tragic result of their efforts held consequences worldwide. In their hubris, the great scholars of the Huru accidentally caused the complete and utter destruction of their civilization and nearly destroyed human settlements in faraway lands. Several millennia before the Etruscan peninsula suffered an explosion of its own in Pompeii, the kingdom of the Huru was destroyed in a tumultuous blast. In one catastrophic moment, an island the size of Britannia sank beneath the waters of the south Atlantic. The after affects of the devastation caused earthquakes, tsunamis and apocalyptic tempests worldwide.

In the end, it is believed that only one, pure-blooded Huru survived. He has taken the name 'The Pilgrim' since that time and only reveals his true name to very few.

After suffering many years of grief in solitude, The Pilgrim ventured south to the desolate continent of Antarctica for he knew it would take humanity many centuries to discover such an uninhabitable place. Taking refuge far from the reach of the blossoming cultures of the world, he labored long and constructed a home deep beneath the ice and rock. He named it Abanis.

From there he occasionally ventured forth disguised as a quiet pilgrim, crossing the great oceans to walk among the lesser developed people of our little planet. The more he ventured forth from his demesne in the ice, the more he desired to make contact with his human brethren. After all, despite his immeasurable age and wisdom, The Pilgrim was still a social creature and longed for simple company.

In his travels, The Pilgrim discovered that although he was among the last of the Huru, there were some living among the humans who possessed Huru heritage. These are called the 'Hurum'. The matter of the Hurum is clearly addressed in the following script, compiled by Usher Ravenscrawl, Librarian of Twilenos:

"On one of his pilgrimages, he journeyed far to the north-east side of present day Africa where he marveled at the newly constructed pyramids of Egypt. After spending some time admiring one of humanities greatest achievements he continued eastward.

Crossing a mighty mountain range, he came upon a lush and fertile land inhabited by an ancient and peaceful people. Upon his arrival to the settlement, however, instead of finding it thriving with men, woman and children, he found only death. A pestilence was unleashed not long before The Pilgrims' arrival and all of the 10,000 or so inhabitants of the settlement had died rather quickly - all except one.

Despite his medicinal knowledge, the chief Shaman of the settlement was no match for the pestilence which came. By the dozens, people had come to him for help. He brewed potions, ground herbs, mixed pastes of all kinds to combat the disease but nothing seemed to help his people. In the end he was alone. All had died and he was left to wonder why he was spared.

The Pilgrim arrived to find the middle-aged shaman prostrate before a well near the settlement's communal center, humbled and wracked with grief. It was a market place of a sort but instead of bustling with merchants and shoppers, there were only corpses and scavengers. Surrounded by lifeless bodies in varied states of decomposition, the Shaman wept. As he approached with heartbreaking curiosity, The Pilgrim greatly pitied this human who had devoted his life to helping others but was now penitent before an unseen illness. As the Pilgrim came to stand silently behind the Shaman, he could hear the man repeating one sentence over and over.

"Why do I live? Why do I live?" The Shaman asked over and over.

The pilgrim now noted, as was his ability, that the blood coursing through the Shaman's veins was not unlike his own. It was faint, somewhat weakened by a few generations but it was there anyway. The Pilgrim was suddenly seized with the notion that there could be others in the world with similar heritage. He recalled that some of the Huru, before the destruction of their realm, had secretly taken husbands or wives from human settlements around the globe. These unions resulted in hybrid children. Most of these offspring were oblivious to their Huru heritage, even if it manifested in a physical manner. Although it was forbidden for Huru to mingle with humans, even they were not impervious to the power of love, and even more so, lust.

Gripped with anticipation and resolve the Pilgrim greeted the man by answering his repetitious enquiry. He answered: "Because you have much more work to do."

And so it was The Pilgrim began searching among human civilizations for those who possessed Huru heritage. In the following centuries Abanis slowly grew as more and more Hurum were discovered. The home eventually became a city and a place of learning. Some of the citizens of Abanis were trained to become Emissaries and upon completion of a certain amount of study, were sent back into the world. Not only would emissaries venture forth in search of more Hurum but they also resumed the responsibility of watching and nurturing humanity as their ancestors once did. In so doing, The Pilgrim and the citizens of Abanis were able to uphold the First Promise of his lost realm: to nurture without contact. For there was a sacred maxim that all the Huru held dear: that all humanity was precious beyond measure.

Nicholas finished reading the page and looked up at Ravenscrawl. "A lot of this makes sense now." He said pushing the huge volume to the side. "But you are pure blooded Huru, are you not?"

Ravenscrawl nodded. "My kin and I are pure but the writer of this book did not know at the time. We have remained inside Twilenos for a very long time and keep its existence secret until emissaries are ready to move forward."

"Who are the Huru? And the Nelfilem, sir?"

Ravenscrawl seemed to consider something. "We are not men. We are the children of men. That is all I can tell you for now."

Nicholas accepted this and placed in his mental filing cabinet on top of the huge pile of other cryptic responses he would someday have to figure out. "Your family is here?" He asked.

"Yes, some of my kin are far below us." Said Ravenscrawl, closing the book. "Which brings us to you, young human. You are an anomaly."

"So I've heard." Said Nicholas dryly.

"Oh yes. You are the first human to manifest traits of the Hurum without actually having any trace of their lineage. This is something we have never seen before."

"So what is this training? I don't understand wh-"

"Somehow," Ravenscrawl interjected. "You are manifesting the Hurum traits despite your humanity. We must bring them out." He raised a finger between them suddenly and Nicholas looked at it almost cross-eyed. "We must extract them and make them ready for you to use, whatever they may be. Do you understand?"

Nicholas hesitated. "Can I just say 'no' and you just pretend like you heard me say 'yes'?"

Ravenscrawl stared at Nicholas placidly for a moment. His faced twitched and he suddenly let forth a bellow of a laugh that echoed around the room. It was a rich and deep laugh that made Nicholas smile and laugh too.

"Come." Said Ravenscrawl after a few moments. "We will begin immediately."

Nicholas groaned as Ravenscrawl began to climb the stairs. He hastened after him, onward and upward.

After climbing a few more levels, Nicholas glanced over the ledge of the stairs and caught his breath. They were about seventeen levels up now and he was not comfortable with heights. Two levels later, Ravenscrawl stopped and pointed to a relatively small room with a simple door at the back.

Like most of the walls inside Twilenos, abstract crystals lit the room with twinkling colors when they approached.

The door was simple and reminded Nicholas of the door to The Pilgrim's home in Abanis. It had a little, circular window with four panes but there was only darkness beyond them.

"This is the Room of Black, human. Let's see how you are able to cope inside." Said Ravenscrawl, opening the door.

Nicholas was surprised to see the subtle light of the small room did not penetrated the blackness beyond the door. He felt suddenly nervous although he couldn't guess why.

"What's inside?" He asked timidly.

"Only what you find in there, young human. Remember that." Said Ravenscrawl. "But she will have to remain here, I'm afraid. It is no place for familiars."

Nicholas looked at Kara. "It seems I have to do this alone. Take care of our Librarian?"

Kara saluted and buzzed up from his shoulder and landed on the outstretched palm of Ravenscrawl.

"Very good." He said, patting Kara gently. "The Room of Black is like a cup of coffee to the manifestation of the Huru inside you, lad. Do not fight it. Let yourself get caught up in the experience. This will give you a stepping stone to focus on your innate skills. When you are ready, simply walk inside."

"Ok." Said Nicholas. He breathed deeply. Not knowing what lay in the darkness beyond the doorway was somewhat distressing. With a nod to Raphael, he stepped into the darkness.

He was immediately smothered in absolute blackness. His first reaction inside was to turn around but when he did so, he couldn't see the doorway, or Ravenscrawl, or anything at all.

"What is this?" He called out but his voice was even drowned in the impenetrable blackness.

He stopped suddenly, thinking he heard something. There were whispers in the blackness, or at least the sounds of whispers. They seemed to be coming from all around him and Nicholas suddenly felt goose bumps on his arms and legs. He felt afraid. More afraid than he had ever felt before.

The whispering, although subtle and unintelligible, seemed to be drawing closer and getting louder. Nicholas reached around in the darkness but could feel nothing. Then he pulled his arms around himself as a primal fear gripped him.

A few moments passed and the whispering seemed to stop. He listened intently but there was only silence now. Then something grabbed his wrist.

Nicholas heart nearly jumped out of his chest and he screamed in terror. He yanked his hand and tried to back away but whatever gripped his wrist would not let go. Anger suddenly welled within him and a flame roared out of his other hand and rocketed away into the distance. It did not give off any residual light but he clearly saw what came out of his other hand. The icy grip on his hand vanished and he was left massaging his wrist and backing away.

"Ravenscrawl!" He shouted. "What is this? What do I do?" But there was no answer.

He staggered around in the gloom and became aware of a light far off into the distance. He didn't want to imagine what horror it could be but he could just make out the cries of a child. A baby was crying far off into the darkness. Somewhere near the subtle light.

He didn't want to move, not knowing what was in the blackness staring at him but the cries of the child overwhelmed his fear.

He ran towards the light. His heart was racing and tried not to imagine what *things* were possibly pursuing him. He thought he heard moans, snarls and jaws snap behind him as he sped across the black infinity towards the screaming baby. But as fast as he ran, he seemed to be no closer to the light. He pushed himself to run faster and faster until his chest began to ache and his vision began to blur. Once again anger welled up within him and he felt himself flow as if in the water. But he knew he wasn't in water. He felt the familiar sensation of his body becoming attuned to the water but in here he became attuned to the blackness. His body dematerialized and he raced across the expanse at great sped in the form of a cloud. He reached meteoric speed as the light drew closer and closer. Just as he thought he was going to reach the source of the sound, he roared out of the doorway.

Nicholas couldn't stop. As his body reformed outside the door, Raphael deftly stepped aside like matador without the cheers of 'ole!' to accompany his movement. Nicholas sailed passed him in a drunken stagger like someone running too fast down a steep hill and flew off the edge of the balcony.

He hung in mid air for a millisecond and his stomach heaved as gravity decided to kick into gear. Ravenscrawl watched with curious indifference as he fell out of sight. Plummeting to the stone floor nineteen levels down, Nicholas realized with horror that he was going to die if he didn't think fast. He decided screaming in terror was the best course of action.

"Ahh! Ravenscrawl! Help!" He screamed as the stone floor approached much faster than he wanted it to.

Help yourself Nicholas. Said a voice in his mind. *Flow!*

Nicholas' mind kicked into self preservation mode and didn't want to argue about the fact he wasn't in water. He closed his eyes and concentrated.

Just as he was about to meet the floor in an extremely terminal way, his body dematerialized and took on the form of a black cloud.

Suddenly aware of what a mushroom cloud must feel like, Nicholas exploded around a large area of the floor. Unless showing up uninvited when the forecast called for sunny skies, clouds generally don't look embarrassed. Nicholas' cloud form achieved this affect, however, by pulsing and billowing around the area in some state of confusion. After managing to pull himself together, at least as much as one could in the form of smoky mist, he regrouped and flew up the massive open space inside the library. When he reached the nineteenth floor, he hovered around the landing near Ravenscrawl and rematerialized. Nicholas appeared manic and disheveled as the vapor receded.

"Wow!" Exclaimed Nicholas, breathing heavily and staring at Ravenscrawl. "I did it!"

After a few moments, his expression went wooden and his face drained of color. His body suddenly felt like it was too heavy to control. Feeling like a five-ounce hermit crab carrying around a seventeen-pound shell, Nicholas collapsed at Ravenscrawl's feet.

"That," said Ravenscrawl, looking down at Nicholas with bemused curiosity "is something I haven't seen in a few centuries, young human. Well done."

JingleJingle***Jingle***

The Greyman looked around at the devastation. In his anger he destroyed every living thing within half a mile of the reef. He looked up at the ruins of the city of Adamis and then to the broken, crystalline doorway. It was lifeless and dark. Any sign of The Hag Nosis was no more than a shadow on the floor. He knew that he should have destroyed her the moment he acquired this putrid, meat-sack for a body but he thought it could wait. To see her in such a state was more than he could bear so he ended her quickly.

There was a time when he might have felt something but now all he was able to feel was hate and malice for those in his way. But it would all be better when he was home. All wrongs would be set right. All scores would be settled. Loved ones would be resurrected. He would start with her, she would be made beautiful again.

He leaned down to the area of the dais where the doorway had been. Here, a multitude of sedentary life had made this place home. Now it was lifeless. He ran a boney finger along the shadowy impression of Hag Nosis and remained there for some time.

Sensing a presence other than sea life, The Greyman stood and spun around. He gripped the scythe and stared into the blue abyss.

After a moment, an apparition appeared. The Greyman slashed at it but his scythe went straight through the image of a grinning figure. It was familiar to him. At least, it appeared to be a familiar face. The Greyman realized it was a swarming school of tiny lantern fish. The pulses and throbs of their undulating swarm formed the face and body of a familiar creature indeed.

"The Maggot Master faces me finally." Said The Greyman while looking around the reef for more uninvited guests. "A wise, if not cowardly decision, to employ sea life."

"I thought you might be here, Halaam."

"How dare you call me that, imp-ling! I was the one who awakened you! I gave your people life!" The Greyman moved suddenly, coming closer to the swarm of fish. He leered at Pantilius and noted the little fish even got the large, upswept ears and explosive hairdo correct. "Your deceit and enslavement of my people was only the beginning of the crimes you have committed. You earned that name, party-pooper." Said Pantilius.

"Look at what your failures have done to our beloved Kingdom." Said The Greyman, waving a boney arm around at the coral-crusted ruins. "Your miscalculations about the gates resulted in this destruction. And yet you were able to make one that led to a prison designed for me. Indeed? Who then is the traitor?"

Pantilius snorted. "Kingdom? We were not gods or emperors! Or have you forgotten why the Huru came here in the first place. We were caretakers, nothing more."

"Why were we created if not to rule. The primates are imperfect. Malicious. They treat this paradise like a cesspool. You know what is to come. You know what they will become. And still you think of me as an enemy."

"It is not for us decide. This world is theirs, Halaam. No matter what they do with it. We do not know what they will become or what our interference has done to them as it is."

"Bah." The Greyman waving a dismissive boney arm. "I have no interest in this old argument. My whelp tried the same thing but none of you understand. I had to punish him. Surely you know he is gone."

Pantilius face froze in the swarm of fish.

Sensing the effect this had, The Greyman leered again. "Yes. Pity I had to end him but he was a bad boy. I'm sure you understand."

"Gabriel was your son, you mercenary wretch. How far you have fallen."

The Greyman shrugged disengaging.

"Despite the gravity of your crimes, I must ask you to repent. It is what *he* would want me to do. You are among the last of the Huru. Repent before there are none left. Repent and you will be taken back to your prison."

"Repent?" The Greyman laughed. The water surrounding him seethed and boiled. "Me? You will bow before me or I will exterminate all life on this planet and start over. You will serve me as you once did, maggot. As for prison," he shook his head and the skull sockets flared, "I escaped once. Only I have the skill to traverse the distance and infect one of these monkeys. Long I searched for this world from out in the darkness. He underestimated me."

"You are a virus, Halaam. We are many and you will be purged. If you do not repent, The Pilgrim, along with all who remain faithful will be forced to end you."

The Greyman stared at the swarm of fish for a moment and then burst into laughter. "You dare challenge me? I will tear you apart piece by piece and make you watch as I devour every single usher and emissary." He cackled. "As for my brother, he is quite lost. Or have you not realized why he has been absent since his so-called progeny got nailed to the cross in Jerusalem. I imprisoned him. He is lost forever. No one can challenge me now, you simple little worm."

Pantilius looked shocked and for a moment there was a flash of fear.

"Yes." Said the Greyman, seeing the crack in Pantilius confidence. He swam closer. "You thought he would appear in just in time, didn't you? You expected him to return and challenge me." He shook his head and waved an admonishing finger at Pantilius. "The Pilgrim is gone. He cannot save you. I see this pains you. And his progeny, the one you hoped could challenge me, is long gone too. But of course you know this. I am so sorry." He tilted his head. "By the way, it was I who whispered to Pilate to use nails you know. Nails are much more," he paused waving a boney arm, "final in the crucifixion."

"Bastard! You are a bastard, Halaam."

The Greyman cackled, thoroughly enjoying Pantilius pain. Then he stopped suddenly and raised a boney finger. "Give me the human and the key. Do this and I will spare your precious hurum. Do not, and I will destroy all life on this blue paradise and start over. Do not test me on this, imp. I am more than capable of doing so."

"Yes I believe you can." Said Pantilius, looking afraid and nervous now. He appeared to consider something and looked around frantically. "We do not wish to have this confrontation. Leave the humans out of this, please. If all you want is to go home, then do so. Let them be." Said Pantilius. "You once listened to me, Lightbringer. Please leave them at peace."

The Greyman considered this. "How is it that you have come to love them so dearly and hate your own maker. You astound me Pan."

Pantilius looked pained. "I am as you made me."

The Greyman looked down at the shadowy remains of Nosis. "Very well. The human and the key. Deliver them to me and I will spare the monkeys who roll in their own filth, along with your precious emissaries. Once I have constructed a new gate at the heart of Abanis, I will leave."

Pantilius hesitated. "You know they are unstable. It could destroy this world."

"Now you lie, Pan. You know the gate leading to Enefka is stable. I simply magnified your design. I have found a way home at last."

Pantilius stared at The Greyman for a while and considered this. "Alright." He sighed. "Will he suffer then? Will the boy suffer?"

"Not if I am satisfied."

"And Abanis? You will leave and let us have our home back."

"If it survives the gate construction, I care not. But only after I have what I want. Not a moment earlier."

Pantilius face looked pained. He appeared to lose all of his confidence and looked old and weary. The swarm of fish changed somewhat and the image of Pantilius sagged. "Agreed. I will arrange for the human to go to Sin. He will be alone. You can have him." Then he lowered his head. "If there is any Huru left in you that I can appeal to, if there is any love left in you for the woman you once cared for, take him swiftly. I beg you. He is only human. Do not make him suffer."

The Greyman stared at Pantilius for a moment. "He will not suffer. It will be instant when I take him." He said quietly. "But if I sense that you are devising some trickery, I will make him suffer. I will make him watch this world destroyed and everything he holds dear along with it. His human mind will go quite insane and I will continue to make him suffer for all eternity."

Pantilius lowered his head. "Agreed. Four days from now, the human will be in front of gates of Sin. I will make preparations." The school of fish dissipated and the image of Pantilius vanished.

Good. Thought The Greyman. *The worm hasn't forgotten how to betray his own kind. The fool thought to challenge me. Indeed.*

He looked down at the broken gate and the shadow of a woman's body. *After I unmake all the life on this world, including the simple-minded Hurum, I will finally....go home.*

Chapter 25: The Right Stuffing

Nicholas opened his eyes and stared up at Ravenscrawl. He felt elated but completely exhausted. "What's happened?" He managed to croak as he sat up.

"You have demonstrated an interesting skill but it requires rest or nourishment after a short time. I bet milk and cookies or some other simple snack would get you charged up again. Changing one's form is not a natural thing so it requires payment. You must remember that doing so should only be for a short time or you will be too weak. In time, you will be able to endure longer periods of change. For now, drink this." Raphael handed Nicholas a small bottle of ambrosia.

Nicholas took it, popped the cork off and drained the small bottle, not caring what flavor it would be this time. It was just as delicious as the first one only this time it had the distinctive flavor of a tropical fruit salad. He smacked his lips appreciatively and nodded to Raphael. "Nice. I love this stuff."

Feeling suddenly revived and not at all fatigued, Nicholas got to his feet and sighed. "Why didn't you tell me that room was going to scare the life out of me?"

Ravenscrawl shrugged. "It would have defeated the purpose. The room stimulates your fears. Through fear, we find ourselves and there is nothing more frightening than that which you cannot see or know. Your imagination does all the work. In your case, you have discovered two things. You have a fiery temper. An affinity with fire or combustion, I dare say. You are also able to change your form into something insubstantial. Like mist. Another skill. Tell me, what else have you been able to do thus far?"

Nicholas considered this. "I have ushered someone before. But I don't understand it. I don't understand what I did or where he went."

Ravenscrawl looked surprised. "Ushering. I see. Very few of us manifest that skill, rarer still for a human being able to do so. You have ushered someone?"

"Yes."

"Who did you do this for?"

Nicholas cringed and looked down. "Gabriel." He said.

Ravenscrawl stared at him and then walked to the edge of the staircase. He leaned heavily on the ornately carved, stone railing and sighed. "I see. I had hoped I was wrong when I felt his departure. Was it him?"

"Yes, I think so. He confronted The Greyman in Abanis after the evacuation."

"Once again our father has taken one of his sons." Ravenscrawl sighed.

"I'm sorry. I wasn't sure how to tell you after I found out you were his brother." Said Nicholas awkwardly. The memory of losing his friend was an ache he couldn't triage. He couldn't imagine losing a brother.

Ravenscrawl turned and leaned on the balcony, looking at Nicholas with sympathy. "No, don't be sorry. He loved you Nicholas. He spoke of you often. It must have been hard for you."

Nicholas nodded.

"Walk with me." Said Ravenscrawl, and the two began to ascend the staircase once more. "Where did it happen, Nicholas. Where was he ushered?"

"It was after the evacuation. He instructed me to go to Rongo-rongo Island. He passed away on the beach there." Said Nicholas, as he walked slowly beside Ravenscrawl. "His wounds were more than I could manage." He said quietly.

Ravenscrawl nodded.

"What is it? Ushering, I mean." Said Nicholas, shaking his head. "You are referred to as 'Usher' Ravenscrawl. I don't understand it."

"That was another part of training you would have completed here in Twilenos, Nicholas. Apparently you completed the field test already."

"But what is it?" Nicholas persisted. He had only witnessed two 'usherings' before.

"To usher someone is to help them move beyond this world and to... another place. Only few of us can do it and the fact you can is even more reason to be astonished. For one reason, you are young, and another you are human. It is unheard of." He paused looking down at Nicholas as they walked and continued. "In religious jargon, this would mean helping them go to heaven, or reach nirvana, or whatever. In reality, it is much more complex." Ravenscrawl paused again. "But I think you want to know what Empyrean is. You have heard of it, yes?"

Nicholas nodded. "Yes. I didn't understand it."

"Empyrean is a place between places. It is not heaven or anything so egotistical as the human idea of 'afterlife'. If life on this world were to be compared to the coliseum of Rome, then Empyrean would be the 'stands' where spectators watch the games."

Nicholas nodded. "I think I understand that. Although 'space between spaces' is something I hope to understand more."

"Oh, you will Nicholas. You will. You are just beginning to see the way of things. More will become clear in time." Ravenscrawl stopped suddenly.

Nicholas stopped too and realized there were no more stairs. He was temporarily dumbfounded by an architectural marvel before him.

At the top of the grand staircase in Twilenos was a huge domed area at least twenty meters in diameter. Tall, round pillars supported the dome and between them was open air. Nicholas could see the horizon and stars filled the clear, night sky. Nicholas breathed deeply and could still taste the fresh, salty ocean breeze.

Inside the dome were white, marble tables and benches of varying designs but between them were natural rock springs. Some of the formations had mildly cascading waterfalls, fed by springs deep in the roots of the mountain. The resulting pools of water flowed along an aqueduct system carved into the rock floor. The aqueducts snaked in and around the marble tables to eventually fall out the edge of the domed area down the side of the mountain. It was breathtaking and Nicholas had never seen its like before.

"It's gorgeous. And peaceful too." Said Nicholas.

Ravenscrawl nodded. "Yes. A human designed this place for us as a gift of thanks very, very long ago. Such creative genius your species possesses. I am thankful for that virtue every time I come to sit here. We call this place 'Lowgarden'."

Nicholas hesitated. "Umm, Lowgarden? Was 'Highgarden' already taken? I only ask 'cause that would've been a more appropriate name. Don't you think?"

Nicholas said, looking over the balcony railing as if to emphasize his point.

Ravenscrawl looked at Nicholas coyly and grinned. "Some day, if you figure out the reason why we chose to call this place Lowgarden, then you will also understand why Highgarden is not an appropriate name at all.

Ravenscrawl gestured to a table and the two sat down opposite one another. Kara flew down from Nicholas shoulder and buzzed around the waterfalls, enjoying the scenery. Nicholas shook his head and decided to add 'Lowgarden' to the ever growing list of mysteries piling up in the storage area of his mind.

"So, what else have you discovered about yourself, young human?" Ravenscrawl asked. He pulled out two bottles of ambrosia from the apparently infinite supply within his robes and passed one to Nicholas.

Nicholas realized something and reached into his backpack. He pulled out the peculiar heptagonal pendant Aryu Veda had given him when they were escaping Abanis. Several of the onyx crystals were glowing now.

"I have this. I think it represents my education or training. Could you tell me more of it?"

"Ahh, quite an artifact you have there." Said Ravenscrawl, taking the pendant gingerly and turning it over in his huge hands. "These were used long ago in Adamis by hybrid hurum to help identify the manifestation of their Huru traits. Who gave it to you?"

"Aryu Veda gave it to me." Said Nicholas, popping the cork off the green vial and sipping its contents.

"I see." Ravenscrawl pointed to one crystal. "You see this one?" He pointed to one jewel which glowed yellow. "It means 'inspiration'. I can tell because of the color of the hue in the jewel. The colors represent skills. Just as there are an infinite number of hues, so are there infinite possibilities of the manifestations of the Hurum. This means you have inspired someone to see their true potential. A valuable skill for any emissary. And this," he pointed to a turquoise colored jewel, "represents flowing. Another necessary skill for fast travel. And this one," he pointed to a jewel that glowed white, "represents ushering. A skill very few of us, Hurum or Huru, possess. You have completed six of the seven necessary skills to become an emissary. You must complete one more, although its nature is not clear."

Nicholas pointed to the other crystals. "What do they mean?"

"This one is earthly location." Said Ravenscrawl, pointing to a green jewel. "A common manifestation of the Hurum. You have an instinct for knowing where you are. And this," he pointed to an orange glowing jewel, "represents your affinity to fire and smoke. Thus your transformation into a cloud. A useful skill for both defense and offense. You can escape physical harm and inflict great pain on others, although I would hesitate to use the latter for no other reason than defense."

Ravenscrawl looked closer at the last jewel. It glowed a deep violet. "This last one must have manifested itself by your proximity to Gabriel while you were raised in Abanis. It is the ability to heal."

"Heal? Yes!" Said Nicholas suddenly. "There was a whale in the ocean. It was injured and I healed it. I once saw Gabriel do that to a deer."

"Yes. You can heal wounds." Then he looked sternly at Nicholas. "But you must be wary of this skill. It cannot heal terminally wounded people or cure diseases but it can waylay a virus. However, to do so, you must seek permission from elders because it could interfere with natural human progression. Remember this."

Nicholas nodded solemnly and sipped the ambrosia. This one tasted like chocolate milk, one of his favorite drinks.

At this point, a sparrow flew into the dome and began chirping as it flittered around the waterfalls. Kara sat up from where she was sitting beside one of the aqueducts and looked at Nicholas and Ravenscrawl.

"Curious." He said, standing up and watching the bird fly around and chirp. "Sparrows do not come up here."

The sparrow flew down to the table and Ravenscrawl watched it with extreme interest. It bounced around on two legs and looked at both Nicholas and Ravenscrawl for a few moments with twitchy movements. Then it spoke.

"Nicholas?" It asked.

Nicholas gaped at the bird.

Ravenscrawl smiled. "Who is asking?"

The sparrow turned to Ravenscrawl and saluted with one wing. "Sergeant Lurp, Second Airborne Company. Lyons."

Nicholas looked at Ravenscrawl, his mouth hanging open. Then the bird faced him again.

"Are you Nicholas?" It asked with a voice too deep for a creature the size of a jar of mustard. "Christopher Nicholas of Abanis?"

"Uhh - "

"I'll take that as a yes. I have a message for you sir. Please answer the following questions so that I may verify your identification."

Nicholas stared at the little bird. He was pretty sure that sparrows didn't speak. They were sparrows. He looked at the ambrosia and wondered briefly what was in it.

"Sir. How do you make an egg laugh?"

Nicholas hesitated. Growing up in Mirthmyst Castle with Pantilius gave Nicholas the only kind of education that could successfully navigate the murky waters of bad jokes. He did some mental acrobatics to a) speak to a bird and b) answer a joke. The little sparrow waited patiently.

"Umm, tell it a yolk?" Said Nicholas, hoping this was the correct answer but not knowing exactly why.

"Correct." The sparrow now looked skyward and began to recite another. "Sir. What can one hold without ever touching it?"

Again Nicholas dug into the recesses of his mind and tried to think of what Pantilius would say.

"A conversation?" He said timidly.

"Correct. Sir," now the bird was pacing back and forth in front of him with its wings behind its back. "What did the rug say to the floor?"

This one was easy. Nicholas heard Pantilius use this one when he was very young and never forgot it. He couldn't imagine why.

"Don't worry, I have you covered." He said confidently.

"Correct." Said the Sergeant Lurp. "Sir, I am told to give you the following message: One sin sorrow, two sins joy, three sins a pilgrim, four sins a boy, five sins burning, six sins cold, seven sins a fortress never to be old."

Nicholas frowned. The fact that he was talking to a bird was only slightly underwhelmed by the fact he had no idea what it had just said.

"Uhh what?"

Ravenscrawl stood up suddenly. His face drained of color and he looked deeply concerned. "Sin." He said.

He walked around the table and leaned closer to the little sparrow. "Sergeant Lurp. Who gave you this message?"

If sparrows could appear to be uncomfortable, Nicholas imagined this one was. The little bird looked back and forth to Nicholas and Ravenscrawl. "Sir. A small, blue creature with ears so big they could hear an acorn drop one hundred miles away, sir. He instructed me to come to this place. Sir."

"Pantilius! He told you to come here? At this time?"

The little sparrow saluted. "Sir. Correct sir."

"Very well Sergeant Lurp, the message is received. Thank you. Off you go."

The little bird saluted them both and flew away. Nicholas saluted back and watched it fly through the space between the pillars and out into the evening sky.

"Pantilius sent this? Why? What does it mean?" He stood up and looked expectantly at Ravenscrawl.

Ravenscrawl turned and looked about to run to the edge of Highgarden but suddenly the floor beneath their feet shook. A hammering could be heard echoing from the ground floor. It was a deep, penetrating sound that made the entire inner sanctum of Twilenos shake to its very foundations.

A deep sound echoed around them. It was if the air itself decided to take on vernacular tones. It was three voices speaking simultaneously.

Long we have slept. Long we have dreamed of going home. Give us the boy. Give us the key.

"Riders! They are here!" Bellowed Ravenscrawl. His face darkened and his lip curled in anger. "They yet live! They dare to come here!"

"Who? What is that sound?" But just as Nicholas asked, the foundations of Twilenos shook again and hammering echoed up to the Highgarden.

"Come! Now, Nicholas! You must leave at once. Go now, flow to the ground floor now!" Ravenscrawl grabbed Nicholas roughly and propelled him to the edge. "Flow!" He commanded and pushed Nicholas of the edge of the staircase and into open air. Kara flew after Nicholas.

Not needing any encouragement or thought, Nicholas was easily able to change himself into a cloud. The fact that he was just thrown into two hundred feet of open air aided this transformation.

Not wishing to imagine what horror he was about to meet, Nicholas did as he was told. He flowed down to the ground floor and rematerialized looking around expectantly. Kara joined him shortly and landed on his shoulder. Considering he was weakened by transforming, she felt like a solid lead brick on Nicholas' shoulder.

He looked up and squinted at the spot where Ravenscrawl stood. He saw him jump off the top floor and watched as the air blurred around the huge man. To Nicholas astonishment, Ravenscrawl didn't change into a cloud of smoke. He changed into a dragon.

Huge wings, forty feet across, sprouted from his side. Nicholas was nearly blown off his feet as a massive gust of air buffeted him. A blue scaled dragon landed heavily on the stone floor beside him. Ravenscrawl was huge, bigger than

Gabriel but more streamlined. Great horns coiled around his draconic head and azure eyes fixed on Nicholas.

This is our true form Nicholas. Said Ravenscrawl in Nicholas' mind. *We are the offspring of Nosis and we are the keepers of Twilenos. Do not be afraid. Three beings are here and I suspect they were sent by The Greyman. You must leave this place with Michael's ilk while I deal with them.*

"Where do I need to go? What do - " Started Nicholas but the ground beneath his feet shook once more and he nearly fell over. This was followed by an ear-shattering hammering coming from the passage Nicholas used to the enter Twilenos.

There. Ravenscrawl pointed a huge claw at a set of large, metal double doors beside the grand staircase. *Take the passage under the stairs to the chamber below Twilenos. My kin are there. Tell them to take you to Sin. They will know what to do. Peace be with you, young human. We will meet again soon. Go now!*

The commanding shout in Nicholas' mind jump-started his legs and feet

before his mind knew what was going on. He ran to the doors, flung them open and dashed into the darkness beyond.

The passage beneath the staircase of Twilenos was tall but rather narrow. It soon became a stone wrought staircase like the one up in the library but this one coiled long and deep into the roots of the mountain. Down and down, Nicholas ran as fast as he could, taking the stairs two at a time as crystal lights in the walls flared into life as he passed. Eventually he ran out of stairs and into a huge, dimly lit cavern.

Stalactites and stalagmites met here and there about the cavern. Pools of spring water sparkled in the subtle light of the crystals jutting out from the walls. Nicholas staggered about in the gloom not really knowing what he was looking for. Again, the foundations of the mountain shook and he staggered sideways right into a stalagmite.

Nicholas blinked. He was quite sure stalagmites didn't have helpful hands that assisted one's balance. He looked sideways and then up.

"Hello, young human. Our Uncle told us you would come." Said a three-meter tall man who looked strikingly like Ravenscrawl and Gabriel. Only this man's hair was streaked alternately red and white, like the skin of a zebra with an attitude. He pushed Nicholas back to his feet and grinned down at him. His eyes were ruby red and his face was youthful and friendly. "I am Rudolph."

Another man, looking quite similar to Rudolph stepped out of the shadows to Nicholas right. And then another and then another until Nicholas was surrounded by eight, young-looking 'Gabriels'. Each man seemed to be created in the same mold as Gabriel and Ravenscrawl. They were exceedingly tall with opaque eyes, streaked-hair and the curiously gold-colored skin. Each wore wearing deep-blue robes, as emissaries of Abanis.

"Uhh, hi." Said Nicholas, realizing he might be surrounded by eight dragons. He suddenly wished to appear inedible.

"Is that the human's name?" Asked one, looking around at the others.

"I don't think 'Uhhi' is a human name." Said another.

"Could be. You know how the eastern people speak. Might mean 'John' in their language." Said a third.

"Uhhi does sound rather northern though." Said a fourth.

By this point Nicholas jaw fell open.

"You know, I once knew a 'Uhhi' over in that land down under, charming fellow." Said a fifth. "He was a fisherman and -

"My name is Nicholas!" He suddenly blurted out.

Rudolph extended a hand. "There you go. Well met, young Nicholas. Uncle told us you need to go North." He nodded grimly.

"Uh, I guess so."

Rudolph turned to the others. "Boys, let's get our friend out of here shall we. We have ourselves road trip."

The others nodded and some were grinning at Nicholas in that peculiar way that teenagers do when they are about to do something entirely too fun.

"Come." Said Rudolph. He grabbed Nicholas by the arm and pulled him into a gloomy passageway. Although he couldn't see very well, he was able to hear the others running down the passage.

They emerged into a larger room that lit up with the same kind of crystals as the rest of Twilenos. To Nicholas, they appeared to be at one end of a long, hollowed out tube carved out of the stone of the mountain. Parked in front of them was a Roman-style chariot. Or what Nicholas thought was a chariot.

It appeared to be made of wood and metal and had a large padded, leather seats with a backrest that could have doubled as the throne for the Emperor of China. Along the side of the carriage were intricate linear designs and subtle knot-work patterns that gave the entire vehicle a misguiding fragile appearance. Unlike Roman design, however, this chariot was lacquered richly dark brown and black. It was a gorgeously designed vehicle that spoke to the inner-male-teenager in Nicholas. Kara gave Nicholas two thumbs up and nodded in satisfaction.

"Sweet." Said Nicholas nodding, not exactly sure why he said it.

The others were watching him and some grinned.

"Boys, time to ride." Said Rudolph. If the man had sunglasses, he would have put them on at this point.

The others nodded to Rudolph and joined him as he walked to the front of the chariot, standing in two rows of four. They picked up a leather and chain pulley array attached to the chariot and slung them over each other's necks.

The air suddenly blurred around the men and Nicholas' eyes watered as he tried to make sense of the morphological shift. After a few moments, there were eight camels standing in front of the chariot.

"Camels?" Said Nicholas.

Yep. Said a voice in Nicholas mind. It was Rudolph's. *Very resilient creatures and they blend in with the local livery. Climb aboard, grab the reins and hold on tight, kid.*

Nicholas jumped into the chariot and picked up the reins. Again, there was a thunderous hammering above them. This time, some small chucks of rock fell to the floor.

"What of your uncle?" Nicholas shouted above the noise of the hammering. "Should we not stay to help him in some way?"

Trust me, Nicholas. Said Rudolph. *It is best for friend or foe alike to be quite some distance from his wrath. To say that he can handle himself is a fairly ridiculous understatement. Ever heard of the cities of Sodom and Gomorrah?*

"No, I don't think I recognize the names."

My point exactly.

The chariot suddenly jerked and Nicholas was flung back in the leather seat. If Nicholas thought that camels couldn't move fast, he was certainly changing his opinion at this point.

The camels charged forward and Nicholas could see that the end of the rocky tunnel was rapidly approaching. Apparently they were not at ground level and the backside of the mountain must have a tall cliff. He knew this because, in addition to the end of the tunnel, he realized there were stars twinkling ominously beyond. And where there were stars, there was also a lot of open sky.

"The-the tunnel! The tunnel is ending!" Nicholas shouted, pointing ahead. Out of the corner of his eye, he saw Kara do a nosedive into his backpack. "There's nothing out there! There's nothing! There's..AHHH!

The chariot shot out of the rock tunnel like a trident missile and roared up into the evening sky with Nicholas screaming at the reins. The chariot's wheels left sparks trailing behind it as it left the stone launching-tunnel. To Nicholas' expectation, it didn't plummet to the ground at all but kept rising, higher and higher. He thought he could hear laughter inside his head and suspected it was Rudolph.

For the third time in one day, as the chariot peeled across the starlit sky and into the night, Nicholas' stomach lurched. Only this time, it was holding on for its life. If he had to change his body into smoke, he just hoped he would be able to do so without any error. He chanced a look down to the rapidly blurring landscape and added to himself that it would certainly be the last 'error' he ever made.

****Jingle***Jingle***Jingle****

The three ghouls stood before the metal door and examined it closely.

"It appears to be impenetrable brothers." Said, the larger of the two.

"But the human and the spike are within. I would rather hammer at this door for eternity than go back to him empty-handed." Said the second.

"Agreed." Said the third.

After receiving a telepathic scream from The Greyman, the three ghouls had immediately diverted their search from faraway lands. It was not difficult for them to follow The Greyman's instructions and track the blue whale's movements to the lagoon and lonely mountain. However, they were not prepared to deal with an impenetrable metal door. At one point, two of the ghouls picked up a third and used its head as a battering ram. This didn't have the intended affect but certainly made a lot of noise.

Just as they were thinking of trying the larger of the three as a second battering ram option, the ground shook beneath their feet. There was a loud crash behind them followed by a deafening roar. At least, it would have been deafening if the ghouls could feel.

"Mindless meat sacks!" Ravenscrawl roared. His huge draconic body eclipsed the stars and great leathery winged buffeted the area near the metal gate. "You dare disturb this sanctuary?"

One of the ghouls tilted its head sideways and stared at Ravenscrawl. "Dragon." It said. "Spawned from the master. We rode such creatures once. I remember this one in dreams."

"Blue scaled." Said a second. "One of the younger."

"Sensitive. An artist. Easy to defeat." Said a third.

Ravenscrawl considered something for a moment. "Yes." He said, watching them carefully. "I am... easy to defeat. Why do you want to enter this sanctuary?"

"To retrieve the key." Said one of the ghouls.

"And the human who carries it." Said a second.

"So that we can go home." Said a third.

"I see." Said Ravenscrawl. He realized that he was in the presence of creatures who long ago were Huru. However, they were shades of themselves. Their minds were infantile and broken despite their extreme age. He could use this to his advantage. "All you had to do was ask. After all, we are brothers." He said finally.

"Yes. We are brothers. We are Huru." Said one of the ghouls, nodding to the others.

"But," said Ravenscrawl, watching them intently, "the door can only be opened from the inside. And only after a secret question is answered."

"Is the human within?" Asked one.

"I detect a deception." Said a second.

"I am hungry." Said a third. He appeared to look guilty as the other two stared at him.

Ravenscrawl stared at all three for a few moments. "The human is within. He is tired and sleeps. You know how pitifully weak humans are. I shall open the gate if you promise to leave quietly with him."

"This is agreeable." Said one ghoul.

"Yes, humans are weak and pitiful creatures. I recall that." Said a second.

"I am hungry." Said a third. Again it looked mildly uncomfortable when the others stared at it.

"The Gate is simple to open but it was designed by a human. There is a question that must be answered to open the locking mechanism. Do you understand."

"We can answer any question devised by pitiful humans." Said one of the ghouls.

"Yes. We are old. The master told us as much."

"We are hungry...and smart." Said the third.

This is too easy. Thought Ravenscrawl. *Their minds work like those of children.*

"Then you must answer the following question correctly." He said, pacing in front of them. "Are you ready to answer the question designed by a simple human and retrieve the items for your master?"

"Yes." They chorused.

"Very well. Answer me the following question. If a turtle loses its shell, is it homeless or naked?"

The ghouls blinked at Ravenscrawl and then looked at one another.

"I shall wait for your answer brothers. The human is sleeping inside so there is no rush." Then Ravenscrawl stretched his wings and took off into the dawn sky and out of sight.

"The answer is easy." Said one of the ghouls.

"The shell of a turtle is its home. Therefore it is homeless." Said another ghoul.

"But it is also naked." Said a third. "Its shell is also its clothing. Therefore it must be naked."

"You are both wrong." Said a voice that sounded like the first ghoul.

The two ghouls looked at the first one. "Why do you say we are wrong?"

The first ghoul looked at the other two. "I said the answer is easy. The turtle is homeless."

"But to have a home is to offer safety and security, by definition." Said a voice that sounded like the third. "It's shell is not a home because it can be consumed entirely by prey. Therefore the answer must be naked."

The first two ghouls rounded on the third ghoul.

"And to be naked is to be without clothing. Turtles do not wear clothing. They wear a shell." Said the first ghoul.

"Aha! You said 'wear'." Said the second ghoul looking back and forth to the first and third. "Whether it be a shell or a tunic, a turtle is wearing something. Therefore it is naked when the thing it is wearing is not there."

The other two ghouls considered this. After a few moments the argument started all over again, this time involving deep philosophical theories of 'not there', 'nakedness' and 'homelessness'.

Ravenscrawl looked down from a hidden nook in the side of the mountain a watched the argument for some time. At one point, one of the ghouls ripped a decaying arm off the shoulder of another ghoul and started beating the third over the head with it. It was probably meant to demonstrate a point but Ravenscrawl couldn't be sure. He considered attacking them but as long as Nicholas was racing away with his nephews, he would entertain himself. Besides, it might be a considerable amount of time before they agreed on an answer. Ravenscrawl didn't mind this. For the time being, Nicholas was safe and he had all the time in world.

Chapter 26: Army Soup with Ash Croutons

The three opponents glared at one another. They had squared off for centuries and now - this night - it would go to the finish. Despite the cool evening wind whipping up sparks from the small campfire, sweat nevertheless beaded on their brows. Their eyes twitched in the flickering flames and shifted nervously from one to another. The demise of one was rapidly approaching. Whatever happened in the next few seconds would determine that outcome. Even then, only one would survive.

Harry rolled the stone cubes.

"Seven!" Shouted Fuzzy happily. "You owe me two hundred gold sovereigns, Mr. Boot."

"Bah!" Harry stood up and shook his head. "Who get's three roads and all the utilities? This game is fixed, I tell you! Fixed! And you two," he shook an old finger at them, "are both in on it."

Fuzzy and Buddy chuckled.

"Oh come now brother." Said Fuzzy, sighing and picking up the game pieces. "Why would we bother to cheat, eh?"

Harry paced away from the fire and waved an arm dismissively. For the past week the three old teachers made camp beside a small lake in a land that would later become known as Korea. It seemed a pleasantly distracting place to hide until they could figure out what their next move was going to be.

Since they abandoned Abanis some weeks ago, the three old fools had been moving from place to place around the world, making sure that their younger siblings were safely hidden. In addition, they were able to speak to one of their oldest friends, an emissary named Saja who was as old and as experienced as they. And one whom, they recently discovered, had encountered The Greyman.

Harry lit a pipe and sighed as he looked across the glistening surface of the lake, then up into the evening sky. The mountains were dark but the moon was out in full form and lit the surrounding countryside with a tranquil, silvery hue. It was a beautiful country, Harry thought. With the exception of the winter months, the tree covered mountains offered shady coolness, day or night. The rich, green rice fields in between the mountains were home to a quiet, generous people he had come to respect. They worked hard, liked to drink hard, and for some odd reason, enjoyed singing. He found them to be quite similar to the Greeks. They even had the same, apprehensive caution regarding foreigners. But then again, Harry chuckled to himself, who likes foreigners anyways.

The breeze around the lake was particularly pleasant this evening. Harry felt calmed as he watched subtle ripples on the lake surface lap against the shore. As the others whispered quietly to each other, he decided to sit down beside the burning bush and have some more rice mead. It was a tasty alcohol and indigenous to...

He stopped suddenly. His brain did the mental version of slamming on the brakes, putting Harry in reverse and backing up. He slowly turned his head to the bush that was on fire beside him.

"Dahhh!"

Fuzzy and Buddy looked up from the small campfire to see Harry move at a staggering run across the clearing with the hem of his robes on fire. They watched him leap over some large rocks near the shore of the lake and heard a splash.

Buddy was holding a small cup up to his lips as his eyes followed Harry, then he continued what he was saying to Fuzzy. "Anyways, this is a particularly interesting mead. One of the oldest recipes in the world."

Fuzzy nodded as he inspected his cup. "It's a little sweet for my taste but a hearty concoction. I think they may have developed it from an old recipe taken from the middle kingdom. But I can't be sure."

After a moment, the two looked right then nodded to each other. After placing their cups down, they stood up and walked over to the burning bush. Among the crackling embers of the mildly flaming shrubbery, they could just make out the grinning face of Pantilius.

"Well, it's about time. Good to see you, brothers." Said Pantilius grinning up at both of them. "I've only been burning here for about three quarters of an hour you know. Where's Harry?"

"I believe he was rather startled just now." Said Fuzzy happily.

"And decided to have a dip in the lake." Added Buddy, nodding pleasantly.

Pantilius winced. "Ahh, he may be in a bit of a mood. Let's wait for him shall we?"

"This is quite a skillful entrance Master Pantilius." Said Fuzzy gesturing the burning bush as a whole. "I quite like it."

Pantilius face brightened in the burning embers. "Yes. A tricky skill The Pilgrim taught me some years ago." He grinned. "He used it a lot in the old days, you know, back when he was more- " He stopped and appeared to look around Buddy and Fuzzy. "Ahh there you are brother. I'm so sorry I startled you."

Buddy and Fuzzy turned to see Harry slosh his way towards them, looking quite bedraggled.

"I'm sure you are." He said dryly, which was a remarkable achievement considering he was soaking wet. "Good to see you, Pantilius. Nice trick." Harry sputtered.

Fuzzy pulled out the tiniest of handkerchiefs from his robes and passed it to him. Harry looked at it in the way a firemen looks at a glass of water next to a raging inferno. He glared at Fuzzy as he snatched it up and began dabbing his wet forehead.

"Listen carefully brothers, I haven't much time." Said Pantilius, looking at each of the old men in turn. "I bring sad news. I fear that Gabriel is lost."

Harry dropped the handkerchief and gaped at Pantilius. Buddy nodded and looked away. Fuzzy lowered his head.

"I am not The Pilgrim but I sense that he has been ushered to Empyrean. Although I cannot imagine who could do such a thing." Pantilius continued quietly. The burning bush crackled in the sudden quiet as the three old men tried to compose themselves.

"In addition, I have confronted The Greyman."

Fuzzy looked up suddenly. "What? How? Where?"

"The details can wait but you should know that I goaded him into a trap. He thinks I will betray Nicholas in exchange for our solitude and the safety of humans everywhere. This, of course will not happen. The Greyman is mad. If he succeeds in his plans, he may wreck this world and everything in it."

Harry blinked. "Trap?" He said incredulously. "Trap? Mice cannot trap a lion no matter how much cheese they eat. If he is a pure Huru and one from our ancient past, how do you suppose we are to trap such a being?"

"Have faith brothers. I ask that you have faith in The Pilgrim. I believe something is in motion that has been gaining momentum right under our noses." Said Pantilius. "And Nicholas is the key."

"What of Nicholas?" Asked Harry suddenly. "Is he ok?"

"As far as I can tell, he is safe. I believe he has gone to Twilenos."

"He will be in good hands with Ravenscrawl then." Harry nodded to the others.

"The Greyman, if I understand the histories correctly, is too old, too clever and too powerful." Said Fuzzy, shaking his head and frowning. "He will suspect that we are deceiving him."

"No." Pantilius. "I wasn't sure before I confronted him but now I am certain that he is only a being of hate and malice. There is no more Huru left in him. He may not understand why some would face impossible odds to sacrifice themselves for the good of others. He only understands betrayal and easily accepted that I would do so."

"If this is the best course, then we will follow it Master Pantilius. What would you have us do?" Said Buddy, stepping closer to the burning bush.

"Listen carefully then." Said Pantilius. "We must assemble all emissaries. All of them. Find as many as you can in the eastern kingdoms and come to Hyperborea. We will await your arrival. There we must have council before the confrontation. Blessed are the meek."

The face of Pantilius faded amidst the small flames and the bush dissipated into a small pile of ash and crackling, orange embers. Harry, Buddy and Fuzzy stood looking at it and remained quiet for some time.

JingleJingle***Jingle***

The camel-flown chariot sped across the night sky. After gaining altitude just long enough to keep all the blood in Nicholas' body somewhere near his feet, the carriage leveled. Nicholas started to breathe again and eased his white-knuckled grip on the reins as he looked around.

Peering cautiously over the side, it was evident to Nicholas they were moving at great speed. Although the silvery, starlit dunes of a great desert moved slowly below, he knew that seeing them do so from this altitude meant they were traveling very fast indeed. The air around him, however, was curiously calm. The wind force, while traveling at this speed, should be keeping him smeared against the back of the chariots grand seat making funny faces. Instead, the breeze inside the carriage was rather like being at the summit of a small mountain.

He leaned right and was able to make out a vast, dark ocean under a grayish-blue horizon. Forward and sprawling endlessly to his left was an ocean of sand. He realized with sudden burst of excitement that he may be near Egypt and traveling over the Great Desert, as Pantilius once called it. And that would mean he may be near the pyramids!

Nicholas looked at eight the camels pulling the chariot across the evening sky. They galloped lazily through the air with no shred of remorse for breaking the (apparently flexible) laws of physics. Nicholas briefly mused that 'galloping' may not be the right word because 'to gallop' indicates that four-legged creatures need something more than just air to 'gallop on' and thus make 'galloping' noises. Regardless, they galloped silently across the sky, pulling the chariot on into the night.

"Are the pyramids nearby?" Nicholas shouted, hoping the sound of his voice could reach the camels.

Indeed, Master Nicholas. Said a deep voice inside Nicholas head. He recognized it to be the voice of Rudolph. *They will pass under us as we move closer to our destination. Shall I inform you as we do so?*

Yes please. Responded Nicholas internally. *I have always wanted to see them. They are a remarkable architectural achievement, or so I have learned.*

Indeed they are. It will be sometime before we pass them, however. Please sit back and rest if you wish. There is a container near your feet with ambrosia and other food items. Our uncle enjoys such human things when we travel this method.

Nicholas looked down and saw a large leather sack bolted inside the front of the carriage. He leaned down and opened it, finding a few bottles of ambrosia and some odd looking packages inside. He pulled a package out and inspected it.

The colorfully painted package material made crackling noises as he turned it over and over in his hands. It appeared to contain some small objects Nicholas assumed were nuts or some other food. After struggling unsuccessfully for a few moments to get the packet open, he gave up, threw them back into the sack and decided to drink some ambrosia.

He leaned back in the carriage and popped the cork top off an ambrosia bottle. It made a pleasing 'thunk' sound. This one smelled different than the other two he had in Twilenos but somehow familiar. He took a sip and was surprised to find it tasted exactly like Mrs. Bakersbee's famous *Peaches and Cream Cobbler.* He smacked his lips contentedly and tried not to worry about his former, doting Matron at Mirthmyst Castle. He missed her and hoped she was safe from whatever evil The Greyman was up to.

Master Nicholas. Said Rudolph in his mind.

No response came.

Master Nicholas, this is Captain Rudolph. I hope you are enjoying this evening flight on Camel Air. I'd like to inform you at this time we are passing over the Great Pyramids of Egypt.

Nicholas suddenly sat bolt upright, realizing he drifted off to sleep. "What? Pyramids?" He blinked looking around.

Yes, Master Nicholas. Look ahead. North by north-east.

Nicholas peered into the horizon and caught his breath. There they were!

On the horizon, he could just make out three, small triangular silhouettes getting larger as they approached. Despite the moonless night, he could just make out one of the four sides of larger pyramid. He didn't anticipate they could be so beautiful in their magnificent simplicity as they now appeared.

Built by the Egyptians thousands of years ago, the Tombs of Pharaohs, are indeed one of humankinds greatest achievements thus far. Said Rudolph. *But their construction involved much suffering. The Pharaoh at the time used hundreds of thousands of slaves over a period of more than twenty years.*

Nicholas stared at the rapidly growing pyramids and frowned. *How can something so wonderful be constructed from so much suffering?* He asked as the full splendor of the pyramids came into view.

Great suffering is often the price of great achievements. Said Rudolph as the chariot and camels veered east. *It is the way of things. It is equally important to remember those who give much for an achievement as the achievement itself. But I suspect you already know this.*

Well, not really. Said Nicholas feeling suddenly solemn and guilty.

Blessed are the meek. Surely you have heard this many times in Abanis.

Nicholas nodded. He considered this in silence for some time as they passed high over the pyramids and continued north east. He looked down at them and wondered how much death and suffering humankind must have endured trying to achieve 'great things'. He suddenly felt that 'great things' were frankly 'not-so-great'.

It dawned on him that the adage 'blessed are the meek' was perhaps the reason why there were emissaries in the first place. So that the 'meek', while suffering for 'greatness' were not forgotten. Otherwise, if emissaries of Abanis were not looking out those who could not do so for themselves, then what was the point? Nicholas pondered this train of thought for some time as he leaned on the edge of the carriage and watched the pyramids fade into the dark distance.

After a long while he noticed they were flying over water and could see populated coastal areas to the east. He guessed they were flying over the eastern edges of the Roman Empire, somewhere over the Mediterranean sea.

Rudolph, Ravenscrawl said something about 'Sin'. Is that a place? Are we going there?

Yes but first we are going to a place where our grandfather first appeared to Humans.

Nicholas did some mental calculation. *You mean The Greyman?*

Yes. You must understand what is to come and what has happened before. Our uncle frequently asks us to take emissaries there when they reach a certain understanding in their training.

Nicholas nodded as he stared at the rapidly approaching coastal villages. He watched them pass underneath the carriage and reckoned they were near Syria. Then a large mountain range appeared in front of them and he felt the carriage slowly descend.

The camels pulled the carriage down in a wide arc around the mountain range and headed towards a certain spot at the highest of the peaks. As it glided down, Nicholas wondered if they were going to need a landing strip or if his camel-companions had something else in mind. He gripped the reins tightly as the carriage dropped further and further towards the summit. He really, really hoped a smooth landing was incoming.

Sure enough, he felt the chariot slow in mid air as the snow capped peak came closer and closer. Nicholas held his breath as the chariot hit the snowy summit and skidded to a halt. Nicholas looked around. Deciding it was safe to do so, he started to breathe again.

He stepped out of the carriage and the snow covered summit made crunching noises as he looked down to the populated areas of Syria and Judea. It was quite a breathtaking view and the air was not as cold as he expected it to be. He heard some organic sounds behind him and turned to see eight, tall men stretching and yawning. Rudolph rubbed his shoulder a little as he stepped closer to Nicholas.

"As I'm sure you have guessed, we are able to shift our forms easily." Said Rudolph. "This is the nature of our manifestation of the Hurum." Then he turned and gestured to the other seven. "Allow me to introduce my brothers Uriolph, Sariolph, Raguolph, Ramiolph, Chamuolph, Zadkiolph, and Haniolph. Sorry we were a little rushed before introductions were made."

The assembled giants nodded and grinned at Nicholas. "G'day Nick" Said one.

"Good to meet ya' Nicholas." Said another stepping forward and crushing Nicholas' hand in a vigorous handshake.

"Hope you liked the ride, mate." Said another, pointing to the sky in general. "Nice night for it."

"Nice to meet you." Said Nicholas massaging his hand and cringing slightly. "And thanks."

Rudolph suddenly eclipsed his view. "For some reason, The Greyman cannot see us as he can see others of the Hurum. We suspect it has something to do with us being part of his ilk. This is why Ravenscrawl asked us to bring you here."

"Ahh." Said Nicholas, looking around. "And, uh here is what?"

Rudolph put a huge hand on Nicholas shoulder and guided him to an isolated spot on the summit of the mountain. "This is Mt. Hermon. And here," he said pointing to a spot on the peak that looked much like any other spot, "is where some of our ancestors made first contact with humans."

"I see." Said Nicholas, looking down.

Rudolph kneeled and brushed away some snow near Nicholas' feet. After a few moments Nicholas could see a smooth round plate appear. It looked to be made of metal and bolted to the very rock of the mountain. In its center was an indentation that looked familiar.

Rudolph stood up and held out his hand. "I believe you have a pendant, Nicholas. I require it."

Then Nicholas realized why the indentation looked familiar. "Ah! The pendant!" He exclaimed. He reached into his backpack and pulled out the seven-sided pendant. Six of its jewels glowed slightly as he passed it to Rudolph.

"Our uncle spoke to me as we left Twilenos." Said Rudolph as he turned the pendant over and over in his hands. "This is quite old. Few survived the cataclysm of Adamis."

He stared at Nicholas for a moment as if to consider something. "You have only completed six of the seven required skills to be called an emissary Nicholas. We suspect this place may yet release a seventh. But we are not sure. I know it may have all seemed rushed but The Greyman is not going to wait around until you are ready. He is hunting you."

Then he kneeled and Nicholas was surprised to see the pendant fit perfectly into the metal plate. The jewels within the pendant glowed brightly as Rudolph stood up.

"This," he said ominously as he spread his arms and backed away, "is the Conflagration. Every emissary must understand why we do not interfere."

Flames suddenly erupted around Nicholas and he was encircled by a ring of fire. Around him, the quiet mountain summit and the eight nephews of Ravenscrawl vanished. They were replaced by tall beings much like those he saw in the vision given to him by Nosis.

He saw the golden-haired Huru among them and realized this was The Greyman before the destruction of Adamis. He was speaking to human leaders. They appeared to be kings and emperors of various cultures. Nicholas looked down one side of the mountain and saw huge armies fighting a war of such epic size that he had only read about their like in books. He saw machines and other weapons of war destroy entire legions of men. Massive explosions and balls of fire, smoke and ash covered the battlefields. Nicholas turned on the spot and saw that there was war all around the mountain. Armies of thousands fought each other and he saw great city walls torn down by great explosions. The skies were filled with smoke and choking ash. Under those skies, countless soldiers of men slaughtered each other in innumerable ways.

Nicholas, in all his pampered life, had never seen such horrible destruction. He turned on the spot and watched the destruction continue all around him. "No." Was all Nicholas could say.

Nicholas never imagined the battles of men, despite all of his studies, could be so awful to behold. Everywhere he looked, he saw death, mayhem and suffering. Throughout all of it, he could see the Huru.

He watched The Greyman telling lies to one King and other Huru whispering in the ears of others, causing many leaders to pit their armies against one another. He saw women being raped by some of the Huru and children slaughtered mercilessly by armies mislead by greed, arrogance and self righteous pursuits. It appeared that much of the destruction was fueled by the Huru.

Nicholas felt tears welling in his eyes as he watched the unceasing calamity. Thousands died around him in a battles that covered all the lands on every horizon and seemed to have no end. Lakes in distant lands were turned red with blood and sickeningly grey with ash. Babies were torn from the desperate grasps of their mothers and thrown upon rocks while their ill equipped fathers were torn to pieces by legions of marauding armies. Amidst the blood, fire, explosions, ash and the fall of cities, the screams of terror, the cries mothers and fathers as they struggled to defend their children, Nicholas could hear laughter. Despite all the mayhem, the golden-haired Huru surveyed his handy work from the top of Mt. Hermon and laughed.

Nicholas stared at him through his tears. A feeling welled in him that he had never felt before. It was a hatred so strong that wanted to rush at the laughing Greyman and tear him to pieces with his bare hands.

Just as he felt his chest about to explode under the pressure of vengeance and hate, the vision ceased. Nicholas fell to his knees beside the glowing pendant and whimpered slightly.

Rudolph and his brothers watched him tenuously for a moment some distance away.

"He is only human, Rudy." Whispered one of Rudolph's brothers. "It may have not been wise to drop this on him all at once. You know what primates are like. Their sense of empathy can be overwhelming."

"Do not call him that." Said Rudolph. "And yes it was a little early but he needs to see before we go to Sin. It is a necessary step for him, human or not."

Rudolph walked over to Nicholas and helped him to his feet. Nicholas looked away and shook his head but said nothing.

At this point, Kara flew out of Nicholas backpack with her spear at the ready. She looked at Nicholas and then looked at the others as she buzzed about in confusion. Then, seeing Nicholas was under duress, she landed on his shoulder and snuggled close to his cheek. Then she pointed her little golden spear towards Rudolph in a manner that said 'not one step closer you big meanie.'

Rudolph raised his hands in the air. "I yield, little friend. You are in charge."

"What happened here?" Whispered Nicholas, managing to look up at Rudolph.

"Some, lead by The Greyman, rebelled against our ways and decided to rule over humans. He was motivated by many things and that story is long and sad. In the end, our grandfather simply wanted to go home." Said Rudolph, keeping his hands raised. "But you need to understand that he has done much against humanity. You need to understand that we must not interfere with them." He pointed to some human settlements down one side of the mountain.

"But why didn't The Pilgrim or anyone stop him? And where is 'home'? What does that mean?" Said Nicholas a little testily.

"They did eventually. It was on this very spot that Michael, his son and my father defeated him. But he was deeply wounded and fell into twilight. As for home," Rudolph shrugged, "I may not be able to explain that well for I do not completely understand." Rudolph pointed to the sky and looked up as he recited slowly. *"From the stars we came, From the Earth we began; Through oceans of rivers and rivers of sand.*

As Dusk looks back to admire the dawn, E'er shall we as time flows on."

"What is that? I've never heard it before." Said Nicholas, pulling a bottle of ambrosia from his backpack.

"Something I read many years ago, in a book my uncle likes to keep safe. I don't know what it means exactly. Nor do I understand what The Greyman means by home."

Nicholas nodded and thought about the recitation. He shook his head and decided to file it under the ever-expanding 'things to ask Pantilius about' category of his mind.

He looked at Kara and grinned slightly. "It's ok Kara. He's helping me." He said and Rudolph lowered his hands.

Kara looked at Nicholas and tilted her head in such a way as to say 'Yeah. And I'm the Queen of Sheba.'

Nicholas paced in front of Rudolph. "Why must we not interfere? Why shouldn't we use our skills to help them? To stop people from having wars and dying and all that?"

"That is a question better answered by someone else, Nicholas." Said Rudolph. "I bring some emissaries here for their training. The Conflagration is meant to make us all remember what happens when we interfere, whether that interference be benevolent or otherwise."

Nicholas turned his back to Rudolph and looked down to a quiet village some distance down the mountain. Dawn was lighting the eastern horizon with a deep scarlet hue. He considered something then he turned to Rudolph. The latter was mildly surprised to see a dangerous light in Nicholas' eyes.

"I hate him. I hate him more than I can say in words." Said Nicholas coldly. "After seeing this, I want to end him. I want to face him. I want to go back to Abanis and face him and take our home back."

Rudolph grinned slightly as the others came to stand behind him.

"You and me both, mate." Said one of the brothers.

"He's no blood of ours." Said another, shaking his head and looking at Nicholas.

"He is older and more powerful than you can imagine, mate." Said another. "He took on the host of the Huru and defeated many, almost single-handedly."

"Only our father's rage strengthened by one you know as The Pilgrim was able to overcome him." Said another of the brothers, stepping around Rudolph. "But it seems just temporary. In the end Michael fell but The Greyman was able to return."

"The more who are against him, the more he seems to gain strength." Said another to Rudolph's left. "And now that he is back, we don't know what other skills he has or what his weaknesses might be, if he has any. You sure you want to confront him?"

"I feel that if someone doesn't stand up against him. No one will. Maybe others will come." Said Nicholas shaking his head and frowning. I'm sick of running from him already and I've only just begun my work as an emissary. Just help me get close to him."

"I don't know why," said Rudolph after a moment, his red and white streaked hair whipping about in the morning breeze, "but our uncle asked us to take you to Sin. It was a fortress of The Greyman long ago when he broke the Huru into factions and left Adamis. Maybe he also wishes you to confront The Greyman. If you wish to do so, that is where he may be. Not back in Abanis."

Nicholas nodded. He leaned down and picked up the seven-sided pendant. The seventh jewel was glowing light, sky-blue but Nicholas didn't know what it meant. He held it up to Rudolph who smiled.

"You are not an emissary yet but you are well on the way Nick. The first human emissary." Said Rudolph nodding to the others in satisfaction. "Never thought I would see the day. We are sworn to follow emissaries and more so, sworn to protect humans as best we can. Since you are both, what do you want to do?"

"Sin." Said Nicholas quietly, staring at the pendant.

"Gentlemen." Said Rudolph loudly, turning to his brothers. "Let's ride."

Chapter 27: Sin Buffet

Far to the north of modern day Reykjavik, Iceland, Pantilius stood before the assembled multitude of emissaries and thought about the past. From distant lands all over the world, the emissaries arrived at the place called Hyperborea. Although Greek mythology identifies Hyperborea 'somewhere north of Thrace', the citizens of Abanis adopted the name for their own use.

What many younger emissaries didn't know, was that this secluded cliff top was the spot where the Host of Adamis once launched an assault on the Fortress of Sin, so very long ago. Some of the oldest emissaries, Pantilius for one, believed that the battle between The Greyman loyalists and the Huru was so powerful that it may have caused environmental havoc worldwide, resulting in the last ice-age. The last struggle between The Pilgrim and The Greyman resulted in the utter destruction of Adamis and the imprisonment of the latter in the Enefka Babellux.

It was Pantilius, working secretly with The Pilgrim, who crafted the Enefka Babellux prison as a safeguard in case The Pilgrim fell to his brother. Sure enough, Pantilius' greatest fears came true. The Pilgrim fell and the unstable gate destroyed their kingdom, along with Nosis, who loved Pantilius as a mother. Only Gabriel was able find the broken body of The Greyman, desperately trying to return north to his sanctuary, and send him properly to the prison built by The Pilgrim. The Greyman cursed them all, Pantilius especially, when he was thrust into the only known, stable gate beneath Twilenos. The Pilgrim, shortly after completing the construction of the Great Sphere of Abanis, moved the gate and built his home around it at the heart of its city.

When The Greyman returned a second time and marshaled humans kingdoms against one another, it was his own son Michael who vanquished him atop Mt. Hermon but fell himself. And yet again, Gabriel sent him back to the prison. However, during his second revisit, The Greyman enslaved Pantilius people, the Nelfilem, who vanished shortly after The Greyman's second imprisonment.

Pantilius and The Pilgrim searched the fortress of Sin and all the lands of the earth for his kin but gave up after many years. They realized the Gate pool in the Chamber of Stars within Sin was the only possible explanation how The Greyman kept returning to earth and perhaps also answered the mystery of the Nelfilem disappearance.

Like most gates crafted by Nelfilem and The Greyman, the one in the heart of Sin was unstable. Gate construction was invented by the Nelfilem to offer a solution to the Huru, who did not belong here at all but they were found to be unstable and unpredictable. Pantilius worked with The Greyman on their peculiar construction, in exchange for the proper treatment of his people but he was betrayed in the end.

For that reason, The Pilgrim and Pantilius dared not venture into the Sin gate or touch it for fear of offering a beacon for The Greyman to return again. And so they remained ever watchful over humanity, knowing that The Greyman may yet return while they trained and schooled hurum as emissaries for humanity. And now, Pantilius thought, it is happening again. And now, he felt so very, very old.

Pantilius stood on a rise near some icy cliffs and looked out across a frigid plain under a glittering, night sky. Aurora borealis danced among the stars and many of the assembled emissaries, about 1200 in all, admired one of nature's grand spectacles. Himtall, Claire, Buddy, Fuzzy, Harry, Saja Goryo, Maurice, Robin of Britannia and numerous other apprentices and emissaries of varying ages stood silently near him. With the exception of Clair, Robin and some other apprentices, the host of Abanis' emissaries wore deep blue robes. In addition to the robes, many emissaries wore protective gear of varying designs, knowing full well that conflict could be in the immediate future. As the eldest living being on earth besides possibly Raphael, The Greyman and The Pilgrim, Pantilius took it upon himself to call the host together. He had instructed Mrs. Bakersbee and Aryu Veda to take all of the younglings to the Himalayas where they could rebuild in secret if the inevitable struggle turned bad.

As Pantilius pondered the past in silence, he wondered how many of the people before him knew the details of the struggle before and what would come. He knew the histories were misleading and sometimes completely wrong but, quite frankly, after the first and second imprisonment of The Greyman, the Huru were scattered and broken in heart and spirit. Only The Pilgrim pulled them all together. Only The Pilgrim was able to bring the scattered and broken remains of a people not meant for this earth to flourish under one sanctuary again. Only The Pilgrim, who taught Pantilius everything he knew from childhood to the recent past, could stand against the might of The Greyman, oldest of the Huru. Only The Pilgrim had the incomparable love for his pupil to forgive Pantilius' early alliance with The Greyman. Only The Pilgrim gave everyone around him more than he ever received. And now, Pantilius was going to show The Pilgrim how deeply he respected his patron by simply having faith. The only problem, he thought as he prepared to speak to the assembled host, was convincing the younger emissaries before him to have as much faith as he. Could they have faith in a being not seen in nearly sixty years?

"Citizens of Abanis, elders , teachers, acolytes and," he glanced left and up at Himtall, "really, really, tall people..." he grinned as some of the emissaries chuckled, "please listen to me carefully."

The emissaries hushed and silently waited for Pantilius to continue.

"Some of you know truths more than others and some of you know others more than truths. But everyone here knows that a being of incredible strength and power has returned to this earth. He is older than you can imagine. And he is the personification of a misanthrope. No human will survive his wrath if we do not stop him."

Buddy and Fuzzy looked at Harry as Pantilius paused.

"This whole doom and gloom thing was your idea wasn't it?" Whispered Fuzzy loudly.

"I just asked him to be honest." Harry whispered, contriving to look innocent but wilting like a weed under the sun-like glare of Buddy.

"You should have asked to be him to be a little less harsh, there are young people present and they may not see home again, ever thought of that?" Whispered Buddy.

"Now look - " Whispered Harry, but he wasn't able to finish.

"Since when does the Master Giggler listen to you?" Whispered Fuzzy.

"He always listens to m - "

"You are such a downer."

"What the hell does that mean?"

"I'll tell you what it means, Mr. Poopy pants, it means you!"

Soon the three old men were whispering loudly and facing each other arguing over who has more "Poopy pants" than the other. This continued for a few moments until Buddy, realizing the skies in his world were a different color, looked around.

The entire host was watching the mild argument with equally mild amusement. Pantilius was looking at them happily. Himtall was looking less than happy and more likely to throttle someone as he glared at the three old men.

Buddy grinned and tapped the other two on their respective shoulders as Harry was about to heave Fuzzy up from his diminutive height to a more suitable one for yelling at. They froze, realizing everyone was looking at them. Grinning stupidly at the crowd, the old men pulled themselves together and graciously indicated for Pantilius to continue.

"Thank you brothers. I am glad to see you are ready for battle." Said Pantilius. "Or at least a lengthy debate." Claire snorted as the old men tried to look sheepish and apologetic.

"As I was saying," Pantilius continued, addressing the host in general, "The Greyman is no laughing matter. Forget what you have read about him or heard about him. He is wholly evil and hates each and every one of you. I most of all. But all we have to do is buy time."

"Buy time?" Said one emissary, stepping forward. "If he is as The Pilgrim in strength and age, what do you think we can do Pantilius?"

"Maurice, I know you have doubts about what we will do this day and night but all I ask is for you to have faith."

"Faith in what?" The emissary known as Maurice turned to the host. "We can hold against him! If he is not in Abanis, we should go there and keep ourselves safe. We can lock the Gate pool and defend ourselves. The Pilgrim and Pantilius teach us that to perish is to deprive a million humans of help in the future."

"Faith is all I ask." Said Pantilius calmly. "The Pilgrim will return to us. I believe it, don't you?"

"Why? Because a sparrow told you?" Maurice laughed and turned to the host again. "Faith doesn't protect us against whatever horrors The Greyman may be capable of.

This is folly to assault an unknown being with all of us exposed as such."

"I know him. I have faced him long ago." Said Pantilius. Many of the emissaries stared at Pantilius in shock and disbelief. "His weakness is his arrogance. He thinks he is more powerful than all of us together, but he is wrong."

Maurice shook his head and looked at Himtall pleadingly. "Himtall, The Pilgrim didn't even save his own progeny! He even asked some of us not to interfere if it should ever happen." The crowd seemed to murmur agreeably at this and many emissaries looked questioningly at one another.

"Pantilius has never let you down. Ever! He is more human than any of us." Shouted Himtall. He looked grimly but not unkindly at the dark skinned man.

"The Nazarene could have helped us," Maurice continued, "it was rumored he was more powerful as a child than The Pilgrim himself but he is gone! And now you want us to have faith in one who has been absent for nearly sixty years?"

"Enough!" Said a booming voice that echoed across the plain. It was if the skies opened up and thundered down an objection. This, in fact, was mostly true. "Strange are The Pilgrim's ways but he never abandons anyone!" Said the booming voice as it continued to echo across the plain.

Pantilius stuck a finger in his ear and winced as he looked up. Several of the emissaries near Pantilius shouted and some screamed as the dazzling display of northern lights and stars above were eclipsed by a great winged form. Emissaries who were gathered in front of Pantilius scattered as a massive, blue-scaled dragon landed heavily on the ice and rock. Great leathery wings buffeting the entire area and some emissaries were blown off their feet and stumbled in to one another.

"Raphael!" Claire shouted and grinned appreciatively as the dragon winked at her.

"Raphael..." Said some of the emissaries, whispering to each other excitedly. "Raphael comes!"

"Raphael comes to avenge Gabriel!" Said others, nodding to each other. "He comes to defend the first promise!"

A huge draconic head turned to the assembled emissaries and everyone stopped breathing and tried to appear inedible. The air around his massive body blurred and after a few moments, a three meter tall man, resembling Gabriel is almost every aspect stood before them.

"I prefer," he looked sternly at Maurice now, "Usher Ravenscrawl."

Then he turned to Pantilius and walked over to the slight rise along the icy cliff. "Good evening." He said formally to those standing near Pantilius. "Hello Claire, my dear. Nicholas is safe and thinks of you every day. A fine boy with penchant for fire. He loves you so don't screw it up. I daresay he would move mountains to be with you."

Claire's eyes lit up but before she could say anything, Ravenscrawl turned to the others. "Himtall, well met. Looking as well fed and as loyal as ever. Good man." He turned to Harry, Buddy and Fuzzy. "Aristotle, Siddhartha, Confucius, still arguing I see. Well, that's no surprise since you each think the other is an idiot. School boys will be school boys. Well met, again."

Harry opened his mouth to speak but Fuzzy and Buddy clamped their hands across his mouth at the same time.

"Saja," Ravenscrawl continued, "nice to see you agile as ever. The young girl is safely living with another tribe and thinks of you as her angel. Well done. My, what a sharp looking sword. Use it well young man."

"Hyung-nim." Said Saja, grinning at Ravenscrawl and bowing respectfully.

"Pantilius," Ravenscrawl stood beside the tiny Nelfilem and looked down, "greetings again, old friend."

"Really, really good entrance." Whispered Pantilius out of the corner of his mouth while wiggling his white eyebrows up at the librarian. "Epic, at the very least I'd say."

Ravenscrawl nodded and looked at the assembled host of Abanis. "I stand beside Pantilius and will be loyal to him to my dying breath!" He shouted. "I have faith in The Pilgrim and I will go to Sin with or without you. You have sworn oaths to our cause. This is the time to prove your worth. The Greyman threatens us all whether we hide in a library or a submerged city. No place is safe until he is gone."

"Will you have faith in The Pilgrim?" Said Pantilius stepping forward. His voice was quiet but reached everyone on the snowy plain. "Will you come to fight for everything we have worked for?"

It took only a few moments for Maurice to make the necessary considerations. He looked at the two beings, Ravenscrawl and Pantilius, who were alive when his Afrikaan ancestors were great kings of vast empires long before the Etruscan wolf children rose from the north. He looked around to the assembled emissaries and nodded. "I will follow." He held up his walking staff, a symbol of his station as a pilgrim from of Abanis. "Faith." He said.

The emissaries looked at each other for a moment in silence. A nearby emissary raised her staff. "Faith." She answered.

Then more emissaries raised their staves. "Faith!" They shouted.

Pantilius grinned at the assembly and leaned over to Ravenscrawl. "I have a simple plan regarding the boy. You need to hear it." He whispered.

Ravenscrawl looked down at the small, blue skinned Nelfilem he had befriended so very long ago and considered this for a moment.

"In the words of Brutus when speaking to Cassius about the demise of Julius Caesar," he said quietly, "this had better be a damn good plan."

JingleJingle***Jingle***

Nicholas and held on to the chariot's reins as the reindeer glided down to the icy, rock strewn shore. Rudolph and the rest of Raphael's nephews decided that flying camels wouldn't be the right form in the northern climate. They thought huge, horned reindeer were more appropriate for their present location and would blend in better. Nicholas wondered if flying as *anything at all*, with a big chariot in tow, would be appropriate anywhere on the planet. But they seemed to like the new forms so who was he to spoil it for them?

An overcast evening sky and a light snowfall, whipped into a mild frenzy by icy winds coming in off the bay, made the shoreline seem less pleasant than Nicholas expected. Up from the shore, the horseshoe shaped strand stretched about a half mile until it came to an abrupt end at the base of a snow-capped mountain. If the mountain were a gigantic pudding, it was as if a spoon the size of a glacier had scooped out part of it nearest the shore to leave a large flat area. At the base of the mountain was a massive doorway carved right out of the rock. Although the entrance was hard to see, Nicholas guessed it was one hundred feet high and didn't have a doormat that said 'Welcome'.

A series of organic sounds signaled to Nicholas that Raphael's nephews assumed humanoid form once more. He turned to watch as they relieved themselves of the chariot harnesses and stretched in the snowy gloom.

"This is Sin Sanctum, Nicholas." Said Rudolph, walking over to him. "We think The Greyman is here but we're not sure if we can survive this encounter."

Nicholas considered this and looked at each of them for a moment, then turned to the massive doorway. "I don't know what to expect but just get me close to him." He said quietly.

"Nicholas, I will fight to the death by your side. You have my word." Said Ramiolph, stepping forward. "But it is rumored The Greyman took on fifty pure blooded Huru with only three henchmen at his side."

"And still managed to penetrate the Gate Room in the Old Kingdom and defeat The Pilgrim in single combat." Said Zadkiolph, standing beside his brother.

Uriolph joined them. "Raphael told us as much when we were young. What do think you can do? If you have a plan, we would like to hear it."

Nicholas turned and placed Kara inside his backpack. He patted her gently and whispering soothingly to her. Then he looked up at Rudolph and his brothers. "Your grandmother showed me something. Just get me close to him."

The dragon-men looked shocked but said nothing.

"Yes, I met the one who calls herself Hag Nosis. In a dream, she showed me much more than I originally thought. It was not until I spoke to Raphael recently that I was able put it together."

"But -" Rudolph began but he was cut off by the sound of eerie laughter on the wind.

It was a dry, mocking laughter echoing in the wind around them. Rudolph and his brothers froze and appeared to be afraid. A chill went down Nicholas spine and he wondered if this idea was more foolish than valiant.

"Family and friends, do not be afraid." It whispered but the eerie voice made Nicholas and his companions feel exactly what it said not to.

"My grandchildren are here with you, Nicholas, what a happy circumstance."

"Who are you?" Said Nicholas pulling out his compass and looking down at it. "Show yourself!"

The compass dial spun erratically for a moment then stopped and held steadfast on 'naughty'. Nicholas looked up and tried to peer across the snowy plain but the snow whipping around him and the darkness of the area visibility difficult.

"Naughty is a point of view young man." Said the voice. It was soft and Nicholas felt almost mesmerized by its tone. *"I am but a simple traveler who wishes to go home. Is that so wrong? Don't you want to go home?"*

"Yes." Said Nicholas weakly. "I- I want to go home."

"Then let me help you. Home is where the heart is. Surely you have heard this before." Said the voice.

To Nicholas it sounded almost pleasant and he fought internally to get a grip on why he was here. Home is certainly where the heart is. Mrs. Bakersbee said that all the time. How could something *she* said be so wrong?

"Come to me, young man." Said the voice. *"Come and let us help each other go home. I am here for you. Can you see me?"*

Nicholas looked up. Far across the strand, he could just make out the giant door set into the cliff-face had opened. Despite the snowy gale around him, he could see a bright light within. Silhouetted against the door frame was a tall, dark figure.

"Come to me, young man. Let us speak of home and warmth and loved ones."

Nicholas had only been away from Abanis for a few short weeks but felt an urge to be home so strongly that everything else seemed unimportant. He took a few staggered steps forward and thought he could smell Mrs. Bakersbee's freshly baked 'Peanut Butter and Chocolate Chip' cookies. Part of his mind said *'there can't possibly be a good cookie in this place'*. Another part of his mind said *'who cares?'*

As he took a few more steps, Rudolph yelled. "Nicholas! He is here! Wait! He is deceitful! He is the Master of Lies! Do not Listen to him! Do no-

"Silence!" The word exploded across the strand and echoed out into the bay. Ice and rock shook about the area and small avalanches dropped from the cliffs on either side of the door. The explosive command sliced through Nicholas' entrancement like a cold blade through an unfortunate tuna.

Nicholas regained his senses and looked around. "Rudolph!" He yelled. But Rudolph and his brothers remained still.

"Rudolph?" Nicholas ran back and stood in shock before his eight companions. They were entombed completely in ice, their faces frozen in various expressions of surprise and anger.

Nicholas spun around and looked at the doorway. "Greyman! That is you! Show yourself to me! You want me, come and get me!"

Laughter echoed on the wind once more. *"Why should I spend any effort to cage a monkey? I have zookeepers for that."* The voice laughed shrill and maliciously in Nicholas mind.

Sitting on the flat, white strand about fifty yards away, Nicholas spotted a small, black object. It must have been a box because the top suddenly flipped open.

"Bring him to me." Said the voice.

Not knowing what else he could do, Nicholas reached up to his chest and ripped the iron spike from its chain, thinking it might protect him in some way. To his astonishment, the rusted, iron spike uncoiled in his hand. He held it like a dagger. "Well, ok then." He said looking down at the spike in disbelief. A crash made him look up.

Standing over the black box, and towering above Nicholas, was the largest creature he had ever seen. It stood thirty feet and appeared to be a featureless humanoid made out of the rock and ice of the ground. Huge hands swayed back and forth as it took an unsteady step towards Nicholas. It's footfall shook the ground and Nicholas staggered as it approached.

"Holy Sh -" Nicholas stopped suddenly as Kara flew out of his backpack and buzzed around his head.

"Kara! Back inside! Now!" Nicholas commanded.

Kara tilted her head and looked at him as if to suggest she was asking 'what the hell is going on?'

"Kara not now! I have a really big problem here!" He gestured frantically at the approaching colossus. "I'm not leaving Rudolph and the others either!"

Kara stared at the approaching colossus. Her little jaw fell open as it took another step towards Nicholas. Then she dived back into the backpack.

The ground shook again and Nicholas' mind raced as he tried to maintain his balance. He looked at the spike in his hand and then looked at the approaching monstrosity with despair. *Think Nicholas, think!*

One more step and the colossus would be in range to turn him into a pancake or worse. Nicholas decided to run back to the water. Perhaps he could drown it some way by leading it and flowing.

He started to walk back but a cold voice echoed around him.

"Leave this strand and I will shatter my grandsons into unidentifiable scraps. Abandon them will you, primate?"

Nicholas faltered and looked at the ice-encased figures of Rudolph and the his brothers. He sagged and looked around for another option.

"You have no hope of overcoming such a creature. Give yourself to it and I will not harm your companions."

"Will he take me to you? Will I meet you finally?" Said Nicholas to the wind around him.

"Indeed it will. You cannot be harmed."

Kara stuck her head out of his backpack and leapt on to his shoulder, shaking her head furiously.

"It may be the only way, Kara. I need to get close to him. I can't let Rudolph and the others be harmed. I would never forgive myself."

Kara lowered her head and appeared to consider something. She turned and saw the colossus towering over them both. She suddenly kissed him on the cheek and leapt off his shoulder with her spear at the ready.

"Kara wait!" Nicholas shouted. He tried to grab her but she was out of reach before he could react.

Kara flew towards the approaching stone colossus. Higher and higher she climbed like glittering, shooting-star going in the wrong direction. The colossus swiped a huge, stony hand at her but Kara coiled and danced on the cold slipstreams. Finally, she reached the head and pulled back her golden spear, launching it as she dodged another swipe.

Nicholas, watching open-mouthed from below heard a *chink* as the spear landed a blow. A small section on the side of the colossus head fell from its body and dropped to the ground. He heard a high pitched ringing around the area and Nicholas guessed it was the colossus resounding frustration. Then a massive hand swung at Kara.

"Kara!" Nicholas screamed but he was too late. The little Golden Valkyrie was struck by the colossus so hard he heard the resulting *plink* from thirty feet below. Nicholas watched in horror as his companion was launched out of eye sight. He turned and saw a tiny splash in the bay. "Kara! No!" He screamed again.

Again Nicholas heard laughter on the wind. *"Valiant little plaything. Yield now or your other companions will follow her fate."*

Anger like he had rarely felt before welled in Nicholas as he turned to face the stone monstrosity. A ball of fire appeared in his hand and launched it at the creature. The fireball rocketed across the remaining space and struck the colossus square in the chest. The resulting explosion caused it to stagger as Nicholas looked at his left hand with shock and disbelief.

"Well, well." The eerie voice began to laugh. *"A human with a proclivity for fire tricks. How wonderfully unexpected. Do you have any other tricks, monkey?"*

The stone colossus, although blackened here and there, looked unimpeded and continued to advance. Nicholas turned to look at the frozen statues of Rudolph and his brothers and his heart sank. *I was a fool to come here.* He thought. *Pantilius, I'm sorry.*

Nicholas lowered his head. "You bastard." He said dejectedly. "I yield."

"Ahh, good monkey. Do not look so downtrodden. Come, let us meet at last. We can eat some bananas if you wish." The eerie voice laughed mockingly at Nicholas.

The colossus reached down a huge rocky hand. It's fingers were the size of Nicholas' arms. Not knowing what was going to happen next, Nicholas brought his hands up to his chin and held the spike in defense.

As the hands of the colossus were about to encompass him, they shuttered and cracked. The colossus raised its hand and appeared to be in some confusion. Then again it reached down and again it hit some barrier Nicholas could not comprehend. One of the fingers broke off and fell to the ice at his feet.

"Bring him to me!" Said the shrill voice on the wind. *"Bring him now!"*

The colossus froze. Nicholas heard a cracking sound and looked up at the creature. Cracks appeared all over its body. First at the torso, then on the arms and legs. Despite not having any eyes to see with, the colossus appeared to look down at its body. One of its arms broke off and fell crashing to the ice beside Nicholas. It staggered around for a few moments then, without any indication it was about to do so, exploded. Nicholas' immediate vicinity was filled with a multitude of colossus-bits. He covered his head and fell to his knees as he was showered in a wave of icy shards and rock fragments.

"What is this? Obey your master!" Screamed the voice on the wind.

Nicholas blinked and tried to get up, wiping bits of rock and ice off himself as he staggered away from the pile. He stared down at it in confusion, then looked towards the doorway to Sin. The dark figure was still there.

A peculiar grey cloud rose from the pile of icy rubble. Nicholas knew it was peculiar because clouds hardly ever, as far as he could recall, reassemble themselves to look vaguely humanoid. This one did.

A ghostly figure stood before Nicholas. It had no features other than being three meters tall and resembling the Huru Nicholas' had seen in visions.

"We are Nanos." It said. The odd voice sounded like someone speaking from inside a bathtub. It also sounded like several thousand voices, male and female, speaking in unison without the inconvenience of extreme volume.

"Subject 4-9-4. Classification: Human. Initiating assistance protocols. Command?"

"Uhh." Nicholas said after a considerable amount of gaping and blinking at the ghostly image.

"Command not recognized. 'Uhh' requires more information." It paused and took a step closer to Nicholas.

Nicholas squinted and thought he could see glittering particles in the cloud-like figure before him. He stared at the apparition in confusion.

"We are Nanos. We serve humanity. Subject 4-9-4 is human. Command?"

Subject is human. Nicholas thought, then he grinned. "I am human." He said flatly and nodded to Nanos.

"Primate! Maggot!" Said a cold voice on the wind. *"You will suffer for eternity. I will shred your mind into fine slices of pain and misery after I destroy everything around you."*

"I am human!" Nicholas screamed as he looked at the doorway in defiance. The dark figure didn't move or respond.

"Subject number 4-9-4, command?" Said Nanos.

Nicholas opened his mouth and caught himself before he said 'uh'. He considered something for a moment. "Nanos. Can you protect me?"

"Nanos. Can you protect me?" Nicholas heard his own voice mimicked by the ghostly figure. The particles in the ghostly cloud glittered for a moment then its own voice returned. "Analyzing command. Subject 4-9-4, please standby."

For a moment Nicholas thought he was surrounded by some new terror but realized there was....but it couldn't possibly be...there was music coming from the ghostly figure!

If his present situation wasn't dangerously bizarre, Nicholas would have found the sounds to be oddly pleasant. The music had, at its core, a simple 2/4 rhythm using mild percussion and string instruments. He also detected a soft male voice singing nothing other than do-da-da-da-da-do-do-dee. Thoroughly perplexed, he felt himself being drawn into involuntary slumber by the soft rhythms. Nicholas didn't know what an elevator was. If he did, the music would've made him feel like he was presently inside one.

The music suddenly stopped.

"Command accepted." Said Nanos. "Initiating shielding protocols on subject 4-9-4." Then it exploded.

The ghostly figure of nanos vanished in the explosion and its glittering particles expanded around the area. Nicholas wondered if he killed the thing by talking to it. Or perhaps the ghastly music damaged it in some way. Before he could react, however, the particles imploded around him.

Nicholas was surrounded by a light, transparent film and heard Nanos speaking all around him. "Shielding protocols on Subject 4-9-4 complete. Physical resistance 97%."

Nicholas looked down at his hand and then to the other holding the spike. He was coated with some shimmering cloud. He poked the sharp end of the spike on his arm and felt resistance there. The spike didn't touch his skin. "Wow!" He exclaimed.

"Clever." Said a cold voice. This time it was not on the wind but real and close. "Do you really think such a toy can protect you from me?"

Nicholas heart stopped as he looked up.

The Greyman stood before him. His black, hooded robes rippled in the breeze around a skeletal frame. His scythe flashed in the dull light of the shoreline as he raised a boney fist and gripped the air between them. Red lights flared in his skull sockets. Nicholas was seized by an invisible force and hurled away from the spot at meteoric speed. He sailed clear across the strand and before he could concentrate on turning himself into smoke, Nicholas crashed into the rock and fell to the icy ground fifty feet below. The force of the impact left a Nicholas-shaped crater on the cliff face. Nicholas was unconscious and bleeding.

"Shielding reduced to 0% physical resistance. Initiating repair protocols. Command?" Said Nanos.

Nicholas didn't respond. His blond hair was matted across his face and blood seeped from a gash on the side of his head. His backpack had exploded on impact and book papers flittered about the area on cold drafts. Although, his deer horn pipe and compass were broken and lay some distance away, he still held the iron spike in his left hand.

"So fragile." Said The Greyman as he materialized at the feet of Nicholas' broken body. "So meat-like. Disgusting thing I must wear for eternity. How did they survive so long, I wonder?"

He reached down to grab the iron spike with a skeletal hand. Before he could do so, a lightning bolt struck the side of the cliff and showered him with heated bits of smoldering rock. He stood and turned. The red lights in the skull sockets dilated.

A small figure, only about three feet tall, stood on the shoreline near the frozen statues of Raphael's nephews. The figure was joined by a thousand others of varying sizes who rose out of the icy water of the bay and began marching up the strand.

"Care to pick on someone your own size, Halaam?" The tiny figure shouted.

"Pantilius!" Whispered The Greyman as he watched Raphael's draconic form land on the rocky shoreline.

"For The Pilgrim!" Shouted one of the emissaries, breaking into a run and raising his staff.

"Nicholas!" Screamed Claire as she ran forward with Himtall.

This was followed by the deafening roar of a thousand others charging forward as Pantilius climbed atop Raphael's back and took to the air.

The Greyman raised his scythe. Red lights in his skull sockets flared once more as the entire host of Abanis stormed The Fortress of Sin.

Chapter 28: An Order of Take-Out

Enlil fell to his knees and gasped. "The time has come." He whispered to himself.

"Enlil!" Aurelia ran forward and put her arms around him.

"It's ok, my dear. You are too kind. I'm an old man you know." He swayed unsteadily as he stood, smiling grimly at Aurelia's concern.

Since coming to the bridge or 'Prochariot, as Arkilius called it, Enlil had been explaining quite a few things to his companions. Nicholas, Longinus and Pilate were particularly interested in why they could see so many stars outside the huge window but no land or water. This had taken some careful explanation on Enlil's part and only Pilate seemed to understand.

The bridge was more like a coliseum to Longinus and Nicholas, although the latter had never actually seen it. The giant, circular dome was constructed entirely out of some smooth, black metal neither Pilate nor Longinus recognized. At the center of the room was a three meter wide pool of brightly lit, turquoise colored water. Although it was smooth and without ripples on its surface, Cassie peered into it and thought she could see more than just the reflection of her surroundings. One side of the dome had a huge, single paned window, ten meters across that looked out into a multitude of stars. Many of the Nelfilem were presently sitting in front of it and watching the celestial dance with dreamy eyes. Pilate stood among them, staring at eternity until he turned to see why Enlil gasped.

"The time has come." Said Enlil, gesturing for Pilate to join them. The companions gathered around him and he spoke hesitantly. "As you know, I have been trying to explain what this place really is and that," he pointed to the pool of water, "is the only way out."

"What about the people? There are thousands down there." Said Longinus.

"The ones you saw sleeping below are truly dead, Long shanks." Said Arkilius quietly. "They are shadows of their former selves. Copies. Nothing more. The former warden of this place has strange skills that even I can't understand. Apparently he uses them for some kind of power source but I cannot fathom what kind. Or how it is achieved."

"Are we...?" Said Aurelia, suddenly looking afraid to finish the question.

"No." Said Arkilius, walking over to her and looking at the others. "You and the others were brought here alive. You do not belong here. As was I and my brethren. The wounds you suffered prior to arrival must have healed here. This place....does that. Time is still here. I'm sorry I don't know how to explain more."

Aurelia nodded but said nothing. She grabbed her husband's hand and nodded to him.

"Then let us get out of here." Said Erik.

"Yes." Said Enlil. "On the other side of this pool is the lair of the warden. I believe his attention has been drawn elsewhere. We must move quickly if we are to avoid detection. Come my little friends!" He yelled at the Nelfilem.

"I and my brothers will go through first and secure the other side." Said Arkilius. "We know what's on the other side of this pool because we built it. "Long shanks, Cassie, Goldilocks and Aurelia should follow Enlil through. Oliveoil, you take the rear. Any questions?"

"Did he just call you Goldilocks?" Longinus leaned over and whispered to Erik.

Nicholas snorted and shrugged.

"One more thing." Said Enlil, facing the companions as the Nelfilem lined up in front of the pool. "You are going to see more things beyond that pool that may be terrible or defy explanation. I don't know what is beyond this gate pool but I will do what I can to assist you. Do you understand?"

"Not even remotely." Said Erik, nodding happily at Enlil.

Enlil stared at him for a moment and his face twitched. Then he burst out laughing. It was the kind of laugh that infected bystanders to, at the very least, grin themselves.

"Humor, good. See the universe as one big joke and nothing will surprise you. Good man." Said Enlil, slapping Erik on the shoulder. He turned to Arkilius. "Warden Arkilius, now is the time."

Arkilius gestured for the first of his brothers to enter the gate pool. To the astonishment of Aurelia, Cassie, Longinus, Nicholas and Pilate, the Nelfilem didn't fall into the translucent emerald pool as he stepped on to its surface. He simply walked across it and stood in the center. After a few seconds, there was a blinding flash of light shooting up from the little creature's feet and he vanished.

"Wow!" Longinus exclaimed, looking at Nicholas incredulously. "Where did he go?"

"He traveled across creation, Long shanks. Believe it, 'cause that's where you're headin' too." Arkilius snorted as another flash of light signaled another departure.

One after another the Nelfilem vanished in a series of flashes. After a while only Arkilius, Enlil and the companions remained.

Arkilius stood on the water and nodded to Enlil. "I will never forget this, my Lord. Just in case....well, thank you." He said and with a wink at Cassie, he vanished.

Enlil stepped on the pool. "Pilate. You have proven to be a good man after all." Then he too was gone in a flash.

Longinus grinned at Nicholas, then he grabbed Cassie and kissed her so deeply and passionately that Aura and Nick felt compelled to look away out of simple decency. This lasted several moments until finally there was a sound like a plunger being released as Longinus backed away and stepped on to the pool. Cassie swayed a little and looked giddily at her husband.

"See you guys on the other side! Love ya' bab - " But he vanished in a flash of light.

"See you there, I love you both." Cassie said as she stepped on to the pool. Soon she was gone too.

Pilate gestured to Nicholas. "You next, Centurion." He said softly.

Nicholas turned to Aurelia and kissed her. "Everything will be ok." He said. "Follow quickly." Then he was gone in a flash.

As Aurelia was about to turn and say goodbye to Pilate, a terrible sound echoed through the domed bridge of the Enefka Babellux. It was like a horn blast and nearly deafened the two of them as they looked around in shock. It was followed by what seemed to be a thousand male and female voices speaking in unison all around them.

"Warning. Enefka Babellux must have a warden. Subject 3-9-1, Arkilius 1, Classification: Nelfilem Primus. Status: Unknown. Location: Unknown.

Subject 6-6-6; Enkidu Lightbringer; Classification: Huru Progenus. Status: Unknown. Location: Unknown. Warning.

*Enefka Babellux must have a warden. Warning. Gate collapse and termination protocols initiated. *Ding* Have a nice day."*

Aurelia looked at Pilate. "What the hell was that?" She screamed over the looping alarm sounds.

Pilate lowered his head and repeated the message he heard over and over in his mind. *The prison must have a warden....*

"Warden Arkilius!" He said, looking at Aurelia in disbelief. "Jupiter's lightning! Arkilius was the last warden! Enlil called him 'Warden'! One of us must remain!"

"Warning: Gate collapse imminent. Warning. Enefka Babellux must have a warden."

Pilate's mind raced as Aurelia stared at him in confusion and growing dread. The alarm continued to resound deafeningly around them. He considered something then grabbed Aurelia and thrust her on to the pool.

"Tell them I'm sorry!" Pilate yelled. "I'm sorry for everything!"

"Pilate! Aurelia screamed and reached out to him. "What are you doing? No! You will be tra - " But she was gone in a flash before the sentence finished.

"Warning! Gate closing. Please step away from the pool."

Pilate watched dejectedly as the light of the emerald pool faded until it was completely black. The alarm stopped as he turned to the window of the bridge and looked out into the face of the universe. He watched the innumerable stars and vast nebulae stretching into eternity as he tried to grasp the magnitude of his isolation. It took only a few seconds for him to realize that he was truly alone and possibly lost forever.

The voices returning was signaled by a sudden *ding* sound.

"Termination protocols aborted. Subject 2-4-1; Pontius Pilate. Classification: Human. Status: Current Warden of Enefka Babellux. Location: Bridge. Command?"

Pilate slowly pulled his gaze from the giant window and looked around in astonishment.

"Subject 2-4-1; Pontius Pilate. Classification: Human. Status: Current Warden of Enefka Babellux. Location: Bridge. Command?" The voices repeated.

As Pilate looked around in confusion. He suddenly grinned like farmer whose just discovered his hen just laid a 24 karat gold egg.

"Warden Pilate." Said the voices. *"Command?"*

Pilate turned slowly back to the window and continued staring out at the endless universe. "Tell me everything." He said quietly.

Jingle*Jingle***Jingle**

The Greyman turned back to the unconscious body of Nicholas and hesitated. Then he turned to consider the incoming surge of a thousand emissaries. Deciding an army of enraged Hurum was a much more pressing issue to deal with than an unconscious human child, he turned to meet the incoming host.

"Rise! Rise and feed!" He hissed. Some of the emissaries faltered in their charge as the ground suddenly heaved and shook.

"Nanos!" Roared Raphael from above as he circled cliff face. "Protect your master!"

"*Command accepted.*" A shimmering dome erupted around Nicholas' body.

The Greyman spun around and placed his skeletal hands on the transparent shield. "I will rupture this feeble shield whelp! But not before annihilating this rabble!" He turned and walked towards the incoming emissaries with his skeletal arms raised. "Rise, beasts of ages past! Rise and feed!"

Skeletal legs and skulls emerged from the icy ground amidst the charging emissaries. Many of them stopped and turned aside to address the threat. The skeletal horrors emerging from the ground were not human, however, they were the remains of beasts who walked the earth millions of years ago. A huge skeletal head, with more teeth than a beast should have, snatched up one emissary and hurled him into some others with so much force that the whole group was knocked unconscious.

"Asia group, Europa Group, stay in formation. Afrikaans take center point!" Yelled Pantilius from the air above them as Raphael flew around in a circle above the strand. "Defend each other! Stay in groups! Concentrate on proximity threats!"

Claire, Himtall, Harry, Buddy and Fuzzy joined the Europa group on the west side of the strand and kept their backs to each other. A huge beast called 'Hornaplentius' by Pantilius, zeroed in on Claire and tried to impale her as it rushed forward. Not knowing what else she could do, Claire changed into a falcon and flew just barely out of horn reach. Himtall spun around to protect Claire and growled.

"Not my little Claire!" He bellowed. In one movement, his fist transformed into a granite hammer and struck the beast full in the face with the kind of force normally associated with one planet colliding with another planet. The sound of the resulting impact echoed across the plain. Despite its size and power, the skeletal monster shuddered and collapsed in a heap of broken and twisted bones.

Gigantic skeletal beasts rampaged and roared amidst the formed groups of emissaries. Fire, ice and electrical bolts flashed wildly here and there as numerous emissaries employed elemental forces to directly damage the skeletal horrors. This had little effect on the beasts so many emissaries were having to resort to more creative methods of defense and offense.

Harry, Buddy and Fuzzy faced a group of smaller skeletal beasts with no apparent lack of viciousness or strength. Despite their diminutive size, the creatures appeared to have more razor-sharp teeth than evolution's credit card should have been able to for.

Buddy deftly stepped aside as one of the beasts launched itself at him. He watched with momentary interest as the skeletal creature was 'spaghettified' into a small, black void hovering in the air behind him. It vanished into the center of the tiny black maelstrom and made a *thok* sound.

"Welcome to Nirvana." He said happily and turned to confront some other attackers.

Harry was only slightly less creative in his defenses. A charging skeletal raptor found itself turned into a large olive tree. Ripe, green leaves and fruit popped into existence around its head to form a halo of olives. It simply remained there as Harry walked away from it to address other concerns. If it had eyes, the raptor would have blinked in confusion.

Fuzzy was incredibly fast despite his apparent image of extreme age and infirmity. One of the raptors found itself slowly being taken apart as Fuzzy appeared in front of it, took a bone off the skeleton, then appeared left of it and taking a rib out.

"*Oh... the leg bone connected to the hip bone.*" He sang as he reappeared at the creatures side. *"And the hip bone connected to the spinal bones.*" He took another bone out and dropped it as the skeletal beast tried to turn and snap at him. *"And the spinal bone connected to the...rib bone!"* He vanished just as jaws snapped where he was standing.

This repeated for a few moments until only a harmless head lay on the icy ground, snapping at Fuzzy's feet. Fuzzy beamed at Harry from beside a neat pile of bones. "I always loved that song!" He grinned childishly.

Do you always have to sing, brother?" Sighed Harry. He waved a hand at a charging raptor and transformed it into a gigantic and, rather surprised, boletus mushroom.

At the center of the strand, a creature resembling a huge crocodile charged into the Afrikaans emissaries and knocked several of them far from their formation. Considering those who were trampled and crushed under the massive skeletal juggernaut, they were the lucky ones.

Maurice spun his staff and leapt in front of the creature as it turned slowly on the shoreline to prepare for another charge. Huge jaws with teeth that could slice several men in two at one time, snapped at him but his staff knocked the creature off balance. Again and again it snapped at the dark skinned emissary but he danced and spun out of the way as his staff repeated blows to the creatures skull. Roaring in frustration, it charged at Maurice but he flipped high into the air and landed on the creatures back. Spinning his staff faster than humanly possible, it became a whirling blur. To the modern observer, it would have appeared to be the biggest electric saw in the world. The spinning staff lowered as the creature bucked and writhed to dislodge the rodeo-riding Maurice. The whirling staff met bone and an ensuing screeching buzz erupted from the contact. Maurice's staff cut through the upper spine and showered the cheering Afrikaans emissaries with powdered bone. The creatures head fell off its body and the legs collapsed.

On the eastern side of the strand, the Asian group was suffering losses. A creature called 'Teethalotus' by Pantilius was ripping and slicing its way through emissary defenses. Saja Goryo faced the creature and was moving adroitly out of biting range as the massive skeletal head snapped at him. He drew a thin, curved sword from a scabbard on his back and darted in between the creatures legs, slicing upwards as he did so. The creatures ribcage fell from its frame but did little other than enrage the beast. It spun a massive tail around as it faced Saja. Several unlucky emissaries were struck by the scythe-like tail and blasted across the strand. The faster thinkers managed to morph themselves into mist or lesser animal forms to avoid the tail swipe as Saja squared off against the creature. It roared and charged at Saja but his movement was too fast. His sword sliced at the massive skull as he dodged the snapping jaws but this did little other than to further anger the creature.

Suddenly Saja stopped and drew the flat end of his blade up to his face. Closing his eyes, he concentrated momentarily and shouted. "Yosae!"

The creature hesitated for only a second and snapped at the motionless emissary. As the huge jaws closed around Saja and threatened to bite him in half, fifty blades erupted through its skull like a steel porcupine exploding. The creature, attempting to pull away with its torso, ripped its own head from its body and collapsed.

Saja emerged from the skull as the blades receded and whirled his sword around to face some more of the beasts. The Asian emissaries cheered in appreciation as he nodded to them.

"Reform!" Pantilius shouted from the sky. Defend yourse-"

"Silence!" The Greyman's command drowned out all other sounds, including Pantilius shouts and the battlefield was suddenly still. The remaining skeletal creatures collapsed. "What delightful spectacles your performances have made." The Greyman laughed mockingly. "Such wonderful party tricks your students have Pan. Perhaps I will spare some to entertain me later."

Raphael dove from the sky. A blast of lightning erupted from his mouth and smote The Greyman. The immediate area exploded into a cloud of vaporize ice and rock as electricity danced up the side of the cliff face. Raphael and Pantilius circled around for another blast but stopped as the cloud dispersed.

The Greyman stood unharmed amidst the devastation around him and laughed. It was a shrill, mocking laughter that echoed across the strand and seemed to be carried on the wind.

"My son, my dear child. Such brutal advances you attempt on me. Shame on you."

"You are leaving this world tonight father!" Raphael roared from the sky.

"Oh, I see." Said The Greyman, whose voice reached every emissary on the plain. "Then come. Come to me and let us settle this one and for all."

Citizens of Abanis. Said Pantilius, his voice reaching the minds of everyone on the plain below. *Hold your ground. Have faith. We must keep him occupied.*

The groups of emissaries assembled at the center of the plain as Raphael landed on the shoreline. Many emissaries remained scattered about the plain in various states of unconsciousness or injury. However, the majority of the host of Abanis survived the skeletal beasts and rallied before The Greyman, who stood less than fifty yards away.

"Remember what we talked about." Whispered Pantilius as he leapt from the dragon and began to walk towards the assembled emissaries. "Take Nicholas to Twilenos if this takes a turn for the worst. Blessed are the meek, old friend."

Raphael nodded but moved towards the frozen statues of his nephews. He changed into human form and began speaking in a strange language as he walked among them.

Although attempting to appear brave and determined, Claire and some other crimson-clad acolytes trembled in front of The Greyman. To them, much less educated than their comrades, this *being* was only referred to in the darkest of nightmares. To them, he was not supposed to exist at all. He was, until now, considered myth and a summation of all natural fears. *If you don't clean your teeth*, said Fuzzy once, when she was little girl, *The Greyman will come and pull them out when you sleep!* Now she was facing the proverbial bogeyman of legend and felt her resolve shuddering under the weight of her own fears.

Pantilius reached the front of the gathered emissaries and looked across the strand to his ancient enemy. The Greyman stood motionless, surveying the emissaries through empty skull sockets beneath a blackened and tattered hood.

"Was this really necessary, Nelfilem maggot?" Said The Greyman. "Do you really think mongrels and younglings can stand against me? You have led them to their deaths."

"You are as arrogant as expected, Halaam." Said Pantilius, standing in front of the assembled host.

"Do not!" The blast of The Greyman's retort made several emissaries cringe and cover their ears. "Call me that!"

"The truth is a cruel wind, Halaam." Said Pantilius. Raphael joined them now in human form and stood beside the tiny professor. His nephews, freed from their icy imprisonment, also joined the assembly.

"How many of these children are you prepared see die at your command, maggot? A dozen perhaps."

The Greyman moved a finger and an emissary was yanked from where he stood by some invisible force and thrown across the plain. He hit the western cliff face with a sickening crunch and fell to the ground.

The emissaries reacted in a variety of defensive forms and offensive attacks. Lightning bolts, fireballs, streaks of ice and screams of angered protest erupted from them. They struck The Greyman all at once but he emerged from the tumult laughing despite of it all.

"Petty parlor tricks and physical attempts!" He laughed as he stepped slowly through the chaos. "Is that all you have taught them, Pan?"

Brothers and sister! You are safeguards for humanity! Hold your ground! Pantilius mentally commanded.

The Greyman took a step towards the host and again his finger twitched. An acolyte in crimson robes screamed as he erupted into a pillar of blue flame. Emissaries nearby immediately doused him with summoned water and ice but the flames could not be extinguished.

"Our skills are ineffective, Pantilius!" Yelled Fuzzy. "He breaks through our protections like they don't exist! What can we do against such overwhelming force?"

Time. Time is all we need! Yelled Pantilius in the minds of every emissary.

The young man, who Claire knew from Mirthmyst Castle staggered about screaming in agony and reaching out to his elders for help. Harry ran forward and tried unsuccessfully to smother the flames with is bare hands but the young man fell and was still.

"Bastard of all bastards!" Screamed Harry as Buddy and Fuzzy shielded younger emissaries with their arms and backed away.

Raphael leaned down to the blackened and lifeless body of the acolyte. He was only forty-two years old but pleaded with his elders to join the assault. Raphael waved a hand and Claire thought he could hear 'Empyrean' in his words as he continued to whisper. The body vanished and only a few blackened spots remained on the snow where the young man had collapsed.

For the first time in her life, Claire saw heartbreaking anguish in Pantilius face.

"Halaam!" He shouted. "Murderer of children! How far you have fallen! How could you betray your makers with such crimes?" Pantilius breathed hard.

Hold your ground! Said Pantilius to the citizens. *Or this world is lost!*

Still The Greyman advanced and laughed. "I am a force of nature, maggot-master. It is you who have murdered that child. I do what must be done." Again he twitched a boney finger and an elder emissary began to choke as if an invisible hand of was crushing his windpipe.

Again the numerous emissaries responded with attacks and shields of force and other such defenses but to no avail. The emissary fell to the snow, his eyes wide and his lips blue.

Again The Greyman stepped forward through walls of flame and ice and rock erupting from the ground by emissaries trying to mitigate his advance. Yet again, they heard him laugh at their ineffective skills as he passed through them.

Pantilius! Perhaps we should - One of the emissaries pleaded mentally.

Hold your ground! Pantilius voice echoed in the minds everyone present. *You have sworn oaths as citizens of Abanis! Just a little longer!*

Several of the younger apprentices began to tremble in fear. Jack Frost, a young man and friend of Robin from Mirthmyst Castle, wept openly but held his ground and didn't run. Claire felt Himtall put his arm around her as she, in turn, held the hand of another apprentice who sobbed in terror.

"How many," said The Greyman, as stepped closer to the assembled host, "will you watch die, maggot-master?"

Raphael suddenly leapt forward. He changed into a dragon in mid-leap and faced the advancing Greyman.

"Enough, murderer!" He roared and attempted to snatch The Greyman in his giant talons.

The Greyman raised his scythe and there seemed to be a moment of two forces pushing against one another like two inverse magnets.

"Good boy! Good!" He laughed. "You have some strength in you!"

The Greyman took a step back in the snow for a second and some of the emissaries cheered as Raphael seemed to gain the upper hand. Pantilius ran forward and added his strength of force to Raphael's. In one movement, The Greyman spun and the dragon was hurled from the spot with incredible force. Raphael sailed several hundred yards into the mountain side like a winged meteor and lay still amidst the ensuing avalanches and devastation of his impact. Pantilius was blasted back and caught by Himtall who snatched him out of the air with a giant hand like a professional shortstop.

"Thank you brother." Pantilius breathed hard. "I might not have landed until I reached Britannia had you not stopped me. His strength is immense." He staggered forward and resumed his position at the front of the assembled host of Abanis. Many emissaries looked at him nervously.

The Greyman turned and resumed his advance towards the assembled emissaries. "And so, the punishment continues, Pantilius. How many more shall I erase?"

Again an invisible force yanked an emissary from the assembly and his body was smote upon rocks some distance away. Then another erupted into flames and yet another simply fell to his knees, unable to breath.

"No!" Screamed Claire. "Pantilius! We can't just stand here and do nothing!"

"Ahh, I suppose I'll leave the young ones alone. How can children be blamed for the misgivings of their elders?" The Greyman said, mocking concern as three more emissaries fell.

"Take me, you bastard!" Pantilius yelled finally, staggering forward. "I caused your imprisonment. I made the gates to Enefka! I tricked you time and time again. And still I live. Still the Great Party-Pooper is unable to finish Pan!" Pantilius sneered and stepped well in front of all the emissaries.

The Greyman stopped. The red lights in the skull sockets flared brighter than before. He pointed a skeletal finger at Pantilius. "You will watch for all eternity as I destroy everything that lives. Then I will go home and leave you here, with your thoughts." His voice was shrill and razor sharp in the ears of the emissaries.

"Pantilius! What are you doing?" Himtall bellowed.

Have faith, brothers and sisters. Pantilius voice echoed in the minds of everyone present. *No matter what you see. You will hold your ground.*

Pantilius froze. He smiled at The Greyman in that annoyingly trademark expression that made him appear to know everything before you did. His dark blue robes rustled in the cold wind blowing across the strand as dawn tinted the sky. His large, pointed ears sticking out from under an explosion of white hair, ceased to bob. His hair suddenly flattened and his pale, bluish skin took on an even paler grayish tone. His blue robes ceased to rustle and they too appeared to become grayish white.

"Pantilius! No!" Harry ran forward but slowed to a anxious tread beside the old professor as he realized what had occurred. He lowered his head and looked despondently at Buddy and Fuzzy as they hastened forward.

The Greyman laughed. It echoed hauntingly around the rest of the emissaries as they ran forward to see that Pantilius had been turned completely into stone.

Chapter 29: Out to Lunch

Aurelia emerged from the pool and gasped, fully expecting another series of mind-blowing images to assail her. That would pretty much describe the trip she just took. One second she was screaming at Pilate, the next, she was moving down a tube of light so fast that all things peripheral became linear blurs. Then she simply appeared at the bottom of a pool of turquoise lit water.

"Come!" Said Erik, grabbing her hand as she sputtered and gasped for air. He pulled her out of the icy pool and several Nelfilem covered her with thick, white blankets.

The pool of water was at the center of a huge dome, not unlike the bridge of the Enefka Babellux. The only differences being the dome itself was much larger, the ceiling appeared to have a map of the constellations and there was an oddly constructed chair on the edge of the pool.

"Thanks." She breathed and shivered as she gaped at the Chamber of Stars. "Wow, so beautiful." She looked down. "Thank you little ones but where did you find such soft fabric in -" She stopped and stared for a moment at two Nelfilem.

One was pointing both hands at another and spraying white lines of fabric out of the ends of his fingers like a overzealous spider on a high fiber diet. The strings formed neatly folded stacks of fabric as they landed in the arms of the second Nelfilem, who looked threatened to be buried under the load.

"Ok." Aurelia said as she stared. "I am officially *not ever* going to be surprised by anything for the rest of my life." She said, shaking her head at Erik in disbelief.

"Clever little munchkins aren't they." Said Longinus grinning beside her and shivering in the cold. He and Cassie were warming themselves under similar fabric.

"Where is he?" Barked Arkilius, who was wrapped in his own mound of blankets. To Aurelia, he appeared to be a disgruntled dollop of whipped-cream with a Nelfilem head. "Where's Oliveoil?"

Aurelia looked apologetically at the others and sank. "He's..." She started, then he looked at her husband. "He saved me, Erik. Pilates not coming."

"What? What happened?" Said Erik, turning to face her.

"He is the warden now." Arkilius nodded as if this was expected.

"Could you run that by those of us who are not versed in the unbelievable?" Longinus leaned down to Arkilius.

"We were correct." Arkilius grunted as he looked around. "We have little time so I'll make this short. All I can say is that Enlil hoped it would be the case. I was the last warden, albeit I was put into a comatose state by my predecessor so that he could leave. The safeguard in the design of the Enefka demands that there must be a warden or the gate closes. There was a reason we asked Pilate to be the last. I'm happy to see he didn't succumb to selfishness and let 'gorgeous' be stuck there. All will become clear in time. For now, we must get you some winter clothing. It's going to be a cold one today."

He turned and spoke to some of the lingering Nelfilem in a language Cassie thought sounded like chipmunks arguing. After a few moments, several other Nelfilem surrounded the companions and began taking arm and leg measurements.

The companions looked at each other guiltily. Although there was little love lost between Pilate and Longinus, the latter felt that being trapped for eternity all alone was a bit harsh. Cassie lowered her head on her husband's shoulder and held his hand as they tried to grasp the terrible extent of Pilate's incarceration.

"He could have come himself." Said Aurelia, looking at her husband. "He could have come and left me but he shoved me on to the pool. He wanted me to say 'sorry' to everyone."

Erik nodded solemnly but said nothing for a few moments. He gave her a sudden grin. "He called you gorgeous."

Aurelia flashed him a demure smile and batted her eyelashes dramatically as if to say 'but of course he did.'

"Arkilius, where are we?" Said Longinus, as a Nelfilem standing on the shoulders of another, was measuring his wrist to his shoulder and speaking to others nearby.

"We are in a fortress. One that has been buried under ice and rock for much longer than I honestly want to know. It's called Sin."

"Sin?" Longinus frowned.

"What is it babe?" Said Cassie snuggling closer to him.

Longinus shook his head as he tried to recall something. "I've heard that before. Sin, I mean."

"Yes, I thought you might have." Grunted Arkilius as some nearby Nelfilem began weaving thicker fabric of varying shapes. "Stationed in Jerusalem were you? Enlil filled me in on what occurred there."

"The Nazarene!" Said Longinus. "That's it, some of my men told me he wanted to be arrested because of 'Sin'. I wasn't there at the time though. They thought it was just religious gibberish."

"He wanted to be crucified, Arkilius?" Nick said testily. "I was there. He..." He paused as the others looked at him. "It was a horrible death until they came." He felt almost guilty for talking about it but something nagged at his mind.

"The one you call the Nazarene did something that even his father may not have the skill to do." Said Arkilius. "Or so I was recently told by Enlil. That is a matter to be seen, though."

Suddenly the nagging thought at the back of Nicholas mind jumped up and demanded to be noticed. Nicholas looked around the Chamber of Stars and the down to nearby Nelfilem who were weaving winter clothes with archaic skills.

"Where is Enlil?" He asked, looking at Arkilius and somehow nervous to hear the answer.

The others looked around in shock as they too realized their elder companion's absence. Then they turned to Arkilius.

He didn't say anything for a moment until his old, scarred face slowly turned into a roguish grin.

Jingle*Jingle***Jingle**

The Greyman stood a short distance from the remaining emissaries. Harry, Buddy and Fuzzy stood side by side with Rudolph, Raphael's other nephews and Himtall. The petrified statue of Pantilius, whose face was frozen into a knowing grin, was between them.

"Hold your ground!" Shouted Rudolph to the host in general. Then he turned to The Greyman and took a step forward. "We will not run from you, grandfather. Your crimes will be answered!"

"I have no intention of destroying anymore of my ilk." Said the Greyman, his gaze sweeping across the emissaries. He pointed the gleaming scythe at the icy ground. "Kneel before me and I will spare you. Resist," he suddenly pointed behind him, "and the human anomaly you call Nicholas will suffer for all eternity beside your beloved maggot-master there."

The emissaries froze and remained silent. Some were staring at Rudolph, who took command of the host after Pantilius and Raphael. Some of the acolytes were still sobbing in terror at what must certainly mean their inevitable death. Elder emissaries put arms around them and stood stoically beside their counterparts as The Greyman awaited a response.

All but one of the emissaries were staring at Rudolph or at each other. Claire, who had was looking beyond The Greyman in horrified fascination suddenly stepped forward. A grayish cloud of mist or smoke was racing across the plain towards The Greyman. It had no form but judging by its trajectory, she knew it wasn't natural.

The Greyman spotted her and turned to stare at the smoke. He waved a hand at it and the smoke dispersed slightly but soon reformed and continued its course. He raised his scythe as it approached.

"Nicholas no!" Rudolph roared suddenly.

The Greyman slashed at the smoke with his scythe but this had little effect. He took a step back as Nicholas appeared at a run and bore down on him with the iron spike in his left hand. His blond hair was streaked with red from a bleeding gash on the side of his head. His crimson robes and cloak were torn in various places but his movement was agile and not impaired. Nicholas was an imposing two meters tall and built like Himtall, wide and powerful. When he drove his iron spike into The Greyman's upper chest, it would have instantly killed a man. But The Greyman was far from being made of flesh and further still from normal.

The assembled emissaries erupted into shouts and warnings to Nicholas as Himtall, Claire and other elders ran forward.

"Nicholas no!" Screamed Harry, Buddy and Fuzzy in unison.

"Nanos protect them!" Nicholas shouted. A glimmering dome suddenly erupted around The Greyman and Nicholas as the host of Abanis ran forward and screamed in protest. They were stopped by the nanos-shield and Rudolph pounded great fists upon it in frustration.

A skeletal hand darted forward and grabbed Nicholas by the throat and pulled him close.

"So, you are as foolish and as stupid as your primate brethren. Pity." Said The Greyman as he drew Nicholas closer.

The skull sockets flared bright red as Nicholas struggled to breath against the vice-like grip. He tried to resume a form of smoke but felt weakened by the previous transformation. Besides, his mind was being invaded by some presence and he couldn't concentrate. He looked into the skull and imagined The Greyman would be licking his lips in anticipation, if as he had any.

"Nicholas! Get out of there!" Shouted Harry as he pushed ineffectively at the glimmering shield of Nanos.

"Despite what you may think," Said The Greyman, pulling the spike out of his chest and looking at it, "this is not some miracle weapon that can harm me. But I have to admire your bold attempt. It is a key, nothing more. And thank you for giving it to me."

He raised the scythe. "And now for the main course! This blade will sever you from your body and leave the shell intact. I'm afraid it might also hurt a bit." The Greyman whispered.

Nicholas tried to speak despite being choked to death. He grabbed the bony wrist with two hands and could only utter "He-heh."

"What is this? You wish to say something monkey?"

As Nicholas struggled under The Greyman's grip, Himtall broke his attention away and blinked through the shield. He took a few giant strides around the glimmering dome and pointed to the gates of Sin.

"Who in Hades are they?" He pointed and looked back at Rudolph.

Rudolph stared at several hundred beings running towards them. They appeared to be Nelfilem, led by two men and two women in thick white robes.

"I don't know." Said Rudolph, sniffing the air. "But some of them are human"."

A voice suddenly entered the minds of every emissary on the strand. *Away, brothers and sisters! Stand back now! Have faith! Stand back!*

The screams of protest stopped and the emissaries looked around as Arkilius ran forward.

"Arkilius! How?" Rudolph shouted in disbelief as he watched the old Nelfilem approach. "Do as he says! Back, back ! Away from this struggle!" He shouted. The emissaries obeyed. All except one.

"Nicholas!" Claire cried as she struggled against Himtall who was pulling her away. "Nicholas!" She screamed. "Nicholas no!" Himtall managed to pull her some distance away from the struggle within nanos' shield.

Back, brothers and sisters. Said the gruff voice in the minds of all the emissaries. *Stand back and watch as your faith is rewarded!*

The Greyman, not noticing the newcomers, focused on Nicholas face as it began to turn purple. "What would a monkey say to me? Huh? Would you like a banana before you are devoured, monkey?" He hissed and the grip lessened. "Speak monkey, if you can. Hoot me a song perhaps?"

Yes, my son. Said a soft voice in Nicholas mind. *Have faith in your assumptions.*

Nicholas was terrified and could see the ring of emissaries now departing the strand or standing back at some distance. He coughed and sputtered as he grasped the skeletal wrist. Summoning all his concentration, thinking of Blue the whale, and Gabriel holding an injured reindeer, and his love for Claire, Harry, Buddy, Fuzzy, Mrs. Bakersbee and Pantilius, and his sheltered, happy life in Abanis at Mirthmyst Castle, he said one word.

"Heal."

The Greyman froze. The red lights in the sockets dilated. Then he laughed.

It was a shrill, lengthy explosion of laughter that reached all ears on the strand. The emissaries froze and stared at The Greyman in confusion. Arkilius stood beside Cassie, Longinus, Aurelia and Nick as they looked on.

A seed of unnamable terror grew in Aurelia's stomach but she couldn't identify why it was happening. She watched the blond haired man struggle with what appeared to be a walking skeleton in black robes carrying a farm implement. Despite a growing dread she couldn't indentify, Aurelia wasn't the least bit surprised at the impossibility of it all.

The laughter suddenly stopped.

"No." Sobbed Claire, not wishing to look as Himtall held her close.

The grip on Nicholas throat lessened somewhat. The skeletal hand released and The Greyman looked at it questioningly. Red, sinewy flesh began to grow along the fingers, then the wrist spawned tendons and cartilage.

"What?!? What is this?" The Greyman grabbed the mutating hand with his other and noticed it too was developing fleshy stings and tendons.

"No! No! He is mine." He grabbed Nicholas by the throat with two hands.

Nicholas closed his eyes and experience a sensation that could only be described as a battering ram slamming at the doors of his mind. *Let me in or I will rip your consciousness apart! Let me in, primate! Open this -*

You will not infect this host. Said another authoritative voice in Nicholas mind. It sounded a lot like The Greyman's own. *This one is immune.*

No! You! How did you escape? He is mine! Mine!

Harry began to take a few steps forward as The Greyman dropped the scythe and struggled with Nicholas.

Hold positions! Shouted Arkilius. *Wait!*

Nicholas opened his eyes. The skeletal hands and arms he expected to see were now covered with muscle tissue and tanned skin. The skull beneath the black hood had changed into flesh. He looked into the face of a handsome, middle aged man who cringed and spat at him.

"No!" The man screamed. "He is mine! He is - " The man's eyes suddenly rolled up into his head which snapped back. His mouth opened and a wail pierced the air around the strand with the sonic strength of ten thousand people screaming at once. On and on it wailed causing several emissaries collapse while others sobbed and fell to a fetal position on the icy plain. Longinus, Cassie, Aurelia and Nick cringed at the sound and held each other in terror, fully expecting some new insanity to emerge from the struggle. Then the wail died away and vanished into some unfathomable distance.

The spot where Nicholas and The Greyman stood went white for a brief instant then the glimmering shield of Nanos exploded. The entire strand was flattened by a concussive blast so powerful it caused major avalanches on the mountain side which buried the gates to Sin. Every person who was still standing on the strand was blasted of their feet and blown back several meters. The explosion echoed around the area for some time then everything and everyone was still. Only the statue of Pantilius remained standing on the strand.

A short while later, the onlookers stirred and rose to their feet. Some of the emissaries cheered, feeling that The Greyman was somehow overcome.

"He falls!" Yelled Maurice. "The Greyman has fallen!"

Others joined the cheering. "He is fallen! We have prevailed!"

Some emissaries had no interest in cheering. As others raised their staves and cheered, some of the emissaries immediately began to tend to the injured while they had the chance. Some were moving about the strand and checking to see how many of the fallen emissaries were still alive and required aid.

Claire was knocked unconscious by the blast but revived by Himtall who shook her gently. She opened her eyes to see Himtall's giant, rosy cheeked face and white beard. Although somewhat disorientated, she rose at a run.

"Nicholas!" She screamed, half staggering, half running towards the spot where Nicholas and The Greyman had stood. She was followed by others who were yelling at her to stop.

Claire reached the spot and stared down in disbelief at what she saw. She was soon joined by others until eventually the entire host, along with Arkilius and his companions, surrounded ground-zero of Nicholas and The Greyman.

Lying on the snow were two unconscious men, a third creature whose species Claire didn't recognize, and a huge Roman spear. One of the men was Nicholas. The other was a middle-aged man with tanned skin, curly, black hair and, quite strangely, wearing the robes of a Roman politician.

The other was unlike any creature Claire had seen before. It was vaguely humanoid but had elongated limbs and very long, white hair. She thought it must be over three meters tall but at the moment it was wrapped up in some sort of fetal position. Although its eyes were closed, Claire guessed they would be three or four times larger than they proportionately should be. But all this was not nearly as odd as the creatures skin. It wasn't exactly grey but more like dull silver.

The spear gleamed in the light of dawn as Claire kicked it away and knelt beside Nicholas. She held his head in her lap and stroked his blood stained, blond hair back. "He...he's not breathing. Help please." She cried and looked up at the others in desperation.

Buddy stepped forward and examined Nicholas for a few moments. He looked up at Fuzzy and Harry, who looked on despairingly, and shook his head.

"Very few of us manifest the ability to heal, Claire. Aryu is one." He said softly, putting his hand on her wrist. "But no one has the skill to bring back those who have passed on."

Claire lowered her head and put a hand on Nicholas' face. The emissaries stood in shock around the scene as they tried to understand what had just occurred. With the exception of a few swallows chirping as they went about their business in the light of a new dawn, everyone was silent.

Chapter 30: Frosted Galactic Bunches of Oats

Nicholas concentrated on blocking his mind against The Greyman. It wasn't quite like, say, blocking a door against a persistent rhinoceros, although it certainly *felt* like it. It was more like trying *not* to think of something that really, really wanted to be *thought of.* Which is really, really hard. Especially on the rhinoceros.

Just when the mental pressure was too great to endure, Nicholas heard his immediate universe filled with a horrifying scream. Then it exploded.

Sometime later, Nicholas opened his eyes. He blinked at several billion galaxies and realized that he was lying on his back, looking up into a clear, night sky. He lifted his head and wondered briefly if he consumed an unhealthy amount of mead sometime prior to lying on his back. His head apparently decided this was the case because now it was throbbing in unison to his heartbeat. Having a heartbeat was all well and good but Nicholas wished it wasn't announced every second or so like a painfully loud Chinese gong.

"Yes. You took a mental beating back there, young human. The pain will go away momentarily." Said voice nearby. It sounded so old and raspy that Nicholas wondered if the owner didn't have a pulse of its own.

He sat up looked and around. He had apparently been lying on a moonlit beach and it looked oddly familiar. Standing some distance away, leaning on a staff of white, birch wood, was a tall figure in black robes. It was facing an ocean and watching waves as they broke softly upon the sandy shore.

Nicholas felt his heart skip and his head throb painfully as he jumped to his feet. He staggered backwards in the sand from the black, cowled figure.

"It can't be!" He shouted. "I felt you leave. I heard you scream and depart my mind!"

"Calm yourself, Nicholas. I am not The Greyman, as you call him." The figure turned to face him.

Much like the beings Nicholas saw in the vision from the Hag Nosis, this creature was not human. Not...exactly. It would have been three meters tall at some point in its life but now leaned so heavily on the white staff that Nicholas could look at it eye to eye. The creature looked like a lanky, old man with eyes far larger than they should be. A wrinkled face looked at him from under a curtain of white hair that almost reached the ground and made more wrinkles as it smiled. To Nicholas, the whole image, black cloak and all, looked vaguely familiar.

"Come here, young man. Let me have a look at you."

Nicholas legs, not caring what Nicholas' brain was thinking, propelled him forward until he was face to face with a Huru. Albeit a really, really old one.

"You are quite the unexpected anomaly, young man. And you have my thanks."

Nicholas hesitated as he looked into the huge, opaque eyes and ancient face as it examined him. "Uhh. You're welcome?"

"Yes. Good response. I'm hoping we have time for a conversation. That means you will have to participate. Otherwise, I'm just an old man muttering to himself on a beach." He cackled. Nicholas was surprised the ancient creature had the strength to stand, let alone laugh heartily.

"Where am I?" Nicholas blurted, looking up and down the starlit surf. "And who are you? Am I dead?"

"Wow! Coming out, guns blazing I see." Said the old creature, appearing to give up by lifting huge hands in mock supplication. "Well let's see. First things first. I am called The Pilgrim by those who know us both. And it is a pleasure to finally meet you." He nodded to Nicholas, whose mouth decided it was the perfect time to gape open.

"You're... The Pilgrim! You made Abanis and ... and gathered the Hurum. You fought The Greyman! You - " He paused to breath and considered something. Now he knew why the creature looked familiar. He had seen a younger version of him in the vision offered by Nosis. He fought The Greyman at the gate which ended in the destruction of Adamis.

"I am honored to meet you, sir." Nicholas said finally, bowing slightly and blushing under his blond beard.

"Yes. Yes. I am 'the one and only'. But you fought The Greyman too. Let's not forget that small mountain of bravery."

"Yes. I did. Foolishly, I think. But how did we get to be wherever here is?"

"We are here because I made a foolish gambit too." The Pilgrim paused, "I was.. *personifying* a young man when The Greyman accosted me. He didn't realize it was me though. It was all part of a plan that was hatched some years ago in

Jerusalem. From that point on, I was secretly attached to him but only in a small way. It's difficult to explain but that's why I haven't been around in Abanis for some years."

Nicholas sighed, not having the slightest clue to what context 'personify' meant.

"And yet," continued The Pilgrim, after considering something, "foolishness can yield positive results if the reason for foolishness is fueled by a good intentions. Don't believe all that nonsense about the 'road to hell being paved with gold bricks'. So many people forget that good intentions are, for the most part, good." The Pilgrim grinned.

Nicholas nodded but said nothing. He was still soaking in the fact that he was standing on a strange beach talking to The Pilgrim.

"To answer your third question, no. I think we are both ok and not quite dead."

"But where are we?" Said Nicholas, looking around and feeling the beach looked familiar.

"Look at the mountain behind us." Said The Pilgrim. He put a wrinkled hand on Nicholas' shoulder and pressured him to turn.

Nicholas looked at the mountain and realized they were on the strand in front of the gates of Sin. But there was no snow, ice, gates to Sin and quite noticeably, no other emissaries. In fact, the area had healthy, green trees growing near the mountain and the beach was almost a tropical setting.

"But. Where is everyone?" He turned around on the spot, recognizing the iceless geography.

"We are where we were, only not in the right time I think." Said The Pilgrim, nodding to himself. "It's been known to happen."

Nicholas stared at the legendary patron of his people. So many questions had piled up in his mind since he left Abanis and he desperately wanted at least *some* answers.

"Yes." Said The Pilgrim, guessing what Nicholas was thinking. "I bet you have. Walk with me."

The Pilgrim's huge hand remained on Nicholas shoulder as they walked towards the water. To Nicholas' mild astonishment they did not step into the water. They walked onto the water. As they walked far out on the ocean, Nicholas wasn't surprised at all anymore. He half expected this.

After a while, The Pilgrim looked at Nicholas expectantly.

"I don't even know where to begin or what to ask, sir." Nicholas sighed, looking up into the multitude of stars.

"Well, let's get a better view then." The Pilgrim nodded happily.

He raised his staff and moved it about. Some of the stars Nicholas had been admiring suddenly fell from the night sky like a light snowfall. One by one they fell into the ocean and flashed as they hit the surface. Some of the falling stars landed on what appeared to be an invisible stairway in front of them. After a few moments, Nicholas was staring at a glittering staircase that reached far up into the heavens.

"Come with me." The Pilgrim beckoned as he began to climb.

Together, they walked up the twinkling, shallow steps. Nicholas chanced a look down and was not even the least bit surprised to see that the earth was getting significantly smaller with every step. He felt a touch of pride in this. Getting used to the ridiculous and the amazing was getting easier.

After a while, The Pilgrim stopped and turned. "Behold. The most beautiful jewel in the known cosmos. Well, according to my opinion. And that has considerable weight, I think."

Nicholas turned and smiled in genuine astonishment. Although they only walked about twenty or thirty steps up the stairs, he could see the entirety of planet earth in all of its splendor. Swirling cloud patterns drifted across the continents ever so slightly as the globe spun slowly on an axis. To the left of the globe were the western continents Pantilius liked to call 'Mayawhatabigland' or 'Incalotatrees'. Across the ocean was Afrikaans, The Roman Empire, Britannia, Scandinavia, and further on, the massive Asian continent.

"I've seen maps of the world in remarkable detail." Said Nicholas quietly. "But this is breathtaking."

"Yes. I never get sick of seeing it." The Pilgrim nodded. Then he whispered something, almost to himself:

"*From the stars we came, from the earth we began.*
Through oceans of rivers and rivers of sand.
As dusk looks back to admire the dawn,
E'er shall we, as time flows on."

He turned to Nicholas and smiled. "From Raphael, my dear and artistic nephew. Something he wrote long ago."

"What does it mean?"

"Sit down, young man, and I will tell you. I think we have time for a tale. I am going to divulge some truth to you that many even in Abanis may not have figured out yet."

Nicholas obeyed. They sat beside each other and looked down at the blue planet that spun slowly beneath them.

"Once upon a time, humans evolved from primate animals because they were clever. They were so clever, in fact, that they were able to make languages and tools to show and tell each other how clever they actually were. Sometimes they would do terrible things to each other in terribly clever ways just to make that point. More and more they spread across this beautiful planet making clever things and saying clever things for their clever lives until finally they knew everything there was to know about everything on the planet. Well, almost everything. You see," The Pilgrim pointed to a small object leaving the earth and coming straight towards them, "as clever as they were, they were not clever enough to feel less lonely."

The small, sparkling object Nicholas stared at was getting larger and larger at an incredible rate. Suddenly, a huge white tube propelled by fire roared past the staircase and Nicholas turned to see it fade away into the cosmos.

"What was that?!"

"Well, as I was saying," The Pilgrim continued to stare at Earth, "they were lonely and wanted to share their cleverness with others. They knew that this planet was one among many worlds in creation that could sustain life so they began searching far and wide for other clever beings like themselves. They used clever devices to see far past this planet and then built cleverly designed ships to take them far from home to meet others." The Pilgrim turned to look back at the stars and the big, white tube now just a faint sparkle of light. Nicholas turned around too.

"As I'm sure you know, the universe is big. Really, really big. In fact *big*, I'm sorry to say, is rather *small* when trying to describe it. It is unimaginably huge and in it, are a lot of stars like our own sun. And spinning around those stars are a lot of planets. Far and deep, the clever primates searched for other clever beings like themselves in the vastness of the cosmos but they're search yielded negative results. Some clever people argued with other clever people that perhaps the human race was truly alone in the cosmos. No matter where they went, no matter how far or for how long they searched, they could not find anyone as clever as themselves. This was deeply distressing to humans but they didn't give up searching. After many thousands of years, they became so clever that they didn't even need big, white tubes to go anywhere. The clever people found ways to simply walk along the light of the stars, much like the way we are sitting on this staircase. This allowed them to search farther and for longer periods of time." The Pilgrim grinned and tapped some of the stars on the steps with his grayish hand.

"Then something marvelous happened!" He said suddenly and Nicholas nearly jumped. "They were so clever that they didn't just travel to the end of the universe. They went beyond it!"

Nicholas frowned. "Uhh, what is beyond the universe? I don't really know what all this means, or what the universe *is* but I'm trying to understand."

"They didn't just go from point 'A'", The Pilgrim pointed to a random star which flashed in recognition, "to point 'B'." He continued, pointing to another flashing star. "They went from point 'A' to another point 'A' entirely."

Nicholas blinked at The Pilgrim.

"And do you know what they found?"

Again, Nicholas blinked and contrived to look as if he knew what The Pilgrim was talking about. He shook his head. "What did they find?"

"Life!" The Pilgrim pointed to the planet earth. "They found others just like themselves!" He beamed at Nicholas.

"You mean," Nicholas tried to make sense of the story thus far, "humans found more humans on a planet just like they're own?"

"No, not humans but similar, yes." The Pilgrim nodded appreciatively. "I know this is hard to understand but I'll be making a bigger point really soon." He sighed and looked at earth for a moment as if to recall something. "I was told they rejoiced at the discovery. All the clever people felt less lonely. One by one they went beyond the veil of this universe to that other place to meet with the others until no one remained on Earth. It was considered the most glorious time in human history - to make contact with *other* clever beings after searching for so long. But sadly, it came with a terrible price." The Pilgrim paused for dramatic effect in the same way Pantilius did whenever telling a story. Nicholas suddenly realized where the latter may have adopted this technique.

"When they returned to earth, the clever humans realized they were cursed in some way by traveling to the 'beyond'.

They were not able to survive. Many of them faded from existence or simply fell into a sleep from which they could not be stirred. The most clever of the humans realized that the only way the human race was going to survive was to return to the place they visited and remain there. Understandably, this caused terrible grief among the clever humans because they were being forced to either abandon this beautiful world or perish entirely. And so, after much clever planning and extremely clever design, they made children."

"Replacements." Said Nicholas, suddenly. He was trying to make sense of all that he was hearing and that word popped up in his mind for no apparent reason.

"You're instincts are correct, Nicholas." The Pilgrim nodded. "And what do clever caretakers do if they cannot survive themselves?"

Nicholas considered this. Caretaker was a word he usually ascribed to people, for example, like Pantilius or Harry, Buddy, Fuzzy, Gabriel, or Himtall. They were like parents to him. Parents want they're...

"Children!" Nicholas exclaimed. "Raphael said something odd to me. He said 'we are not men, we are the children of men'."

The Pilgrim nodded. "Raphael is correct. And what does Huru mean?"

"Huru." Said Nicholas, frowning in recollection. "Sumerian I think. It means..." He paused as something occurred to him. "The Huru are the children of humanity!"

"Indeed, Nicholas. You are getting the hang of this. The clever humans didn't *have* children, though. They *made* children. Why would people *make* children instead of *having* children?"

"Because…they didn't want the children to be the same. Because they were dying?"

The Pilgrim nodded. "Yes. They were dying. And what do progenitors do to their creations in light of dying?"

Nicholas searched his memories and summoned lessons about zoology, biology, physics, astronomy, history, sociology, philosophy, ethics…then it came to him.

"They make them better. Humans made their children better than themselves in order to survive. That is what happens naturally but you are saying they did it artificially?"

"Indeed. They did. The Huru were created to survive cleverer beings than ourselves. We were made in their image and given the ability to control matter and energy in a variety of different ways. We do not age, or get sick or die unless by extreme violence. We were intended to be a master race and caretakers of the Earth until the return of humans."

"So, you are one of the last of the Huru. The Greyman was too?"

"Yes. Until Gabriel's untimely passing, only four of us remained. One of us was imprisoned. I'm sure you can guess to whom I refer."

"The Greyman." Nicholas nodded. "Why was he called 'The Greyman'? Oh! And I learned that humans evolved from primates up to present day. Were there humans before us? I know the earth is older than people think but - " Nicholas stopped suddenly. He realized the filing cabinet in his mind just exploded and showered The Pilgrim with bits of unanswered questions.

"In time, my clever human." The Pilgrim raised his hand. "When the Huru were created, we enjoyed a brief period of companionship with our makers until they departed. They left three of us in charge of the rest. Two brothers and one female. Take a wild guess who they were?"

Nicholas thought about the vision Nosis gave him and did some quick calculation. "You, The Greyman and the Hag Nosis."

"Exactly. Very good, young man. But as the centuries passed, our people became restless. As our makers before us, we became lonely. Many of us felt like abandoned children and they were partially correct. It did not please our makers to leave us, however. In fact, I know it upset them greatly for they loved us dearly. Anyways, many of the Huru forgot that we were made to survive. We forgot that we were caretakers of this abandoned world. Driven by passionate convictions, The Greyman and his followers built a 'gate' to try and find our human makers and join them. Some of us, including myself, opposed this motivation. We were made to care for the earth until our makers found a way to return. Not to abandon our charge. But The Greyman didn't listen. He was the most powerful of us all, the most intelligent, the most creative and the most charismatic. Against my better judgment, I gave in to my brothers plea, for there was a time that I loved him dearly and would have followed him anywhere. Together, I and the assembled Huru passed through a 'gate' that he constructed." The Pilgrim paused and looked at Nicholas with sadness in his large eyes.

"Where did the gate lead to?" Nicholas said, completely engrossed.

"It lead here."

"Here?"

"Although we were designed to survive, we are not as clever as our human makers. The Greyman's gate design was flawed. It lead us here, only it was not what we expected. We arrived around twenty-five thousand years in earth's past and have been trapped here ever since."

"You..." Nicholas paused and gaped at The Pilgrim for a moment. The latter let it sink in and waited patiently for Nicholas to catch up.

"Yes, my clever human. I was born nine thousand years *from now*. You are an ancestor to the humans who created me."

"Time was broken in some way? Is that even possible?" Nicholas looked at The Pilgrim with horrified fascination. Until recently, he thought that lighting a pipe with a flame on the end of one's thumb was real amazing. This, however, was beyond his scope.

"According the cleverest of the Huru, it was considered impossible to go back in time. There are too many paradoxes involved. My brother vehemently defended the gate construction project and laughed at the notion."

"Para-what?"

"In other words, we screwed up so bad that we broke the laws of the universe itself. Or so we assume." The Pilgrim snorted. "We were so arrogant, Nicholas. So proud. And so foolish to even try."

"So that's what The Greyman means by 'going home'." Said Nicholas quietly as they watched the Asian continents spin lazily under the curtain of evening.

"Yes, my boy. And the rest, as they say, is history. Since we were trapped in the past, we made a pact to never interfere with humanity unless it seemed appropriate but that has been a messy business to control. We split into factions and argued over our purpose. The Greyman became increasingly disgusted with humanity as he watched civilizations kill each other in wars over greed, self righteous pursuits or such nonsense. He couldn't believe that they would evolve to become our progenitors. Eventually, he grew to hate humanity and wished to rule over them while others wished to remain absent from human history altogether. Hurum, for example, are the offspring of Huru and humans so who knows what damage we may have caused to future events. All I can say is that we, in Abanis must remain vigilant emissaries, ever watchful of human progress and ever absent from its unfolding."

"Wow." Nicholas shook his head as he tried to make sense of it all. Then something occurred to him.

"But what of Pantilius? Who are the Nelfilem?"

"As our makers before us, we also wished to make 'children of our own'. The Greyman was in charge of their creation, as was Nosis and I. They were designed to have an extraordinary understanding of physics so that they could assist us constructing gates. Some, however, regarded the

Nelfilem as a failed experiment because many of them didn't wish to be enslaved to one task. As for me, I think the creation of the Nelfilem was our greatest triumph."

"So do I." Said Nicholas, grinning. "Pantilius is a great teacher."

"I believe it, for he was and still is my greatest student." Said The Pilgrim, nodding happily.

"What of The Greyman? Has he been destroyed? And why is he called 'Greyman'?"

The Pilgrim considered the questions for a few moments and shook his head. "He has become a kind of virus, Nicholas, and no longer a Huru. He is malice and hate wrapped in bad news. A tragic loss, for he was the greatest and the most gifted of us all. Although his body is old and feeble like mine, it is still trapped in a remarkably clever prison. Now, however, he has learned to survive without a 'host' but not for lengthy periods, I think. That is why he wanted you. He is gone for now but I suspect he can still be a considerable threat sometime in the future. If my plan worked accordingly, he is back in his prison and more than likely quite vexed for being there. As for his name," The Pilgrim sighed, "maybe you should ask Pantilius that question, for he coined the term and best tells its meaning."

"I see." Nicholas remained silent for a short time as he considered the meaning of 'threat sometime in the future', then pressed on.

"So healing him was the right course of action then?" He felt a sudden and strong draft of air as he asked the question. He also heard peculiar 'whooping' sounds but couldn't identify the source.

"Incredibly insightful, young man. Force against him will always end in failure." The Pilgrim nodded appreciatively. "I'm sure one of the others might have guessed it sooner or later but I'm afraid they would have perished to The Greyman's wrath before taking action. Sometimes the simplest answer is also the most elegant one. And that," he slapped a huge hand on Nicholas' shoulder, "brings me to you."

"I'm human. That's what you mean, right?"

"Yes." The Pilgrim stared into Nicholas' icy blue eyes and considered something for few moments. "You truly are manifesting traits of the Hurum. Like them, you can control certain aspects of matter and energy, not to mention the fact you look pretty damn good for a fifty-two year old. That is what the Hurum carry from their Huru heritage. For some reason, that gift has completely ignored the fact you shouldn't have it at all. My guess is we just see what happens. All I can say, is that you acted as any emissary from Abanis would have and then some. A job well done, with flying colors, I might add."

"Thank you, sir." Nicholas blushed. He didn't have a clue what 'flying colors' meant but decided to take it as a compliment.

"It's 'brother', Nicholas. No need to call me 'sir', although the sentiment is appreciated. I may be quite older than you but considering you are human and, as such, one of the makers, call me Brother Enlil."

"Enlil." Nicholas smiled. "Thank you Enlil."

"I sense our time is running short, young human. Is there anything else you wish to know?"

"Are we going somewhere?"

"We are going back soon. I suspect our brothers and sisters will be working on it."

Nicholas mind raced. There were other questions but one was jumping up and down and stomping around his head.

"Pilgrim, I mean uhh... Enlil. What is Empyrean? I mean, *where* is Empyrean?"

"That's an easy one Nick! Haven't you figured that out by now?" Said a rough, but not unkind voice from behind them. "For you are *in* it."

Nicholas turned to see a great, red dragon flapping massive leathery wings beside them.

"Gabriel!" Exclaimed Nicholas, jumping up and smiling.

Chapter 31: Hot Cocoa

"Saja." Said Himtall, staring down at the figures in the snow. "Do you know where the younglings are?"

Saja looked up at the giant Viking and nodded. "They are in Shambhala, near Aryu Veda's ancestral home. He and Mrs. Bakersbee are caring for them. Why?"

"We need Aryu. Quickly. You are the fastest among us so can you - " Himtall stopped and blinked at the spot where Saja had been standing. Out of the corner of his eye he saw a blurred streak of black hair and a glint of steel race towards the shore. There was the faintest impression of a splash and the swordsman was gone. "-bring him here?" Himtall finished lamely.

Aurelia looked down at one of the men and gasped. She yanked off Longinus' newly woven cloak and covered him with it.

"Erik, it's Pilate!" She exclaimed as her husband and some others stepped forward.

Buddy kneeled down to Pontius Pilate and placed a hand on the man's forehead. "Giant pudding cakes! Harry, he lives!"

Harry, who was staring at Arkilius, the Nelfilem and the recently arrived humans with some considerable confusion, broke from his reverie and kneeled beside Buddy. "He is human? Well, he is in good hands, my dear." He nodded to Aurelia.

Harry placed his hands in the air above Pilate. After a few moments of concentration, the ground around the bodies was warm and grass began to grow.

"There. Warmth will bring him around." He said gruffly, looking at Claire with deep concern.

Fuzzy was sitting beside Claire. She sobbed quietly and tried to wipe the blood off Nicholas face.

Longinus, Cassie and Erik looked down in disbelief as Harry finished making the ground warm and cause vegetation to flourish.

"We are among the gods." Longinus whispered to Erik, shaking his head in disbelief.

"Who are you?" Claire whispered, looking up at Aurelia.

Aurelia, recognizing the fact that she wouldn't possibly be able answer that question with ease anymore, simply said. "We were lost and found. Is your friend hurt? Can I help?"

Claire eyes welled up again and she looked down. Her long, chestnut brown hair fell over her face. "No." She said softly.

Cassie, whose gaze fried Erik and Longinus into embarrassed silence, sighed and draped her own cloak around Claire's shoulders. "It's cold out her, love." She said quietly and sat beside the young woman. She guessed the blond haired man was a loved one and felt sorry for the young woman.

A few minutes later, Himtall spotted Aryu Veda running up the shore towards the group with Saja Goryo jogging lazily beside him. His white robes rippled in the morning wind and his sandals flapped on the snow. Slowing to look at the statue of Pantilius with horrified shock for a moment, he tore himself away and rushed into the crowd.

"Over here, doc. I don't know what you can do but, uhh...." Himtall trailed off as Claire looked up at him.

"Out of my way brothers and sisters." Aryu elbowed his way in and was briefly shocked when he looked at the strange creature beside the two men. He looked at Pilate and nodded. "That one is simply sleeping. He is fine. Stand back, dear." He said as he turned to kneel beside Nicholas and examined his unresponsive eyes.

Claire put Nicholas' head gently down on the freshly sprouted grass and looked up at Aryu with a mixture of panic and hope. "He's not dead?"

"Yes and no. He is in a state of twilight. And he is human. That is why you did not recognize it." Aryu placed a hand on Nicholas' forehead and closed his eyes. After a few moments he began to mutter to himself.

"Human?" Claire said incredulously. She looked around at some of the gathered elders.

Maurice was whispering to others and nodding his head. "All makes sense why The Greyman wanted him. A human that can be infected by him would be able to infiltrate civilization on a more permanent level. He would not deteriorate due to their extraordinary immune system and could father hybrid offspring. Some of us could sense it, child. Although, we did not understand it fully." He said quietly.

Aryu opened his eyes and winced. "He is so far into twilight. I cannot reach him." He looked over Aurelia's shoulder to the creature behind them. "But *he* can."

Aryu jumped to his feet, ran over to the large, silvery skinned humanoid and knelt down. "Master. Awaken. Please help us."

"What is this, Aryu? He is dead! The Greyman has been vanquished and you try to bring him back?" Maurice bellowed, stepping forward.

"He is not The Greyman!" Said a deep voice in the crowd. Raphael limped forward and nearly fell but was caught by Rudolph and two of his brothers. He was bleeding from several wounds along one side of his body but looked well enough to shout. "Aryu, awaken him now or the boy is lost to Empyrean. Do it now!"

"Master," Said Aryu once more placing his hands on the creatures head and closing his eyes. "Please help us. Please awaken."

The wind suddenly rose and a voice erupted around the assembled emissaries. It was soft but deep, like an echo from a vast distance.

And why must I waken, old friend? Said the voice.

"As you once told me, so long ago, master...because you have much more work to do."

Some of the emissaries screamed in shock and others fell back on each other as the creature twitched and came alive. It sprang upward rigidly as if driven to a standing position by an invisible hand. Coils of black fabric sprung from non-existence and wrapped around the creature until it's entire body looked like an Egyptian mummy going through a 'Goth' phase. A staff of white birch wood burst up from the ground and showered some astonished emissaries with dirt as the creature snatched it up. Long black hair spouted from its silvery head as the alien, equine face grimaced like a newborn child. Black robes materialized around the creature's body and within moments the huge, opaque eyes opened and looked around. The eyes locked on Aryu Veda from beneath a black hood. It's thin lips curled into grin.

After several moments of shock, Maurice fell to his knees and bowed his head. Many emissaries followed in suit while others began to cheer and slapped each other on the back. Several apprentices, including Claire, looked around in confusion.

"The Pilgrim!" Some whispered to each other, kneeling in adoration.

"Rise." Said the creature with a voice that sounded like trees groaning. "I am not your master but the gesture is appreciated." It looked down at Claire who was gaping at the tall humanoid and struggling with the feeling she knew who it was.

"Hello, my dear. I am The Pilgrim."

"Enlil. The boy! He is in twilight." Said Raphael, gesturing to Nicholas. "Oh, and welcome back, Uncle." He bowed.

"Ahh yes." At three meters tall, The Pilgrim looked like a tree leaning down to inspect an injured deer when he knelt beside Claire. "Hold out your hand, dear."

Erik, Longinus and the others looked at each other in shock. *Enlil* they mouthed silently. Apparently, Enlil was not exactly human. They looked at The Pilgrim and again at each other as Longinus snorted.

"Clever old bloke." He said, shaking his head. "Why does he look so ..odd?"

"He camouflaged himself on the ship so that you wouldn't be afraid, Long shanks. He's not exactly human." Whispered Arkilius gruffly. "Now watch this."

Claire held out her hand as instructed. The Pilgrim extended a huge finger and tapped the center of her palm. A little white rock appeared, making a sound like a *pop* when it materialized. It crackled and grew into a cylindrical shape that was soon filled with a steaming, brown liquid.

"Take two sips and call me in the morning." He nodded sagely to Claire.

Claire looked down at the steaming mug. "Hot chocolate?"

"Yes." Said The Pilgrim with wide eyed encouragement. "Fantastic stuff. Better with marshmallows, of course, but I understand Mrs. Bakersbee is rather busy at the moment. Give him a sip, dear. Go ahead."

Claire lifted Nicholas' head and poured some of the cocoa into his mouth. Nothing happened.

"One more, dear. Go on." The Pilgrim goaded.

Again Claire did as instructed, only this time, when the hot chocolate was poured, Nicholas lips moved. He coughed suddenly and opened his eyes. After looking around in confusion, he looked up at Claire and smiled.

For a brief moment, Claire was speechless. She looked into Nicholas' icy blue eyes and, without any warning, grabbed his ears and kissed him. The emissaries watched and decided it was a good time to erupt into cheering.

"Well done, old boy." Raphael nodded to The Pilgrim. "And the hot chocolate was a nice touch of style, I might add."

The Pilgrim winked at him but said nothing.

"Nice couple. That fella's some kind of hero I think, fighting that skeleton creature." Nodded Longinus, putting his arm around his wife. "Glad he's ok. Who are they Arkilius? Friends of yours? Arkilius?"

Aurelia grinned at the young couple but was staring a Nicholas strangely. "He was right here a minute ago." She said, standing up and looking around.

The Pilgrim stood and, having the advantage of being able to see over everyone's head, spotted Arkilius some way off.

Arkilius was standing in front of Pantilius' statue. Some of the other Nelfilem were standing with him and looking concerned for the old leader. "Sorry brother. Sorry I wasn't here to protect you." He said gruffly.

Pilate was awakening at this point and telling Cassie and Aurelia what occurred on the Enefka Babellux.

"One second I was standing on the bridge and the next, I woke here. I have no idea what happened." Pilate breathed hard as several Nelfilem helped him to his feet. After a few moments of staggering and squinting in the morning sun, he followed the rest of the emissaries over to Pantilius.

The Pilgrim marched over to the stone statue of Pantilius and stared down at Arkilius. Some others were tending to wounded emissaries across the strand and checking bodies for signs of life. Nicholas limped a bit and had his arm around Claire as they walked over.

"I know of no means to make a creature become stone, much less undo such a thing, brother Nelfilem." Said Aryu, inspecting Pantilius stone grimace with a professional interest. "This malady is beyond me, brother."

"His name is Arkilius Stoneward. Pantilius' brother." Raphael whispered loudly, so that everyone could here.

"Pantilius! No!" Nicholas stumbled forward and fell to his knees with Claire in tow. "What happened?" He looked up at Harry, Buddy and Fuzzy.

"He stood before The Greyman." Said Maurice, standing beside Arkilius and looking down at the old Nelfilem. "He sacrificed himself to buy us time. It was remarkably brave but foolish."

"Two sides of the same coin, little brother." Said The Pilgrim, peering into Pantilius frozen, stone face.

Arkilius looked mildly surprised. "Butterfly-chaser stood his ground, huh? Good lad. I learned him well."

"Yes." The Pilgrim sighed. "To stand before him willingly is somewhat foolish." He cast a quick glance at Nicholas. "But sometimes foolishness is necessary."

The Pilgrim turned and looked around the strand. He saw the emissaries tending to the wounded and acknowledged them. He smiled at some young apprentices who were staring at him like wasn't supposed to exist.

"You all stood your ground." He said finally. His voice reached everyone on the strand. "Despite of his wrath, The Greyman was put down for a time. I am proud of each and every one of you."

He turned to Harry suddenly. "Harry, my boy. Do you recall the gift I gave to Pantilius for his birthday some centuries ago, shortly after he and Himtall built Mirthmyst?"

Harry frowned for a moment in recollection. The expressions on his face changed from sudden realization to shock, then disbelief followed quickly by despair.

"Oh please, don't say it." He said quietly as his face drained of all color.

"Would you be a good man and bring the gift here please, brother. Arkilius and the rest of us would be eternally grateful." The Pilgrim whispered loudly. Buddy snorted.

Harry cast an evil glance at Buddy and Fuzzy. "You two are coming with me. You need to help me get the blasted things here. No questions. Come on."

Harry marched towards the shore and, after a quick nod to The Pilgrim, Buddy and Fuzzy followed him.

Sometime later, emissaries heard splashing and arguments coming up the strand from the shore.

"Ahh. Our 'foolosophers' return." Said The Pilgrim happily, nodding to Raphael.

"Blasted, infernal things!" They heard Harry shout.

"Wait, stop smothering them!" They heard Fuzzy shout. "They are fragile creatures, brother.

"They are from hell itself!"

"Actually, I don't think Hell really exists." Said Buddy breathlessly. "Be at peace with that fact, brother."

"Look, go Nirvana yourself in the ocean. I'm the one who is getting sprayed to de - ouch! Ack!"

The emissaries watched with mild amusement as the three very old men struggled up the strand with a clutch of animated sunflowers. One of the sunflowers was spraying Harry repeatedly in the face with bright pink liquid. The other two were miraculously untouched by the spray.

"Ahh, very good brother." Said The Pilgrim. He stepped forward, grabbed the sunflowers from the old teachers and coddled them like a newborn child. The flowers writhed and twitched in The Pilgrims hands as if they appreciated the new attention. Well, as far as sunflowers can appear to appreciate something.

"Hello my beautiful, little children. Do you miss Pantilius?" The Pilgrim whispered encouragingly. "Pantilius is not happy. He is sad. Show him what you do to unhappy people."

The sunflowers looked at Pantilius stone statue and leaned closer to the frozen, stone face of the old, Nelfilem professor. Then they looked back to The Pilgrim.

"That's right." Said The Pilgrim, as if he was coaxing a pet. "Pantilius is sad. What do you do to sad and unhappy people?"

The sunflowers appeared to look at Harry who sighed and tried to wipe the eye-watering, pink dye from his face. Then, turning to face Pantilius, all three sunflowers blasted the stone statue with pink dye. The bright liquid covered Pantilius completely.

Many of the onlookers waited and wondered what the point was. Soon everyone was still and only the soft chirping of sparrows flying here and there about broke the silence on the strand.

Pantilius blinked while the emissaries held their breath and stared at the old professor in wide-eyed shock.

Arkilius leaned closer. "Pan?"

"You will never defeat us! We will stand our ground. We - !" Pantilius shouted and stopped.

He looked around at the various expressions of shock and surprise. He saw Nicholas and smiled. Then he looked up at The Pilgrim and smiled even more. Then he looked into the face Arkilius, the brother he thought lost forever and whose face was suddenly wet for some reason. His smile grew so wide it threatened to displace his ears.

"Alright." He said, still grinning as his eyes swiveled here and there. "What did I miss?"

Sometime later, after much cheering and congratulatory sentiments had swept through the assembled emissaries, the icy strand before the Gates of Sin was becoming quiet. Some emissaries were standing in small groups and talking about all that had occurred since abandoning Abanis.

Claire was holding Nicholas close while he relived all that occurred since their separation in Abanis. He was giving an animated account with his hands, pointing to Rudolph and his brothers. He pretended to struggle with something around his neck and shrugged as if it was all just luck. Claire, however, looked out into the ocean and bid him to follow as she walked towards the water.

Arkilius and Pantilius were laughing with each other as the latter tried to summarize world history for the last several thousand years. Pantilius was pointing to the other Nelfilem surrounding them and asking Arkilius hurried questions while pointing to the sky. Arkilius was speaking in a low, gruff voice telling his younger brother of his own awakening. He pointed to Pilate and the gathered Nelfilem, then burst out laughing.

Cassie, Longinus, Erik and Aurelia were listening to Pilate tell of how he simply fell unconscious on the bridge of the Enefka Babellux and awakened on the strand. What he didn't divulge, however, was how much the voice of the Enefka Babellux told him about the Huru and the Hurum. Whatever he learned, Pilate was regarding Enlil, The Pilgrim, with a kind of reverent awe since awakening.

In fact, many of the citizens of Abanis were staring a Nicholas in the same way. Already they were whispering of how the first human apprentice of Abanis fought The Greyman and lived. Robin in particular stared at Claire and winked at the Nicholas in the odd way that young men do when a brother wins the heart of 'fair lady'.

The Pilgrim was not among them, however. He took time to walk across the plain before the gates of Sin to say goodbye to many that had fallen before the wrath of The Greyman. Numerous times he kneeled and, after speaking a few silent words, the bodies of fallen emissaries were simply gone.

Down at the shoreline, Nicholas watched sadly as Claire waded out into the frigid water. "She's gone Claire. She sacrificed herself for me."

"We'll just see about that." Claire winked and submerged herself in the water. A short while later she broke the surface and ran up the beach to where Nicholas was waiting. She mimicked wiping herself off with a hand and her crimson apprentice robes were bone-dry.

"OK. You really have to teach me that." Nicholas snorted. "I've been drying my robes in the sun."

"As Pantilius says, it's all in the wrist." She grinned at him. "Look here." She held out her hand and Nicholas could see the little gold figurine. Kara was battered and lay still. One of her gold wings was bent and the little Valkyrie's spear was broken.

"Can she be fixed?"

"I think so. C'mon Nicholas. Let's see if The Pilgrim can help."

They ran back to the emissaries and found The Pilgrim had completed ushering the fallen and was talking quietly with Aryu Veda, Raphael, Arkilius and Pantilius.

"My lord." Said Claire, holding up the lifeless, gold Valkyrie so The Pilgrim could see. "I made this for Nicholas but she was felled defending him. I don't know how to fix her."

Erik, Aurelia and the others stepped forward and stared at the little gold figurine with curiosity. The Pilgrim took Kara and held her up to the sun, admiring her craftsmanship.

"There was only one other I knew of long ago who could make such toys, my dear. Quite an impressive skill." The Pilgrim looked to Raphael who nodded in agreement. Fuzzy grinned proudly at Claire.

"Nicholas." Said The Pilgrim loudly. "Since you are its current *master*, would you be so kind as to allow me to use Nanos for a moment.

Nicholas looked around the ground with sudden shock. "I nearly forgot! Nanos? Are you here?" He turned on the spot and looked to the ground. Some of the onlookers did the same.

After a brief moment, a grayish cloud formed at Nicholas feet. The cloud quickly assembled itself and soon a ghostly, featureless form was standing before him.

"Command acknowledged, Subject 4-9-4, Classification Human, Christopher Nicholas. Command?"

Aurelia's faced drained of color. She wasn't in the least bit surprised to see a talking ghost. After all that she had seen in the last day or so, this was but a small miracle. On the other hand, she was looking at Nicholas with disbelief.

The Pilgrim handed Kara to Nicholas and nodded to Nanos.

"Uhh, would you mind repairing this little gem?" Asked Nicholas, taking Kara and holding her up to the ghostly apparition.

"Processing. Please hold."

Once again, Nicholas heard the strange music when he took control of Nanos earlier. Some nearby emissaries looked at each other in confusion as some soft male voice, emanating from Nanos, sang gibberish that sounded like 'dee-doo-daa-daa-daa'.

After a few awkward moments, the music stopped.

"Command accepted." Nanos suddenly dispersed and enveloped the little gold Valkyrie in Nicholas' hand. The cloud pulsed a few times with a flashes of bright light then reformed. "*Command complete. Reconstruction complete.*" It said.

Kara blinked and stood up in Nicholas' palm. She looked around and drew her spear. Then she spotted Nicholas and buzzed wildly around his head.

"Kara!" Nicholas exclaimed.

Nearby emissaries laughed at the reunion. The little gold figurine snuggled closely to Nicholas cheek and remained there as Claire looked on happily.

"Don't you ever do that again!" Nicholas waved a finger at her, mocking admonishment.

Kara tilted her head and looked at Nicholas as if to say *'Yeah. You and whose army?'*

Nicholas spotted Aurelia staring at him with some kind of wide-eyed disbelief as he place Kara on his shoulder. He walked over to stand in front of the companions. He looked at Pilate, Longinus, Cassie, Erik and Aurelia and nodded to them.

"I am told we have you to thank as well. You have my gratitude and I want to hear the tale." He grinned at them.

"Longinus Massimiliano, former Commander of Jerusalem." Said Longinus stepping forward and extending a hand.

"Jerusalem? Really?" Nicholas glanced at Pantilius as he shook Longinus hand. "I am too! But, I've never been there."

"Huh?" Longinus frowned at him in confusion.

"Sorry, it's hard to explain."

"Well, pleasure to met 'ya. That was some kind of bravery, young man. Eh Erik? He did some serious fighting with that skele - Erik? Aura? What's wrong?"

Aurelia and Erik were staring at Nicholas. Erik had the look on his face that resembled someone realizing something that couldn't possibly be true.

The Pilgrim stepped over to the assembled humans and put an arm around Nicholas' shoulder. He looked from Aurelia to Erik then nodded.

"Forgive me but I wish to be part of a happy meeting." He said. "A baby came to us long ago when he was found with this." The Pilgrim held up the iron spike which had reformed into a broach once more.

Erik stared at it in disbelief. "The spike." He said, mesmerized by the stained loop of iron.

Pantilius, Harry, Buddy and Fuzzy looked at each other with happy astonishment, realizing before anyone else what was occurring. They walked over and stood beside Nicholas, facing Erik and Aurelia.

"And he was a good student." Said Harry proudly.

"A kind, young man with an almost supernatural sense empathy for those around him." Said Fuzzy, patting Nicholas on the shoulder.

"With a particular skill for identifying only the very best baked delicacies around the world, I might add." Said Buddy happily.

"And an uncanny knack for laughing at all my jokes, no matter how bad they might be." Said Pantilius. His wild, white hair and pointy, upswept ears bobbed up and down as he nodded to everyone around him.

Nicholas looked at his old teachers with some confusion then stared at The Pilgrim.

The Pilgrim nodded. "Nicholas, allow me the extreme pleasure to present to you Aurelia Firenze and Erikssen Fisherman. Long ago they were taken by The Greyman and now they have returned. Your Mother and Father."

Nicholas jaw dropped open. He stared at Erik and there was recognition in his eyes. He looked at the woman, Aurelia, and saw himself reflected back in the sudden well of tears in her eyes.

Aurelia stepped forward and put a hand on Nicholas face. She brushed aside the long, dirty blond locks and softly touched the jagged scar on his cheek. "My boy." She said softly. "How is this possible? How long were we - " She stopped and looked at The Pilgrim, who nodded silently, answering her unfinished question.

"I thought I lost you!" She said. Suddenly she grabbed him and hugged him. Erik stepped forward and after looking into the face of his son, he pulled him close. The three stood hugging each other for a long time. Longinus and Cassie looked on with happy amazement.

Claire found herself being pulled close to Cassie and Longinus by the latter's huge arm. He winked at her and nodded. Claire rather liked the giant man and felt he was more than just a friend to Nicholas' apparent father and mother.

"I don't' believe it." Whispered Longinus to Claire. "But he was just the size of a watermelon when we saw him last. Unbelievable." He shook his head.

Despite the occasional happy sniffle from the crowd of onlookers, the icy plain was silent for a long time as mother, father and son were finally reunited. Only sparrows chirping in the morning sun and the soft sound of waves crashing along the shore broke the bittersweet silence on the strand.

Unnoticed by anyone, a tiny of trickle of snow and rock moved near the gates of Sin.

Chapter 32: Starblossom Afternoon Tea

Shortly following the happy reunion of Aurelia, Erik and Nicholas, the host of Abanis spent some time debating with each other on the next course of action. The fortress of Sin had to be dealt with but with the immediate presence of The Greyman gone, some opted to return to Abanis with their injured brothers and sisters. The Pilgrim ordered Aryu Veda to lead the majority of emissaries back to the damaged city but asked some to remain. Word was sent via sparrow to Mrs. Bakersbee to have the younglings return there as well.

"Twerp, Lurp and Churp." Said The Pilgrim, smiling down at three sparrows who, for lack of a better expression, stood to attention at his feet. "Thank you for a job well done. We are in your debt."

"The pleasure was all mine, my lord." Corporal Twerp, raised a feathered wing and saluted smartly. "Will there be anything else sir?"

"Return to Jerusalem for now, I think. I'm afraid that whole region is going to be a hotbed of activity in the centuries ahead. You have my thanks. Dismissed."

"Wing company!" Corporal Twerp nodded to The Pilgrim and addressed his fellows. "Back to the eagle's nest!"

Longinus watched the sparrows fly away as he was reaching down to pick up his spear. "You are able to speak to birds too , Enlil?" He said, grabbing the spear and checking it for damage.

"Of course. It's all about listening carefully, young man." The Pilgrim grinned. "Is your heirloom intact?"

"From what Pilate told me, it shouldn't be but looks fine."

Longinus was about to say more regarding the condition of his family spear when he was interrupted by Pilate, who ran over in a panic. "Wait! Longinus! Don't touch it!"

"Pilate. Don't fret." The Pilgrim patted him reassuringly on the shoulder. "He is gone for now."

Raphael peered around The Pilgrim and saw Longinus caressing the spear and inspecting the bladed tip. His eyes widened. "Uncle! It has been reforged? Your sp -"

"The spear of Longinus is back in its owners rightful hands." The Pilgrim cut him off loudly and looked at Raphael meaningfully.

"Of course. Yes. Well done, young warrior. Keep it well." Raphael cleared his throat and glanced at The Pilgrim.

"Ahh." Pilate looked relieved but reluctant to step closer to the spear. "You have no idea what that thing did to me, Commander. Sorry."

"Noted." Longinus nodded, not unkindly, to Pilate and looked around. "Where's Erik and the kid?"

"Up near the cliff face." Said Cassie, who bustled past with some Nelfilem carrying trays of hot cocoa. She was assisting emissaries care for the wounded and was instructed by The Pilgrim, for some strange reason, to bring them the hot beverage.

"That," Said a voice behind Longinus, "is a remarkable weapon, Commander. May I take a look?"

Longinus turned to see a very tall, dark skinned man admiring the spear he inherited from his uncle.

"Certainly. Maurice is it?" He said, handing the spear to the man.

"Indeed. A pleasure to meet another warrior." He said, taking the spear and admiring the ornate metalwork along the shaft and pommel. "Incredible craftsmanship. Do you know what this means?" He pointed to some intricate linear markings on the spearhead.

"Yes and no. The first part means 'Aegis' but the other markings in the metal are a mystery to me." Longinus said, peering closer to the linear script and frowning. "I know it's been passed down for many generations in my family though. Do you know what it means? I've not been able to discern the language."

"It's called cuneiform, Commander. It is an old language developed at a time when some of us made contact with humans. It means 'guardian'. Quite an old weapon but a most elegant example of a time when some of us lived side by side with early human civilizations. Come let me tell you some of its history."

Longinus listened intently to Maurice talk about his spear as emissaries prepared to return home. Cassie, Aurelia, Erik and Pilate were listening to Buddy explain that they were going on a trip back to their home. It was a rather difficult explanation.

"We're going where?" Pilate exclaimed.

Harry bustled past with some younger acolytes and snorted as Buddy attempted to explain why their 'home' was on the southern side of the planet. When he reached a point that the companions seemed to grasp, he then attempted to explain why it was under two miles of ice and rock...and had artificial sunlight. This was considerably more difficult. Cassie was looking at Buddy in the peculiar way people do when expecting 'kind' people to show up at any moment to usher him back to a safe and happy environment.

A short while later, the emissaries of Abanis were all but gone except for a few stragglers. Although The Pilgrim asked Raphael, Pantilius, Nicholas and Claire to remain behind for some unfinished business, some of their human guests were having difficulty accepting the only mode of transportation.

Nicholas came back from the cliffs near the gates of Sin, where he had been trying to gather his backpack items. He ran up beside Claire who was listening to Longinus argue about their method of travel and tried to help the situation.

"Longinus! Dad! You will love this!" Nicholas exclaimed to the reluctant commander and pointing to the black, wood and metal carriage.

The human companions, not having the means to *flow* as emissaries, were forced to take a trip in the carriage. At first, they were astonished to see Rudolph and his brothers morph into giant reindeer and take the harnesses but not nearly as much as hearing *how* they were going to get to Abanis.

"Let me get this straight." Said Longinus, glancing at the reindeer with a worried expression. "In the sky? As in, up there? I'm not sure if you noticed but these guys," he jerked a thumb towards Rudolph, "have hooves, not wings."

"C'mon babe. After all we have seen, do you really think they would let us come to harm?" Cassie pulled her husband's arm.

"Why do I suddenly feel old?" Erik grinned at Longinus.

"Old?" Longinus said, looking at Erik in hurtful surprise. He considered this for a moment. "Old?" He said again, looking at Nicholas and considering the idea some more. "Bugger that!"

He jumped up on to the carriage and was soon joined by the others. He nestled his giant spear in beside him so that it stuck out of the open-roofed carriage like a mighty antenna.

Arkilius, who volunteered to escort them, sat in the center holding the reins. Cassie, Longinus, Pilate, and Nicholas' mother and father squeezed in on either side of him.

"We'll be home soon." Said Nicholas, coming up beside the carriage. "Don't worry, Rudolph and his brothers will have you there in no time."

Erik and Aurelia smiled down at their full grown son. "I want hear everything, son. Hurry home. We have a lot of catching up to do." Erik winked at him.

"Hold on to y'er war-stick, Long shanks!" Arkilius bellowed. "Rudolph! Let's ride!"

Nicholas felt his stomach lurch in empathy as Rudolph and his brothers took off. He watched carriage shoot across the strand at a speed normally associated with cheetahs. Longinus decided that this was a perfect time to scream.

"Nicholas!" Longinus screamed, holding on to the side of the carriage with white knuckles. "You are as nuts as your old maaaaaaaan!"

The carriage left the icy strand and roared up into the air. It rocketed past a flock of thoroughly terrified geese and Pilate heard them squawk in protest as the flock dispersed. Turning south in a wide arc, the reindeer driven carriage rose higher as it sped across the afternoon sky.

After a time the carriage disappeared from sight and only five figures remained standing on the strand. Six, if counting the ghostly form of Nanos that trailed after Nicholas.

"Unfinished business Uncle?" Said Raphael as he watched the carriage vanish into the blue sky. "I'm assuming you mean Sin?"

"Yes. We must enter that place and begin to harrow it." Said The Pilgrim. He noticed Claire look nervously at Nicholas and smiled at her. "It is quite safe for now, my dear. There is something we must do and I want you and Nicholas to see it.

Together, they walked towards the gates of Sin. Raphael was limping only slightly now, thanks to the healing efforts of Aryu Veda and pointed to one side of the mountain above the snow covered gates. "I believe I landed there, Enlil. His strength was immense."

"Yes." The Pilgrim sighed. "I know all to well his strength."

"Would you like Nanos to clear the avalanche, sir?" Said Nicholas, wondering how they were going to pass into the fortress.

"Very kind of you, young man but no need." Said The Pilgrim. He waved a hand as they advanced on the enormous gates. A twenty-meter high snowdrift covering the gates of

Sin was blasted aside as The Pilgrim waved his hand. After a moment, the massive stone gates slowly opened.

"It's all in the wrist." Pantilius whispered loudly to Nicholas, wiggling his eyebrows and giving Claire a wink.

They passed into the grand hallway leading slightly down into the roots of the mountain. Strange lights and linear patterns lit the walls and floors as they passed deeper into the darkness until they came to the chamber of stars.

Nicholas had never seen its like before but recognized the style to be similar to the buildings he saw in the doomed city of Adamis. The star chamber was very similar to the chamber he saw The Pilgrim and The Greyman dual in his vision, only this one was really huge. The dome had hallways branching off to other parts of the fortress but it seemed The Pilgrim wanted to focus on this room. Across the domed ceiling were constellations as if all seasons were being represented at once. One star in particular lit the sky brighter than the others and Nicholas recognized it to be Polaris, the Northern Star.

They approached the circular pool of water at the center of the room and Nicholas wondered why there was a stone chair at its edge. The Pilgrim turned to the others and gestured for everyone to come closer.

"Come gather around." He said, looking kindly at his companions. His large, opaque eyes settled on Pantilius and he sighed. "It is obvious that he can return through here, old friend. He has found a way beyond our wildest paranoia. This gate must be closed."

Pantilius nodded. "I think I know what you have in mind. You want to seal it right?"

"As its original engineer, I was hoping you would see it done properly. That is also why I asked Claire and Nicholas to join us." He said, nodding to the others. "With Nanos." He added quietly.

"I understand. But is it necessary?" Pantilius shook his head and stared into the pool with the air of a craftsman admiring some sort of machinery.

"Umm." Nicholas almost rose his hand. "What's this all about, sir?"

"Nicholas." Raphael turned and gave him and Claire a mildly sympathetic look. "This gate was designed to keep him from returning. It is the gateway to a prison. He is there now and not destroyed. He will try to return. He is cleverer than we are and I think you understand now how strong he is. Therefore we must seal this gate. Forever."

"Ok, makes sense." Nicholas nodded. "I understand some truths." He said hesitantly, glancing at The Pilgrim. "But, frankly, what does this have to do with Claire and I?"

"Long ago, or long from now, however you wish to see it," said Pantilius, "I was told humans had tools and servants of an artificial nature to do all sorts of physical tasks. I believe Nanos was given to The Greyman long ago and may, in fact, be the last of its kind. I believe that only it can seal this gate properly but there is a problem. Nanos is yours. It recognizes you as one of its *makers* which is why you were unharmed when The Greyman ordered it to attack you. As a human, your command supersedes all others. Once a 'Nanos' finds a human master, there is no being in the cosmos who can order it to do anything until the master is gone."

"I see." Said Nicholas, sensing he was being prepared for possibly bad news. He looked at Claire and noticed she had the same sense of anticipation. "Can't I just order it to obey someone else?"

"Possibly." Said Raphael, looking at Nanos. "But it would still be attached to you, Nicholas. All commands would have to be cross-checked through you. My father owned this Nanos temporarily because it's maker does not exist in the universe as we know it anymore. I was told you now understand that truth."

Nicholas nodded but said nothing. He held Claire's hand.

The Pilgrim turned to the gate pool and sighed as he stared into the emerald colored depths. "The gate must be sealed." He said. "And Nicholas, he is afraid of you. You defeated him with my aid and he has never known such a defeat. Not from a human, anyways. He may find a way to return. Therefore, I want you to order Nanos to seal the gate and become watchguard of this Northern gate." He turned to Nicholas and came closer. "A sister gate exists in Abanis. It is sealed within my home, the silver dome in the plaza. I built my home around it and feel it is safe against use for now but I need to know this northern gate is also safe. Considering you are the master of Nanos, I am asking if you will remain here and be the watchguard. Think carefully, young human. This is no small service I ask of you."

"Is there no other way?" Said Claire, looking at Raphael , Pantilius and The Pilgrim in turn. "After what risk Nicholas took to challenge The Greyman, you would ask him to do this?"

"I am sorry my dear. And to you, Nicholas." Said The Pilgrim. "But you are the only one who can command Nanos to reseal the gate if ever it is breached again. I am sorry to ask this but - "

"I'd be honored, sir." Nicholas blurted. "If I must spend eternity, or however long I live, making sure that monster never returns, I will stay here, Alone, if needs be."

The Pilgrim smiled at Nicholas and patted him on the shoulder.

At this point, Pantilius thought it was the right time to spew hot chocolate out of his nostrils. He had summoned a steaming cup out of nothingness while The Pilgrim spoke and was just taking a sip when Nicholas said 'alone'.

"Alone?" He coughed and sputtered. "My dear boy, you are not doing this alone! Mirthmyst needs a new atmosphere anyways. I was thinking of franchising the castle." He winked at Claire.

"And the library is dangerously close to human settlements now." Said Raphael. In time, the forlorn mountain where I reside will become habitable to them. I was also thinking of relocating." He looked around and down one of the many hallways branching off from the star chamber. "I daresay this fortress has enough space to house the library and then some."

"But this place is so..." Nicholas paused and looked around, "odd. It's alien to me and not as friendly for younglings as Abanis, Pantilius."

"I was thinking of a northern campus for years, my boy. This may be the answer. The kids can have Abanis *and* this place." Pantilius nodded.

"You really want to have Twilenos come here Raph - err Usher Ravenscrawl?" Nicholas turned to Gabriel's brother.

"Hello?" Pantilius waved his hands about, gesturing to the ghostly form standing a few meters behind Nicholas. "You have Nanos. After it seals the gate, we can do some remodeling."

Pantilius strode away from the others and placed his hands on his hips as he paced around like a interior decorator with a penchant for ballet. "It must be Germanic, yes. *Vith* a touch of Roman and a *sprinklink* of Asian for tranquility. Yes. It *vill* be *mah-velous*." He beamed at Nicholas.

"Uhh, ok."

"Good man." Pantilius winked at Claire. "And you my dear? Will you help us design a *vonderfool* home for *ze younglinks*?"

Claire looked at Nicholas and grinned at him in disbelief. "You just became an apprentice and now you are running a franchise of Abanis. You have *got* to be human." Then she looked at The Pilgrim and nodded. "I'm in, if Fuzzy allows it. He has been teaching me."

"Splendid!" Said The Pilgrim. "We will make the arrangements. But Nicholas, there is another matter. 'Sin' is such a dreadful name. It carries such a negative implication. As watchguard of the northern gate, you must name your new home. What will this home be called?"

Nicholas looked to Pantilius, Claire and Raphael. He was never really good with things like this but something came to him that just seemed to fit. "Neithernorth." He said.

"Neithernorth." Said Pantilius, nodding to The Pilgrim and Raphael. "The Fortress of Neithernorth. Nice ring to it. Almost fairytale-like, I daresay. The kids will love it. Why so, lad?"

Nicholas shrugged and looked around. "Well, it's neither here nor there. It's just north."

****Jingle***Jingle***Jingle****

"A moment of silence for the ushered." The central plaza in Abanis fell silent for a long time. There were some sniffles in the crowd as The Pilgrim lowered his hood and bowed his alien head. After a few moments he raised his head and addressed the assembled emissaries.

"But this time," he continued, "will not be filled with sadness for those of our brothers and sister who stood their ground against such a terrible enemy of humanity. We will rejoice their sacrifice with the knowledge they are gone to Empyrean having done their duty and upholding the first promise."

He walked to another spot where Cassie, Aura, Longinus and Erik stood and looked around. "Pontius Pilate." The Pilgrim continued. "Please stand forth and be recognized."

Pilate stood and looked around nervously. A thousand sets of eyes peered at him with an odd mixture of admiration and curiosity.

Since taking the spear in his domicile in Jerusalem, Pilate endured a rigorous ride filled with horrifying revelation. The last several hours, however, were more along the lines of 'terrifyingly insane.' After a gut wrenching, white-knuckled ride across the sky and half the entire planet, Pilate was pushed down an ice-shoot at the base of a mountain. The ensuing slide seemed to last several minutes, after which he dropped into an icy pool of water. After being pulled from the water by kind men in blue robes, he was fed hot chocolate told that he was now two miles underground. This matter would have been acceptable to believe until he emerged into the central plaza of the city of Abanis and saw that it was in fact daylight. Something, he was quite sure, didn't exist two miles underground. To further add to his disbelief, a portly chap named 'Buddy' said The Pilgrim was making repairs to the 'great sphere' and that there would be a fantastic victory celebration in the plaza. His only hold on reality at that moment was a kind of morbid satisfaction that Longinus, Erik, Cassie and Aura were feeling looking as perplexed as he felt.

"Pilate." Longinus whispered. "You look green. Are you quite ok."

"I'm fine, Commander, thank you." He said looking at a spherical woman who seemed to be in charge of the food and the young children.

"Pilate? Come here my good man." Said The Pilgrim who was standing in the center of the plaza with the many others, including some of the Nelfilem.

Pilate walked slowly up to The Pilgrim and stood before him as asked. He did not wish to think of the multitude watching and waiting for whatever came next.

"Pontius Pilate, Aurelia Firenze, Erik Fisherman, Longinus Massimiliano, Cassiopeia Athenus." The Pilgrim called out their names. "You stand before a grateful family. You are human and without your involvement in the events which recently threatened us, the world may very well be different. You have our thanks." The Pilgrim bowed to them.

To Pilate's surprise, the thousand or so emissaries assembled in Abanis bowed to them. He recalled later that it was an odd moment. Never in his life was he genuinely thanked for doing something worthy of it. He felt an odd frog-like feeling in his throat and decided he would pursue more of that feeling in the days ahead.

"Pontius Pilate." The Pilgrim continued. "You lived a cruel life and missed your potential. Although you have redeemed yourself in my eyes, your mortal life has been forfeited. The world thinks that Pilate is gone. Will you stay with us and live a new life? One that you have earned."

Pilate considered this. He knew this was coming and a sudden urge overwhelmed him. "I understand there is an extensive library among your people. Someone named "Ravenscrawl' is it's librarian. Any room for an assistant?"

Raphael stepped forward and looked sternly at Pilate for a moment. "Ravenscrawl is known to me, human. How did you come to know of this?"

"I was the warden of the Enefka Babellux for two hours. The voice on that ship told me much." Pilate shrugged apathetically and tried to grin at The Pilgrim.

Raphael and The Pilgrim exchanged a brief glance and the latter nodded.

Raphael grinned at Pilate in a friendly manner and laughed. "So you love books do you? Well, then, you shall have your wish."

The emissaries cheered and called out Pilates name, welcoming him to Abanis. Pilate sat down at the table with Raphael and some elder emissaries and was passed a mug of wine.

"And you four..." The Pilgrim paused, looking at Longinus, Cassie, Aura and Erik. "I daresay this isn't Rome or Greece or Germania but we have good food, good fun and the weather is under my direct control if I want it. The sphere of Abanis is one home for us who are not entirely human. A second home is being constructed as we speak.

And we have much work to do. Will you help uphold the first promise and help us in our efforts? Will you stay?"

The plaza of Abanis went silent. Claire put her hand in Nicholas' and leaned her head on his shoulder. "That's a bit rhetorical isn't it?" She whispered to him.

Nicholas snorted and grinned at his mother and father.

Cassie and Aura looked at their husbands. Longinus nodded enthusiastically and gave Maurice a 'thumbs up'.

"We wish to stay in Abanis, Enlil." Said Erik. "Thank you for having us."

"It is done!" The Pilgrim raised his staff and a stream of bright lights shot up to the heavens above and exploded. The city of Abanis was showered with falling stars of all colors as The Pilgrim shouted to the assembled host. "The first human citizens of Abanis. Welcome!"

The emissaries erupted in cheers and shouts. This lasted for quite some time as more food and wine was brought out by Mrs. Bakersbee's legions of busy bakers. Children of all ages, some of whom had never seen an actual human before ran up to the central spot and greeted the four newcomers. Longinus found himself shaking hands and laughing with some of the Nelfilem who seemed to be Pilate's personal body guard. Claire and Nicholas ran forward too and congratulated them.

"What is the first promise, Enlil?" Said Aurelia as the cheers seceded and emissaries returned to their respective tables. Music was playing, people were singing and food of all kinds were being passed along tables longer than some streets in Jerusalem.

Pantilius stepped forward at this point and nodded. "My dear, it is that all humanity is precious beyond measure."

Sometime later, the celebration was in full swing. Longinus was talking at length with Maurice about the Roman Empire while Cassie made paper animals for children from Mirthmyst castle. She made a ridiculously huge paper hat for Himtall, who placed it on his head and let the younger children 'go for a ride' on the walking giant as he staggered around in a silly swagger. Pilate was already making notes and talking to Raphael about how move the library up north while Arkilius and Pantilius attempted to catch up after the longest loss of contact in history.

"Seven thousand years is quite a long time, brother." Said Pantilius, draining a mug of mead and winking at Aurelia. "Let's start in Mesopotamia shall we?"

Harry, Buddy and Fuzzy were reminiscing with Erik and Aurelia about how they found Nicholas wrapped in cloth and holding an iron spike. Claire and Nicholas sat with Rudolph and his brothers at the same table and listened to the story while Mrs. Bakersbee told Aurelia about all the silly things Nicholas did as a child.

The Pilgrim walked among the tables talking to everyone as much as he could and even found time to dance with a tiny girl from Mirthmyst castle. She had never seen The Pilgrim before, along with many of the young acolytes, and was absolutely convinced that he was either the tooth fairy or Jack Frost. In fact, Jack Frost was sitting at a table nearby and coughed on his mead when he heard the little girl talking to The Pilgrim. Jack was an emissary who lived in Britannia with Robin but even he couldn't convince the little girl otherwise.

After a while, Nicholas found himself sitting with his mother and father. He tried to tell them all the fantastic things that happened while growing up and all that he had learned. They were quite surprised to hear that he was fifty two years old and that the time they spent on the Enefka Babellux was much longer than they originally thought.

"We are fortunate to be so young still and have time with you, son." Said Erik. "You have no idea what we went through to get out of Jerusalem. Your uncle Longinus and aunt Cassie helped us."

"Damn straight." Said Longinus, sitting down with Cassie on the other side of Claire and Nicholas. "And you were this big when I held you in my arms." He mimicked holding a small object. "And now look at you! Do you have any idea how long it has been since I've had to 'look up' at someone? You're a big boy now." He elbowed Nicholas in the shoulder and nodded at Claire. "Look forward to getting to know you two."

"We never had a chance to see you grow up, Nicholas. I'm sorry." Said Aurelia, looking a little saddened in spite of all the surrounding merriment.

"Mom, please. I understand." Nicholas started.

"Grow up?" Said a deep voice behind Aurelia. She looked up and saw The Pilgrim lean down and sit with them.

"You will have ample time to see your son grow, my dear." He said, putting a huge, silvery hand on Nicholas' shoulder and the other on hers. He looked at the companions in turn and nodded. "He will grow and grow and you will see it happen. Why? Because we are all children and we are all growing up continuously."

And so it was, that the man who grew up in a strange place under peculiar circumstances, performed a few good deeds and was happy for a time. But that man, who seems here and there to be a bit Santa-like, still had much work to do.

His uncanny resemblance to that jolly old character from modern-day folklore is in no way tied to the fact that he prefers cookies for breakfast, lunch and supper. Nope. Nor is it happenstance that his reindeer driven carriage can fly across the sky at great speed while he works to uphold the first promise of the Huru. Nope not at all. Furthermore, it's purely coincidental that he will live in a fortress somewhere near the north pole shortly after these events... and have little pointy-eared, ancient Nelfilem help him rebuild the fortress. Nope, no affiliation there at all. *Ahem*

But this still isn't a good spot for saying that he 'lived happily ever after'.

After all, 'happily ever after' is all about endings. This story, on the other hand, was all about beginnings.

The End.

4/13/2013

FOR THE PRIVATE COLLECTION OF RICHARD COOKE,

THANKS FOR EVERYTHING BRUTHA!

HOPE YOU ENJOY THIS PLAYFUL WORK-IN-PROGRESS.

ANY INSIGHTS YOU MAY HAVE ARE WELCOME!

ALL THE BEST!

ERCHAMION

& 곰와

Made in the USA
Charleston, SC
23 February 2013